THE
GREEN
LINE

THE GREEN LINE

Monica Mears

HAMISH HAMILTON
London

First published in Great Britain 1987
by Hamish Hamilton Ltd
27 Wrights Lane London W8 5TZ

Copyright © 1987 by Monica Mears

British Library Cataloguing in Publication Data

Mears, Monica
 The green line.
 I. Title
 823'.914 [F]   PR6063.E3/

ISBN 0–241–11975–8

Typeset at The Spartan Press Limited
Lymington, Hants

Printed and bound in Great Britain
by Butler and Tanner Ltd Frome

Contents

Map of Beirut viii

Part I	:	TROUBLES	1
Part II	:	CONFLICT	69
Part III	:	TAKING SIDES	154
Part IV	:	BATTLE JOINED	225

To all my friends

Author's Note

Apart from the names of the political figures of the time and that of the radio reporter mentioned in the first few pages, all names are fictitious and any resemblance to the names of real people is entirely coincidental.

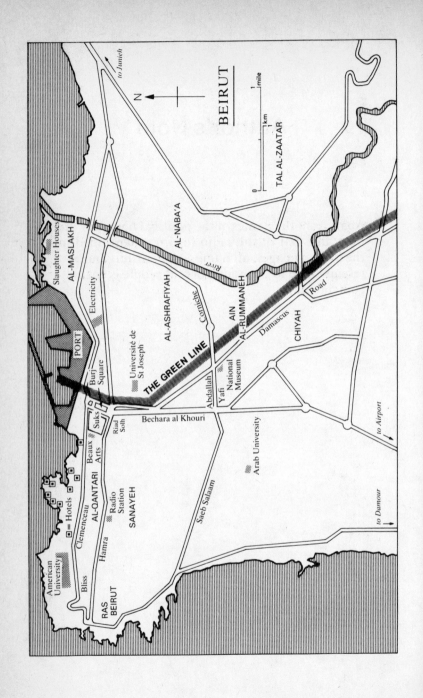

Part I

TROUBLES

'You will be as good as committing suicide if you go out,' said the radio reporter in Arabic, his voice crackling a little through bouts of interference caused by the machine-gun fire. 'Stay in your homes. Whatever you do, don't go into the streets. There's nowhere in Beirut that can be guaranteed safe today. The gunmen are everywhere and they are shooting at anything that moves.'

I should not have gone out that day, Samia told herself, remembering. It was so stupid of me. But the thing was this, that . . . Oh, never mind. What happened would have happened anyway, sooner or later. It's not important.

I remember every word, though, that the newscaster said that morning. Bless him, everybody had so much faith in him, in Sharif al-Akhaoui, during the Troubles. He would tell us exactly what was *happening*, and he would burst out with such emotion too, telling us exactly what he *thought*. So different from the official reassurances that everything was under control.

'Hundreds of people have died this weekend alone,' he said. 'Don't forget: hundreds of people. And they have been mostly civilians, taking a chance, popping out for a minute to buy food and essentials when they thought things were quiet outside. Don't go out. It's just not worth it. People are being kidnapped at every road block.

'And if you live in the Ain al-Muraysi area, or in al-Qantari,' he said – his message could not have been more specifically meant for me – 'if you live there, then stay well away from the windows, or preferably move into a basement or cellar if you possibly can.'

He meant what he said, of course. From my back window, if I had dared to go into my bedroom at the back of my flat at all, I could see the unfinished top stories of the new office block, the Murr Tower, which the Mourabitun militia had been holding since the night before. And from which, terrifyingly, they kept bombarding the Phalangist positions in buildings quite close to me, so that all night long there had been the thunder and vibration of rockets exploding round about, and of mortars screaming by – two or three a minute sometimes. The windows of the flat were all wide open, or I should have had no glass left in them, and the noise was sometimes as if an express train were hurtling through my sitting room, making the corridor shake where I lay huddled with my protective mattresses.

This morning things were quieter, but with these modern weapons which they have, with those rifles which have telescopic sights, one would be a fool to stand anywhere in sight of the Murr Tower, even in the supposed safety of one's own bedroom.

It was simply impossible to believe what was going on. Here, in a modern city! Nearly all my life I had lived in Beirut and look what was happening! Just in the last few days the port had been partly destroyed, the whole commercial district was being pounded by night-long artillery fire, the lovely old warrens of the *suks* were being utterly devastated. Short of nuclear war, surely there is nothing that could be more destructive in a city, a densely populated city, than guerrilla war by tower block, with every high rise luxury hotel – the Holiday Inn, the Phoenicia, the lovely St Georges, silhouetted against the deep blue of the sea – every one of them turned into a guerrilla citadel.

'One simply can't believe it possible,' Sharif al-Akhaoui was saying, almost sobbing. And, referring to what he had seen that morning where a crowded building had collapsed,

'I can't describe the sight, it was . . . it was . . . The little children . . . ' There was a pause, a crackling of the radio.

'Now please, remember. If you absolutely must – must! – go out for any reason, remember that there have been some changes during the weekend in the position of the various fronts. There's now a barricade at . . . '

Then he gave his usual detailed report of which routes to take to avoid snipers, armed hold-ups and so on. By the time he had finished, my finger-nails must have scratched a layer of enamel off my front teeth. I was so frightened. Because I knew I would go out, whatever he said.

It was Monday, 27th October, 1975. We had been living with this terrible fighting, in one form or another, since the spring – which is something I can't describe, the way it drains you I mean, because there is not even any hope of anything but destruction coming out of it. And the strain, all the time the strain of living like that. The noise of the fighting, the danger, the impossibility of anybody carrying on normal working and instead being cooped up all day at home, day after day, with no end in sight . . . The electricity supply kept plunging me into darkness every so often, leaving me with nothing but my very old and erratic little transistor radio to keep me in touch with what was going on out there, and to block out the shelling and my fears; while all the time its batteries were running lower and lower. I had nothing left to eat, during those last few days, but chickpeas. And a little sugar. I was lucky. I wasn't starving. But it hadn't occurred to me how important it would be to buy in extra salt and also things like garlic, olive oil, lemon juice, tahini and so on, to make the chickpeas taste palatable. And to have to eat nothing for days but a *mezze* of chickpeas with no flavouring whatsoever – all the time it made me long for something, some proper food to eat, so that in the end I couldn't stop myself picking at the chickpea mush all day long even though I hated it, cursing myself of course because the more I ate, the sooner it would all be gone. Which I suppose is how Beirut's poor must feel much of the time.

Chickpeas with sugar – errgh! I tried it. It was terrible.

If only I had not been alone. If George were still alive, or if one of the children were still living at home, perhaps I would not have made myself ill. What I mean is, I would not have eaten and slept so irregularly and upset every rhythm in my body, like they do to people sometimes as a form of torture. When one is young, such things don't matter so much, but once one is past a certain age . . . The trouble was, of course, I kept the curtains drawn day and night against the noise and against the possibility of being seen by a sniper, so that I lost all sense of time. All in the heat of the Beirut summer! My air conditioning was not working, so that I sweated and itched and was scratchy and irritable for days on end. And I had sores in my mouth too, lumpy ever-present sores. Which didn't surprise me. Nobody can possibly be in good health when the state, the body politic, is sick. The sickness intrudes into every aspect of life, as we in Lebanon know so well.

And yet in those last few days, when the artillery battles were just outside my own windows, it seemed . . . it seemed as if these events must at last be reaching a decisive climax. Things couldn't go on like this. They couldn't possibly! It was inconceivable!

Whereas in fact the fighting, the civil war as it later came to be called, had another year to run, or – no, no, much more than a year, depending on how you look at it; a decade or more by now – and it was to go from bad to worse, to infinitely worse.

And something else which I didn't know then: that day, that Monday was to be, for the time being, my last day in the thick of it.

What struck me that morning, I remember, was how oddly disorientating it was to step out on to the streets of Beirut. It was as if my acoustic map of the city had been scrambled so that it no longer made sense. Over the months we had all grown used to the sound of rifle fire and heavy machine-gun fire coming from the traditional battle fronts, as we used to call them – from the suburbs of Ain al-Rummaneh, Chiyah, Hadeth. We were used to the barrage each night of mortars and rockets pounding and smashing, almost always at familiar targets and from predictable directions. But now, since I had last been out of doors, the fighting had spread throughout the centre of the city, not only to al-Qantari but also to the hotel district, to some other very beautiful residential areas, to Ras Beirut even and the area of the embassies.

And today, instead of coming as they had recently done from the commercial area just to the east and from the south-east, the daytime sounds of sporadic fighting burst as well from any number of different places to the north and west. And from so near at hand! Also the traffic – what little there was of it – the noise of the traffic had changed. Whereas previously the roads here near the centre of the city had still been relatively busy, now all the traffic had veered away from the new danger zones and I could hear it quite some distance off towards the south, tracing out new paths round the battlefields. Going, I suppose, to wherever there was left to go. Which was all so odd. I mean, cities on the whole are not prone to such massive acoustic shifts. It was as if Beirut had swivelled on its axis, so that the sounds in the air and the buildings on the ground had changed their relative positions. It was as startling as if, for example, the sounds – only the sounds – of the land were to have changed places with those of the sea.

The change made me feel expectant. And other people too, I think; there was a certain look about the few people, the very few people I saw that morning scurrying furtively about . . . After all, anybody who stepped out of doors in Beirut that morning had a good chance of dying before lunch time.

And yet people, myself included, did go out. By now, taking risks was just a part of life. One no longer thought about what was safe (nothing was safe) but only about what was not likely to be totally disastrous. During the course of the summer I had often seen children out playing in the streets, groups of them, often quite small, playing skittles with empty cartridges or having gun battles. Their young parents would let them out. What else could they do, month after month? To keep them indoors all summer, in a tiny flat perhaps, in that heat and humidity, all day every day while the schools were closed down, must have been a torture; for everybody.

Once I saw some people queuing up to buy sweet pastries piled in mouth-watering heaps on trays in a baker's window – *baklawa*, *ghraibeh*, sticky *zalabieh*. The gorgeous smell of baking wafted down the street and the queue of people curled out of the baker's door and longingly round the window, right round an unexploded shell which was lying on the pavement. They looked at the shell abstractedly and kicked it almost, they were standing so close, then each of them turned away again to gaze anxiously as the pile of pastries grew a little smaller.

I went out.

I remember that when I pushed open the street door of our block of flats I felt such a pain behind my eyes, as if they were about to burst, a sudden fierce intensification of the headache which had been troubling me for days. For a momenr or two my vision went strangely blurred, as if I were dizzy. I might have known, if I had stopped to think about it, that my blood pressure was up too high again, much much too high.

I waited on the doorstep close to the wall, until the pain had lessened, instinctively scanning doorways and balconies, ready to dash back inside at the least flicker of movement. I stepped, very gingerly, out on to the pavement and waited again, feeling terribly conspicuous on the empty street: a well-dressed woman from another Beirut, from a by-gone Beirut; a woman grey-white haired, very erect, in a smart tapestried suit, ready to leave for her office on a Monday morning. I was out of sight of the Murr Tower down here at street level, but all the same, it was as if I could *feel* a sniper's rifle pointing at me from behind every window and every pile of uncollected rubbish in the road, a thick tight feeling, as if at any moment a bullet would explode inside my head.

The huge acoustic shift was unnerving. I became very conscious of the altered sound of the city and conscious with it, frighteningly conscious of the new complexity of the battle round about me. Because of course there was nothing to be seen, the fighters were all hidden in buildings and behind barricades, and yet the battle might suddenly flare up to surround me at any moment.

Even the sky had moved. A great thick brown blanket of

smoke had been hanging for days over the commercial district and the port, where countless fires raged. But today the blanket had been brought westward by the slight wind, so that it hung heavily over my own street, turning the sunlight lurid and apocalyptic. And there, just down the street, where it should not have been, was a gaping hole, tooth-edged and filled with a brown tongue of this terrible sky, where yesterday the upper floors of the life insurance building had been. I was shocked to see the building destroyed: one more thing gone which I had always taken for granted.

Such an accumulation of smoke, with the last days of the Beirut summer anyway so muggy! It made the air too thick to breathe so that I stood there trying not to, almost eating it instead, half tasting, half smelling the sweet hot fetid summer odour of cooking and shell-damaged drains, mixed with the stench of the uncollected rubbish piling up by the roadside. Such unaccustomed smells! It was like the return of a forgotten primitivism to my deodorised sanitised high-class quarter. As if the blasting of the *suks* had let loose all the odours of the city's ancient gut.

All of which made me so angry, so head-splittingly angry. At the fighting I mean, at those who brought the whole thing about and relentlessly, cold-bloodedly kept it going. At . . .

The roar and squeal of a car rounding the corner at speed made me leap back against the wall for cover and set my taut nerves shrieking. The car pulled up in front of me, just on the other side of the debris which littered the kerb. I recognised it. Thank goodness. It was a bright yellow service-taxi, with its red service-taxi numberplate. A Chevrolet. I recognised it at once by the rolling motion with which it came to a stop, scattering a rabble of cats which were scavenging or rat-catching in the rubbish: Mustafa's taxi.

Mustafa's sun-tanned face leaned out.

'*Tfaddali*! Be quick! Trust good old Mustafa to arrive in the nick of time,' he said, chattering loudly and cheerfully as usual, in his hearty Beiruti Arabic, as he leaned across his fat front-seat passenger to throw open the door for me; for all the world as if it were perfectly normal for him to be here today, on *this* route! But then, yes, he *would* be. He was one of life's great opportunists.

'*Tfaddali*! In you get if you're coming.' He sounded more irritable this time as I hugged my wall still. He was on edge too, after all. We were both, at this moment, sitting targets.

As I hurried to the car, across the rubbish, a swarm of flies rose up around me with a loud buzzing and a cat slithered against my ankles, then sped off, hissing. Cats. They were everywhere recently. Cats and armed looters. They prowled and scavenged the empty streets. And thrived. Horrible.

'It's *hadret el Mudira*,' Mustafa told the passengers on the back seat. Madam the Director. He liked to call me that, it amused him. For some reason – perhaps because I am a woman – he had been terribly impressed when he first found out that I was a director of the imposing-looking Literacy Centre where he dropped me off each day. He had spent the whole journey rolling his eyes towards me and clicking his tongue up and down, the only time I ever knew him with nothing to say.

'Move over, *khalti* my old dear,' he said to the woman who, with her wide bottom and her lapful of bags and baskets, was taking up most of the front seat. 'Make room for *hadret el Mudira. Yallah ya, khalti*! Hurry up! Apart from anything else,' – this with a big grin – 'it costs me money to spend the day sitting here.' And he drummed his fingers on the steering wheel.

The woman heaved and shuffled and her bags and baskets undulated on her lap, but she managed to make very little difference to the amount of space left for me. I felt sorry for her. She had bags between her feet, bags hugged to her chest, bursting with the most unlikely collection of things: plates, a lacy house-robe, a spare set of false teeth, a cuckoo wall clock. She must be fleeing her home in a hurry with whatever she had managed to grab, there was such a look on her face of misery.

'I ought to charge you double,' Mustafa grumbled at her. 'You take up enough room for two.' He put one arm around her shoulders to help to squeeze her in a little closer. 'Cheer up, aunty.'

I climbed in beside her, with difficulty, and Mustafa roared off as soon as both my feet were in, so that I had to shut the door in a hurry.

The car was hot and stuffy. Everybody, except Mustafa, had their windows up, for psychological protection, I suppose, against bullets. The fat woman had large shiny stains on her dress, creeping out from under her armpits and each time she breathed they gave off a sweaty smell as her arms sagged against them. I opened my window just a little. Mustafa, squashed in his corner, had his window wound right down and his arm resting on it as usual. The skin on his arm had turned very dark by this late stage of the summer and he looked almost Indian.

Poor Mustafa. I heard much later (was it from Rashid?) that he was killed eventually crossing the Green Line which, in the style of Cyprus or Berlin, came to divide Beirut into two halves. He was one of the few drivers who would make the crossing during the months when the danger was greatest, in spite of the large sums of money which were sometimes offered. But then, for money he would do anything. For money, or out of sheer joyful bravado.

We were a full taxi-load. Mustafa had a talent for that, for finding passengers, even in these empty streets. Behind me were two women in black, with black headscarves drawn in close so that their faces were partly hidden. One was crying and crying into a large handful of tissues which she was pulling one by one out of a box on her lap. Crying pitifully. The other woman was holding and comforting her, rocking with her and moaning sometimes, in unison with her sad keening.

'Her nephew was kidnapped yesterday,' Mustafa explained. 'Vanished without trace.'

'My neighbour saw it happen,' the crying woman said and her voice rose and fell to the rhythm of her wailing, in an incantation to her lost nephew. 'He was pulled into a car, my nephew. Pulled in. By a couple of men, my neighbour said. Pulled into the car and it drove off with him. My nephew! Leaving his little boy standing in the road. Wandering along the road by himself, looking for his daddy, his *abi*, following the way he had gone. My poor nephew, taken away. Gone. *Allah* have mercy.'

It was a dreadful thing. We all spoke at once, commiserating. There was a general hubbub of conversation, all of us relating our own griefs, recounting and reiterating all the dreadful things which the fighting had brought. Each of us had lost somebody or something, a way of life if nothing else. It was like a wake, like the gathering in the house of the bereaved, this group of people thrown together in the taxi, rocking, like the woman, from side to side as Mustafa hurtled round the corners.

'Poor little lad. He'll never see his father again. My nephew! Never again.'

'We'll find him. *Inshallah*,' said her friend.

'*Inshallah*,' we all murmured. 'God willing.'

The fat woman rocked heavily between myself and Mustafa: '*Inshallah, inshallah*.'

Mustafa broke in boisterously, 'We'll do what we can to find him. Tell me what he looks like. I see most things from this taxi.'

'In his thirties, straight black hair, dark eyes . . . ' Any young Lebanese man.

I twisted round as best I could and reached back my hand to the woman. She took it fumblingly and I gave her hand a squeeze. It was all the comfort I could offer.

'*Allah ma'ek*,' she sobbed, returning the pressure. 'God be with you.'

The man sitting next to them on the back seat, behind Mustafa, kept muttering things to himself in French. '*On va payer. On va payer.*' He was the only one who had listened without saying anything to the poor woman's story and now he sat muttering and twitching occasionally in his corner. He kept balancing the knife-edge crease of his pale, expensively tailored trousers on his knee, using his thumb and forefinger. Then he would dart a glance out of the window and stroke the sides of his nose delicately with the same thumb and forefinger, flicking them gracefully in the air – then cover up his nervous shaking once again by re-aligning the crease on his trembling knee. When he saw my gesture of comfort to the woman he flicked his face away towards the window and muttered again, '*On va payer*,' with a knife-sharp glint in his eye.

Mustafa wove his taxi at great speed, to and fro across the tense empty streets, just as if he were haring as usual in and out of the lines of traffic. 'Why should we be an easy target?' he asked when I remarked on it. But it was his sense of style, I think, which was at stake as much as anything. His young man's panache.

The fat woman was the first to get out. We swung even more wildly from side to side of the road as we approached her dropping point. 'To confuse them,' said Mustafa, grinning at me and letting go the steering wheel for one terrible moment to raise his hands in imitation of a sniper.

I stood on the pavement, holding some of the bags and parcels, while the fat woman slowly and painfully got out. Mustafa cursed her irritably for the time it took. '*Yallah, khalti! Yallah*! Come on, aunty, you're costing me a fortune, and giving the snipers time to eat their dinner first. *Yallah, yallah*!' He was really angry with her in the tension of the moment.

Everybody took sides, sympathising volubly with one or the other of them. All of us (the man with the creases I noticed especially) were anxious at having to wait on that exposed crossroads. An old man blinked at me from the shelter of a narrow alley as I stood waiting to get back in. Spread in front of him on the pavement was a selection of Lebanese and foreign newspapers, a very poor selection compared to the usual scores of different ones to be had. How on earth he had managed to get hold of any at all, I couldn't imagine. Nor how he would manage to sell them.

My head ached again. I caught sight of the body of a middle-aged woman, with her clothes twisted around her, lying in the gutter a few yards away. I was a fool to be out.

'Come on, aunty! *Yallah, yallah*!' Mustafa helped to shove the fat woman to her feet. At last she was clear of the car with all her bags and baskets heaped in her arms. I climbed back in.

'Well, shall we go by the public gardens today?' Mustafa asked me with a burst of mischievous humour, relieved to be speeding on his way again. '*Hadret el Mudira* must see the flowers in the gardens at Sanayeh,' he told the others and he stepped on the accelerator.

'For goodness sake, no,' I told him.

'Why not?'

Of course we did not go. Sanayeh was on Sharif al-Akhaoui's list of forbidden territory. The Mourabitun had set up one of their battle positions there and it was no place for a joy-ride. We did not go, but I loved the look in Mustafa's eye while he contemplated it, reminding me a little of Elena. I loved his recklessness.

'So work still calls?' he asked me, curiously, after a moment. There were not many people, after all, who were risking the journey to the office that week.

'Yes. Yes, there are some things I badly need from my office for the emergency advice service I'm setting up. But also, I'm hoping to get in touch with my daughter . . .'

'Ah, how is she, your daughter? Wayward as ever?'

'Not exactly wayward . . .' I said.

I began, without meaning to, to go over in my mind all the things that had come to me in the middle of the night while I lay huddled wakefully in the corridor: the new ideas for my work, the list of things I must fetch today, my plans for contacting Elena; all the things which, along with the thunder of the shelling, had insistently invaded both my dreams and my sleepless spells all night, so that this morning I felt swollen-eyed and groggy. I was exhausted from the pressure – the pressure not only of the battle going on around me, but of forever thinking passionately and urgently about this and that aspect of my work, about the whole new realm of work which had come my way with the drastic breakdown of all the usual public services, new responsibilities, new tasks – On my diet of chickpeas. So that now I was definitely beginning to feel ill. My head was aching badly.

'Not exactly wayward,' I said. 'Yes, it's true she lives most of the time in a tent, on the edges of the desert, but –'

'She's a nomad, then. A bedouin,' Mustafa said with satisfaction.

'Well, yes. And if she stays that way I don't mind. It's not that which worries me. Why should I worry if she's searching after her radical alternatives? She writes – she used to write – such cheerful letters home, spilling out all her news with such enthusiasm, page after page after page. Such bouncy girl-guide enthusiasm –'

'Like my little sister,' said Mustafa, with love. 'Just like my little sister. A bouncy girl guide.' The metaphor seemed to amuse him.

'What does she do in the desert, your daughter?' asked the woman who was comforting her friend, with polite interest.

'She's an economist. She's working on a famine relief scheme in Ethiopia. Which she loves. She loves it there. Only what pains me a little is that so much intelligence,' – what was it I wanted to say? – 'that so much beauty and caring should still be so gawkily uncoordinated in a girl of her age, that they should not yet have fused together into the warm sparkle of womanhood. At twenty-three . . . ' There were murmurs of understanding from the back seat.

Why always the 'buts', the anxiety, the intense mixture of pleasure and pain I felt at the thought of Elena, even then? Is it just the pain of what happened later, obtruding into my memories? No, I think not. Some hurt – (was it because of George and myself? yes, but not only that) – some hurt had kept her prickly and spikey, strangely angular and teenage-gawky beyond the proper age for such things.

'But she writes – ' I said, 'she used to write with such exuberance, such freshness.' Again the understanding murmurs. And I love her, I would have added were it not for the woman whose nephew was lost, I love her, not only because she's Elena, my daughter, but because she's so happy, so wonderfully full of life.

Mustafa said, 'You've still heard nothing from her?'

'How could I have, when no post has been delivered for so many months now?'

'But she hasn't been in touch at all, by any other means? By phone or anything?'

'No.'

The woman in the back said, 'And you're afraid she'll fly home to find out what's happening to you all?'

'Yes, yes! Exactly!' So I had not been mad after all, these last few days, worrying about Elena who was the very one who was, for the moment, safely out of all this. 'Exactly! It would be typical of her just to turn up like that. And now especially, when I know she was expecting to have her holiday. If only I could warn her somehow. The road from the airport is so especially dangerous. There have been so many roadblocks and murders.'

At the mention of murders the poor bereaved woman let out another wail and began to sob and rock all over again. '*Allah* protect him,' she cried between wails. '*Allah yihmeeh.*'

'*Allah yihmeeh,*' we each repeated.

'That's why I've come out today, as much as anything else,' I told Mustafa. 'To try to get a message through to Elena, I hope – I hope! – by our office telex. You see, the trouble is with these tents of hers, she could be anywhere.'

Yes, I could feel now that I was ill. Ill with the fear and tension. With the shock, too, of this other woman's loss. There was a din building up inside my head. The car engine roared as Mustafa accelerated up a rise.

My mind moved on again from the question of contacting Elena to the list of all the other things to be done when I reached the office. And from there, obsessively, to the other list, the more complex list of the things I was working on for long hours each day while I was cooped up at home. My radio series, due to start on the air next week, still had impossibly many gaps. There were so many bits of information I needed still, in order to produce a sufficiently comprehensive set of programmes on how to manage under siege. Nutrition, first aid – there were still scripts to edit and people I was trying to contact in hectic haste, while the telephone system was becoming more and more erratic. Soon it might be impossible to organise anything at all.

And then there was . . . But I was already ill from thinking of ten things at once, let alone twenty, or thirty. And Mustafa was swinging us mercilessly round the corners, making me feel peculiarly dizzy. Not far now . . .

We were on higher ground now, clear of the pall of smoke, and I could see right across the city to the east, to the slopes of al-Ashrafiyah where Yusef lived. It was difficult to make much out from this distance, with so much smoke rising from various buildings in between, but I thought I could just see the hospital where he worked, where recently there had been frequent shelling. Two or three times lately, when I had rung Yusef at home, the line went dead as soon as I had dialled, making me think each time that his house must have been hit. It was terrible, the dead line. A cruel thing.

But today I knew they were all right still. Yusef had rung me three times since midnight, during the shelling near my flat. 'Little mother, are you O.K.?' Dear Yusef, always so loving and thoughtful about me. Latifa had come to the phone as well, in the small hours, and I sent my love to the children, who were awake too, she said, and didn't know whether to be more frightened or excited. Poor children. A dozen or so shells exploded while we were talking and I could hear them quite clearly down the phone as well as through my own windows, making the three kilometres which separated us seem much less.

If I could only keep Elena away from all this at least. Oh, the ache, ache, ache in my head.

The buildings we were passing now shone hot and white against the sparkling sea. They were lovely as ever. And the mountains, there to the other side, the sheer beauty . . . It has all changed of course, by now. Those buildings have mostly been destroyed since then. Which is the tragedy of Lebanon – the throwing away, I mean, of such loveliness.

'What have they done to him, do you think?' the weeping woman in the taxi burst out. 'My poor nephew, oh my poor nephew. *Ya waili*! What do you think they've done to him?'

We rounded a corner and came suddenly upon a road block: a smouldering line of burnt-out tyres. A group of young men – boys, they were only boys, aged about fifteen or sixteen – were fooling around near them, shouting and laughing. A couple of them were playing around with rifles, two very real rifles, Kalashnikovs, with the big crescent-shaped magazines. Almost certainly, in this neighbourhood and with K'lashn's like those, the boys would be Moslems. I began to be apprehensive about my Christian identity card.

But Mustafa, though he slowed down, showed no sign that he intended to stop.

'Bloody kids and their road blocks,' he said and he veered round to bump his way through a narrow gap in the smouldering line. The stench of burnt rubber filled the car and made me cough – a suffocating smell.

The boys were watching us, waving their arms and shouting. The two who had rifles were pointing them at us and making a game of seeming to pull the trigger.

'Rat-ta-ta-ta-ta! Rat-ta-ta-ta-ta!' A dangerous game to play with real rifles. A silly game. It seemed to set the nerves of the man in the back seat, with the knife-edged creases, more on edge still. I could hear him begin to puff and wheeze.

Then, what was more dangerous and stupid still, one of the boys ran out into the road and made a heroic gesture of dropping to one knee and pointing his rifle after our car. Big laughs from all his friends . . .

The knife-crease man went suddenly rigid, as if gripped by an electric shock. Then, so fast it was done before any of us realised what he was doing, he had wound down his window and was leaning out, pointing a pistol back up the road. He fired. And fired again.

I stared. The women stared. We simply couldn't believe it. Mustafa stepped so hard on the accelerator that we sped forward with a lurch and in a moment we had rounded a corner into a quiet side street. Whether the boy was hit I don't know. It's something I shall never know. The man drew his head and arm back in through the window.

Mustafa was cursing angrily. 'Son of a — ! Not when you're in my taxi, if you don't mind!'

The man carefully wrapped his pistol up in a white silk handkerchief and put it in his pocket, looking a little sheepish. He pinched his trouser creases between finger and thumb and arranged them carefully on each knee. He had stopped trembling.

That man. That terrible man. I shall never forget him and his flawless elegance.

We were nearly there and the streets were suddenly peaceful here, in the neighbourhood of my office. Mustafa stopped the car beside the steps of the Middle East Literacy Centre – or 'Center' as it was spelt on the trilingual nameplate by the pillared entrance. I said good-bye to the women, those poor women, in the back. They had shrunk into the corner, as far away as they could from that dreadful man. This time they did not ask God to be with me when I told them, with all the appropriate phrases, how much I grieved for their lost nephew. They looked at me with white suspicious faces. They must have known, I suppose, by everything about me that I was a Christian – like that man after all. Like the kidnappers no doubt were, who took away their young man.

Mustafa leaned back and laid his arm nonchalantly along the top of the seat. He made an exaggerated attempt at his usual cheerful grin. 'You see?' he said to me. 'Here safe and sound. There's no danger when you drive with Mustafa!'

It seemed somehow not quite the thing to say. At any rate, I paid him four times the usual fare. It would have been churlish to pay anything much less.

I have often wondered whether perhaps, if I had sat down to rest even for five minutes after I arrived at my office, I might not have had my stroke that day – the first of my two strokes. Perhaps; perhaps not. In any case I was in far too much of a hurry to sit down. I wanted to find what I needed before anything else could happen to prevent me. There might be a prowler in the empty building perhaps, or . . . I hunted through my filing cabinet with my fingers and thumbs stumbling against each other. The emptiness of the place was eerie, the silence strange, with the muffled sounds of rifle fire away in the distance. My stately office had a funereal layer of dust on everything. The crinkled skeletons of my once huge and beautiful pot plants stood, dry and shrivelled, in the marbled window alcoves. The plaster figures on the frieze around the ceiling stared vacuously down at the icons, my lovely Eastern Orthodox icons on the walls, whose black backgrounds, together with the black, black ebony of the cabinets, today cast dark shadowy reflections in the great gilt-framed mirror, reflections which gave a ghostly flicker as the sun caught the brass handles and fittings in the room and glanced off the glass tables; so that I kept thinking there was someone else moving about.

My poor lovely soulless office, of which I used to be so fond! More even than my flat, my office was important to me, filled with all my own things: the Persian carpets, the icons, I had brought everything here with me. Because I love beauty, I love it. I love to be surrounded by it. And to work as I did, sometimes totally engulfed and absorbed, *living* here it seemed almost at times; my home . . . To work as I did, completely involved in my work, it mattered that my whole person should be here, my whole self; and also, reflected in the mirror, so much more besides . . . It was as if – as if with my huge mirror doubling the size of the room almost, I could think at greater depth.

But today the eeriness . . . And I could not put even half my mind to what I was trying to do.

The boys, with their road block . . . And yes, I was feeling shaken. Much, much more shaken than I thought. I had always imagined that I had developed a certain psychological immunity to the incidents of war, a certain familiarity. After all, I had so often been to where there was fighting going on, places my work had taken me: the West Bank in 1967, in the June War; then Jordan in 1970 when King Hussein had his showdown with the Palestinian commandos; and of course southern Lebanon many times, amid the perennial skirmishes on the Israeli border. But one is never immune, never, to each new instant in which people are in danger or are being killed.

And I could not stop thinking of the way the women in the taxi had suddenly grown suspicious of me. I was still hurt by it: the way they had shrunk from that man and then classed me along with him, as one of his fellow Christians. Yes, yes of course I am a Christian, but to be categorised, without mitigation . . .

I wanted to say to them, look, I belong to the Orthodox Church, I am different. I'm not what you think, not a Maronite and not at all a subscriber to the political ideology you imagine. How can you arbitrarily assign me, simply by one aspect of my life, to one or the other of two opposite camps? What camps? It shocked me to find that people could be bewildered and horrified by the whole business of the fighting and yet, still, out of fear and necessity, begin to draw, as it were, the green line. Constricting, if they were not careful, their whole outlook.

Surely, how could anybody, any reasonable person, be said to belong totally on one side or the other? As if the fighting were so simple as to be about religion only! As if religion were so simple . . .

I wanted to tell the women . . . But it was my radio script I should be thinking about. I should be working out which papers and journals I needed to collect in order to rewrite one of my scripts in the way which had come to me in the middle of the night. I should be thinking . . . But I could not think. The road block, Yusef, Elena, the weeks and weeks of strain . . . It was suddenly all too much. I could think of nothing. There was just a raddled mass of fears and tensions, like matted wool, pressing on my thoughts and getting me nowhere.

I sat down and was just beginning to go through the drawers of my desk, hoping that what I saw there would jog my mind back into action, when the door opened and a man walked in.

It was Rashid.

'Samia! What on earth are you doing here?'

'Oh, Rashid! It's you! *Na-aztni*! You made my heart stop!'

'But what is all this? How did you get here? You didn't run into any trouble on the way?' We were embracing each other with joy, as if we had not met for months, kissing each other's cheeks, a dozen times.

I told him about the boys and their road block. And about that man. 'I don't *think* the boy was hurt. Not as far as I know. We all got a bit of a fright, that's all.'

'That's all? That's all? But Samia! You know perfectly well that if you'd been stopped you might easily have been murdered.'

'They were only boys.'

'Don't kid yourself. You know very well that you risked your life coming here. And why? Whatever did you come for? Just for these little bits of paper?' He flicked, with a great cheerful show of disdain, through the few papers I had so far put on top of my filing cabinet. 'You go gallivanting through the middle of a battlefield just for these?'

'Ooff Rashid! *Haram aleik*! You're merciless! Poor me, you always make fun of me.' I shook a fistful of papers at him, but he grabbed my wrist and shook it back.

'Me?' he said. 'Me? Merciless? You're the one who's treating yourself without mercy, playing Jeanne d'Arc in the battlefields. Or rather, no, that Englishwoman more like:

Boadicea, leaving the mere boys of this world standing gaping beside their puny barricades while you charge through in your chariot of fire.'

I tried partly to free my fist, partly to get it near his nose. 'You! You!'

But he was enjoying himself, playing one of his favourite games, jumping from Arabic to French to English metaphor, according to the mood of the moment, chasing a thought across the three languages in search of *le mot juste*, the most apt way of putting it, *al kilmeh al munasiba*; in his own special brand of Lebanese Polyglot.

He pulled the fingers of my fist to his lips and kissed them. We were both laughing. But this would not do. My papers.

'I said, 'Look, I'm much too busy. I've got no time to stop and joke with you.'

'Exactly. That's exactly why I'm joking. You need to be made fun of. You're trying to kill yourself, not only out on the streets, but with overwork and seriousness too.' He looked at me. So fondly, admiringly, in spite of what he said. I was always lucky to work with him. We made a good team, Rashid and I. And it was his fondness for me, I think, which used to buoy me up in my work in those difficult years when George was ill and dying.

'You know,' Rashid said, standing with his elbows on the back of one of my armchairs, 'you really should come with us to Damascus.'

'Ah, so you've definitely fixed up to go.'

'Well, obviously, yes. It's impossible to work from here. At least in Syria we'll be able to get down to things again.'

I shrugged. He knew my feelings.

'That's why I'm here today,' he said. 'To put some last minute things together. And to check that the building's still secure.'

'And yet you scold me for coming.'

'But that's a different matter altogether! Two minutes. Two minutes is all it takes me to walk here. And there's been no shooting near here today.'

'Aha. And when do you leave for Damascus?'

'As soon as there's another ceasefire and it's safe to go. Next week I should imagine. You'll see: it's nearly the end of the month, it won't be long before they arrange a ceasefire, so the banks can open and the militiamen get their pay.'

'Next week my radio series starts.'

'So you've definitely decided not to come with us?'

'You *know* I'm not coming,' I said.

'I'll find out whether you could broadcast your series from Syria.'

'Yes, there's no harm in asking. But how could I work from Damascus? I need to *be* here to know what the problems *are*. There's so much terror. So much chaos. People are so desperate for support and advice. How can I plan each programme if I'm not in touch with their questions? And Yusef's here. This is my home. No, I shan't leave.'

'But the danger. I can't afford to lose you.'

'You know me, Rashid. You know how I feel about my work. And never before has it been as crucial as now. Just think, people are having to learn again from scratch how to live: how to cook without food, how to wash without water. So far water's not such a problem. But who knows how much worse things may get? Then what shall we have, when there's no more water to flush the toilets and if people flock to the basements for shelter for longer and longer periods? Dysentery? Typhoid? We must tell people in advance what to do. And the children. We can't allow them to go for months and months with no schools, nothing. There are so many, many things which need to be done. And which need to be done *here*. So many things and so few people in a position to do them.'

I was hot behind my eyes, from the passion I felt about the situation or from illness, I don't know which. The papers in my desk drawer merged into a blur of dancing print, refusing to let me make out the words on them. So many things . . . And myself so tired . . .

Rashid was pacing softly to and fro across the carpet, stopping to stroke the dust off the shoulders of my little statuette in the arched alcove, and then back again. He was saying, 'But here in Beirut we're working with our hands tied behind our backs and – almost literally – a gun at our heads. In Damascus we'll be able to get properly prepared for the day when we can start to put Lebanon back together again.'

'Yes, you're right to go, Rashid. You *should* go. And you'll be able to look after my United Nations work for me, in the Yemen. Which reminds me, you will help Haya for me, won't you, with her training course, for literacy teachers – in Syria? She hasn't set one up by herself before and there's some problem, she said, in getting enough volunteers to work outside Damascus.'

'Don't *worry*!'

'Yes, you should go. In any case, your family's not here. It's different for you. I mean you don't belong here, you don't belong to this crisis as I do. I can't leave. Nothing will make me leave while the Troubles continue.'

Rashid was leaning across the desk and looking at me closely. 'I'll get you a drink,' he said. 'You should indulge yourself just a little, don't you think?'

'You're very sweet, but no thank you. I must finish this before I'm too tired even to stand up.'

The intermittent sounds of rifle fire in the distance had merged with the pains in my head so that I could not tell them apart. I made myself stand up and go over to the bookshelves to sort through my box files, taking out pamphlets, letters, this and that, keeping going at all costs, even though I hardly knew by now what I was doing.

The next thing Rashid said was so unexpected that for a moment my hands did stop their sorting.

He said, 'If you were a Moslem I would marry you.'

If you were a Moslem I would marry you. Again and again during the years which have passed since then, I have remembered him saying that. If you were a Moslem I would marry you. Not that I thought, then, that he meant what he said. No, no, not literally speaking. But to me that sentence came to stand for Rashid, to be my symbol of him. It said so much about him. About me.

'You would marry me,' I said. 'I see. And what makes you think I would marry *you*?'

Why so uppity? I might have been Elena's age with a retort like that. Rashid deserved better. And, rightly, gave as bad back. He threw up his hands histrionically, waving his fingers as if they were tendrils feeling for a non-existent hold above his head. He said, in English, 'Ah, you emancipated

Christian women with your European husbands and your fancy European ways.' Then, '*Que vous êtes impossibles!*' And in Arabic, 'You won't even let me get you a drink.'

'Please, Rashid, you know I don't appreciate your low humour. And you know very well that I was emancipated long before I married an Englishman.'

'And I know very well that you will always rise to the bait.' He chuckled and shook his head at me. 'Samia, Samia.'

I turned back to the bookshelves. Blobs of pale grey blindness were swimming in front of them. I would soon have to sit down.

Rashid said, 'If I can't make you cry for your own good, then I *must* laugh at you. You're incorrigible, Samia my dear. Look at you, you run about in the middle of all this – this shooting,' – and here he made an extravagant gesture as if to suggest that the shooting were some sort of grand theatrical folly – 'you get yourself embroiled, nearly, in a duel, and then what do you do? You talk to me pleasantly about the boys you saw passing the time of day by the roadside, leaning on their shooting sticks – ' I opened my mouth to protest at this, without success. He waved my protests away. 'But I know you, Samia *habeebti*, my very dear Samia. You show the world only your cool, your so very dry and cool and capable exterior. But I know that you're hiding a very lovely and a very fiery woman. And I also know that at this moment you're very ill. Only you won't show that either if you can help it.'

'Cool? But I told you I was frightened. And besides, you know my fears about Elena – '

'Ah, yes, your magnitudinous fears about Elena, who is three – perhaps four – thousand kilometres away from the dangers which you say are lying in wait for her. But as for yourself, you told me you had a slight fright in the voice in which my English headmistress used to say: "How do you do? So airless today, don't you find?" You can be so cool, Samia, that butter wouldn't melt in your mouth. Isn't that the phrase? Or do I muddle my metaphors again?'

She was Rashid's standing joke, this headmistress of his from his schooldays in Egypt. She had herself become a metaphor. (If one can believe that she ever actually existed.)

I said, 'Rashid, your metaphors are always muddling. You should keep to proposals of marriage.'

'At last,' he said. 'Good, at last you're beginning to melt a little. That's better.'

He laughed, his warm happy laugh. How is it, I often wonder, that Rashid survived being brought up as both an Arab and an imitation Englishman – survived and survives everything else in his life, even the loss of his wife whom he loved so dearly – without ever losing his coherence, his wholeness, his light-hearted humorous self? Whereas in my own case... Look what my schizophrenic English-education-cramped Arabness has done to me. It's as if I were made up of a pair of warring dragons, or rather, no, as if I were a dragon with two heads, each eating the other away with recriminations and resentments and with bitter regrets that they were ever flung together on the same body. But then I often think the Egyptians are a different breed from us Arabs of the Levant. The fire-breathing without the burning. They have an instinct for survival. Rashid's dragon heads seem to muddle along, like his metaphors, in unlikely harmony.

But the two-headed dragons of the Levant? Look at Israel/Palestine. A two-headed dragon if ever there was one, two peoples fighting for ownership of the same body. Or the two heads of Lebanon: Christian and Moslem, rich and poor, European and Arab, call them what you like. There are so many definitions of what the conflict consists of.

And the names of my own two heads?

I know, at least, what Rashid would call them. Puritanism and Passion. Christian Puritanism and Arab Passion. There has always been in me that combination of puritan striving and straining, of hard-working conscientious continually-working purposefulness – all those European ruling class virtues of my missionary college schooling – mixed with Arab passion; leading to such passionately keen striving. So that my blood pressure soared and soared...

But the way in which Rashid assimilated his English education was quite different. His secular English school demanded that his intellect conform to all the notions of empire. But it was not a missionary school. It did not also demand his soul, as mine did. Instead, Rashid stole the soul of his headmistress, to incarcerate it in his never-ending series of jokes. Whether she actually existed or not, she served her purpose in allowing Rashid to enclose his schooldays in a jar; a jar in which, Aladdin-like, he kept the soul of the British-in-Egypt firmly trapped, at his beck and call for ever more.

But where was I?

Yes, in my office, with Rashid and proposals of marriage.

I may have sounded better, but I didn't feel it. The grey blobs had by now obliterated the whole bookshelf. Although I blinked and blinked again, I could not manage to see it. I remember thinking, I'm losing my balance. I mustn't fall, I must not, not *now*.

Rashid caught me. He had me in my chair at once and became infinitely solicitous, bemoaning the fact that he had no jacket to put round my shoulders. He had come out, for once, in his shirt sleeves. But he had no need to give me his jacket, he had his whole self wrapped warmly round my shoulders.

'Now you must sit still,' he said, 'and do nothing. Absolutely nothing. Do you understand? No papers, no bright new ideas, nothing. While I go and find you a glass of my *araq*.'

He left me with my head propped on a big soft cushion on my desk. I felt so ashamed. Ashamed of succumbing to my own weakness.

So that was it. Finish. The end of my career. I had just twenty minutes left, though of course I did not know it then, just twenty minutes in which to finish preparing messages for Elena which would never be sent, in which to gather the remaining notes for a radio series which I would never present, in which to fail to tie up all the loose ends which I would have wanted to tie if I knew that my life, as I had lived it until now, would be finished when the twenty minutes were up. Just twenty minutes in which to salvage my future, my very committed rewarding future which, in response to the current crisis, had seemed to be on the point of expanding into an entirely new dimension.

Because of course I still kept on telling myself, 'One day I shall do this, or that. One day I shall achieve such and such.' I was already nearly sixty, but I had such a feeling still that everything was just on the point of beginning for me, that the brand of 'Arabness' my generation hoped to create through our work – the synthesis of East and West in a new Arab culture which would have neither the shortcomings of the existing Islamic states nor the pitfalls of wholesale Westernization – that such a world was still ours to create.

Laughable now with hindsight, yes perhaps. But surely one is justified in having a grandiose view of one's life's work? A grand vision of a world to be created out of chaos and schisms? Without such a vision in the eye of God, there would have been no world.

I had only twenty minutes left of my working life and yet I just sat and did nothing, exactly as Rashid had told me to do. And what strikes me now as ironic: my mind, for once, was not even on my work.

I remember I was thinking about what Rashid had said: 'If you were a Moslem I would marry you.' That was so like him, I thought, to say something apparently straightforward, even if it was a little startling, and yet to mean something much more subtle. He was not the sort of person to let tradition stop him from marrying a Christian if that was what he wanted. Far from it. He was too much of a radical for that, always refusing to let himself be hidebound by conventional thinking. No, no, he did not mean that he wanted to marry me but could not because we were of different religions.

And yet, I thought, it's true that in his own personal life he is very much a conservative. His wife, Fadwa, had been a Moslem like himself, very beautiful with her pale eggshell skin and large dark eyes. She was a very intelligent person, very much admired. She had become, in her quiet way, something of an expert on ancient Arabic poetry; she would talk about it with such animation in her eyes, such love for it. To me she seemed very much the traditional cultured Moslem woman. Which she enjoyed being. That was the thing about her, she so much enjoyed honouring the traditions. To her, being a woman and a wife was an art form, like poetry or musicianship, a skill which had to be worked at with imagination and a very self-assured pride. When she laid the table for a dinner party – it was something she always made a point of doing herself, with only the minimum of help from the servants – it was done with intricate craftsmanship. Beautifully. Each dish for the first course was painstakingly decorated, the little filled pastries each individually sculptured with a motif on top to suggest their various contents. And the hand-embroidered cloths and serviettes of her own making – she should have been a designer if she had ever worked at a profession. She would have been quite outstanding.

There was one particular evening when I was invited for dinner, at their former house in Beit Miry, in the mountains just outside Beirut. I remember I came, unfortunately, straight from work. It had become a habit with me, since George had died and the children had begun to lead their own lives, to work late at my office each night, a habit I ought to have been better at breaking from time to time. I had brought my grey and gold kaftan with me, one of my favourites, to change into for the evening. But it's not the same. Not the same, I mean, as going home to have a bath, to dress carefully, to prepare oneself for the spirit of the evening. I came with the city sweat and grime still on me and with my thoughts dishevelled, racing somewhere out of context of this decorous house. Fadwa, dressed in ivory silk, came to kiss me on either cheek with her cool smooth skin and her quiet dignity and I felt vulgar and ashamed to be caught like this in my unpressed clothes, exactly as I had felt once when, at the age of sixteen, my mother had caught me reading a slushy forbidden romance and scoffing sweet crumbling *maamouls* under my rumpled bed quilt, long after I should have been asleep; an uncouth child.

We had dinner that night with all the dining-room doors thrown open to the terrace so that we could smell the jasmine and look down on the lights of Beirut below us. The room looked lovely, as ever, decorated in white and beige and palest ivory. The flowers in the middle of the table were tiny and delicate, like bundles of white lace, and the servants had lace aprons to match. The curtains, the carpets, everything was part of the colour-scheme, even the clay-coloured figures on the Egyptian wall-paintings, standing sentry-like beyond the lamplight. But there was something about the decorousness tonight which made me feel discontented, claustrophobic, itching for the unpredictability of open spaces; for the vastness of the dark pine-covered mountainside just beyond the terrace.

I drank a little too much, I think. It was at the time when I was still grieving very close to the surface for George, but that's no excuse. Something must have gone wrong at work that day too, I think, because by the time the dessert came – a light and delicious concoction of apricots, with brandy, almonds and cream – by then I felt such an overpowering discontent. And I had none of that feeling I used to have when George was alive that when I got home I would be able to let off steam at somebody. (Poor George, was it really as bad as that?)

I must have been a little drunk because I kept seeing the room as a tableau. Even the guests were a part of it. We were Rashid's usual eclectic gathering, speaking three, perhaps four languages round the table. There was a bearded viola player, of outspoken views, a management consultant, even a car mechanic with a passion for botany. All Lebanese life was there. (Except that it wasn't, as Elena would have been quick to point out.) Rashid's colour against Fadwa's shades of calm. A cheerfully contrived tableau. And it seemed to me that I had had my fill of tableaux lately, since a visiting Saudi colleague had insisted recently on having me accompany him nightly to the Casino to see the famous and fabulous cabaret there. It seemed to me that making tableaux had become too much of a cult in Lebanon of late; that the tableaux had become too complacent.

And suddenly I wanted to change this one, to make it move. Not destroy it, no. The intention of the political radicals was never to destroy Lebanon, only to shake it, wake it, disturb it just a little, set it in creative motion. But what am I saying? What had Rashid's tableau to do with politics?

I mean only that I was a little drunk that night. I must have been slumped down in my chair because I remember I was looking at Professor David opposite me through the lacy white flowers between us, watching his pink face and his glasses flickering in and out of the stems. He was a good friend of mine, from the American University of Beirut, full of New England charm. And it must have been something he said . . . Yes, he was saying in his contemplative professorial way – meant, I think, a little as a challenge to me – he was saying that each flower was so perfectly positioned that to change any one of them would upset the whole arrangement. And so I moved one little spray – or tried to turn the flowers round to see how they looked from all sides – I don't remember which. And accidentally knocked the whole bowl over. I must certainly have been a little drunk.

Fadwa said something quietly to a maid and within moments an almost identical lacy bunch was put, with smiles, in its place. How could Fadwa be so impossible to disturb? But then she did not live to see her world destroyed beyond reconstruction by this terrible fighting.

If you were a Moslem . . .

No, I thought, I could never live within such order and contentment, such simple single-aspect beauty, I could never be Rashid's wife. If he ever marries again he will marry a Moslem. What had he meant then? That he was very fond of me, at a safe distance, but that I was really a little too odd with my fiercely turbulent ways of carrying on? He preferred his women to be a little more conventional?

But then again, Rashid would never be so negative. He loves my fierceness, I thought; my turbulence. I know that. It matches his own vibrant love of life. We both have that same quality, Rashid and I, that vibrant rocking Arab flamboyance. But whereas Rashid rocks like a pendulum, perfectly in balance, perfectly in time with himself, when I rock I overturn the whole works.

What did he say? If you were a Moslem . . . Yes, if circumstances had been different, very different; if things in the Middle East had not been as they are, then who knows . . .

Dreams of safe and stable worlds . . .

And then, coming back to myself, I was surprised to find myself sitting, dreaming, doing nothing, leaning on my desk with my head cradled in my arms and my arms on a comfortable cushion. For weeks I had filled every minute with work, work, work. And here I was now, basking in the sweetness of doing nothing!

But no, not sweetness. I was ill. And apart from that, there was already the turmoil in my mind, the recriminations, the self-doubts . . . The lists of things I had meant to do started to churn again in my mind, round and round in jumbled fashion, with a feeling in my head like grinding teeth. I sat up straight, beginning to be restless. Why not get on with it, now that I felt a litttle better? Two more addresses where Elena might be contactable . . . Another bibliography on sewage disposal (the contents of my applied literacy classes for small farmers had their uses) . . . But I felt too tired to get up. My big luxuriant bottle garden on the plinth over beside the mirror looked, as far as I could see through the dust, as if it could do with a drop of water. I ought to fetch some.

Too tired . . .

It crossed my mind that Rashid might not perhaps have meant anything at all by his remark about marriage. Perhaps he was just looking for something to startle me, to shake me up enough to make my mind jump aside from the groove which my perpetual thoughts of work had gouged so deep with their continual day and night grinding. He would be chuckling to himself now, wondering what I had made of his remark. 'If you were a . . . ' Rashid! I knew that chuckle. It followed the visits to the Literacy Centre of ladies from overseas with blue-rinsed hair, who were looking for a worthy cause on which to bestow their charity, the charity of their after-golf benevolent societies. 'Literacy – ' Rashid would say, and in their minds' eyes the ladies would see simple sluggardly peasants being tidied into orderly schoolrooms, learning to read and write. He would show them his films of Literacy Centre advisers visiting poor rural backwaters of the Middle East and they would go away happy. And send more money. Which is why, of course, Rashid was our Organising Director, in charge of our finances. He had a genius for enticing their money out of them.

But he did not share their blue-rinsed naïvety. His ideas were like his guest lists and his polyglot language: eclectic, as he used to tell me, with his chuckle. His approach to his job was so – so florid. And his definitions of literacy were beautifully variegated in political hue. So that while the blue-rinsed ladies were being shown out of one door, the bearded grassroots-power boys in faded jeans were being ushered in at the other. He would talk to them about literacy and they would conjure up visions, strobe-lit revolutionary visions, of the down-trodden masses infiltrating print rooms and script rooms and reclaiming democracy and mass communications for the people. Rashid showed each group the same films. He told them much the same things, only in differently coloured language. And he would chuckle benignly, leaving them each to pick out the tones and undertones they liked from his variegated linguistic garden. And leaving me – this was the point, Rashid had such implicit faith in my ideas – leaving me, the Project Director, free to develop our projects exactly as I saw fit.

My office was beginning to be stifling as the morning grew hotter. There was of course no air conditioning today and the windows were tightly and safely closed. The plants in their urns over in the window alcoves were looking more shrivelled and skeletal still, the dust thicker. My head had sunk down on to my arms again, but the cushion beneath had become hot and damp against my cheek and I pushed it out of the way, resting my head on the piles of papers instead, while my thoughts trailed sluggishly along in search of a definition of literacy relevant to Lebanon now. What is one to make of the value of literacy when more than ninety per cent of the people are literate, by the conventional definition, but are suddenly quite helpless? Literacy for what? For resorting to guns to settle arguments? So much for my precious faith in literacy.

All at once the written word had become almost unheard of in Beirut. In Beirut! The publishing and printing house of the Arab world! But if written communication had become impossible, I was surely right to expand into the medium of radio in order to give people the tools to cope with this crisis? The tools, perhaps, to resolve it? With my radio series I had *carte blanche* from the Education Ministry to begin on the 'education for reconstruction' of Lebanon. Out of chaos, God created the world . . . The tantalising synthesis of Lebanon's multi-faceted culture was perhaps, even now, just waiting to be realised. But through literacy? What did I mean? – literacy. Where to go from here . . .

But it was no good. My ideas came back to me with the stale pre-masticated taste of belching.

Rashid came back, carrying a bottle of *araq* and two glasses.

'I'm sorry, I couldn't find any water anywhere to have with it. None of the taps are working.'

So my bottle garden would have to stay dry too. '*Malesh*,' I said. 'Never mind. It doesn't matter.'

'I would have offered you a Scotch, but this was all I had.'

'I prefer *araq*.' All the same, I would have liked it better with water, fresh and cool in my mouth like aniseed toothpaste. But never mind, he was so pleased to bring it for me.

I could not get my hand to grip the glass he gave me, which was a very strange sensation, as if my hand were just an empty glove. But I remember I blamed the way I had been sitting, with my head leaning heavily against my right arm. I could feel the pins and needles in my fingers.

With my left hand I had no trouble. I raised my glass and thought no more about it.

'*Sihtek* – your health!' said Rashid. 'Is it all right?'

It was like fire, drunk without water. It made things less important than they were before. 'Thank you, lovely. Just right.'

'Good. Now tell me about Elena.'

'You want me to tell you? No, you'll laugh at my worries.'

'You know very well that I'm not laughing at the bits of you that matter,' he said and smiled at me, with such warmth. Almost lovingly.

It came home to me then that he was leaving. 'Rashid,' I said, 'I'm going to miss you when you go to Damascus.' Very much.

'Ah, at last! At last it has occurred to you that you're going to miss me!'

He came round to my side of the desk, drew up a chair for himself and gave me a hug. Then he sat down, with his hand resting on my knee.

'And Elena?' he asked.

'It's just that I'm so worried she'll come here.' I told him about my plans to send messages by the telex machine downstairs, warning her not to fly home.

'But why the urgency? Just now when it's so dangerous for you to be out?'

'Because it's precisely now that she's supposed to be coming. It's supposed to be her holiday time. That's what she told me last year, at least. The end of October, or the beginning of November at the latest, she said. Which means during the next two or three weeks. It's a slack time in her work – something to do with the end of the autumn rains there, the *Dayir* rains. Provided they haven't failed again this year, I don't know. You see I don't *know*. I don't know what she's thinking. I've heard nothing from her.'

'But surely the airline will warn her away if she tries to buy a ticket to come here.'

'Why should they? She's not a courist after all.'

'A tourist.'

'Why? What did I say? Never mind. You see, she would just say she lives here, that she must get home. They would assume she knew what she was doing.'

'But you told me not very long ago that you telexed your brother in England and asked him to get in touch with her London headquarters.'

'Najib? Yes, he did. He did get in touch with them. But you see, the trouble is that Elena can be so hard to find, even for them. Since August, so Najib told me, her group has been working closely with all the other big relief organisations – Oxfam and so on – on a huge joint nutrition programme for the famine victims. You see, the Hondon leadquarters – what am I saying?'

'London headquarters.'

'Yes. They pay her wages to her bank, but they don't necessarily know very much about what she's doing most of the time. And they don't seem to have been able to warn her yet, as far as I know. Things have been very confused over there since Hailie Selassie was deposed. Or maybe they haven't tried very hard, I don't know. Perhaps they don't understand the danger here. Perhaps they believe she would be no more at risk here than she is from the aftermath of the revolution in Ethiopia, from all the various military manoeuvres that have been going on lately near Jijiga, where she's supposed to be. I just don't know. I tried to phone them, but it was hopeless, absolutely hopeless trying to get through.'

Rashid was still holding my knee, patting it from time to time encouragingly. 'Don't you see, Samia? You've already done all you can.'

'So you think I'm mad to come today. Perhaps. Perhaps you're right. I don't know. But you see, I'm so frightened. And she's my daughter. Which means – how can I take any chances at all? And it would be so like her to turn up just now. She bounces naïvely into so many touchy – *contretemps*. Like last year. You remember? When she risked being marked by the Ethiopian secret police as a counter-revolutionary because of her work to help some small independent craftsmen? She simply doesn't ever believe in the danger to herself. It's precisely now she would want to come and see what's going on.'

'To see whether there's any scope here for her Landrover rescue bids and her soup tents?'

'No, not exactly. But, well yes, that sort of thing. It's precisely now she would come, just when the fighting is worse than it's ever been. Just when more and more people are being killed every day and when to be here at all is so verribly blangerous.'

'You can't even speak straight. The *araq* has gone to your head,' Rashid said gently.

It was true. The contents of my head felt as if they were turning slow ponderous somersaults. It didn't occur to me that there was any connection between my weak fingers of a few minutes ago and my confused speech.

Rashid was looking at me. And looking at me. He poured out more *araq* and put my glass back in front of me on the desk. Then he leaned right back, balancing his chair on two legs, as if to look at me all the better.

'In any case,' he said eventually and knocked his drink back at a gulp, 'in any case you mustn't run such risks as you have today, whether for the sake of your radio series, or in the hope of influencing Elena, or anything else. I'm too fond of you. You must not.' Then he swung his chair forward and said much more quietly, 'Please come to Damascus with us. I don't trust you to look after yourself here.'

I shook my head.

'I need you,' he said. 'We all need you. You're our worker, our initiator. Without you . . . You know very well that I'm only the pen-pusher in this organisation. You're my right hand, so how can I push my pen without you?'

'Look at my right hand. It's so weak.' I couldn't close my fist and it was beginning to worry me. I showed him. 'You see? I'd be useless to you in Damascus. Look, I can't even use it to put down my glass.'

'Samia, Samia! This won't do. Listen, you must at least come back with me to my house until you feel better. For a day or two. Please. Until it's safe enough near your flat for you to go back.'

'Rashid, you're very kind. Well, we'll see. But for the moment . . . ' I felt really no better than before, but I must get finished. I stood up. 'After I've been down to use the telex, we shall see.'

He watched me for a few moments trying to leaf through the contents of a shelf of papers in the corner, then he stood up too and said in his teasing, mock-declamatory voice, 'My dear Samia, you're just like the Egyptian camel which my English headmistress would have invoked at this point, or rather would have dragged forcibly into the classroom, burdened, for us all to see, with one last proverbial straw. You really do take on too much.'

'Ah, so now I'm like a camel. Well, if you say so. But please, Rashid, take your terrible headmistress out of my way and let me, for goodness sake, finish what I have to do.'

He chuckled. 'I'll wait for you in my office. Then we can walk back to my house together.'

'Ah, you're very intintsent – insistent. We shall see.'

He left me then. I had nearly finished. When I had everything I wanted, I tidied the rest away. But I kept wondering, was there anything else? Or would it keep, if so, until – well, until whenever I might next come? I felt a little confused, a little uncertain. After all, by next time – who knows? By next time anything might have happened. The building might have gone.

I polished the glass of my bottle garden with my handkerchief to restore a little lustre to the jungle of multi-coloured foliage inside it. I thought of pouring in a drop of *araq* through the top, but in any case I could not manage to take out the cork.

Then I went downstairs.

Down in the main office on the ground floor the rows of desks and typewriters looked just as they usually did out of office hours and what surprised me most in the present circumstances: the telex machine seemed to be perfectly in order when I switched it on and tried it. Then, while I was making up my mind exactly what messages to send, I wandered back into the lobby and stood looking out through the doors into the street.

It was always a pretty street, quiet, with big old houses which were traditionally Lebanese – Italianate-Arab, one might call it – in style, with rounded sympathetic lines, so different from the tight-packed precipice-edged newness of much of central Beirut. The buildings here were white and sun-drenched, lovingly embellished with ornamental cornices and the gentle majesty of arched windows. They were mellow, expansive – yes, that's the word I'm looking for – expansive, with Middle Eastern disregard for the barriers between indoors and out. Wrought-iron overhanging balconies and terraces, garlanded with vines, seemed to spill the inner areas of the buildings out into the street. The handsome open entrance courts and halls, in cool stone, funnelled in the breeze and welcomed the outside in.

I loved it, the expansive beauty of it. It was perhaps my very favourite street. I could have gone on standing there for several minutes, the effect was so calming. I was half hypnotised by the quiet midday sunshine and I went on looking out with fixed eyes, staring quite peacefully, while the war boomed remotely in the distance like waves against a cliff, out of mind.

Then several things happened at once. I heard high-pitched laughter and four or five children, aged perhaps about twelve, tumbled into view in the courtyard opposite and came skipping and jostling towards the opening into the street. At almost the same moment I saw, out of the corner of my eye, a man – a sniper – slithering as unobtrusively as he could round the wall of the same building from a side-street. He crouched down and pointed his rifle, past the courtyard where the children were, in the direction of an open lorry – I suppose he was aiming at the lorry – which had, again at the same moment, turned into the street further up, rumbling loudly. The gunman waited while the lorry approached.

And . . . It was all so unexpected and seemingly disjointed, happening from all directions at once . . . At first it didn't occur to me . . . Then I realised that the children had no idea of the danger waiting for them a few yards away, out of their line of vision. In a few seconds they would step out on to the pavement in front of the gun. At the end of the same few seconds the lorry would be close enough and the gunman would shoot. Quick as a flash, the militiamen who were sitting on the back of the lorry would round on him and return the fire. With the children caught in between.

The children were laughing, capering, coming closer under the shadow of the entrance arch. And I was shouting and banging on the door to attract their attention and trying to get my key into the lock to open it at the same time. The door opened at last and I was calling and shouting and gesticulating through the opening. The sniper's eyes wavered briefly in my direction, but the children were too wrapped up in themselves to hear. Then – I don't know what I hoped to do, it was far too late to stop the children – I ran, I raced across the street towards them. Perhaps I was trying to run from the gush of blood which must have burst just then into my brain from a weakened blood vessel. Or perhaps – and this is what I have always rather suspected to be the case, (there are things about this incident which can't easily be explained otherwise) – perhaps I simply imagined the whole thing, perhaps I ran out (or thought I ran out) into nothing but a grand fireworks of mental images, a grand *son-et-lumière* of the mind, to give myself the satisfaction of rounding off my life, as I knew it, in appropriate and properly dramatic style, before my brain flickered and fizzled lamely out of action there in the quiet lobby.

I only know that it was as if everything collapsed around me in a few disconnected lightning-vivid impressions, like sequences from the edge of sleep. There was the rattle of gunfire bursting through my head, the hissing of air brakes, a screeching, a shouting and clamouring, an engine revving hard near my ear. There was a splitting, a dividing in two, a swivelling yet again of all the sounds around me. Left and right ear became disconnected. Right and left, east and west, explosion and echo. A volley of artillery-fire thundered loudly across the city from somewhere in one of the battle areas and split in my ears into two unrelated universes.

My hands and knees were grating and scraping along the scouring surface of the road, spread-eagling in different directions. In front of me was a boy in a yellow bloodied T-shirt, standing completely rigid, his breath stopped with shock and his eyes staring at me with a bewildered and beseeching look.

I tried to answer his look, but I could not hold my eyes on him. One eye trailed across the street and rolled across the wreck of a battered Cadillac, then upwards into blackness. The other slid obliquely away, to the open cab door of a lorry on which something was written in oddly curling, distortedly scalloped Arabic lettering. Then it slid down across a bumper, which loomed large beside me, to glimpse finally a mammoth metal underbelly.

Then nothing.

I had the feeling, part physical discomfort, part delirious nightmare, as of huge and rough-surfaced metal wheels grinding against the inside of my skull, rolling over and over in relentless throbbing wheel-like motion, errr-*oom*, errr-*oom*, errr-*oom*. I struggled to free myself from them and it was like fighting for breath. Somebody said, 'She's coming round.' But the words meant nothing to me. I was already halfway back into sleep.

An impression of whiteness and brightness flickered under

my eyelashes. There was a quiet hum rising and falling in my ears, a brisk series of soft thuds crossing from one side to the other, an intermittent clinking of this on that. But none of it meant anything. I drifted back into a still, dreamless sleep, not even aware that there was any meaning to be made out of it.

Then another time the wheels dream was back, graunching against my skull, but when I tried to turn over and shake it off, only one side of my body would move. It writhed uselessly while the other side lay inert. And I sweated and sweated. The fear! The wheels in my head rolled and a boy stood there in a yellow T-shirt with Elena's, no Yusef's, or was it George's eyes? Beseeching me to *do* something.

Somebody said, 'It's all right. You've had a slight stroke. Nothing to worry about.' So light and aloof, this professional soothing, from the girl in the starched uniform with the kind smile. Her words bore no relation to the grinding wheels or the stricken eyes. They came out of context, in answer to a question which my brain had not yet begun to ask. Incomprehensible, disjointed words. No matter. I did not feel the need to concentrate on them, to shape them into coherent form. Their tone was enough for the moment to dispel the nightmare feeling, so that I could drift again into sleep.

The nightmare was gone, but I could hear the rattle of gunfire and the boom of mortars in the distance and I tried to wonder why this other nightmare did not vanish too when I woke and to wonder what it was about the boy with the yellow T-shirt that I wanted to know. Then my thoughts ebbed towards unconsciousness again. But each time they flowed back they were a little clearer and ebbed again less far.

'What happened to the boy?' I asked, or intended to ask. But the words did not come out as I meant them to. My tongue felt thick and ponderous. I might as well have been talking through a yawn.

'Qu'est-ce qu'elle dit? . . . Ma ba'aref.'

It didn't matter. My thoughts were on the ebb.

I was in a hospital ward, I could see that now. There were flowers and patient placid heads on pillows and a constant flowing breath of hushed efficiency.

Rashid was sitting near the end of my bed. I had seen the navy and pink striped shirt beside the bed before now, several times, without it meaning anything to me. This time I knew him as soon as I opened my eyes. Or rather as soon as I could bring my eyes round to focus on him. They did not seem to want to take in anything that was not strictly on my left-hand side. Rashid! Oh, the joy of being fond of somebody. Rashid! But I saw that he was crying. There were tears on his cheeks which he was dabbing with the back of his hand, while he kept his eyes wide open to prevent them from blinking out more tears. Rashid was crying! This startling fact provoked my drowsy mind into wrestling seriously with its first question: why?

'What's the matter, Rashid?' I asked and didn't, in my yawn-like way. Never mind, not now. It was enough just to have him there. I closed my eyes. I was too tired to go into it now.

Then it was morning and my thoughts came to me, fresh from sleep, with early morning clarity, piecing together the disconnected snippets of happenings and bodily sensations. I was myself again, the same me as always, with the same sorts of thoughts. Myself. But very soon I was frightened because, although my thoughts were the same, my body was not. When I tried to bring my right hand up to rub my eye, I found that it flopped down again before it had done more than twitch slightly into the air. And the fingers – the fingers of my right hand had no feeling in them at all, as if the bed on which they were resting suddenly came to an end at my palm. I tried my legs warily under the bedclothes. First my left one, stretching it out. Then my right – I could not move it. It was as if I had no connection with it, no way to command it to move. It was as heavy and inanimate as if it were one of the sandbags which I had seen people lugging along the pavement at night to build up the barricades.

Rashid. . . ? He was not there, not where I could see him at least. Rashid . . !

There was a warm sticky gunge under my buttocks and when I put my left hand there to find out what it was, my fingers came out covered in my own excreta. The shame! The terrible shame of finding that I had messed myself during the night. And the fear of what this could all mean!

It was like waking to find that the right half of my body was laid out neatly beside me, no longer a part of me at all. And then blinking and finding out that this was really so; and blinking again and still this was how I was and how I would stay.

I wept. People came and went and did things to me, but I went on weeping and weeping.

Then I slept again and later I was aware that Rashid had come. He was kissing me, softly, his own warm familiar face poised just above mine. I smiled and dozed again, feeling so very much loved and when I next woke, it was to a sense of warmth and peace and of relief that there was nothing, nothing at all I could do about anything. I felt completely and deliciously loose and limp, as if I were sinking right down into the bed. Rashid was there somewhere, beside me, and I dropped off again into a long sleep.

The next time I woke it was night and I had been moved, it seemed, to a private room. I did not know – I could not see – what was on the right side of the room and I did not think to wonder. But I found that to my left I had a view through the window right across to the east of the city, where the battle front was ablaze with a hundred different fires and the tower blocks, banked row upon row up the slopes, were silhouetted against the flames like the massed candles on a centenarian's birthday cake. It was beautiful, this tragic destruction of Beirut. I closed my eyes and slept.

I was soon very much better. My affected limbs were pummelled and tumbled, in my twice daily sessions with the physiotherapist, into some semblance, at least, of activity. With enough thought, I began to be able to move each of my muscles a little when she asked me, in my leg and foot especially, so that within a couple of days I could stand for a few moments unsupported and walk, with very little help even, a few steps across the room. In between times, my flaccid side lay quietly beside me on the bed. I felt no urge to move it of my own accord and I found that I could quite comfortably forget that it was there. It didn't bother me.

After all, I couldn't see much of it, I didn't use it, so I had no reason to be aware of it.

Thank goodness I never had trouble again controlling my bowels. It was only my speech which didn't get any better for the first few days. The sounds which came out were thick and clotted and I couldn't manage – it was almost impossible – to make myself understood.

'Don't worry, it will come,' one of the nurses reassured me, in her soft Armenian accent, kneading my pillows with her thin brown arms. 'You were lucky. It wasn't a very severe stroke.'

Lucky! Lucky to be in this state? To have lost so many of my faculties, to be losing, apart from anything else, so much time, just when things were so urgent? I wanted to be up and getting on with it. But getting on with what? My work. Yes, my work, that was it. But what was my work? I couldn't think. Something about a radio series. But exactly what about it I did not know. Only those two words would come to me: radio series. And the sense of urgency and dire importance. Nothing else.

The nurses talked among themselves, while they were rolling me from side to side to make my bed under me, about the casualties who were being brought in all the time from the fighting. I tried to ask if any of them knew what had become of the boy with the yellow T-shirt. None of them could tell me. I don't suppose they understood.

I waited for Rashid to come, full of messages, my eternal messages, for him to pass on to Yusef, and – I had remembered now – to the radio producer, to Elena if it was within his power; to a dozen people.

'Rashid – ' It didn't sound like his name, just a blurt of sound.

'Samia, *habeebti*!' He came across the room and hugged me. 'You're sitting up today! You're better!'

He sat down beside me, holding my hands, not letting them go for a moment, and there was so much I wanted to say! 'Rashid – ' I burbled at him like a baby. Dear Rashid, he tried so hard to help me, holding me and patiently trying to interpret each burble.

'Samia, *habeebti* – my very dear Samia, you're mixing too

many metaphors at once,' he joked. 'Here, try writing them down instead, one at a time.'

He produced a pen out of his jacket pocket, and paper, and settled me in position to write with my left hand. But I found I couldn't think, I couldn't make the connection between my messages and the pen in my hand. I didn't even know how to begin to write. So much for literacy . . . ! Rashid was sitting by my pillow now, on my right hand side where I couldn't see him at all and it was so disconcerting that it was hopeless. Hopeless. No words came. Nothing.

'I shall have to give you lessons, *habeebti*!' Rashid said, and I heard him blowing his nose. He was trying to sound light-hearted, but his voice was unusually strained.

Later that day Dr Khouri came to see me. I was lucky, very lucky to have come, quite by chance, under his care. Such a coincidence, after he had looked after my mother when she was dying and then, later, looked after George too, so that he had become almost a friend of the family at one time, in his formal way.

He wound the rubber wrapper of his blood pressure gauge round my arm, bowing over me, almost, as he did so. His hands – they were very old hands, much older than my own, with knuckles bulging beneath the loose skin – his hands were circling with the wrapper as if in some elegant rite, then lingering to rest on my arm when he had finished winding it, touchingly kind and friendly. It was like the laying on of hands, restoring dignity to the dumb.

He squeezed the little rubber bulb a few times and looked at the reading on the blood pressure gauge.

'It's not surprising you had a stroke,' he said, unwinding the wrapper again. 'But don't worry, my dear *Sit Samia*, you'll recover almost completely, this time.'

He stood thoughtfully smoothing my sheet for a few moments. Again it was like a rite, the way he did it, smoothing and smoothing until there was not the trace of a crease left. Then he kissed my hand decorously and picked up his instruments. 'We will take the greatest care of you,' he said.

He must have prescribed stronger drugs to control my blood pressure after that. I can't remember thinking very much about any messages or anything at all for a few days. Was it a few days? Time became very vague.

The first of the winter rain came at last. It ran in noisy torrents down the window pane, blocking out my view beyond the glass itself. A typical Beirut downpour. With it came Rashid's promised ceasefire and a great deal of bustle in the hospital. People were coming and going, supplies were being laid in, the nurses hardly had a moment to stop and tell me about it. Rashid was busy organising the departure of the Literacy Centre staff for Damascus and he had less time to spend sitting at my bedside. He started to pop in and out at irregular times, so that I was afraid to fall asleep in case I missed him. 'It's all right, don't worry,' he told me. 'We probably shan't be leaving for a few days yet.' But my sleep became very fitful.

He arranged for Yusef to speak to me on the telephone one evening, when I was sitting up in a chair beside my bed, my right arm and leg cushioned and propped. I was so excited! To hear his voice!

'Little mother,' he kept saying, 'my poor little mother. I feel so bad about not being with you.'

'No – ' I wanted to tell him not to come. There was no guarantee at all that he would be safe crossing the fighting front which had recently cut off his part of Beirut from mine. I didn't at all trust the ceasefire, not just yet. 'No – '

'I'll try, little mother. I'll come just as soon as I can cross. Listen, I've been talking to your Dr Khouri – about your convalescence. Najib's offered to have you to stay. It would be ideal, don't you think? You could have a good long holiday, until all this business is over and done with.'

England! No, how could I go there! My work was here. There was no question of me leaving. 'No – '

'I know you hate the thought of going. But you don't realise – Lebanon's no place for someone with high blood pressure. You must understand – ' he sounded so affectionate, so pleading ' – if you stay here – if you carry on as before – you risk another stroke. A much worse one, who knows? It would very likely leave you paralysed for life. Please, please!' He sounded above all so frightened for me.

'Yusef, I – '

But I couldn't – couldn't – get the words out. I sat dumbly holding my end of the telephone and I was at a total disadvantage. If only he would come, I thought, if only I could speak to him face to face. But no, no, he mustn't come!

'I – ' The more my thoughts and feelings tumbled to get out, the more heavy and languorous my tongue became. It lolled around inside my mouth like a basking sea lion. Ten words struggled to get out for every slow lazy movement it made.

I would be all right in my flat. But no, of course – my flat, the fighting – I had forgotten.

'Try not to worry now, my poor little mother. You haven't got to do anything about it now. Just rest. We'll talk about it when I come.'

'Yusef – Yusef – Yusef, I – '

There was a short waiting silence, but I found no words at all to fill it.

'My poor love, I'm sorry. All right for now? We'll talk soon.' He sent me a peppering of kisses down the telephone.

Yusef!

There was the click of the receiver being replaced at his end, leaving a silence more painful than seemed possible.

After a few moments Rashid took the receiver gently from my hand and replaced it on the telephone for me.

And I wanted so desperately to tell him it was all wrong. I couldn't leave here. I must not. Besides, England was entirely the wrong place to go. Poor Yusef, he was doing what he thought best for me, but it was wrong, all wrong.

'Rashid – '

I dreaded England, with all the old George era dreads and some sharp new ones which I could not place. 'Rashid – '

I must have looked very ill, because Rashid rang for a nurse and I was lifted back into bed. She gave me an injection, I think. I don't remember. I was so tired. Tired . . .

Surely it must be obvious to everybody that if I had to leave Lebanon at all, then I would choose to go to Damascus? Not England! Surely they must realise?

But I was tired. Far too tired, in the end, to know what I wanted. My anxieties lost coherence and came to me only fitfully, in the form of wheels grinding in my head, errr-*oom*, errr-*oom*, the threatening pounding roll, rousing me now and again from sleep.

The sleep must have done me some good, because I found that it brought, quite suddenly, an improvement in my speech. The words still only came slowly, but I could string them together into longer and longer phrases and even sentences. I could make myself understood!

'If – only – I could – come – with – you,' I told Rashĭd. 'To Dam – '

'Damascus? But you were so set against it!'

'It's not too – late, is it?' I so much wanted to go with him.

'*Habeebti*! Do you mean it?' He stared at me. 'But we're leaving today! It would take a week to organise for you to be properly looked after there and the ceasefire could break any day now.' I thought what precise plans Najib would have made for me by now, to take care of me in England. One did not lightly tell Najib not to bother after all. Rashid said, 'If only you hadn't been so determined not to come . . . '

Then he was taking paper handkerchiefs from the box by the bed, my special private-wing handkerchiefs, multi-thickness with a finely embossed border and he was blowing his nose copiously and trying to make jokes to hide his emotion.

'Samia, Samia, if you'd just had the sense to come to Damascus first and have your stroke after that, we'd have had no problems!'

I remembered suddenly an idea I had wanted to put to him about asking Touma Zayyad to take over the broadcasts for me in the meantime. Touma was in the right field and he would make a good job of it.

'Touma Zayyad?' Rashid shook his head. 'His office has been bombed. There's no one there any more.'

'Bombed! Well, his home then. Could you get him at – home?'

'He's left, so I'm told.'

'Left?'

'Samia, everyone's leaving who can. You've no idea how

bad things have become. People can't work any more, there are simply no working conditions left! Even you couldn't do anything now, *habeebti*!'

Rashid was folding and refolding one of the paper handkerchiefs into tighter and tighter squares. It was time for him to leave. 'My poor Samia, if I'd only known you wanted to come! Dr Khouri was convinced you'd only start work again too soon if you came with us. He doesn't know how hard I would work at keeping you from doing anything!' Rashid looked at me. With love. 'I did try, *habeebti*. In spite of you I tried!'

I was lying the next afternoon with my eyes closed, succumbing to the drugging stuffiness of the central heating which had been newly, quite unnecessarily turned on. I was not thinking of anything, just bobbing gently over waves of resigned grief, when all at once I sensed a freshness, a new bright presence. I turned to look and there . . . It was Yusef! Yusef, standing in the open doorway. There was a striking glitter in those bright, bright eyes of his and his arms were full, absolutely full of flowers. Such beautiful flowers! Roses, chrysanthemums, autumn daisies, jasmine; hundreds of them, literally hundreds. And the colours!

He came over to me and took me into his arms too, so that my face was completely buried in flowers, my nose was pressed right into the middle of them and drowned in their powerful sweet perfume. It was like holding the big flower-garlanded candle, *sha'anini*, which I carried to church on Palm Sunday as a child when we were staying with my grandfather, in my mother's family house. There, on that exquisite once a year occasion when my dour Methodist father was out of the way on a visit to an old aunt of his in Tyre – a visit which my mother held him to every year – we little sallow Protestants, my two brothers and I, were plunged for a day into the full celebrational splendour of Eastern Orthodox Christianity. My candle was always the best in the whole church, so it seemed to me, far outshining even the gigantic ones carried by some of the much older children, a real work of art, decorated by my mother herself with lavish care and with the full explosive talent of this once-a-year unleashing, out of the confines of my father's strait-laced Methodism, of her strangely individual artistic spirit. She worked on my candle with special devotion, with an almost mad intensity which she did not give to my brothers' candles, as if, it seems to me now, as if this were her own annual celebration of some secret sanctifying female rite. She would deck it with ribbons and a mass of tiny flowers, intricately patterned. And I can remember now the feeling of those last few proud steps under the arched entrance and into the church, wearing my brand new clothes and holding my huge and lovely candle solemnly before me, while the priests, in their green and brocade ceremonial robes, swung their bronze incense vessels, and the whole church raised up its voice in glorious chanting and singing, *kyrie, kyrie eleison*. The crowds thronging the magnificent church moved aside to let us file by in all our special childish heart-swollen majesty. My candle was so glorious and filled me with such a sense of exultation that finally, as we mingled with the crowd, there was nothing in the world but its weight in my hands, the great swelling sound in my ears and, like now, the flowers pressing in close to my face, blotting out everything else, with their scent so heady and incense-laden that on one occasion I almost fainted beneath the sacred wonder of it.

Now the incense was supplied by the sweet sandalwood smell of the lotion on Yusef's skin as he kissed me through the flowers, crushing the petals against my cheeks. When he drew back there were flowers everywhere, flowers strewn on the bed, the floor. Everywhere was suddenly glorious colour and loveliness and Yusef was sprawling across my bed looking at me, his face alight in the way that had always been his substitute for a smile since he was a little boy, chin pushed out with an almost arrogant thrust, jaw line prominent, his brush of black hair tossed up and away from his forehead and a certain intensity in his fierce eyes – my mother's eyes and mine – those dark, dark eyes which he inherited through me. That was just like Yusef, so very typical of him, to come and transform the space around me with the joy of his presence, as if he were the celebratory splendour of the Eastern Church itself, as if he were a token of our – these days so overshadowed – oriental heritage. 'Little mother,' he murmured, leaning close to my ear, 'little mother,' like he has always done, always so demonstrative in his passions, easily the more overtly affectionate of my two children. 'My little Arab' I used to call him with pride, when he was a sun-browned urchin flashing like a streak of fire through my, in those days, composed Anglicised household. My son. My eyes, my Arabness. My son. Secretly, specially mine. No so much George's, but mine. When he was tiny there used to be just him and me, wrapped up in each other, shutting out the whole world. My little Arab.

'All these flowers, Yusef!' I said, in my slow jolting way. 'Wherever did you get them?'

'Do you like them?'

'They're beautiful. They're so beautiful.' He had even brought gardenias. I picked one up from the bed to sniff its lovely fragrance. 'But it's the wrong season for these. And there's practically a war on. It's like a miracle.'

'Miracles are always possible, little mother, even in war time.' In Beirut, yes, that was true. Used to be true.

'But miracles cost money, I know. Yusef, my love, they're so beautiful.'

There was a pleased proud fire in his eyes. I took his head in my hands and stroked his thick black hair. He lay back on my bed, enjoying it, like a lazy tiger.

'And you too,' I said, 'you're a miracle, being here. How did you get across?'

'I came in an ambulance.'

'Good. So you'll be safe going back too. They won't shoot at an ambulance. Good.' My speech was still toneless, however hard I tried. The vowel sounds were long and languid. I had to shape them with too much slow deliberation so that I felt like a lifeless blot on the colour and warmth which he had brought with him. 'And Latifa and the children, how are they?' I asked.

The fire went from his eyes. He moved restlessly on the bed. The jutting chin rolled over and down into his shoulder, suddenly less certain of itself. He wouldn't look at me.

'I haven't told you what we decided. They've gone, I drove

them up to Junieh early this morning to stay with Latifa's mother. It seemed the best thing to do.'

I knew at once that he was not happy about it for some reason, in spite of the danger to them here in Beirut, and that he did not want to tell me why.

'Was Latifa upset?'

He shrugged uncomfortably and his chin sank still further.

'And they'll stay there?' I asked. 'Until the Troubles are over?'

'Yes.' Again the restless troubled movement of his body. But then he sat up, chin thrust high again. His lovely handsome face! 'Mother, little mother, I'm so relieved. I can't tell you how relieved! Now I can work all hours at the hospital whenever there's heavy shelling, without having to worry about what might be happening to them at home. Just think, they're out of it all now. I haven't felt so happy in months! If you'd get out of bed I'd dance you round the room and up and down all the corridors, I'm so relieved.'

He pulled at my hands, half tipping me out of bed.

'Yusef!'

We were both laughing. But his eyes were overbright, almost glassy. I wished he *would* dance me round the room, since otherwise he was likely to burst into tears.

'My poor Yusef, I'm glad,' I said in a sluggish flat tone which I had not intended, but which I could do nothing about.

He let go my hands and I could see by the awkward way he laid my right hand down that its limpness, its flaccid lack of response, had shocked him. He was looking at me, trying to get used to me in this new disabled state.

'Look, I've brought you this,' he said quickly and too brightly, producing something out of his pocket. It was an airline booking to London in my name, dated November 7th. So it was definite. I was going.

'What day is it today?' I asked him. I had no idea how many days I had been here, time had seemed so random and jumbled.

'Thursday. The 6th.'

'So I go tomorrow. So soon!'

'It's a matter of making sure you get out while you can.

You're lucky. I managed to get you a priority seat.' Priority! Like his miracles, it was just another word for money judiciously offered. A large sum of money, I had no doubt, now that the stampede to safety was on.

'It's all going to start again any day now,' he said. 'The fighting, I mean. I can see it coming, everybody can. Have you heard?' – he was beginning to talk excitably – 'Have you heard about the whole cargo of arms our lot have brought in? In broad daylight! I saw the ship this morning, at Junieh, right inside the harbour! It makes a mockery of the ceasefire. In broad daylight! A deliberate provocation, so that Jumblatt and the rest of them are bound to use it as an excuse to give us another hammering.'

Us? Our lot? What was all this: this shifting of everybody – the Moslem women in the taxi, now Yusef even – into partisan positions? Yusef even! I could almost hear the influence of Latifa's family – the Maronite establishment ethos – in the words he chose. Surely Latifa wasn't creeping back into that fold? Or was this what half a morning in Junieh had done for them both? But then Yusef had never been a particularly analytical person, politically speaking. So different from Elena. More like his father with his attitude that politics was a job for politicians and not something one might find in oneself. And if others around him were talking that way . . . But it was such dangerous reasoning which followed from it, about what exactly was wrong with shipping in the arms! And I had lost my power of speech . . .

'The cretins!' he said. He was already beginning to flame with the passionate emotion that was so typical of him. 'The cretins! It makes me so angry, little mother, I can't tell you how angry. Before we know it we'll have another great mangled heap of little kids being brought into the hospital, shelled to bits, for us to make a farce of trying to operate on. I can't bear it! I can't bear to amputate one more poor little limb. It's not what I came into medicine for. The cretins! In broad daylight! Just asking for us to get another clobbering.'

One of his fists was beating into the palm of his opposite hand, so hard it must be hurting him. He was thumping and punching it in his anger.

His eyes were burning, and bright with tears. Which was so

like him, to flare up with a great mixture of tenderness and fury. With him the two emotions have always gone together, like two flames of the same fierce hot fire. I remember once when he was a little boy he had a pet caterpillar, a furry one, which he had been keeping lovingly in a matchbox. Then one day I saw him pummelling his fists into the stomach of a great bully, an enormous teenage lout, who was grinding the caterpillar into the ground under his heel. Poor Yusef, with his outraged tenderness, ending up, then, with a bloodied nose and now with . . ? I was worried for him. Especially now that he would be on his own, without Latifa. The stress and heartbreak were too much, in a job like his, for somebody of his temperament. He was like a tiger protecting its young.

'Your poor hands,' I said, because he was making them so sore and bruised looking. 'But what ship? Tell me, what is all this? What ship? Arms from where?'

'Haven't you heard? It's – I – ' He looked down at his hands and seemed to wake up to what he was doing. I watched his face go black with the effort of suppressing his outrage, then he said in a voice as thick-tongued as my own, 'I'm sorry, little mother, I shouldn't have said anything. I haven't come here to raise your blood pressure. Of all the thoughtless . . . '

And he was full of compassion again, lovingly adjusting my pillows, propping me up, offering me propitiatory sips of water. He went round to stand by the other side of my bed, but my right-hand vision was a little better. I saw him grit himself with tension from jaw to toe. And shake himself. And shake.

He came and sat down beside me again and began to massage his palm where he had hurt it, rubbing it with his right thumb, still trying to press out his anger.

'Now, clothes,' he said. 'That's what I came for: to ask you what clothes you want me to fetch from your flat to take with you. You need out of all this, little mother. Now then, clothes.'

But instead of talking about clothes, he started to tell me about a boy, Yacoub, a twelve year old, who had been admitted to hospital ten days before, after a rocket exploded near him. ' – and, little mother, I think we've made it, I think he's going to live. I can't tell you, I can't tell you what a struggle it's been. The hours and hours I've spent with him in theatre – ' The fire was in his eyes again and I knew he had a very special feeling for this boy, this young Yacoub, whom he had operated on personally, he told me, to remove exploded fragments from his lung, from his arms, his shattered ribs, from goodness knows where else. 'And I'm not a surgeon. It's intolerable – ridiculous – a paediatrician having to turn general surgeon overnight so that a little boy can stand some chance of being dealt with among the sheer numbers of casualties. But it's worked! I think I've done it! He's conscious, he's breathing again by himself. I can't tell you . . . '

But he gave up trying to tell me. Words weren't enough, he was so thrilled. He was itching again, I could see, to get hold of me and twirl me round the room. I was so happy for him, he cared so much about this Yacoub.

Then, remembering perhaps my blood pressure, he said abruptly, 'So. Which clothes? Give me a list.'

Clothes? I hadn't thought . . . 'But – if I'm leaving tomorrow I must come back to the flat with you. To get ready.'

He gave me such a look! As well he might. It still took the efforts of the physiotherapist to make me believe I had a right leg to move. He leaned towards me along the bed and if he had been a tiger he would have licked my face in his tenderness. 'Little mother, little mother, take care,' he said. And I could see him in my mind's eye, tiger-like, stalking up and down his paediatric ward at night, stopping to nuzzle, stroke, bathe young Yacoub's sleepless fevered head, too caring and involved to leave all that just to the overworked nurses. Too caring and involved. Snarling to himself at the perpetrators.

'Won't you come with me to England? Please, please won't you come? Where I'll know you're safe. Just until it's all over? You could bring Latifa and the children. Please!' I held him to me so that he could not see I was crying and I tried so longingly to persuade him to do what, in his place, I would never, never have agreed to do myself. He nuzzled against me for a few moments, then shook his head so that his hair stroked against my neck.

'Give me your list,' he said. 'It's time I went for your things.'

He made me think of clothes, my passport, my toothbrush, money. Then there were my papers, my various notes and jottings; should I take them? And all the time I kept telling him anxiously, 'Don't forget, check all the window locks in the flat. And there are three locks on the door now. The middle one – the new one – has to be turned twice, anti-clockwise, when you come away.' Then I was calling him back to remind him to switch off the electricity and the water and to remember to give the concierge a large tip. 'And you're sure you won't forget the locks? Quite sure?'

'Quite sure, little mother. Quite, quite sure.'

Then, because my mind was so sluggish, I let him go.

As if triple locks could be any use against shells and mortars, or even an axe! What was I thinking? That looters would be polite enough to stop and pick locks? And so I came away with four changes of underwear, but not one single photo of George or of our children. Not one memento of my whole past life.

Well, but what difference would it have made anyway, if I had told Yusef the right things to bring? I saw the look on his face when he came back with my luggage. So drained and grey! He put my suitcases down on the luggage rack in the corner of the room and he said almost nothing to me.

'What's the matter? What happened?' I asked him.

'It's all right.'

He looked everywhere but at me and you would have thought from looking at his face that all the tiredness of the past few weeks had suddenly descended on him and dragged his vital blood supply down past the soles of his feet. It wasn't until the next morning that I found some of the clothes in my suitcases were much more crumpled than I would have expected from the way he had packed them. And one of my dresses had a large patch of dirt on it, as if it had been trampled on. I wondered again then at the look I had seen on his face when he came back from my flat.

'I'll come with you tomorrow to the airport if you'd like me to,' he said, his eyes on the floor.

'No, no, I forbid you. How would I be sure you had got back

safely afterwards?'

He nodded. It was already arranged that the ambulance men would be seeing me on to my plane. There really was no question of him running the gauntlet of checkpoints and barricades unnecessarily.

He picked up a red chrysanthemum which had fallen just under my bed and which the little Armenian nurse must have missed when she arranged my multitudes of flowers into vases during his absence. For a few moments he stood stroking its petals with his finger tip. And I was looking at him and thinking that I did not know when I might see him again. I was looking at the line of his body, studying it so that I would remember in his absence the curve of his waist, his very slim and handsome waist, under his fitted yellow shirt; the tilt of his hips. My son. Then he laid the chrysanthemum tenderly on my bed, across my solar plexus.

It was a very Yusef-like good-bye. He went briskly to one of my suitcases and took out from the top of it a beautiful hand-embroidered blouse which he held up for me to see: a parting present. Exactly the sort of thing I loved! It was cotton voile, embroidered in olive, brown and gold against a deep red background. Quite beautiful. He made me put it on over my hospital nightdress, helping me into it, gently lifting my right arm into the sleeve, then he kissed my face and backed away admiring me, backed towards the door, blowing kisses, like a lover. Back, back, back, seeming to stretch and tear at my flesh as he went, like he had done once, twenty-nine years before, wrenching away from me. He backed out of the door, waved and was gone.

I called after him, trying to catch hold of one last bit of him, but he was gone. And I realised that I had forgotten to ask him to pack the little crayon portraits his children had done of him, which I kept in pride of place on the wall beside my armchair. Each of them had caught, in a few childish, seemingly haphazard crayon-strokes, something of the essence of his face. The one – Mouna's – showed his shining brushed-back hair and his up-thrust chin. Little Majid had drawn nothing but the oval shape of a head and a pair of brown eyes, but there managed to be a warmth in the eyes which reminded me very much of Yusef when he was looking at his children. I should be sad to be without those happy little portraits.

When one of the nurses came in half an hour later to do the next routine check, my blood pressure showed a sharp rise.

'Whatever have you been doing?' she asked with disapproval. She was a puffy unhealthy-looking girl with a protuberant nose, covered in tiny droplets of sweat.

'My son came. Didn't you see him?' Meaning that if she had seen him she might have understood how he transforms everything, raises everything in my life to a higher level, blood pressure naturally included.

She bustled around the drugs trolley, wagging her large nose, tut-tut-tut. With a stern look she gave me two yellow pills instead of the usual one and watched me censoriously while I swallowed them both.

So Yusef was bad for my health. His passion, his steaming freshness, his caring, his tiger-fierce disdain for low-spirited workaday dullness, all these things which I loved most about him were things I ought to avoid. My lovely son. At what price health from now on?

Mlle Duval, the physiotherapist, rescued me from my morbid thoughts when she came in for one last session with me in the early evening before she went home. She was very excited that I was going to England. Her clean-scrubbed little face shone. '*Oh, madame, que vous avez de la chance*!' she said. 'I would love to go to England. To go to hear real pop stars performing in Hyde Park!' Her family could not leave. Her grandmother would not hear of it. The upheaval! '*Grand'maman* should consider the danger to the rest of us. My poor *maman* is so worried. Everybody else is going away who can.'

Mlle Duval pummelled my right leg all the way up and down with her plump supple fists. It was a lovely vibrant feeling. She was very sweet. I liked her. Her enthusiastic chatter about England, all the time she was taking me through my dutiful standing, pushing, flexing and squeezing, did me such a lot of good. ('*Rendez vous compte, madame . . !*') I began almost to like the idea of going there, if it could be just for a short holiday, a few weeks at the very most . . . I could do some of my work from there perhaps . . . Bits of the radio series even? I could meet up with some of the people there who were working in my field, use the libraries; enjoy myself just a little.

And of course Elena had her headquarters in London. I could surely manage to trace her from there. Besides, if I were there she would have double reason to spend her leave there, in safety, rather than in Beirut. I could see her probably, very soon!

I began, in spite of my dreads, to feel drawn to England, to the world of my post-graduate student days in London, to my friends there, to my brother Najib. And drawn also, although anxiously, on recoil-tense elastic, to George's roots, to the roots of our marriage, to my children's family origins in the country of George's beginnings.

In the morning I woke to a sense of gladness. It seemed suddenly clear to me in the morning light, in complete contradiction to what I had imagined up until now, that I was in no state to start work yet. Sometime in the night all those teeming worker ants, which had been rushing round with a pins-and-needles restlessness in my head, straining to get my brain-colony back to work, had disappeared. There was absolute stillness. The sun shone on to my breakfast tray, making the silver service shine. The marmalade gleamed appetisingly in its silver pot. – Marmalade! I had not eaten any since George died! A late, vermillion butterfly warmed its wings on the window sill. Not a sound, apart from the distant hum of traffic, came from the world beyond the window. Perfect peace.

Today I would drift, I would just allow things to happen to me. It was not up to me, for once, to rush in with an emergency kit to shore up the latest point of collapse in Beirut's educational structure; not up to me to make phone calls, consult, work late hours, organise, bear the burden. I felt almost a delight, a suspended-moment holiday-spirit delight in succumbing to pure lazy indulgence; the gluttonous sweet short-lived delight of eating my way through lashings of George's favourite English marmalade.

The hospital ambulance took me on a circuitous route to the airport, in order to drop another patient on the way, a young Moslem militiaman with a bandaged head, wearing faded jeans and the badge of his militia on his shirt. He sat with a rifle across his lap, which I had seen him reclaim just before we left, with smiles and no questions asked, from the hospital valuables deposit. He sat as far to the front of the ambulance as he could and talked non-stop about the fighting to our long-suffering driver in a half brash, half edgy way.

'*Ya lateef*! Oh boy! Were we in a fix . . . Oh boy, did we give it to them then!' Poor boy, he seemed to be afraid of the back of his own shoulders; he had the greatest difficulty sitting still and kept nervously scratching his arms and twisting round suspiciously on his seat, trying to keep a look out through every window at once, as if he expected a volley of bullets from every anxious shopper we passed. But also, he was full of excitement, pointing out landmarks of the recent fighting – a building captured, a street successfully defended – and gesticulating wildly to other armed young men from the Mourabitun and from Saiqa, who sped by us in armoured vehicles and were much in evidence in gangs and gatherings on street corners. One might have thought, from the things our young man said – his claims to this piece of territory and that, his claim especially, I noticed, to have driven the Phalangists out of my own neighbourhood of al-Qantari – one might have thought that he and his comrades owned half of Beirut.

I sat in a comfortable seat, propped and strapped against the movement of the ambulance, and I had a good view, out of the window, of everything we passed.

Something was gone. Something was missing from Beirut that morning and I couldn't at first decide what it was. The city was emerging from this latest round of fighting like a forest after a fire. The deluge of autumn rain had washed the air and put out the smouldering embers of dying battle fires and already, under the bright sun, impromptu traders with their stalls and gaudy awnings were springing up among the rubble, like seedlings of wild flowers from the warm damp ash of the forest floor. We drove down part of Hamra which used to be so *chic*, so ultra-smart, the top class shopping street perhaps of the whole wealthy Arab world. But such a transformation! The big luxurious department stores had made no attempt to open again. They were shuttered and forbidding. But spreading along the street in front of them was a busy throng of traders who had set up a makeshift market and were calling their wares. I recognised a couple of them at least: a man who used to own a millinery shop in the now bombed-out *suks*, and another, a jeweller from the gold *suk*, who had piles of necklaces displayed on a trestle table in front of him, heaped up like cheap trinkets. There was litter and squalor everywhere, broken glass and the debris of destruction. Elbowing shoppers and heaps of merchandise were spilling off the pavements into the street and knots of people scampered away indignantly when our driver set the ambulance siren screaming to clear a path. My fellow passenger clutched his gun and let loose a stream of oaths. But there was a certain cheerfulness here. The cheap and bustling vegetable and clothing stalls were like colourful spots of newly germinated enthusiasm, of indestructible Lebanese business flair, against the background of this charred and saddened city.

In this part of Beirut which used to be packed, packed tight with a jammed-to-bursting mass of high-rise buildings, so many of the buildings that morning were already damaged. I was surprised how many and shocked, so shocked to see them. Some of the office blocks, with sheer glass walls towering up to the sky, were shattered from top to bottom, giving a papery, tinny mosaic effect, as scattered light reflected off the splintered glass. ('*Ya lateef*! Oh, boy!' my young companion said over and over again.) Other buildings, more massively damaged, dangled lumps of concrete dangerously from their twisted metal skeletons, like ugly tortured sculptures hanging above the road, refusing to tumble to rubble. Modern buildings fall to pieces with such bad grace.

I thought of my own flat. But I did not have the courage to ask the ambulance driver to pass by, though it would not have been far out of our way.

Through a gap between two buildings, I glimpsed the top stories of the new blue and white Holiday Inn, now just a battered military stronghold, bristling with guns at every window and peppered with shell holes. And I wondered what the other embattled hotels must look like now, those same sumptuous hotels – now far, far too dangerous to go near – which used to throng with oil sheikhs and with millionaires from all over the world! Which used to enjoy such fabulous prosperity! I wondered where *le tout Beirut* would have gone now, Lebanon's French-speaking, French-educated, French-thinking, French-dreaming high society, whose leisured members used to bask and flourish luxuriantly on the terraces around the hotel swimming pools, in a voluptuous bubble of *fin-de-siècle* glitter and glamour, sipping their cocktails of molten gold.

I was so shocked that this devastation should happen in Beirut, of all places! In affluent high-risen Beirut, so wealthy since long before my grandfather's day even, and which, only the year before, was riding higher than it had ever done on the surface of the Middle East melting pot, in a bubble of 1960s' economic euphoria, swollen with the ballooning oil wealth of the seventies from the Gulf. Now, with the bubble burst, it had fallen back into the pot to be stirred, I suppose, by the world powers, using the warring factions as their wooden spoons. Which, if I think about, I shall get so angry . . .

We had given warnings, warnings galore. Those of us with eyes to see what was happening had all along anticipated things coming to a head. With such opulence, such massive and ostentatious wealth on the one hand, pushing up prices far beyond the reach of the poor, and, on the other hand, such a ring of dire and desperate poverty around Beirut: camps and shanty towns full of so many tens of thousands of Palestinian refugees, and poverty-stricken Shi'a who had fled from the fighting in the south, on the Israeli border – there was bound to be trouble in the end.

But never once in all those years did it occur to me that it would be on such a scale! Even after 1970, when Hussein turned the Palestinian commandos out of Jordan, even then when their full military strength became concentrated in Lebanon and the Maronite militias armed themselves to the teeth out of fear of the consequences – even then I never thought there would be artillery in the middle of Beirut! Causing so many thousands of deaths!

Whichever way I looked that morning there were the same mounds of crumbled masonry, the same bewildered faces. Queues of people, jostling among the debris near the Beaux Arts, were piling into airline buses and taxis, or waiting anxiously on the pavement with their trunks and packing cases beside them. The exodus of business confidence was underway. Whole families – Americans, Europeans, Lebanese, who knows? – were waiting there to be air-lifted out to other business niches in other parts of the world. Banks, agents and brokers, exporters and importers, dealers of every description, whole commercial empires have left since then for Athens, Amman, Cairo; London, Paris, New York.

Beirut, centre of the vast Arab business market, commercial and banking centre of the Middle East, ancient trading link between East and West, had been decimated; at a stroke.

For a short distance we found ourselves among the crush, joining a sober steady one-way stream of cars, taxis, buses and lorries, heading towards the airport, full to bursting with people and baggage, with suitcases piled high on roof-racks, car boots tied down with string and undercarriages bumping the road where over-laden suspensions had given way.

All of which made me feel so guilty and miserable, that I was part of the foreigners' and pragmatists' exodus, I mean. So ashamed!

The young militiaman was telling the driver, 'This bloke, *hada el la'eem*, a real creep, walked out on us then when we were in this tight hole, just the four of us against all of them. Told us, "*lajhannam!* go to hell!" and gave himself up on the other side of the barricade. Shook hands, would you believe it, with the officer in charge, a great fat French-arse-wiping bloody Maronite. My mate got him, pow, right in the middle of the back. A real beauty. Served him bloody well right.'

Rather I had died at my post. I sympathised, with all the self-disgust I could summon up, with this boy's sense of justice, with the honoured tradition that deserters like myself – deserters to the European fold – should be shot.

We turned off to put the boy down at a place just off the Riad Solh Square, where a group of wary, silent young men were remaking a barricade out of salvaged building blocks and sandbags. It was a sinister empty place now, a vulnerable place, on the edge of a land of rubble. The boy cocked his gun before he got down from the ambulance.

And from there I saw it. There was a clear vista ahead into the huge devastated area which, last time I had been here, not more than a month before, was the great busy commercial district where the *suks*, the banks and offices and buildings of commerce had been. Completely laid waste. It reminded me of the photos I had seen of places like Dresden and Warsaw after the Second World War: the long rows of gutted burned-out buildings, the jagged skyline, the desolate rubble-filled streets. The intense sense of loss.

It was the Phalangists who had reputedly done most of the damage, pounding the area continuously with shells and rockets, hoping (in vain) that by so doing they would force the Army into the affray – with the usual partisan outcome. The Phalangists of all people: purported defenders of Lebanon's prosperity! It was one of those madnesses in which this conflict abounded. So that now, in front of me, there was just an empty no man's land, stretching away from here and up the Damascus Road. This was the no man's land which Yusef had had to cross the day before, when he came to visit me, in order to get from his part of Beirut to mine.

And now that I could see it for myself, I understood, quite clearly, something which had happened while I was in hospital, something which I had heard discussed on my bedside radio but had found it very hard to envisage. Up until now the fighting had been nothing but a confusion of local skirmishes between a variety of rival groups, between the Phalangists and groups of Palestinian commandos, between the Phalangists and Shi'as with all kinds of armed gangs and sectarian murderers joining in to add to the terror. But now, for the first time, this recent fighting had led to gains and losses of territory. And it had happened in such a way that – barring the hotels' area and a few other pockets of resistance – the antagonists now faced each other across this no man's land, this emerging Green Line, each occupying and controlling their own side of Beirut, east and west respectively; creating two identifiable sides to the conflict, amalgamating the disparate armed elements into two more or less cohesive fighting blocs.

I understood now. I could see it now: the clarity of it. And I was afraid once again of what this would do to people psychologically, this clear geographical distinction between the two blocs – to people like the Moslem women in the taxi, to Latifa, to Yusef – this aligning of the population, physically, on one side or the other. Already people seemed to feel such an urge to simplify the conflict, politically speaking, into an either and an or. An us and a them.

I stared at the bombed-out buildings in front of me while the boy got down and I felt such a surge of fear and sadness for Lebanon, for my family, myself, my home; loving Beirut less equivocally now than I had ever done, now that it was less lovable.

'I sure am glad to be getting out,' said an American woman to her husband when we picked them up from a nursing home near the National Museum to take them with us to the airport. They arranged themselves and their luggage in the ambulance with a few quiet contained sighs and a practised air of being used to inconvenient departures. They had all the marks, all the portable affluence, of an internationally travelled business couple: the expensive well-organised suitcases, the self-contained lack of regrets.

'I sure am glad to be getting out,' she said, neatly crossing her legs to fit their allotted space between the suitcases, and patting her lacquered hair. 'I never did like Beirut. It was neither one thing nor the other. You know what I mean?'

I was shifting restlessly in my seat to ease the various nameless aches which had begun to plague me, over in that forgotten right-hand part of my body where I had lost the subtlety of feeling to be able to place them. I knew what she meant: Beirut was too far east, too Arab, to make her feel at home. And yet it was too westernised to be what some Americans liked to call 'authentic'.

'All those nightclubs. And the supermarkets and modern dress,' she said, ' – you could have been anywhere.'

It was epitaph time, it seemed.

'Mrs Holden, if you'll excuse me saying so and I know

you're not well, but I think you're quite wrong.' They had a girl with them, an earnest young woman in a plain skirt and cardigan. Her voice rose and quavered with emotion, then fell sharply away, like a Billy Graham oration. Daring at last, perhaps, to answer back to the boss's wife now that it was all over? She tucked her hair firmly behind her ears and said, 'Beirut is kind of unique. It's beautiful. Can't you see, Mrs Holden? It's special because it's a very beautiful mixture of everything from everywhere. There's nowhere else in the whole world quite like it. I don't think anybody has a right to be *blasé* about it. God's earth is very beautiful.'

The girl stunned herself and Mrs Holden into silence. I was sitting on the opposite side of the ambulance from them and I gave the girl a smile, I wanted so much to encourage her; she meant well, in her way. But the smile was lost on her. She could see nothing but her own embarrassment. In any case it was only half a smile. The muscles on the right-hand side of my face refused, as so often, to do what I intended.

'Sure, honey, sure,' said the man, who must have been Mr Holden, her boss. He gave to each woman one of those deeply anxious, placatory – even sycophantic – smiles which to me are almost a hallmark of a certain type of foreign middle-aged businessman who has never been quite sure of himself in Beirut. His wife's mouth moved back at the corners with queenly cheese. Neither of them reminded the girl that there was a war on and that Beirut was hell itself. Nor that it was no longer her beautiful mixture; that this was West Beirut, and West Beirut only, which she was seeing from the ambulance; that what I had felt earlier to have so palpably gone this morning from Beirut was its eastern half. No traffic flowed across from it, no workers came from it to their offices and factories. As far as this western half of the city was concerned, to all intents and purposes the other side – lying over there somewhere beyond the devastation, out of sight and out of mind – was no longer a part of things.

The streets we took, to avoid the sombre slow-moving cavalcade on its way to the airport, were awash with rushing water after the heavy rain and the wild service-taxis rushed hooting along, throwing up crests of spray as they hared past the ambulance and wove in, out and around each other, more in evidence than ever now that the rest of the traffic could muster no more than an echo of its former throbbing din. There were no clamouring traffic jams today, with irate and hard-pressed drivers stepping on the decibels, no hooting whooping streamer-trailing wedding parties, no young men in open sports cars vaunting their speed and prowess on squealing tyres. A muezzin's call to prayer resounded across the quarter in the unnatural calm. One was left very aware of the surface silence of the five-day-old ceasefire and of the drawn silent faces of a clutch of nervous citizens, venturing out of doors in search of food, who were gathered round the back of a grocer's van and looked up with morbid prognostication as the ambulance went by.

I was reminded of Mustafa and his wild exultant risk-taking as I watched the service-taxis darting about like agitated molecules of steam in this explosively high-pressured city.

The following morning I woke up in a nursing home in Hertfordshire, 'deep in London's rich suburbia,' as Najib had described it to me, in his formal, precisely accented Arabic, when he met me off the plane. Poor Najib, for many years his Arabic had suffered from bouts of a sort of freely translated English, of which he was humourlessly unaware.

The peacefulness of England was breath-taking. It was so wonderful to step out of the door and be almost at once in rolling woodland where, as soon as my stroke-affected leg permitted, I could wander in perfect safety. Safety! To be out of doors and yet to be safe! To know that there is not a sniper behind the next tree, or the next, or the next. I had forgotten that the world had such privilege to bestow. The woods dropped their last thin sprinkling of autumn yellow on to the bracken in front of my feet. A heron rose in slow majestic flight from a nearby stream.

England was alive and well and currently – enviably – preoccupied by nothing more drastic than an unofficial work-to-rule by some junior hospital doctors, which Harold

Wilson's government and everybody else was taking so wonderfully, hearteningly seriously.

Nobody seemed to have heard of what was coming to be known as the Lebanese Civil War.

Part II

CONFLICT

I had come to England for the first time in my life as a student, a post-graduate student, towards the end of the thirties. And for me there really had been no conflict then. No conflict of loyalties.

'You will be going to England,' my grandfather told me, formally announcing the decision that I was to be allowed to study in Europe, 'You will be going to England, Samia *ayni*, my eye, my dearest Samia, for a very good reason: to help redress the balance. To counter the huge influence of France in Lebanon.'

I remember him so well, my grandfather, with his *tarboosh* and his soft white hair, sitting cross-legged on one of the upright sofas which lined the walls of that particular hall in his house, the *akd*, where he held court with other men who came regularly to visit, to smoke and discuss, carrying on endless erudite conversations in classical Arabic.

There were murmurs and deep smokers' coughs of assent from the old men who sat cross-legged on the other sofas round the edges of the hall, dressed, like my grandfather, in baggy *sherwals* and shiny belted *gumbaz*, and smoking their long-stemmed pipes. The sages assembled. They were looking round at me where I stood just inside the doorway, keeping my hands clasped demurely together in front of my belted floral dress, which clung limply round my knees in the style of the time.

The *akd* had its same familiar fusty smell of pipe smoke and old furniture, which seemed not to have changed since I was a child. A little to one side of me, on its own special table where it had always been, was the first edition copy of my deceased great grandfather's dictionary, which he had worked on throughout his lifetime. It was huge and old and thickly leather-bound, yellowed and scuffed and with that ancient mustiness which I used to suppose was the smell of the nineteenth century itself.

And of course my grandfather did not fail to make special mention of it in his short speech to me: 'Let us remember on this proud family occasion, Samia *ayni*, let us remember the superior achievement of your great grandfather, who was one of those visionary scholars of his day in whose eye gleamed the idea of the renaissance of Arab civilisation, of Arab ideas. We are indebted still to those scholars, your great grandfather among them, who, in the dark days of Turkish rule, saw to it that Arabic became a written language once again. They took advantage of the special freedoms enjoyed in Lebanon at that time, to set up printing presses, to found Arabic newspapers, to compile encyclopaedias and technical books, and also dictionaries of the Arabic language – this great dictionary there beside you – so that Arabic could be brought up to date, so that it was capable once again of being used as the foundation for scientific and technical developments, for industrial processes, for literary thought, for modern learning in every field.

'Text after text was translated from the various European languages. The painstaking work was begun of assimilating the bases of modern thought, of rational and scientific thought, of gleaning all the knowledge which Europe had to offer.

'And now, Samia *ayni*, you in your turn are to go too, to Europe, to study . . .'

As I stood there before the gathered company I felt, as I was meant to feel, a great sense of honour – and honour then, still, in the thirties, was a great part of one's thinking, of my thinking, a great part of family life in the Middle East – I felt a great sense of honour that I was now to be admitted, as it were, into the family intellectual tradition; that I was to be entrusted with carrying it on in my own right.

But more than anything this was a time for congratulations and I didn't stay demure and awed for long. It was my day to be honoured, young as I was. There was a lot of puffing on pipes, there were grunts of admiration and some slightly wry smiles, because it was common enough for young men to go to study in Europe in those days, but still a little unusual for a young woman to be offered the chance. The teasing they gave me was all very good humoured though. They were all academics or journalists, these old men, all steeped in the liberal reformist tradition. They teased me, they had always teased me as long as I can remember, because I was my grandfather's favourite. They had known me since the days when I used to sit between his crossed legs, with his warm chuckling breath on my hair, while he used to count out, on my bare toes, the points he was making to the other men – one, two, three, waggling each of my toes in turn.

I must have said something witty in reply this time when they made gentle fun of me, because I remember them all laughing, with deep crackling smokers' belly laughs. My grandfather drew me to him with his dear venerable face wreathed in merriment and, taking both my hands in his, honoured me with as many – at least as many! – kisses on either cheek as the occasion demanded.

But of course he really had no need to have summoned me into the presence of the sages to make his formal announcement of what had been decided. I knew already. I had known for days, for weeks even. It had been the talk of the two households, of ours and his. Even the servants knew all about it. And my mother had consulted me at length. We had gone into all the ins and outs of it, she and I, excitedly hoping and making plans, late in the evenings when she sat by my bed, combing out my hair for me. When I looked round at her once, as she paused in her combing, I could see that her face, which was strangely beautiful in the lamplight, was glowingly animated with the joy of her fervent secret hopes for me; with passionate love and pride.

The only difficulty had been to convince my father to allow me to go. His daughter! – at only twenty-one! – to be allowed to be a student abroad, unchaperoned! There had to be a great deal of negotiating and careful manoeuvring, which my mother gleefully recounted to me; while my father looked graver and graver every time I saw him. But my grandfather was a very aged sage by then and very much the head of the family; especially in things concerning me, it had become the pattern for him to have the final say, so that in the end my father grudgingly consented.

'Just think, she'll be going to England,' my grandfather had said to him – according to my mother at least – 'to your worshipful seat of Protestantism!' But he must have said it with his tongue in his cheek, because he was not a worshipper of Europe himself. An admirer, yes, a humble admirer of European thought, but not a worshipper. He often warned in his influential newspaper editorials of the dangers implicit in the mushrooming of European schools and universities in the Middle East, so that now in the thirties especially, under the Mandates, almost all the education which was to be had was European, a borrowing, foreignising people's outlook and involving a tacit bowing to European superiority. Giving to the mission-school Christians of the Middle East a way of life not our own and setting us apart from our Moslem countrymen.

Also, there was a greed, a self-indulgence in European life he said, especially in those in Lebanon who aped it; a dangerous denial of traditional values. There was a misuse of power, now especially, under Hitler and Mussolini, a growing popular contempt for other sects and other peoples which he trembled to think might be imitated here by the emerging semi-military parties – the Phalange and Najjade for example – based on the Fascist model.

But at the same time he was overawed by his own personal discovery of the European mode of rational thought; by the entirely new and illuminating perspective which the study of cause and effect gave to his view of his own subject, history. He was a great admirer of European achievement. A believer in assimilating the best of the West. He insisted on sending his children and grandchildren to the best schools, even if they were European; schools where we could gain, during the course of our school years, a command of several languages and of the styles of thinking implicit in them. Where, finally, we would be able to make our own judgements.

I was to go to London to study education so that one day perhaps – who knows? – I might set up my own school . . .

My grandfather was a very conservative, old-school nationalist.

But it was really my mother, I think, who had made up her mind that I should go to London specifically and who interceded tirelessly for me behind the scenes, more often even than she told me – my beautiful, very talented mother, with her diffident virgin eccentricity and her very decided ideas.

She had come home one day, furious. We were all in the garden, several members of the family. My father was not home but my brothers were back from the office by midday; and my grandfather was there and my Aunt Sabika and Great Aunt Munira, all sipping cool drinks and dipping into various bowls of *mezze* under the shade of the orange tree. Our garden used to be a gathering place in the heat of summer, for everybody. My mother was late, she had been expected back some time ago. Then all at once she came running down the steps under the bower of purple bougainvillaea, calling out to us. Her hair, which was usually gathered twirling in the nape of her neck in something much more interesting than the then ubiquitous bun, was flying about her head, trailing in loosened strands across her shoulders in a dark glossy fury.

'He can't behave like that, this Monsieur Gonfleux. It won't do. Listen, you won't believe it.'

She at last allowed the servant, who had followed her down the steps, to take her jacket and she twisted her hair casually up into coils behind her head and persuaded it, miraculously, to stay there with a single comb. Its streaks of silvery grey flashed in the sunlight, but in spite of that I thought how dashing she looked, almost as if she were of an age with my brother Najib, wearing the confidence of her late forties like the pride of youth. My brothers slunk down a little into their chairs. Najib especially was always embarrassed when our mother looked less than matronly. It was to please him, and our father of course, that she still wore a version – a cut-down calf-length but still formal version – of the black high-collared Edwardian dresses she used to wear when we were children. But still she looked far from matronly. Najib gave her a quick formal kiss, then tore off a piece of *khobz* which he chewed stolidly, looking morosely across the garden from under his lowered eyebrows.

Grandfather, sitting cross-legged amongst a heap of cushions on the garden bench, smiled at my mother with huge pleasure.

'I see you've been having one of your delicious battles,' he said and laughed. 'Well, never mind, *ayni*. Come and sit down.' He patted the seat next to him. 'Come and enjoy yourself and tell us everything.'

She had had dealings with this M. Gonfleux before. He was supposed to be involved in a review which she was organising. She chaired the Universities' Literary Committee which, under her direction, was undertaking an over-all review of the teaching of literature in the various confessional schools and colleges. But without the cooperation of the Mandatory authorities, nothing could be achieved. M. Gonfleux had to be tolerated; not only tolerated but won over, involved . . .

To hear her mention his name again, with that frustrated edge to her voice, was enough to make me curl up on her behalf. I was sitting on the grass and I drew my knees up to my chin and wrapped my arms around them, hugging them to my breasts. Grandfather smiled at me with twinkling eyes.

My mother kissed us all in turn and sat down on the cushioned seat between me and Grandfather. She tossed her head backwards and shook it a little so that her coils of hair hung loosely and softly between her shoulders. Her face, I thought, looked suddenly a little gaunt; but also defiant. Fiercely defiant.

'He's a rhinoceros!' she said. 'Completely impenetrable!'

M. Gonfleux was a Mandatory official, a professional colonialist, recently arrived from a post in a French colony in Africa; and I suppose he must have assumed he was dealing with a backward tribe. He totally ignored anything which had to do with Arabic, with Arabic scholarship; totally bypassed my mother's prestigious committee as if it didn't exist. Today, she told us, she had arrived to see him in his office, by appointment. But he kept her waiting in the corridor outside, for half an hour, three quarters of an hour, an hour . . . There were benches against the walls of the corridor, filled with a crush of other supplicants, mostly men in ragged *djellabiahs* and *keffiyahs*, who were encamped all day with their flasks and grubby packages of stale-looking *khobz* to eat, hoping for their turn to see officialdom. She kept going up to the clerk, who was on guard at a desk by the doorway to the various offices, and asking him to remind M. Gonfleux that she was waiting. But nothing came of it. Then finally she managed to confront him when he emerged briefly from his room and it was clear from the way he tried to speak to her, dismissively, through the clerk, that he did not at all regard her as a colleague. He completely failed to understand that she was his equal, his superior even, in social standing. And I suppose that the more she harried him for an explanation, in her poised but very insistent way, the more exotic and impossibly primitive he must have thought her, with her intense angry beauty, her staring retinue of supplicants and her elegantly poetic French.

'He told me my services weren't required,' she said, 'he'd already appointed somebody else to look into the teaching of literature. It turned out he meant Pierre Jameel from the *Université de St Joseph*.'

Aunt Sabika's cheeks quivered. 'Pierre Jameel! It's ridiculous!'

We were all appalled. With Pierre Jameel, literature in schools would mean French literature only; European literature at most. He made quite a point of telling people that he never read Arabic. He prided himself on it.

The members of my mother's literary circle were up in arms when they heard this latest about M. Gonfleux. There was already so much anger, accumulated during the years of the Mandate, at the power which was being handed to the French-speaking establishment, to the Maronites. My mother had been, since the twenties, something of a Madame de Staël of the Arabic literary revival in Beirut, with her literary gatherings and her various university committees;

but it was no time now, among the Moslems and Orthodox Christians of her circle, to look to France for literary inspiration. No time, after this latest brush with M. Gonfleux, to look to France for a post-graduate education.

Anyway, my mother had recently become excited by the work of Virginia Woolf and the Bloomsbury writers. They were her own generation. They were a literary ensemble with a very contemporary appeal, far removed from the classical formality of her French-style '*salons*'. They were breaking new ground and gaining prestige and acclaim. And when she found out that University College was in Bloomsbury, there was no question, I had to go there.

And I loved it there. I loved London. The student parties, the freedom – oh, the freedom! to be where and with whom I liked! – and concerts, the theatre, the English people who invited me to dinner in their homes: everything made me feel so euphoric. I was so young and thrilled with the novelty of it all. So much in love with England.

I had a friend, a fellow student called Mary, who used to invite me to her Bloomsbury home to drink endless cups of lemon tea and listen to her wind-up gramophone. We kicked off our shoes and wheeled and twirled through all the brash dance movements of the thirties. Then we collapsed exhausted, lounging there in her parents' drawing room with student abandon, each of us stretching out our silk-stockinged feet on one of those Middle Eastern *suffahs* – sofas – which had become very fashionable in the West (and which I was taken aback to find that she called Ottomans! As if we weren't glad to be rid of the Ottomans!) Mary, laughing, held her Persian cat up above her head and recited poetry to it – one of the Arabic poems I had taught her – with a throaty sensuous lilt . . . I was so happy there, so very happy. I had, as I said, no sense of conflict.

Then in 1939 I went home to Beirut where I met George, who was English in a very special way, and later I married him.

Perhaps, if George's parents had been able to come to our wedding, things would have been different. But we were married in wartime, in 1944. There was no question of them coming. It wasn't until two years later that I met them, when we had a rather belated honeymoon in England after the war was over. And by then I was already thoroughly pregnant with Yusef, joyfully bringing to these strangers, inside my own body, the best present I could give them. Which was one more reason, in the end, for the pain.

Perhaps, if they had been able to be at our wedding, they would have accepted me. That's after all what a wedding is for, isn't it? When one sees a beautiful bride, decked with care and love for the occasion of becoming a member of one's family, then the splendour of the day and her gentle hopeful beauty fill one with generosity. One is delighted to welcome her. But when an already married woman, a foreign woman and bulbous-bellied at that, walks into one's own home on an ordinary morning . . . I think they tried hard not to let their distaste and rancour show. Their uncomfortable unhappy politeness was, most of the time, unimpeachable. George's father asked me all the proper conversational questions with weary well-meaning exactitude. His mother, with her sideways looks and her abrupt laconic speech, seemed to be making an effort to pass judgement on me with humour rather than sourness. But they could not like me. Nor Yusef when he was born. A little black-haired wriggler, claiming to be their grandson. It was not until Elena came, a little girl, the little girl they never had themselves. And so fair! Even her hair was fair. George's mother paraded her in her pram up and down the village street. His father carried her up on his shoulders, with her little hands making white indentations in his ruddy forehead where she clutched him. She was shown off to I don't know how many people.

'Isn't she just like our George? Isn't she?' Talking to other people, their faces broke into the confident jollity which I only ever saw when they were not aware of me. I stood to one side, clinging tightly to little Yusef's hand. 'Isn't she sweet? So English!' They tried to suck her up into their lives. They pleaded with George to come back home to live, coaxing him, cajoling him, reminding him of his rights in the family business. They pleaded with me to persuade him. His mother complained of the difficulties of encroaching ill-health and sniffed back scores of demanding tears.

And I think . . . Yes, in a way George would have liked to

go back. There was that certain . . . wistful melancholy about him. But – well, for one thing there was the work he was doing . . .

But how could we go back! 'We will forgive you for marrying that foreign woman,' is what they were saying. 'We will put up with having her here, with a good enough grace, if only you will bring us our little grand-daughter.' How could we, with all that we believed in, let our children go to live there, to be defined as Arab and English respectively? Yooo-sef and dear little Elly. Unacceptable and acceptable. How could I put their whole identities on the table as the stake for which my mother-in-law and I would inevitably fight?

And of course there was more besides, many more things to prevent us from going there to live. How could I ever have borne to become like Najib, for example? Or to have become a Marie-Claire? To have become like my brother's devoted wife?

Well of course I wouldn't have become like them, not exactly. Not in some ways. But in other ways, how could I have avoided it? If I had given up the work and the struggles I believed in, to become first and foremost George's (foreign) wife?

But where was I? Yes, our wedding.

I think that even if we had been married in peace-time they would not have come. It would have been an extravagance of distance, time and money beyond their rural imaginations. Because they were very rural people in their entrepreneurial way – very local in outlook, with closely-hedged emotions – in spite of all the things about them which had given George himself the impetus to go beyond their world: their business aspirations, the encouragement they gave him to do well at school, and so on . . . and of course there were the telegrams. The telegrams from the War Office, which George used to go with his mother to deliver sometimes, during the First World War, when he was still quite small; when his mother was acting postmistress. There was one for almost every house in the village by the end of the war, announcing the deaths of men in France. It was those telegrams, George used to tell me, which first fired his imagination about foreign places. He would eye each one, as his mother hurried along the street with it, wondering about it and anticipating the great surge of emotion which he knew would burst from the house the moment the door was opened and the telegram was spotted in her hand. Then after that the house would be quite different for weeks and weeks. The curtains would be drawn, the occupants would emerge dressed in black, with sorrowful faces, and everybody else would talk about them in a specially intense and subdued way. It was strange, he said, to him as a little boy to find that everyone in the village attached the greatest importance of all to the things which were happening so far away. It had a very deep effect on him. And his own father too was in France for a while, in the army. So that George grew up believing that it was the world beyond his own horizon which mattered most, whereas for his parents the whole experience of the war was an aberration, a dreadful aberration, which did not shift the permanent focus of their eyes away from their own familiar surroundings in Lifcote End. France, for his mother at least, was somewhere to be thankfully and determinedly wiped from memory after the war was over. And Lebanon . . . well!

Strangely, George's father was supposed to have sailed out, in 1917 or 1918, to join the British force, the 'Egyptian Expeditionary Force', which was helping the Arabs to drive the Turks out of the Levant. But for some reason nothing came of it, he wasn't sent, I don't know why, though I think he would have liked to have gone. He told George about it in one or two rare confiding moments afterwards, about T. E. Lawrence too and the desert war, so that it became one of the special legends of George's childhood, bringing magical feelings to his soul. It was one of his favourite games, to assemble armies of stones facing one another in the desert dust of the back yard. But to his parents, his father included, Lebanon was really still inconceivable, I think, even after George had gone there; a place on a paper map. So that when we were married it was as if it were a paper wedding, barely relevant to the real George they knew. And so their shock when I turned up in body, demanding to be treated as inseparably linked to their George.

And I expected too much too, I suppose. Far too much.

Before we came to their village, to Lifcote End, we spent a week in Cornwall, a real honeymoon week, for all the world as if we had only just been married. It was an idyllic week: bluebell woods and farmhouse scones with cream; rosy-cheeked farm children scurrying in the yard among the dogs and the scratching chickens. And there was George, squatting to point out a clump of primroses to me, which were half hidden in the grass. I can see him still, in my mind's eye, smiling up at me, rapidly combing his fingers through his hair to get it back out of his eyes, the way he so often used to do when he was young. Then as he stood up again, he swung his hand back to take mine and we rambled on up the valley bottom, with George winkling out everything new and special to show me, gently parting the tangled branches of a bush and drawing me in, 'There, look – a nest. – It's a sedge warbler's.' We doubled back on ourselves and scrambled hand in hand up the rough hillside, as well as my pregnant shape would let us, panting and laughing all the way up, up on to the cliff tops above the glinting choppy Cornish sea. The wind caught us, blowing my hair and the skirt of my dress ballooning out in front of me. George, laughing, burrowed his way through my hair to reach my face and we gave each other long deep kisses – and more – rolling with my big round belly in the heather.

Well perhaps it was not really like that. Perhaps it rained some of the time. I don't remember. Perhaps the apparent idyll of it was not born until a week later when Cornwall became for me the antithesis of Lifcote End. I don't know. I only remember that when we came to Lifcote End on the bus from Bedford station there were the same bluebell woods on the way, the same sunshine as in Cornwall; it was in many ways so like Cornwall. I arrived expecting to like George's parents so much.

When we came to their house, we walked in at the gate, and the front garden was beautiful. Beautiful. The brick walls glowed a lovely warm red in the sun and were overhung with thick festoons of may blossom. The lilac and lily-of-the-valley were in bloom and there was a whole jumble, a glory of dust-blue rosemary, of half-wild campions and columbines, of yellow irises and early rambling roses flowering in the sheltered warmth. Bumble bees, replete and dopey in the sunshine, staggered and criss-crossed in the air above a clump of mauve-flowered sage growing by the path. I loved it, the rampant untended beauty of it.

We went round to the back, in at the kitchen door, and straight away, as soon as we stepped into the house, there was something wrong. We had been expected the day before, it seemed. George's mother hardly managed to say hello, she was so busy wiping her floury hands on the kitchen towel and telling us how yesterday's dinner had been spoilt and had to be fed to the chickens. 'There's no fire in the dining room – today,' she said, almost accusingly. 'I'll have to see about getting one lit . . .' There was the noise of doors slamming outside and then she was casting quick glances out of the window, worrying too much about the suddenness of our arrival and about the delivery van which was just arriving at the office entrance, across in the factory yard, to be able to be glad that we had come.

'I didn't know whether you'd be here for dinner today or not,' she said. 'I don't know if the chops will stretch to two more . . .' She kept wiping her hands on the big striped roller towel as if it could absorb all her harassment, all her resentment; all the love she couldn't or wouldn't express.

And George was a different person from that moment, so terribly different, even with me. His boisterous delight changed to a sort of sullen irritability. He put down the suitcases, which he had hardly seemed to notice he was carrying until now, lowering them to the floor as if they suddenly weighed four times as much. Then he went over and gave his mother a stiff peck on the cheek.

'This is Samia,' he said, nodding towards me, but he avoided catching my eye.

His mother gave her hands another quick embarrassed wipe on the towel before she took the hand I held out to her. I could see that George wasn't meant to have brought me round to the kitchen, with such cheerful informality.

He was standing with his shoulders drooping, looking out into the patch of kitchen garden. 'What's happened to the yard wall?' he asked. His phrases, his movements had become heavy and reluctant, as thick and solid as the stuffing in the big sofa by the kitchen range. 'Why that awful fence?'

I stood there in the middle of the room. Nobody was even expecting me to say anything. And I felt the joy go out of me like the air let out of the neck of a balloon. Suddenly, just like that, right down flat. Within a few moments of coming into the house.

I changed, in honour of our first meal together, into a pretty, wide-sleeved maternity dress of Lebanese silk, printed with a red and yellow bird-of-paradise pattern and tied with a broad sash under my bosom. I saw George's mother look quickly at me and away again as I came into the dining room. She was already serving out the food, from the dishes which the maid was bringing in, piling up a plateful for each of us and giving it to the maid to pass down the table. Which was something I couldn't get used to, the way my food was just put down in front of me, just like that, and I was told to eat, quickly:

'Eat up before it gets cold.' She said it to me cheerfully enough, bustling to take off her apron and sit down. It was the sort of thing one might say to a child, or a dog. She glanced again at my silk dress. 'We don't stand on ceremony here, I'm afraid. Not on weekdays. You'll just have to take us as we are.' She poured gravy on her dinner and scattered salt and pepper liberally over it. 'Help yourself.'

I looked at what was on my plate – the chop, the vegetables and gravy – and they all seemed pleased enough with theirs. They were soon chewing vigorously, George and his parents, not stopping to talk until the mounds in front of them were considerably diminished. But I couldn't eat much. I was too nervous for one thing; the sombreness of the dining room, with its dark-stained panelling and its bleak, almost empty walls above, made me ill at ease; and I was not at all sure, in the silences and the talk about the morning's business, what was expected of me. But also the food was so strange to my taste, the boiled cabbage for example and the heap of seemingly flavourless potato.

'I was ready for that,' George's father said when he had finished, leaning back with a contented sigh. He smiled at me encouragingly.

I put down my knife and fork when George did and pushed my plate away just a fraction.

'Have you finished?' his mother asked me, disbelievingly.

George came to my rescue, explaining to her. 'It's different in the Middle East, Mother. You're always expected to leave a little bit on your plate, out of politeness, to show you've been given enough.'

Her bottom lip curled. She thought I was leaving it because I didn't like it. Which was true, of course. And which didn't help things at all. She took my plate, disapprovingly.

'Very nice indeed, dear,' George's father said to her, with a pointedly exaggerated smile, passing his scrupulously cleaned plate up the table to her. To them it seemed, I think, that I was not only rejecting their food, but by implication a part of themselves, a part of their way of life.

Upstairs in our room after the meal was over, George said to me morosely, 'I wish you hadn't got dressed up in that thing.' He was slumped across the bed, fiddling with the yellowed fringe of the bedside lampshade. A faint musty smell of mothballs came from the bed.

'But you love this dress! You're always telling me so.'

'I didn't mean that. Couldn't you see it was completely out of place?'

I felt the pregnant glow of my face turn cold with the sudden unexpected shame. 'You should have warned me. I was trying to show my respect.'

He jerked up into a sitting position and combed both his hands rapidly through his hair at once so that it stood up like hackles. 'Warned you? How was I to know you were putting the bloody thing on? If you'd asked me I'd have told you!'

'In London we always dressed for dinner.'

'This *isn't* London!'

He had never been so angry before. With me, I mean. But he felt, I think, such an urge to protect. And so much confusion, not knowing who to protect against whom.

'Look at you with your flashy bangles and everything,' he said. 'Anyone would think you belonged to the hareem of some great Eastern potentate.'

He stormed out ot the room and I heard him lock himself in the lavatory, across the landing. I didn't know until then, I had no idea he thought of me as foreign. I sat down on the lumpy counterpane so that I could see myself in the dressing-table mirror and I looked at my flowing red and yellow paradise silk, at my cluster of horn bangles, my Mediterranean complexion, my black piled-up hair and I wondered what he – what his parents – saw. A young Arab: sultry, oriental, unknowable?

George came back after a little while and put his arms around me. 'I'm sorry,' he said. He sat looking at me in the mirror too. 'I'm sorry, *kabedi*,' – he used the Arabic endearment deliberately – 'It's just that you look so stunning, it's hard for them to take, all at one go.' But it wasn't the way he had looked at me in Cornwall and his voice, his laugh, his kisses were constrained, here in his parents' house.

He tried, during the fortnight we stayed with them, to explain; to explain me to them, them to me: how by serving the food out for me, on to my plate, they were treating me as one of the family. But he was too bound up in it all, too angry. And he could not explain away the hurt I felt. Their hostility was too real. I could see it in their faces several times a day. And then when they heard that we wanted to call the baby by an Arabic name they were incensed.

'Yoo-sef! Sab-eee-ka! What sort of names do you call those!' said George's father. 'What on earth's wrong with Arthur? Or Elizabeth? That's what I'd like to know.' His face went red and his jowls shook above the collar of his white shirt. (Which is why, I suppose, we compromised when it came to Elena. 'A real mish-mash of a name,' Elena called it once in a fit of teenage pique. 'Neither one thing nor the other.')

George said to his father, 'We do live in the Middle East you know.'

'More fool you.' He cast a quick bitter glance at me.

His mother had just been showing me photos of George as a baby. A toddler. A neat and smiling schoolboy. There was a self-deprecating look on her face as she handed me each one, as if to deny the strength of her love for him.

'You'd be so proud of him,' I said to her, 'if you could see the work he's doing now. The irrigation schemes, to help thousands of poor farmers. He's a very good engineer.'

She pinched her lips together and put back the photo she

had just been showing me, on to the pile: George in his new grammar school uniform. She gathered up the rest of the photos from the dark-polished table between us and wrapped them into their tissue paper package again, holding them against her breast while she secured the ribbon. Acrimony oozed out of every pore in the room.

'Oh, I dare say he's a good enough engineer,' she said acidly. 'But charity begins at home, young man, and don't you forget it.'

George raised his eyes to the ceiling, then stared sullenly down at his legs, stretched out in front of the fire.

'It's a waste of time telling him, Meg,' said his father. He rustled his newspaper and drew it up in front of his face like a curtain to blot us out.

They thought, of course, that I had taken their son away from them. Which was nonsense. By the time we were married he had already been in Lebanon for six years. But I suppose they had always assumed his stay there would be temporary, they had gone on thinking from the beginning that he would come back home in a year or two. Just a year or two more. But then I think it must have hit them for the first time, seeing him married to me, how hopelessly different from them he had chosen to become. And so the hostility and the bitter resentment. But always suppressed, on his mother's part at least. Just the looks and the barbed remarks, never an outright row, and all the worse for that because I was never allowed the chance to justify myself. All of which upset me terribly – I got such cramps and indigestion in the night especially, not just from my pregnancy – because in my own family I had never seen such hostility. Disapproval, yes, my father disapproved of everything. He was brought up at a severe and very austere Protestant missionary school, on cold water, cold looks and icy godliness. His glacial frowns were a part of my childhood; the only time he ever approved was when I married an Englishman, because he had been taught to despise his own culture, everything Arab . . .

The thing was this, that to me, coming from the Middle East . . . I was used to treating my parents with such respect. There was no question, I always had to keep myself very much in check where my feelings towards them were concerned and I believed ultimately, I think, in what they believed in, however much I might pretend to myself at times that I was fighting against it. The tradition of deference to older people was so strong then still, of genuine admiring respect for the value of experience. And also my father was so authoritarian, so high above us. So Victorian. When we knocked at his study door it was like going to see a headmaster. We had to pluck up courage to raise our eyes and look at him behind his great mahogany desk. We spoke to him in small voices, as to a revered and perfect being, across a great hierarchical divide. And so to find how sullen George was with his parents, how abrupt sometimes and exasperated, to feel the antagonism all the time between them, the lack of real regard for each other, that was a shock to me. I had no idea until then that he didn't like them very much. Which made me see him in a new light and which I found very hard to take.

And which made me realise that, paradoxically, he would eventually want to come back to live in England. Because he had left it to *escape*, not primarily for the reasons which I had always imputed to him. I had always assumed that he came to build his bridges in Lebanon for their symbolic value, as it were, to span East and West; that his idealism, his caring, his effusive enthusiasm for his work needed the Middle East in which to survive.

But I could see now, watching him there in front of the fire, irritably shaking off, with a few short-tempered grunts, the opinions on the state of the nation which his father proferred from behind his newspaper – I could see now that his stay, my stay, in Lebanon never would necessarily be permanent from his point of view. When the urge to escape grew less, in middle age probably, he would want to go back, He would be more comfortable, more in tune with life if he were in his own country, in the realm of his own natural knowledge, his own plants, his own birds, his own geography. Which was the beginning of one of the greatest fears in my life, that sooner or later I would be forced . . .

Then when our children were still quite small and Elena was the apple of her grandparents' eyes, Najib bought himself a house in England, in Berkhamsted, not so very far from

Lifcote End, and George became full of a brother-in-law's excitement on his behalf. He was indispensable to Najib, a fund of useful local knowledge and full of restless fancies of his own. When I met him with the car at Beirut Airport, after a week spent in England helping Najib to organise solicitors and builders and so on, he said enthusiastically, with a flurry of fingers combing through his hair, 'There's a lovely thatched house for sale – a holiday house – just ten miles out on the Bedford road from Berkhamsted. At a very reasonable price.'

I was driving. I avoided his eyes by staring straight ahead. 'Let's think about holidays when we're not both so busy, shall we?' I was afraid of the coaxing tone of his voice when he made such a point of saying it was a *holiday* house. 'How did you get on with Najib?' I asked.

'Have you ever seen him in a pullover, without a tie, for a whole week before?' He laughed. 'We got on fine.'

It seemed to him, I suppose – especially since my other brother, Salim, had been so tragically killed in Lebanon, in a car crash – it seemed as if Najib were opening the way for me to follow. Which is one of the reasons why I struggled so hard to prove myself in my career during those years, and which was ironically a very Western thing to have done. But I was struggling to prove my professionalism, my unique importance in the development of the Arab world, so that all my life, whenever George had thoughts of going home, I could justifiably throw them out for him because of my position, his position, the tasks in hand. And so my high blood pressure, which was made worse of course by all the other reasons why I worked, worked, worked . . .

And yet, how could I entirely loathe England when Elena, my own daughter, was so consummately English? And when I had been taught all my life, as Najib had, to love everything English, by our father especially, with his unashamed anglophilia, his old-style colonial-world reverence for the heart of the English-speaking world? George's family home should have been for me . . . what? The pearl in the oyster perhaps? For all my grandfather's gentle wariness I went there with such hope, such faith . . .

What shocked me most, I think, was that damp musty smell in George's parents house, the smell which in Beirut would have been the smell of poverty. It was in the passageway from the kitchen, in the shut-in sitting room kept for visitors, in the bedroom even; especially in the bedroom. By the wash-stand in the corner I noticed it, where there were patches of mould down in the corner of the wall, near the floor. 'Mildewed whitewash,' George said, sniffing. Though it had never occurred to him to notice the smell before.

Well, but George's parents weren't poor of course. They ran a thriving business, they were the local *Bürgers*, the *bourgeoisie*. But there was none of the sophistication I was used to at home, or that I had met in upper middle class circles in London in my student days. And I took the atmosphere for poverty.

Perhaps I was a snob. No, not a snob. I hope not. It's not that I minded who they were, but . . . Well, when George told me his family were ordinary country people, with a small leather goods factory, I thought . . . I mean, I had read so much Jane Austen, I thought they were country gentry, aristocrats almost. I imagined them like my father's family in their old-established Christian enclave on Mount Lebanon, an old influential family in a village where business was the dominant ethos, where the businessmen were the squirearchy in effect; a large flourishing village. And I imagined Lifcote End would be a sort of Jane Austen version of that, only more modern of course, and peasantless. But to find, when I went out for walks with George, just a very small village, with tubercular rural workers congregating outside the village shop; and their wives buying tiny quantities of sugar and flour with their ration books; and outside toilets in every cottage garden, bucket toilets, that didn't even flush . . . To find something like that in England, when I had been taught that Great Britain deserved to lead the world, that it was a perfect model for the world: I felt so let down!

Oh, but of course I was delighted too. So secretly thrilled. When I found out that I had married into a lower social class than I had ever come across socially in my life before, a rural class, it appealed to the young romantic socialist in me. On later visits we spent hours on our walks together, George and I, cheerfully analysing and classifying the local population, making global comparisons, and exercising our political theorising and our wit. It was all part of the holiday spirit, of the tenderness which drew us together in adversity. We lay in the grass, George and I, his face above mine, breathing in the sweet meadowy smell of each other's skin, while the children were indoors with their grandparents, or playing across the fence in the little factory yard.

For all my dread of it, I always loved that village. Hated it, but loved it too. We had so many holidays there, so many happy times with the children. And with Najib not far away – there was so much coming and going, Yusef was not left out of things the way he might have been. I loved the old stone houses of the village with their mottled red-tiled roofs, banked up row upon jumbled row, amongst the trees, towards the tower of the village church. I loved the smell of rural England, the warm sweet smell of growing things after the rain, the hedgerows, the many birds, the deep peace of the English lanes.

George's gentle sweet England.

It was my love for the place which made it so hard – my love for George, for the peace in our marriage which, later on, only the holiday mood could reinvoke – so hard to choose, I mean. To withstand the pressures upon me.

Ought we to go there to live? For the children's sake even? It used to worry me, often, what I was doing to them by bringing them up in the turmoil of the Middle East. Knowing the risks, the accumulating dangers of Lebanon. They were both always so keen, in their different ways, to plunge themselves into the fray. Which was my doing. It was what I brought them up to; how I wanted them to be. It mattered so much that they should care; should feel, as I did, ardently involved. I was proud of them, so very proud, but at the same time terribly afraid, of what I was giving them the propensity to become.

'You owe it to George to come,' Najib used to say, taking me aside at least once on each of our visits to him. He was very conscious of being the head of the family after our parents' deaths. 'The prospects would be better for George in London. And you'd easily get a job yourself if you wanted one.'

I shook my head.

'But Samia, *dis donc*, what is there to stop you?' asked Marie-Claire in her very French accent. 'You could do like us and keep a home in *Liban* too, if that's what you want.'

Najib laid his paternal hand on my arm. 'Think about it, Samia. Let me know. As I've said to George, we can always give you houseroom with us until you find somewhere of your own.'

He would always give us houseroom, it was true, so that as we took over his house holiday after holiday with our noise and bustle, my rejection of a holiday house of our own nearby often seemed purely selfish.

It was a promise which he kept over the years. An obligation laid upon me. An option never closed.

He would always give me houseroom.

One must fit into one's frame.

It had been Najib's maxim for perhaps twenty years past, since the time when he had first begun to be very successful in business, when he had branched out from Lebanon to open his own new head office in the City of London; to swell the ranks of the European Lebanese.

And the maxim was exactly appropriate to him. *Man muss sich dem Rahmen anpassen.* I remember him saying that he had come across it somewhere in one of those German books on good business practice which began to be so plentiful after the war and which, for a while, were very much in vogue.

I was reminded of it as we sat over midday dinner in his oak-furnished dining room, when I allowed myself to be released temporarily into his care from my Hertfordshire nursing home for the length of a winter Sunday. Najib, the image of Lebanese patriarchy, presided at the head of the table with the members of the family ranged down it on either side of him. Henry was here today, sitting opposite me at his father's right hand; Henry, whom I had once, years ago, heard daring to ask, 'Wouldn't it be more to the point to make the frame fit the picture?'

It had been on one of those many occasions when we had come as a family to stay with them, when Yusef and Elena were perhaps in their early teens.

'I am not,' Najib had told Henry severely, 'a picture. I do not have the arrogance to suppose myself to be one. This frame in which I live – this house with its antiques, its gardens – Berkhamsted, this well-mannered part of England – the fairness in business which a basis in London affords – this frame has a grace, an immemorial grace beyond you or me. We have a duty to fit ourselves to grace it in our turn.' It was one of his perennial themes: the way in which so many things in the world today are being jeopardised by people's belief that they themselves are works of art which deserve to have the frame shape itself to them. 'Take the Middle East for example,' he would say to us. 'First the Jews, now everybody else as well – Palestinians, Syrian expansionists, Soviets – all trying to shape the Middle East to fit their own faces, until between them they are ruining it beyond recognition.' He told Henry, 'By the time you have my experience you will appreciate the need to revere and preserve the astonishing beauty and symmetry of this frame within which you belong.'

'Pompous bugger,' I had heard Henry mutter – I was almost sure that was what he said – as he edged out of the room with an uncomfortable teenage smirk, his hands in the back pockets of his jeans; while Yusef and Elena, who were both a little younger than him, sat side by side on the sofa gawping with fascination. I watched the bile rise in Najib at such insolence. 'God grant that your generation doesn't smash the frame to bits,' he said bitterly.

But these days Najib had no such disturbances to suffer. Henry, in good Lebanese tradition, was turned businessman like his brothers and he had a wife and two children to grace his father's table at Sunday lunch today. The children looked very restrained, sitting with solemn faces and turning to their mother with an insistent 'Mummeyh?' from time to time when they needed anything. I felt sorry for Karen. Her face sharpened anxiously every time they spoke. It was not an easy job – it never had been easy – to be the mother of two such young children at Najib's table. They would have to be a lot older yet before they were allowed to be more than token presences. I tried to cheer them up by offering them things which I thought they might like from the plate of *hors-d'oeuvres* at my end of the table.

'Wouldn't you like to try one of these?' I asked the older one, pointing out a little round red stuffed tomato. 'Or a little gris-stick perhaps?' I held one up for each of them in my good hand, but they both scowled at me unhappily. My speech was still a little ponderous and they must have found me odd, I suppose. They would not remember having seen me before.

'What do you say?' Karen prompted them. They wriggled uncomfortably. And I saw at once that I had only given Karen the worse task of trying to make them answer politely. It was best for her sake, I found, not to speak to them. With my fork in my left hand I chased an elusively slithering piece of tomato clumsily across my own plate; then abandoned it where I could mercifully ignore it in the lee of my oblivious right side. For a moment I felt Najib hovering, about to come to the rescue, but he thought better of it and restrained his perpetual attentiveness.

At the far end of the table, beyond the children, Marie-Claire was gathering in the dishes from the first course with her studied smiling calm and what I noticed about her now particularly, in my physically disjointed and unco-ordinated state: she seemed so comely and at one with herself in all her movements, still handsomely elegant in the way the French-speaking Lebanese of her age so often are, the moneyed honeyed elixir-blessed Maronite élite. And Najib still adored her. She was the perfect complement to his life, he told me once: the person on whom he could always smile. Which must be hard again on poor Karen.

Najib sat in his Edwardian oak dining chair, which his body seemed to fill out so personally and though I wasn't looking at him there to my uncomfortable right, I could feel his contentment emanating palpably forth, as if he thought it right and fitting that he should be where he was in life, a man of sixty-three with creditable sons, the owner of a business which was now healthier than ever, thanks to his foresight, as he proudly told me, in withdrawing the bulk of his company's funds from Lebanon well before the present conflict burst its bounds. To fit into one's frame, according to Najib, is to fit smoothly into oneself. To adapt oneself to the market, to keep firmly in touch with the way things are going and take opportunities as they arise: that was his recipe for success.

'Are you as glad as I am,' he asked me with his mellow smile, 'that your children have grown well past the teenage stage at last?'

'Glad?' My right shoulder and my neck had stiffened recently and I felt a stab of irritation as I screwed painfully round to acknowledge him. 'Oh, but you know, our house was so alive when Yusef and Elena were teenagers. I love teenagers. I love their – ' and I held up my good fist, tightly clenched, to demonstrate the quality for which I could find no exact word, 'I love their violence. Their . . .'

'Their violence?' Najib frowned at the offending fist. Ripples of distaste went round the table. Even the children looked up from their plates.

I was unrepentant. 'What's the word? I love their passion, I mean. Their caring. The violence of their emotions. I love the conflicts raging within them.'

'You liked it when your children were like that?' Najib looked appalled. I could see him struggling with images of his own gruff obtuse boys, sprawled about the drawing room like logs, at odds with the chairs they sat on. 'But surely,' he managed eventually, 'what did George think? Surely you didn't expect him to put up with – '

It's one thing I remember particularly about Najib from the time when we were children: his pained anxiety at my failure to conform. I was always the favoured one, the baby of the family, the only girl. Samia: 'the exalted one'. It had been my mother's choice of name. I remember Najib standing on the periphery of the terrace at our grandfather's house in his short grey flannel trousers, looking pale and awkward, politely hoping to please somebody with his quiet willingness to obey; while I was showing our grandfather the strange-looking little people which I had just made out of clay and telling him a story about them, in Armenian, my best Armenian, which I had picked up from the servants and which I must have spoken very comically because grandfather roared with laughter and lifted me into my favoured place, sitting in the crook of his crossed legs, wreathed in the smoke from his long-stemmed *nargileh*. With his arms about me, he then made up a story of his own, perching my little clay figures on his knees.

At least with my father and my father's family it worked, this effort of Najib's to please, to prove himself worthy through timid unobtrusive obedience. Praise and love were meted out by our father precisely according to merit. And Najib was a very good boy.

But it was Najib – that was the strange thing – of everybody in the family it was Najib who took my side and interceded for me when my father was angry, when he had me hauled before him for playing around out of doors with my socks down around my ankles and my knickers showing, kicking my big red ball up against the walls of the neighbourhood like a common street child. 'There was nobody watching,' Najib told my father earnestly. But then yes, he would do that. He always had that determination, that compulsion even, to make everything right, to bring me back into favour when what I did or said was not proper and fitting. Which is why, at times in our lives, I have caused him such terrible hurt. By my refusal, I mean, to be brought.

'I love the fire and the flair in my children still,' I said. 'I'm glad they haven't lost that teenage spirit.'

Najib, looking pained, diverted the conversation by bringing round the wine. As he came behind us to top up our glasses, he laid his arm across the shoulders of each of us in turn, each of the women; across Karen's bony shoulders, eliciting a quick tight smile and then, pausing there, across Marie-Claire's softly yielding ones, which seemed perfectly moulded to the shape of his forearm, to his every mood. He smiled across at me and a look of magnanimity spread across his face, as if some final rightness in the state of things had been confirmed. I felt his hand rest kindly on my shoulders too, compassionately kneading the stiff muscles round my collar bone.

It was excellent wine, from Najib's bountifully stocked cellar, and the main course was delicious too – spit-roasted lamb *shawarma*, specially prepared in my honour. I congratulated Marie-Claire. She always was an excellent cook. Karen asked about the marinade and Marie-Claire told her the details of the recipe with characteristic care, with her precise French-accented enunciation, while Karen helped one of her children to eat and did her best to seem to be listening intelligently.

I turned to Henry. 'And your house, Henry?' I asked him. 'How's it coming on?'

'It's driving me round the bend just at the moment!' he said, making a long-suffering face. 'Goodness knows when we're going to be able to move in. We're still waiting for the special window fittings I ordered and only the other day I went over specially to talk to the decorators and they hadn't even bothered to turn up.'

'It's absolutely maddening,' said Karen.

'The bridging loan's costing us a fortune.' Henry took a gulp of his wine (too fast, he wasn't thinking of the wine) and started to throw his weight about in his chair, as I could imagine him doing, figuratively speaking, to achieve what he wanted in his house. He told me all his plans and frustrations, excitably, letting his arms flail out on either side. He seemed to keep justifying each decision he had made, over and over, as if he were all the time asking for my approval. He was not the son, I remembered, whom Najib had primed to succeed him in the family business, but only in a subsidiary import-export company instead.

'I'm sorry you're having so much trouble,' I said. 'But must you move house? It must be a strain when you're both so busy.'

'It's a question of getting the biggest mortgage I can, so we can have money for other things.'

'So you're moving to a smaller house? No –' I was confused.

'No, a bigger one – to get a bigger mortgage. It's the cheapest way to borrow money.'

Najib cleared his throat and I could feel him stirring beside me. He never did like finance to get mixed up with family dinners, as if it were a question of taste, of separate flavours. Of the proper place for everything.

'What's happening about your flat, Samia?' he asked. 'Any news?'

'You mean my flat in Beirut? I don't know. I don't know if there's anything that can be done at the moment. Whether I could make arrangements to safeguard it . . . I don't know.'

'Are you trying to sell it? Henry asked.

'To sell it?' I looked at him, but I could not for the moment focus. I had noticed already, this new tendency of my vision to flounder whenever there was something that was making me strained or anxious. 'To sell it? Well, in any case I hope to go back very soon, but Henry! There are rockets and mortars blowing up the streets! There's no question of anybody buying or selling. And what would you do about a solicitor, about all the deeds and so on? There are no businesses open. Nobody wants to take the risk of being shot dead behind his desk by some trigger-happy passer-by.'

'It's really as bad as that?' And suddenly it seemed I had captured Henry's imagination. He wanted to know more and more. About the guns being used. The size of the shells.

'105 millimetre . . . Perhaps some larger ones even, by now. I'm sorry, I don't know every technical detail of the weaponry,' I told him. 'Only the effects.'

'How much damage does a shell of that size do exactly? In a city street? It's hard to imagine . . .'

Marie-Claire brought in the lemon meringue pie and all the time we were eating it the discussion was of Beirut, of the devastation. I was glad to have the chance to talk about it, glad to be able to talk at all, to form the words, to express again at last the terrors of what was happening. I would have said more, much more, but I was conscious of a restraint in Marie-Claire and Najib: a *pas-devant-les-enfants* queasiness perhaps; a perfectly proper feeling that wars should not be contemplated where there are children about. A desire to preserve the flavour of the lemon meringue pie. If Henry's interest was all the time in the technicalities of the weapons used, I was grateful at least for his awed sympathy when I explained their power, when I described the pitting and pulverising of parts of the buildings in my own street.

'And you see . . . When you asked me just now what I shall do with my flat . . . My belongings . . . I'm not being honest with myself. There was a look on Yusef's face when he went there to fetch my things . . . Perhaps I already have no flat. I don't know. I just don't know.'

For the first time today my words began to stumble heavily

over each other and my eyes, struggling to fix on Henry, floundered somewhere between here and Beirut. 'The trouble is that since my stroke my mind gets so confused when I try to think what I should do . . .'

The children – at last, poor things – had finished their pudding and were allowed off to play. Karen, released from her duties, wiped her mouth and folded her serviette. Then she entered the conversation, determinedly, as if she felt it necessary to prove that some essential part of her had survived the children unscathed. She was a bright girl, she had been a maths teacher in a polytechnic before she became a mother and I remembered how this had made Najib suspicious of her when he first met her. He abhorred what he called the distempered female pushiness of some modern young women. And it was difficult, I could see it was still difficult for her, not knowiing how best to make herself acceptable to this family which lived with one foot still in Lebanon; not knowing Lebanon well, not knowing the Lebanese. I think it reassured her to find me so ill-matched to this occasion. A fellow struggler in the family. She began to smile, to look less tense, as if I might be an ally perhaps. She wanted to know more about me. About where I fitted into all this.

'Why literacy?' she asked. 'I thought Lebanon was supposed to be a highly literate country.'

'Yes. Yes, it is, but – well in any case we work not only in Lebanon but throughout the Arab world – but also the thing is that we look at literacy in a different way from most people –' I glanced sideways towards Najib to see the expression on his face, but my eyes did not quite reach him. '– You see, you have to ask yourself what is literacy *for*? And in a country of so much change . . . You can't bake a cake, or run your business or whatever, by the same old handed-down recipe if suddenly the only ingredients you can get are totally changed. You need to know about finding new recipes. You have to know how to "read" the new situation, to ask appropriate questions about how to tackle it. People must be able to take control of the new decisions, the collective decisions – the choices – being made. Otherwise they are powerless, as good as illiterate.'

'But that's politics!' said Henry and he gave a loud uncomfortable laugh.

'Yes, of course,' I told him. 'Why not? Education, politics. Does it matter what you call it?'

'Oh, come now, Aunt Samia . . .'

But Najib did not care to hear any more. It was time to remind us once again of the tenor of the household. 'You're welcome to your politics,' he said, rising from the table. 'But let's have coffee in the drawing room, shall we? Then I can shut my eyes and sneak benign glances at you all from under my lids, in comfort.'

It was hard to get up from my chair, after so long sitting, and I was limping on my weakened leg as we walked through to the lounge. Najib was ready to offer me his arm, but I pretended I had not seen it, hovering there at my side. I plumped down, much more heavily and clumsily than I had hoped, into an armchair and again there was the look on Najib's face of pained forgiveness, that I had preferred to do without his sevices.

But Karen did not take Najib's hint. She followed Marie-Claire into the room, carrying the coffee pot for her, and while she stood holding it, waiting for Marie-Claire to lay out the little hand-painted porcelain cups, she persisted, 'Isn't it a bit left-wing, though, Aunt Samia, this idea of ordinary people taking control of important decisions?'

'It sounds like revolutionary politics to me,' said Henry and, with his blustering laugh, 'You're not a Communist are you, Aunt Samia?'

Oh, but I was impatient with him, with these European's left/right labels! 'Or am I a democrat? Or a nationalist?' I suggested. 'Or I wonder, am I after all a conservative, teaching people how to prevent changes from taking place?'

Marie-Claire's bone china fingers were pouring coffee into the thin-lipped cups. Karen silently passed me mine, with a frown of concentration.

'Does it ever happen to you, Karen – ?' I asked and once again for a few moments I found myself delving uncertainly for words, they seemed to slip clumsily from my tongue, just at the moment when I wanted them. 'Does it ever happen . . . that you think . . . you are quite clear what you believe in . . . and then something happens . . . When the moment comes you flout every principle you stand for?'

'I'm not sure I –'

'What I mean is, this stroke I've had – I knew all the things you can do to try to prevent high blood pressure. Work less, relax more, avoid stress . . . I'd read all about it. And yet I did nothing. I didn't bother to use what I had read. Concerning something as serious as that! I was as good as illiterate. Me! And now still: all I want now is to go straight back to my work in Lebanon, even though the stresses would be ten, a hundred times greater than they are here, even though I know – I've been warned in no uncertain terms – that is precisely what would lead to another stroke.'

Karen nodded uncertainly, still with her frown. 'Yes . . .'

'But why don't I take this opportunity to engineer a change into some other way of life entirely, now that the strain has become too great for me? Why not? Some new synthesis . . . for Lebanon . . . But enough of that. Najib wants his peace and calm. Marie-Claire, this coffee is delicious.'

'Something should be done about Lebanon,' said Henry, looking enthused. But there was a cry from the garden and he and Karen, with an enquiring glance at each other, went out together to see to the children. They must have gone for a walk then, quite a long one, through the winter woods, because there was no sign of any of them for an hour or two.

Najib had already closed his eyes and he was sitting sleepily ensconced in the deep cushions of his armchair, smiling indulgently. It was as if he could shake his head over me, his little sister, and smile, now that my body was letting me down with age, now that I was trapped here, dependent upon his charity. Yes, charity. Najib loved charity. The constraints of charity.

As the winter afternoon closed in around us, with its fireside heaviness, I suddenly had such a desire to break out, to do something outrageous. To go donkey-riding in the Pyrenees perhaps. To live like a gypsy. To marry my Moslem . . .

Najib slept soundly in his chair. To keep a sense of order in one's affairs, to accommodate oneself to one's frame, that, according to him, was the way to perfect contentment.

'Which I can't stand,' I told Rashid when he rang me – at last! – from Damascus. I was sitting in the phone booth of the nursing home, with my red kaftan wrapped around me, hugging the receiver to my ear. 'I can't stand Najib's contentment. When things in Lebanon are so desperate. His contentment seems so much at odds with everything I care about, with everything I'm aching to say.'

Rashid chuckled down the phone and even at that distance it was very definitely his particular chuckle, full of warmth and affection. 'Samia, Samia, as incorrigible as ever! Samia, *habeebti*, what a delight you are. So now contentment is a crime.'

'But . . . I can't explain to you . . .' Soon, when I left the nursing home, I would be living in Najib's house. For weeks on end. 'Perhaps it's not Najib's fault, only I can't bear it, to be here at all. So far from everything that matters to me. When so much is going on in Lebanon! When there's so much I could be doing there to help all those poor unfortunate people.'

'My poor Samia. But your voice! You sound so much better! My very dear Samia, if you only knew how much I cried to see you like that in the hospital! But never mind, it's just such a joy, isn't it, to be able to eat fresh bread again! After eking it out in Beirut for a fortnight!'

'Is it? Yes, yes, I suppose . . .'

'It can't be so bad there, is it? My poor Samia, don't worry, I'll come and rescue you before long.'

'Yes, I wish you would!'

He laughed at the vehemence with which I said it. '*Habeebti* . . .'

Back in the glass-roofed sun lounge of the nursing home grey heads nodded on wheezing dressing-gown-clad chests. The institutional easy chairs were arranged – for companionship's sake I suppose – in an arc; but the arc was much too wide and too public for companionable chatter. Nobody spoke. The convalescent air was stale with boredom.

A little to one side of me, just beyond the arc, two men wearing towelling bath robes sat solemnly in deck-chairs side by side, staring out at the landscape. I was reminded of a David Hockney painting: the deck-chairs, the two men just sitting. It was Elena who first introduced me to David Hockney's work during one of her enthusiasms: her enthusiasm for desert art. But no, she would not have liked this one. She had studiously ignored the 'English' Hockneys, as if they didn't exist. And it was a very English Hockney, this.

Outside, the blue, blue autumn sky, the green grass and the yellow autumn woods in the distance seemed artificial. Such blatant primary colours looked unreal. The perfection was unsettling; the stillness. (Stillness! After Beirut!) It was the whole motionless paint-on-canvas atmosphere which disturbed me, with my fellow stroke patients waiting, doing nothing, just waiting quietly. Waiting to go back to their own lives.

It made me so irritable. All I wanted was news, news, news; of Beirut, of Yusef, of Elena, of Rashid again. Instead, there was just this terrible waiting. The doctor, on her afternoon round, stood in front of my chair frowning into her folder of notes. She couldn't understand why I was so on edge, in spite of the tranquilisers she was giving me.

Was it because of Najib? Something to do with the memories he awakened? I don't know. But I felt such a fear, that old deep-rooted fear of staying here in England, an irrational fear perhaps, but it had filled me with a determination to scurry back to Lebanon, almost from the moment I arrived.

It was crazy to have come here, returning like this to the very source of the tensions in my life.

Just as soon as Elena had been here . . .

I was in my room, sitting in a chair by the window, when the nursing home's occupational therapist came to see me. She put a bowl of water, a flannel and some soap down on the table beside me.

'Right, Mrs Gilbert, let's get all those muscles in your right arm working again,' she said. She rolled up her sleeves. 'Practice, that's what they need. Constant practice.'

For the next fifteen minutes my reluctant right arm was

bullied good-naturedly into some semblance of activity. She took me through all the motions of washing my face and hands, my neck too, chivvying me relentlessly.

'Use them, use them. Use those muscles all the time,' she said, standing with her hands on her hips watching me do a two-handed act of guiding the flannel across my face.

At least my right hand could squeeze the flannel so that it did not drip too much. That was something.

But I felt such pain, such an ache. Of my emotions, I mean. To find myself so absurdly in possession of only one half of my body, only one half of myself! Mrs Gilbert without Samia. And I kept asking myself, how can I exercise my absent side if it's not here but in Beirut?

It seemed to me that if I were only back there, in Beirut, I would be able to summon these parts of me back into being and feeling, this right elbow, for example, which seemed not to know that it was part of a chain of command, so that every so often the occupational therapist had to help it to move, with her hands cupped around it. If I were back at home I might be able to persuade my eyes, without such difficulty, to acknowledge the existence of the soap, there to the right of the wash-bowl. As it was they kept wanting to close every few seconds against this unacceptable place; to conveniently black out the occupational therapist's roundly determined face.

If I could only have news, news, more news. Something to latch on to. I sat in the reception area of the nursing home going through all the different newspapers which I could persuade the bemused secretary to order for me, but for the first fortnight or so after my arrival there was barely any mention of Lebanon in the English papers, and nothing about Ethiopia, nothing at all, though I scoured every one of them from front to back.

Latifa wrote from the Greek islands, where it seemed she and the children had gone with her family for a week or two, to stay in a holiday villa. It was a hurried letter, full of autumn picnics and sailing sprees and late-night dinners in a restaurant by the water's edge. My grandchildren were once more in the world of school holidays, swimming and horse-riding and thoroughly happy. Which delighted me, to know that they were safe and well. But it was a very artificial letter.

Of Yusef, Latifa wrote: 'I managed to speak to him on the phone the other night, before we left for Greece. The sooner all these troubles are over the better, or he'll collapse trying to go at it all the time, the way he does. It seems he's worried about that kid of his, that patient, Yacoub, the one he adores. He's caught a cold or something and it's gone to his chest. Could end up being serious in his condition. Just when he seemed to be on the mend. And you know what Yusef's like. Up all night etc. etc. That's not the half of it either. Anyway, he sends you his regards.'

His regards! As if Yusef could ever send anything as wishy-washy as his regards. So now this was how it was to be. With the postal service from Lebanon non-existent, or arrangeable only at great expense, from now on Latifa's family would see to it that he was only let through to me in translation, on their flits abroad; filtered, watered down, de-flavoured, run through ice; de-Yusefied. So it seemed to me on bitter convalescent afternoons.

Then at last I had a letter from Elena's head-quarters. I had tried several times, without success, to get through to someone there who might know whether she had received any of my urgent warnings. The letter said:

'Dear Mrs Gilbert,

'In reply to your telephone query, I have to inform you that your daughter Elena is at present working on a field assignment and we are not able to make direct contact with her unit at the moment. However we shall let you know next time we receive a report from her regional office. I confirm that she is currently expected to take three weeks leave.'

It was signed by an illegible somebody in the absence of somebody else who had a position but no name.

This letter, more than anything else, helped to remind me

what it was like to be back in my own mind as it had been before my stroke. It stirred my fitfully sleeping anxiety and returned me to the web of fears and dreads and powerless frustration which had entangled me so debilitatingly during my last days in Beirut, until I had broken out and rushed headlong past the battlefields . . . The letter pushed up my blood pressure enough to keep me in the nursing home for a full week longer than anticipated.

At night I had graunching, pulsing nightmares, as of wheels grinding against the inside surface of my skull in rhythmic rolling motion, errr-*oom*, errr-*oom*. Mortars pounding relentlessly, boom, boom. On my delirious eyelids was the red epiglottal sight of the mouth of the child whose breath had been taken away by terror. And there was Yusef, bending over the child's bed at night, over the child in the yellow bloodied T-shirt. But, no, it was myself the child was looking at now, looking at me with Elena's eyes, beseeching me to prevent it happening . . .

To prevent what happening? I woke up then, but the fear and the question, relating to something present and future, were still with me all day.

My numbed brain had woken again to the seemingly cosmic despair of the Middle East. My sense of endemic disaster, that pan-Semitic sense, of catastrophe waiting on the corner, was back with me, to stay.

Black Saturday. Yusef rang me, at the nursing home. By some rare miracle he got through on the phone without any trouble, very early on the Sunday morning.

'Little mother, I wanted to tell you before you had a chance to hear it on the news.'

'What's happened?'

'There's been a massacre. About three hundred people killed or wounded.'

'Three hundred! But what happened? Who were they?'

'Mostly port workers. Unarmed. They were just mown down, yesterday.'

'But why? Why?'

'Retaliation. Half a dozen Maronites were murdered

earlier in the week. We've been up all night, little mother. A lot of them were brought here. We've been working all night.' The weary grief in his voice! 'I think we've lost more than we saved.'

'My poor Yusef. So now it will begin all over again, the fighting.'

'Yes. I'm sorry, little mother. Is there somebody who could sit with you? I'm so sorry.'

Yusef was the first, but friends rang all morning to commiserate. Rashid too, my very dear, dear Rashid rang again all the way from Damascus. I spent the morning hovering in the lobby near the phone, thinking of poor Yusef; the task he had to perform. There had been a death in the nursing home during the night and relatives kept wandering through, or waiting in the lobby too, sitting around in sorry groups, their faces red and swollen with grief. Flowers arrived. It seemed fitting that I should be in the house of the bereaved.

Connie Maddox rang, my very old friend who had spent many years in the Middle East as a doctor with W.H.O. and who was still always one of the first to know what was going on. She sounded very concerned in her tough dispassionate way. She offered to come, to be with me. But I put her off. I was due at Najib's for lunch. I went upstairs to get changed.

At Najib's, the discussion of the news was like the toast before we raised our sherry glasses to our lips. Brief and formalised. Except that I think by that stage it was already impossible to discuss the war without bitterness.

'Firm government is what's needed,' Najib said, shaking his head. 'Judicious use of the Army.' And with a wistful smile he added, 'It's all very well this collective decision-making of yours, Samia, until the trouble starts.' He said it quite without malice, as if he thought that any sane and sensible person must agree. I didn't at all see the connection, and said so. 'All these jumped-up private militias,' he explained, 'taking things into their own hands.'

'I have never been an advocate of militarism,' I said acidly.

Henry filled the awkward silence by taking a large audible gulp of sherry. 'Well, at least some good may come out of it,' he said. 'It'll show those Moslem gunmen that they can't just go round murdering people willy-nilly without their own people suffering the consequences.' It didn't seem to me that any such conclusion was likely to be drawn, but I couldn't see how to explain that to Henry.

Karen was looking at me, her eyebrows contracted with concern. She was about to say something I think, but Marie-Claire called us at that moment to come through to dinner. Najib placed his arm firmly under mine to lead us through to the dining room, without giving me a chance this time to protest my independence. It was as if he felt that yesterday's events, or our reactions to them perhaps, had somehow confirmed him yet again as the stronger of the two or us. He patted my arm with grave, measured sympathy.

It was when he was taking me back in the early evening to the nursing home that I told him, 'Najib, next week when I leave here, I thought – I hope not to be in England very long . . . Would you be very offended if I find myself somewhere in London to stay?'

We were just about to go in through the main door of the nursing home and in the half-light – half artificial, half moonlight – his face turned bluish. His features puffed up with the blue blood of his affronted dignity.

'I see,' he said.

'When Elena comes – You know what she's like. She could be here any day and she'll want to be near her friends. If I'm right outside London, in Berkhamsted, she'll come and go and I'll hardly see anything of her . . .' Did it sound very lame? But it was true, perfectly true, along with everything else.

'I see.' It was all he could find to say. 'I see,' in English, though I was speaking to him in Arabic.

Then when he had been to inform the nurse-in-charge of my return, he came back across the lobby to me and said, 'Samia, you know what Yusef told you . . . the grave danger to your health . . . We fully expect you to make your home with us, for some months to come. Permanently, if that's the way things work out. Of course if, when Elena comes, you want to spend a few days in London –'

'Najib, I –' I what? What could I say? There was silence between us. But he must have seen how I shrank from his hospitality.

He kissed me good-bye with solemn formal dignity. 'Well, we shall see. But of course if you insist, then we shall have to see what can be arranged.'

Poor Najib, with his unimpeachable kindness. I felt guilty, when he had gone, that I had not hugged him. Hugged him with all the love I felt.

I went to bed and dozed the evening away, propped up against my pillows. I had the television on in my room, with the sound turned down low, waiting for the news. Then all at once – I must have been asleep – my eyes half opened to a scene which was peculiarly familiar, flashing up on the screen at the foot of my bed. Buildings, a blue and white façade . . . the Holiday Inn! More shell-battered even than I remembered it, but yes, unmistakably . . . There was a quick, out-of-focus shot of a shell bursting, a gunman running, darting behind a sandbag barricade; then a flurry of activity, which was hard to make out, in a high-up window.

And of course it was what I had known was coming, what we had all expected, all day. It had been bearing down like an added pressure in the air. I caught snippets of the commentary: '. . . renewed violence . . . life brought to a standstill . . .'

The camera cut to a stupendous view of the beauty of Lebanon: of a steep scrub-covered mountainside, with mountain upon mountain ranged behind, their slopes plunging down to the blue of the sea. Then the advertisements followed, for cat meat and herb shampoo, and my world snapped shut like the eye of a lizard.

We had returned from our honeymoon, George and I, in the summer of 1946, to find a subtly different Lebanon. No, no, memory distorts. We had only been away a month and things don't change in such a short time. But we were hardly back home again when the problems of Palestine were blasted explosively, tumultuously before our eyes with the bombing of the King David Hotel in Jerusalem, by the Irgun, and we found ourselves in the middle of so much anger at what was happening there, in Palestine, so much anger at the British for having allowed it all to happen.

Then, two years later, in 1948, when much of Palestine was declared a Jewish State, there was again such violent emotion! Everybody blaming Israel on the English. So that I was ashamed, terribly ashamed to be married to an Englishman. I blushed – I remember it. I remember hearing the news on the wireless when the last British soldiers crept ingloriously away – we were gathered that evening in my father's house and in front of my whole family I blushed. And blushed. George had a cold at the time. He was gruff and violently sneezing. He coughed and spluttered for days. Yusef was small then, an exhausting two year old, so that in any case at home between ourselves our tempers were like wire brushes. It was the wrong start completely for such a marriage. There was such a conspiracy of circumstances.

And all the time there was such bitterness between us, between myself and George. Such love and such bitterness.

Because . . . What was it that had happened on that fateful honeymoon in Lifcote End? I had developed doubts, frightened unhappy doubts about this person I had married. Such guilty painful doubts mixed up with all the love; all the tears, the scenes, the fears. It was not, after all, some streak of cherishable Bloomsbury bohemianism which made George unlike all the other Englishmen I had met in the Middle East, all the public-school-educated colonialist types of the era. He was not like them because he was not one of them. Instead he was a rebel peasant. Which was delicious, of course. And infinitely mysterious, because I had only caught a glimpse of the life from which he had broken away.

But also . . . But also I had seen him for the first time from the point of view of an outsider, from the point of view of a stranger in his family, and there he was, a sober irritable countryman who was threatening to rusticate me from my own world.

Such guilty frightened doubts. I kept accusing him in advance of all the things I was afraid he might do. 'I know what you want. You want to send Yusef away from here. To boarding school! The moment he's old enough. I expect boys are much better behaved where you were brought up!'

'What on earth gave you that idea?' George stood still, staring at me with anger, it was so unjust.

Little Yusef was slipping and sliding out of my clutches, twisting the seams of my stockings awry. He was crying and struggling to free himself, he had had such a scolding – was it for spilling ink on one of George's drawings? I think so – but I was clinging to him with the anguished inadequacy of a young mother with her first child, with passionate wringing love, trying to persuade him to be comforted. I felt so contrite at the amount of adult anger pouring upon him. 'You always think he's badly behaved,' I shouted at George aggrievedly. 'You're always scolding him!'

But I was the one who had slapped him and slapped him in my anxiety over what he had done and who now finally, in a rage of spurned love, sent him out for Rasha to deal with, he continued to struggle and kick so much.

George turned stolidly back to his drawing board, turning his back on me, refusing, absolutely refusing to say anything more. Holding in his anger. So that I felt so sad and ashamed, and cut off from him.

Which set the pattern for our marriage from then on. All that bitter, bitter, bitter-sweet ambivalence.

It was so very threatening. He was a strawberry plant. I often thought of him like that. He had even begun to look like a strawberry with creeping middle age, in his anger especially: red-faced and heavy-jowled. Like his father. But more so than his father, thanks to Middle Eastern heat and good living. He was a strawberry plant, happily sending out a runner to root down in foreign soil, but then letting it grow only as big as the little plant from which it came, content just to let it go on producing soft sweet homely strawberries, for all the world as if the soil made no difference. An Englishman always; and who would then, quite contentedly, if circumstances had been right, have broken off from the new plant and confined himself once again to the patch where he had begun. Whereas I am a vine, I used to think, vigorously climbing and spreading, with my roots deeply fastened to just one place, but trailing adventurous lavish tendrils everywhere. I used to be so afraid he would want to make a strawberry of me, to uproot me, transplant me, take away the sun and cut me down to size.

Which was a terrible analogy for a wife to think up. Poor George. I diminished him so much, found so much to criticise. As if it were his fault that in the early years of our marriage the English were stumbling and blundering through the last violent throes of colonialism in the Middle East, with Arabs everywhere snarling round their heels, passionately resenting their presence.

Then in 1956 there was Suez and all the hatred of the British and the French. Which had, of course, so many repercussions in Lebanon, opening wide once again the split between the two ideologies, the two – well yes, in a way one might say, the two populations: the western-educated, westward-looking supporters of Chamoun's government – Christians mostly; and on the other hand those who saw themselves as Arab, part of an Arab world, supporters of Nasser and pan-Arab unity. And which meant that everybody automatically relegated me, with my Christian religion and my English husband, to the pro-Western side of the political divide. So that I went madly house-hunting in districts away from the smart French-speaking area where by chance we were living at the time – we had inherited the house from Najib when he moved to England – I went madly house-hunting in the more 'Arab' areas of the city. George came along with me sometimes, out of curiosity. It intrigued him, I think, that I was so passionately determined about it. Then in the summer of 1958 when there were armed clashes and rioting going on in the streets, in a hectic rush of removals men and alarmist phone calls, of excited children and boxes and forgotten items, I moved us one weekend to our new house where we had Moslem and Orthodox neighbours, a mixture of neighbours of all kinds. Which seems a crazy thing to have done, to invite so much new tension at a time like that. We lost one box of belongings in transit and we were lucky not to lose any more. But it was no joke, with Lebanon teetering on the brink of civil war, at least to me with my younger woman's tense impetuousness it seemed no joke to live in the wrong neighbourhood, to have one's allegiances defined for one, often by complete strangers in the street. Years later, many thousands of people were to be kidnapped and murdered in Beirut for no more than that.

It was none of it George's fault. On the contrary, he agreed with me, he supported me all along in trying to tie myself more securely to the ethos of Arabism. He loved the Arab world. He loved it the way it was, the abundant joyful richness of life in the Middle East. It must have been such an explosion of experience for him, after being confined all his childhood in the parochialisms of Lifcote End. When I met him he was living in a crowded bustling part of Beirut, in a street in Bab Idriss which then was full of tenements and young single men, where affluent foreigners were hardly ever seen, and he already spoke fluent Arabic, he was living very much as a Beiruti. Then when he met my friends, and my family – my parents and brothers – he took such pleasure in them, in Middle Eastern family life, in our house with its courtyards, and *akds,* and vaulted kitchens below. I married him precisely because he flattered my budding and growing conviction that there was something exotic and special in my Arabness.

And he wanted me to stay that way, to stay exotic. He was a strawberry plant, a little afraid of the world-wide gales of post-war change; afraid of the changes bringing so much negativism to the Middle East, when 'Arab' came to be a word full of resentment and defensiveness, of conflict and aggressive defiance – involving a contortion of perception with which Elena's generation have been saddled since birth.

George wanted me and my Arab world to stay as we were. Which made it all so unfortunate that I should come home in the evening with the general contempt of the West upon me, insidiously clouding my pleasure in the man I had married. It was all so 'unfair' to George. He was not the sort of European whom the quarrel was against.

And I loved him, he was so loyal. Such fun to be with: on the family trips to Baalbek with a picnic, the way he took me by the hands and dragged me running and panting, before the sun got too high, off to play hide-and-seek with the children; crouching with me silently among those lovely columns, holding his breath, his fingers resisting the impulse to comb rapidly through his nineteen-fifties' creamed and glistening hair as he waited in suspense for the moment when Yusef and little Elena would see us and come crowing and shrieking to grab us. Such a delight to be with. He made us all laugh that day by standing on a high stone platform, underneath the very tallest columns, reciting some grandiloquent passage from Shakespeare, sending it resounding through the ruins – and the little ones joined in too: all of us shouting, sending our voices echoing right up the columns to the sky; and the fondness in his face as he watched the children. I loved him, this Baalbek George, the George who, as on this occasion, would sometimes – and so surprisingly, endearingly, quite without warning – would sometimes send a daring runner reaching out to new more lofty worlds beyond his strawberry sobriety.

My mother was gesticulating to us from afar and George raced the children over there, to the picnic lunch, which was spread out on a cloth from the wicker hamper which George's parents had given us as a wedding present. George helped my father to tuck his rug more tightly round his legs. He was an old man now and in late September the breezes could already be quite cool at times.

My mother had become very thin, painfully thin. She had lost her fine-featured artistic pensiveness, her beauty. Her face had grown a little crabbed. She seemed vulnerable, much more so than she used to be – or than I used to think her, at least. She was old. And a little difficult, in her lack of trust in the world.

'You look hot, George,' she said fretfully. 'You should sit down. You shouldn't overdo it.'

'Those young rascals give you too much running about to do, that's the trouble,' my father said to him, smiling at young Yusef. He was much milder and more informal with his grandchildren than he had ever been with us when we were small.

'George is perfectly all right,' I told my mother. I brushed a fly for her off the black padded shoulder of her dress, just at the edge of the shadow cast by the brim of her hat. George's forehead was sweating from his exertions under the midday sun and his skin was blotched with shining ruddy patches. An Englishman abroad. A 'red monkey'. It made me angry and irritable to see him like that. 'He's perfectly all right!' I protested 'It's just the way he is.' I was always defending him, again and again, to other people, against my own resentment at being married to him.

Yusef scuttled in close to the food with schoolboy gusto. But little Elena wouldn't sit down. She hopped round about us, from foot to foot, warily out of range of my mother. She was always unsettled when my mother was with us. She was afraid, I think, of her seemingly haughty elderly ways.

'Any more news from your parents, George?' my father asked, when George had arranged his rug comfortably for him and we had provided him with a little plate of stuffed vegetables and vine leaves, perched on his arthritic knees.

'Yes, I had a letter from my mother again a couple of days ago. She's still not well.'

'She's hoping you'll come?' said my mother. It was as much a statement as a question. She knew very well what George's mother was hoping and in her elderly pinched way she looked as injured and disdainful, for my sake, as she used to look at the mention of M. Gonfleux.

'Yes.'

'Well? Will you go?'

George was looking at her, not at me, but I knew by the rigid way he held his head averted that he could sense the tautness of my body while I waited for him to answer her.

'Yes, I might go,' he said. He looked across at the columns, tapering up into the blue. 'For a short visit. For a fortnight or so.'

'Poor George, he always *hates* going there at this time of year. It gets so foggy and cold!' I said in a sudden loud voice, gushing with guilt.

Why always the need to apologise? First for George, now for myself? Not to my mother this time but to my father, for the fact that I, a woman, rated – continued still, obstinately, to rate – my own career above my husband's mobility. But yes, obviously. Why not? – I was a very determined brisk young woman – Why not? My work: the promotion of pan-Arabic political literacy, almost the *cause célèbre* of the Nasser era, without which . . . How could I possibly have capitulated? How could I possibly, in dutifully following my husband, have given in to the values of the pro-Western lobby and gone off meekly to live in England? It was unthinkable, in the politics of the times, that we should go. (How on earth explain all that to George's mother?)

My father knew better, after all these years, than to be waylaid by my talk of the English weather. He lowered his eyes and chewed, with slow ruminating dignity, on his cabbage *mahshi*. Elena's little silk-soft knees bobbed and skipped.

George laid an arm protectively around Yusef, who was sitting curled up against his knee, eating his crumbling *sambousik* out of his cupped hands. 'It shouldn't really be too bad, just now. In Lifcote End. Not really . . .'

If he did, very occasionally, talk about maybe one day going home to live, it was in that voice that he said it. Wistfully. Accepting that it was not to be. It was one of the few things we did not fight about. The battle was entirely with myself.

Which made it so painful, so long-lasting and irresolvable. If only he had fought; if only he had definitely said he wanted to move to England, we could have fought to a conclusion. Divorce? 'Yes, why not?' I used to think. That way I could have got rid of the Englishness from my life, drawn a line around it and disposed of it for once and for all. So it seemed at the time. The politics of the fifties were full of potential solutions.

But he would not do battle. He would not talk about it: the big issue of our life together. He just retreated into his irritability. He grew into the habit of shutting himself away in his study – during breakfasts, evenings, weekends, most of the time he was home – working away at his papers and his engineering drawings, constantly on the telephone. When he opened the door, it was to give vent to a hot, choking cloud of pipe smoke and irritation and to stump heavily out – he was becoming very heavy in middle age, much too heavy – he stumped out to demand food from the cook for him to take straight away on a site visit, or to thunder at the children for playing in a noisy gaggle on the terrace, with their friends and their bouncing balls, too near to his ears.

And he was away a lot. Which was the trouble with his

job: that because he was designing bridges and dams for the Litani River Project in South Lebanon, with all its complex schemes for irrigation and hydro-electric power, he was often away from home for several days at a time. And I was working long hours too, terribly long hours, throwing myself into that vast problem of illiteracy in the Arab world, building up influence with governments, and with UNESCO and so on, designing a workable international programme for the Middle East. So that at times George and I hardly saw each other and then usually only when we were too tired and fraught even to care. I uused to lose sight of him, of George, my George, George whom I loved.

We would meet in the kitchen perhaps, when I came in late at night and went there to find myself something to eat – a peach perhaps, or a *baklawa* to sweeten me after such a long day spent shepherding an important proposal through an international meeting. I would find George there, in his dressing gown, stirring sugar into a large mug of cocoa. We greeted one another with nods and sighs of tiredness and sat down opposite one another to eat or drink, each immersed in our own thoughts.

'I've signed on for the introductory classes,' I told him, scraping the flesh off my peach stone. 'To join the Orthodox Church.'

'I tell you, you won't like it.'

'But why ever not? It's a wonderful church!' My mother's church. The Eastern church of her beautiful artistic younger days. It was a church of glory and music and a powerful heart-stopping liturgy.

'All the same,' he said, 'I can't see you stomaching it. The priests there are a bunch of bumpkins. Swinging their incense and muttering strings of absurdities! You'd lose patience with them in no time.'

He went on pulling holes in my intentions, humorously enough; but months later, after I had been received into the church, I found that the change-over left me feeling dissatisfied, in limbo, and I felt he had spoiled it for me. It was true, I missed the tradition among the Protestant clergy of making the church a forum for intellectual thought and discussion. But more than that, I had to go to worship alone, without George, and I knew at once that I had wilfully lost another part of my life with him – one of our times for being together. It was as if, by denying my Protestantism, that other much resented blight on my Arabness, I were churlishly disowning George too – like Peter denying Christ. Strawberries, Christ: such misleading comparisons. But yes, as I walked in alone among the crowd in the Orthodox church, with my face set in the hard self-sufficiency of my middle age, it was all at once as if I could hear nothing but raucousness and cacophony. The magnificence of the music and the liturgy were lost on me, they were raucous in my ears; like the crowing of cocks. Maybe it was that I had thought my loyalties would be simpler, so very much simpler, if I returned to the original church of the Middle East. But instead I was confronted there before the candle-thronged altar with nothing but a mass of my own shaming angry disloyalties. Mocking my solitary pride. Complicated beyond my understanding.

Blame, recriminations, sparks flew between myself and George. Over anything, everything. It didn't matter what. And yes, usually at meal times. It was at meal times that the family met to clash over who, where, when and over which plans for tomorrow.

'Paint your room! Why on earth should you paint your room?' George would pounce on Elena like that, objecting for no particular reason, to anything she wanted to do.

Elena sat hunched aggressively. She had been late reaching puberty and she was, at fifteen, still at the stage when her breasts were just bumpy elevations on an elongated child's body. She sat, saying nothing, waiting for the onslaught.

'And just exactly what colour do you propose to paint it, madam?' he asked her.

'Purple, if you must know!'

'Purple!'

'Two walls white and two walls purple.'

To George it was lunatic. He had never seen a room painted in white and purple, or any of the bright bald psychedelic colours of the sixties. Creams and pastels were still the order of the day. Lunatic!

'Why not daub on mud-coloured spots while you're about

it?'

'Oh, very funny, I don't think,' she muttered.

I warned her, 'Elena!'

It was something else he couldn't bear: that habit she had acquired of spitting ill-formed lumps of schoolgirl sarcasm rudely back at whoever was making her annoyed. And yes, usually at George. He and she used to clash terribly. He was suffering by then from heart trouble, from arteriosclerosis and it made him more irritable than ever and so ill-tempered and unreasonable. He looked crossly down the table through his gold-rimmed spectacles, which had slipped a little down the smear of sweat on his broad red nose, making him look agitated and sour.

'Who said you could paint it anyway?'

'I did,' I said.

He turned to me. 'She can't, it's ridiculous.'

'But, George –'

'No absolutely not.'

The hurtfulness! Elena was almost in tears. She had been busily telling me for weeks what she planned to do with her room, now that I had said she was old enough to decide for herself. It was a sort of treasured rite-of-passage, this room-painting. Yusef had been allowed the same privilege five or six years before.

'George, please – !'

We argued then and Elena sat there, chewing with her mouth open, mumbling hatefully to herself through each mouthful and casting him schoolgirl-venomous glances up the table. She was very bitterly hurt, that was the trouble, that because of his ill health he took so little patient interest in her, just as she was beginning to flower and mature.

'George!' I was exasperated. 'George, you can't just come and walk all over what Elena and I have decided!'

'What! What are you playing at now?' he said, 'Trying to undermine my authority in front of the children!' As the argument went on it became more and more acrimonious, with George agitatedly clattering a fork against the polished table top, bellowing his dudgeon. It was my fault, I suppose. I always had to thrash things out. It was my nature to go on and on, to worry about each thing until it was resolved.

Yusef sat there between us, opposite Elena, and suddenly in the middle of it all, of all the shouting, he exploded:

'Stop it! Stop it!'

His anger was quite, quite different from Elena's. He exploded, like a firework: his hands, his jutting chin, his shining shock of black hair, his eyes, all of them flashed one after the other in a fast rain of fiery gestures before he hammered his fists down several times on the table – boum, boum, boum, boum, boum – to put out his own anger. He sat there, as he always used to do while the arguments raged, burning with sympathy and tenderness for whichever of us was being most hurt: with me if my voice was rising and rising and the lines on my face creasing and deepening; with George if, as on this occasion, deflated by the sheer determination of my maternally aroused scorn, he finally went sullen and flabby-jowled and as pulpy and squashable as the stuffing in his mother's furniture. It was the one thing at that time which shook my confident pride in my ripening half century of age: the way that Yusef, with his young man's virtue, had begun to protect and cherish each of us as if we were already old.

George needed meal times. (Perhaps he needed the arguments). He needed them to tease out of everybody what we were thinking, to find out, assess; to gather nutrients, as it were, for his strawberries. Then he would retreat back to his study sourly satisfied, self-contained. If I would let him. But I caught him, as he was leaving the table:

'George, those socks!'

They were awful, his rustic diamond-patterned socks, bought the holiday before in – of all places for a man living in smart fashionable Beirut to do his shopping – in Northampton. I had caught sight of them while he was still sitting down and was waiting for my moment, in revenge – counter-revenge was it by now? – for the scathing remarks he had just a moment ago heaped on something I had said, some opinion I had voiced on one of his colleagues, which he had insisted on rooting out of me when I would rather have kept it to myself. Battles, battles, always the setting up of battles. From the purple walls we plunged straight into the next one.

'George, those socks!'

He lifted the bottom of his trouser leg, showing a white strip of aging skin and displaying the offending sock in all its garish tasteless glory. He looked down at it with sudden roguishness, then he came down to my end of the table and rubbed his finger playfully against the tip of my nose. But no, no, no, I was unrepentant:

'Those socks, George! How can you be so boorish?'

But I cried sometimes for my rebel peasant, whom it was hard to get close to in the fields and counter-magnetic fields of tensions which between us we managed to set up. After our move to the flat in al-Qantari I went to his study sometimes when he was not at home. One had to cross the terrace to reach it – it was cut off from the main part of the house. There was a fig growing on the terrace just outside his study door, a large rampant fig. Which I had taken in hand and tried to train. Its branches ran all along the walls as far as the balustrades, round and over the door, until his study was buried from sight behind a wall of greenery. Down under the sill of the doorway I had trained it, so that one had to step across and through a green thicket to go in at the door.

I went there in his absence, to sit for a while, in his armchair; just to look, absorb. He had some framed drawings on the walls, pen-and-ink sketches of railway and canal bridges designed by Thomas Telford: Ironbridge and three or four other examples – chosen, it seemed, for their pretty settings. Why Thomas Telford? Only one other bridge designer, also an Englishman, rated a place – just one place – on the wall: that one with the foreign origins and the glorious name. Isambard Kingdom Brunel. Thy Kingdom Come, in Lebanon as it is in England. Was that what I found so disturbing about his seemingly innocuous choice? This suspicion of graven images, of English ancestor worship?

In the middle of all the clutter of books and papers on his side table, always somewhere near the top of the heap, was a big book of John Constable's paintings, George's bed-time quieter of tangential thoughts. Or for his other loftier mood, his Baalbek mood, there was a slim book of Gainsboroughs which he kept on the shelf with the telephone directories, just above his desk. He had no plants anywhere in the room, no trophies, no knick-knacks. Just his work, his shelves of books on engineering, plus these pictures, these . . these strawberries. And some literary works, mostly by Thomas Hardy, in one corner of the book shelves, near the light switch. If only he had preferred Gainsborough – whom I rather liked, liked a lot in fact – if only he had preferred Gainsborough's superb and stunning women, his shapely refined upward-reaching images, to Constable's farm children, if only he had preferred the far-ranging ships and suspension bridges of Isambard Kingdom Brunel to pastoral-scale Thomas Telford, if images of grandeur had overcome his affection for the soft sweet reliable parochial side of rural England, I might have forgiven him for shutting himself away here. I would have felt less excluded. But to be so blatantly a Lifcote Ender!

It was only later, quite a time after he died, that I finally took Hardy's *Jude the Obscure* off the bookshelf and read it. It had been his favourite book, but I had resisted reading it until then. And it occurred to me, reading it, that possibly George was afraid all along to go back to England to live. He was afraid of being a Jude, of being sucked back to where he began. As afraid of England as I was. It struck me for the first time that in George's terms his life had probably been a success, that he would have been happily content if I had not goaded him all the time, pressing on to him my own sense of instability; driving him to this shrine of his native graven images. Was that true? I don't know. Even now I don't know. I only know that there were so many things about him which I could not take.

And yet I had loved him, loved him passionately when we were on my own ground, or on outings and holidays of my own choosing; or whenever we had moved to a new house where we could begin all over again . . .

But at other times: blame, recriminations . . .

'What's the matter with you? . . . with the situation in the MIddle East? . . . with our marriage? Why can't we just be happy?' Cries from our bed in the unproductive dark.

And if, instead, I had married an Arab?

I got out writing paper and wrote a letter to the Greek islands, to Yusef's – Arab – wife, hoping (why with such anxious doubtful hope?) that on her return to Junieh, she would read my messages over the phone to him in Beirut.

As if I could, I thought, as if I could possibly stay for any length of time in Najib's house when he confines me so within a side of myself which I don't even like; when he restricts me to some pincered censored version of myself in which everything I feel strongly about, everything I have ever tried to be, to achieve, to create for my children, is put down as upstart folly. And he smiles now on my present decrepitude, as if it were only what he would have expected of me, after a lifetime spent scrambling indecorously after suspect ideals. As if I were doomed from childhood on.

I sat there on the sofa of Najib's town flat in Knightsbridge, in a nest of brocade-covered cushions which Marie-Claire had provided for me and yes, of course I was terrified of coping on my own. I felt such helplessness at the thought of the simplest task. There was really not much wrong any more with my right side; I could dress myself, make my bed, go out walking – a little slowly perhaps, but really without too much difficulty. But whether it was the drugs or still the effect of my stroke, I don't know: even to organise myself a meal of just a few nuts and grapes seemed to require a major effort which made me want to weep. Well then, I would weep. So be it. I would sit alone and weep.

I had offended Najib terribly by refusing to be a guest in his own household. By all the traditional laws of hospitality my right place was with him. I insulted him by refusing. But with his usual kindness, his pained and solemn desire to make amends, he had offered me the use of this flat, which he had recently acquired for business purposes he told me. I would disturb nobody, he said, if I used it. And now he was doing everything for my comfort, calling in two or three times a week, arranging for the cleaning woman to buy food for me and sometimes to cook it, though I much preferred it when I could persuade her just to bring me ready-prepared salads from the counter in the local salad bar.

And of course he sent Marie-Claire to help me organise myself. Of which I was glad. I could bear the thought of living under Marie-Claire's guidance. She did not presume to judge me.

'Yes, please,' I told her. 'Please choose them for me – vases, rugs, a foot stool – whatever it is you say I need.' Marie-Claire smiled. She was re-making my bed for me, her deft finishing-school-refined fingers flying over the sheets and covers, rapidly smoothing out every wrinkle. 'Please,' I told her, 'you have such good design sense. I give you *carte blanche*.'

It was just what Marie-Claire loved. To have her sense of style appealed to; to be given scope to exercise it. Her style was not my style, of course. Far from it. She was a true daughter of Lebanon's *beau monde*, brought up on the benefits of *la formation française*, on French femininity and drawing-room accomplishments. '*Mais nous sommes des phoeniciens. Nous ne sommes pas des arabes*!' she had said to me on several occasions in the past, whenever I had talked of Arab this and Arab that, we Arabs, our Arab heritage. And she had said it each time with a toss of her voice on the last syllable and a toss of her elegantly coiffured head: '*Nous sommes des phoeniciens*!'

When she had finished with it, the flat would have the dralon and candelabra look of the grandmother glossies, it would be all *élégance* and stockbroker-belt good taste, a true reflection of Marie-Claire's cut glass, polished silver and fresh dahlia world. But what did it matter? I did not intend to be here for longer than absolutely necessary.

'I give you *carte blanche*, Marie-Claire,' I said.

She inclined her head with a quiet smile. 'It would be a pleas*eur*.'

Karen was with us, helping Marie-Claire to push the bed back into place. It surprised me that she came so often to help. Certainly, in her case, it wasn't for love of housekeeping. It was more as if she were organising a schoolroom, with her sharp face and her quick efficiency. I got the impression she was – I don't know – cultivating me? Is that the word? But that sounds too cold, much more cold, I'm sure, than she meant to be. She had invited me to dinner at their house, while I was still in the nursing home and normally I wouldn't have gone, I wasn't interested in that sort of polite let's-discuss sociability, but she seemed genuinely to care very much that I should come. And Henry too. He had fetched me, and taked me back again in his car, and I was touched by his friendly boyish enthusiasm. 'I'm helping to organise a big fund-raising effort,' he told me, 'among the London Lebanese. We're collecting for Yusef's hospital. To help the wounded.' He had beamed at me, sitting with his big hands loosely clasped at the base of the steering wheel, and had made a point of saying again: 'For Yusef's hospital.'

Karen and Marie-Claire were discussing visions of a breakfast area for me at one end of the kitchen. And adding and adding to their list of things I would need – table linen, matching curtains . . .

'We should have a party when it's all finished,' said Karen. 'A Christmas party.'

'Najib wants to give a party. For you. In your *honneur*, Samia,' said Marie-Claire and I knew from the searching interrogatory look she gave me that this was a first hint of some very definite proposal of Najib's. 'Not at Christmas, that would be too soon, but in the spring, perhaps, when you're well enough *récovèred*.'

'A party!' I thought of the sad scenes from Beirut which I had seen on the television news the night before – the deserted shuttered shops on Hamra, which every other Christmas of my life had been festooned with lights and filled with throngs of people busily shopping to the sound of carols sung out across the Christmas-spangled air; the tense gun-ridden streets. And I couldn't see that I was likely to have the slightest desire for a party, even by the spring. But knowing Najib, this would be his way of satisfying his slighted desire to do the right thing by me. A question of honour and duty. Certainly it wouldn't be something I could refuse, not on top of everything else.

'It's very kind of him,' I said. 'But please, let's not make any plans yet. Just at the moment I'm afraid I have no heart for a party.'

'But when the troubles are over we could have a celebration, *n'est-ce pas?*'

'Yes, certainly. Yes, why not? When the troubles are over . . .' But I felt very depressed.

I turned back to the newspapers which I had spread all around me on the sofa and across the coffee table in front of me. I pored over them once again, looking for that key paragraph, somewhere, which would answer my most anxious questions about Beirut. Looking in vain of course. Yes, there was plenty of news coverage. Plenty. Compared to three or four weeks ago at least. On the front pages even (where the South Moluccan terrorists, who had captured a Dutch train, allowed space). The battle for the hotels raged on and there was fighting now in most parts of the city. But which? Which parts, which streets specifically? What damage? Six hundred people had died in the previous week. Six hundred! In just one week! Plus another nine hundred injured! And they were mostly civilians, just ordinary people. But who? I had to know! Who?? Who were they?? 'Looting, arson and indiscriminate kidnapping are rampant, spreading terror and anarchy,' I read. Yes, I know this, I thought, I know this already, but who, where, what does it mean? Is Yusef still unhurt? And what about my flat? My acquaintances? My friends? What's *happening*?

Such a pincered censored description, I thought. But where did the pincering and censoring begin? People are confined – restricted – to their own side of the Green Line, I read. And I thought: yes, to one version of themselves. Najib has nothing on this.

I tried ringing two or three of my London friends, who might know something more. But nobody answered. Nobody was in. I sat.

And sat. Grey fingers of winter infiltrated round the central heating of the flat, chilling my spirits still more and making my toes feel cold and damp like pieces of fish on a slab. That one's mood and the weather could be so bound together in miserable harmony I never would have believed if I had not been married to George. His empathy with rough wintry weather in Beirut had been something dreaded by our whole household, the servants included.

I did not seem to have been doing the right thing to the switches over the boiler. The radiators were always going cold. But for the moment I would rather suffer the intermittent cold than appeal to Najib to help me yet again.

I went out – it was the only thing to do – in search of news of Elena.

'She's been transferred. Quite some time ago now,' said the Field Director at Elena's headquarters. She seemed surprised that I should ask, surprised that such old news should be of any interest now.

'Transferred?'

'Didn't she tell you? Oh, of course, I forgot, she couldn't reach you in Beirut. Excuse me just a moment . . .'

A young woman in a long wrap-around Indian skirt and a leather Afghan jerkin had come into the room, in need of something, I didn't gather what. The Field Director leafed through the papers in her stack of trays, scrabbling at their corners as she searched. Like a dog, I thought. She reminded me a little of a dog, with her round inquisitive paws. She tossed various papers out one by one into a heap. The girl gathered them up and, after a brief discussion between them, left the room.

'I'm sorry, do forgive me. We're a bit hectic at the moment. Since we reorganised . . .' Then gradually, piecemeal, interrupted all the time by phone calls and by people darting in and out in reorganised bustle and enthusiasm, she put me in the picture. 'Yes, Elena's based in Somalia now. Mogadishu. She's responsible for the relief camps on the Somali border with Ethiopia. For supplies and so forth, bringing in the convoys of lorries. Sorry, be with you in a moment . . .' She turned as she was going towards the door and asked, 'Coffee?'

'Yes, please. But black, if you don't mind.'

I heard her talking in the outer office for a minute or two, busily sorting something out. Then she came hurrying back, with two cups of coffee on a tray.

'Oh, I *am* glad to meet you at last!' she said, with a quick friendly smile. 'We've been worrying about you being in Beirut.' She handed me my cup. 'Is that chair comfortable? Do say if you'd rather –'

'Thank you. Very comfortable.'

She crossed the room once more to shut the door then she sat down behind the desk with her cup on her lap. 'I don't know how much you know about what's going on in Ethiopia,' she said, 'but Colonel Mengistu has recently begun to step up the pressure against the Somali-backed secessionist movement in the Ogaden. And what with the famine at the same time, the desert nomads are absolutely pouring across the border into the Somali relief camps.' I must have been looking anxious because she said quickly, 'Oh, it's all right, there's nothing for you to worry about. Our reshuffle wasn't caused directly by the war in the Ogaden. It was the famine initially, plus of course all the upheavals in Ethiopia since Hailie Selassie was deposed last year, which made it more logical to try and organise the relief effort from Mogadishu instead.' She smiled, a warm grin of pleasure. 'I must say, Elena's marvellous about going all over the place at a moment's notice. She's always the one who dashes off when anything urgent crops up.'

'And do you have her address, where I could get in touch with her?'

'Yes, of course. Several addresses. Just a moment.' For some – frequently interrupted – minutes, she stood picking her way, with her plump fingers, through a large dog-eared folder. 'As I said, there's nothing to worry about. She's not likely to be sent to the war zone itself. Of course, we are trying to organise relief supplies there for the famine victims, but Elena wouldn't be sent anywhere near the front. There's no particular danger involved.' I couldn't be sure, but I wondered afterwards if I hadn't heard her put the emphasis on *particular*.

She gave me the addresses when she had finished noting them down. 'By the way, I did pass on your message, when your brother got in touch with me – about not going to Beirut. I expect she's got it by now. I shouldn't worry. Though you're right of course, it would have been just like Elena to turn up there without a word of warning! Especially if she thought something was going on which she ought to get involved in! Bless her, I don't know what we'd do without her.'

I saw all at once that she was fond of Elena and I liked her. I liked her busy involved office, her friendly talkativeness. When she heard about that letter I had received in the nursing home, that dreadful obfuscating letter, she said, 'How awful! You poor soul! My new secretary hasn't quite got the hang of dealing with things like that yet when I'm away. I'm ever so sorry! Anyway, if there's anything you want to know just give me a ring. That's the best way. Or drop in. I'd love to have a proper chat with you about Beirut, one day when there's more time.'

She showed me out, hustling and fussing kindly round me, like a friendly beagle on a leash. When she shook my hand at the top of the narrow stairs leading to the street she said, 'Of course, with Elena having a boyfriend out there we haven't seen her yet this year.'

'A boyfriend?'

'Oh, didn't you know? Perhaps I shouldn't have said.' She grinned cheerfully. 'Can't be helped.'

'And you don't know when she plans to take her next leave?'

'Well, her holiday was delayed of course by the re-organisation, but she's bound to take it soon. She's bound to turn up here sooner or later!'

When I left the building I felt as if I had just been showered with sand, as when my grandchildren's roly-poly dog had bounded up to me on the beach at al-Damour last Easter and had shaken itself right next to me, while I was sitting back on my elbows idly watching the children jump and tumble among their sandcastles. A roly-poly good-natured deluge.

Once, when Elena was six years old, I took her shopping in the *suks* and I lost sight of her in a large crowd. Which was so typical of her. She had no fear. She was always wandering off like that, even when she was quite tiny, fascinated by that very Eastern smell which pervaded the *suks*, of spices, garlicky meat and wood-smoke, of old walls and urine and pungent sheep-smelling new wool. She went darting after gaudy or glittering objects which her magpie eyes picked out in the yellow-lit nooks and crannies. Or, while I was busy choosing from among the big sacks of almonds and pistachios at the nut and grain merchant's, she would sneak into the mouth of the cavernous shop of her favourite baker a little further down the *suk* and watch, legs sturdily apart, thumb in mouth, while he tossed bread dough between his hands to flatten it into rounds as thin as cloth and slapped it against the back of the fire to cook. In the back of the shop a pyjama-clad Iraqi used to sit, Buddha-like, with his belly resting on his crossed legs, bubbling volumes of smoke through an ancient-looking *nargileh*, and staring out at nothing with the same calm rapt concentration with which little Elena stared in at him.

On this particular occasion a gun-fight broke out, there in the midst of the *suks*. It was 1958, the year of those riots and disturbances which had very nearly erupted into full-scale civil war. We were in one of the fabric and clothing *suks* and to please Elena I had gone with her for a few minutes into that other favourite shop of hers, that treasure trove of a shop where later, when she was a little older, I bought her one of those flamenco skirts which were all the rage at her riding school. It was a wonderful place, more like a theatre dressing room than a shop, packed with racks of the oddest mixture of clothes: wigs, *tarbooshes*, top-hats, sequinned evening gowns, furs, *burnouses*, silks, white cricket trousers, sea boots; all smelling of camphor and moth balls. The little Moroccan, who used to lurk furtively in dark corners behind the high racks, had just popped into view to blink, blink, blink at me three times by way of asking what I wanted, when there was a terrific burst of gunfire from the alley just outside. There was the usual calm one moment, with shoppers busily poring over goods all down the *suk*. Then the next moment – an explosion of sound. And suddenly little Elena was nowhere in the shop; nowhere to be seen.

Outside people were fleeing in all directions from shots which seemed to come from hidden places all around, ringing ear-splittingly in the confined alleyways, smashing the muffled placid hum of the ancient hollows; making people scream. But there was no Elena.

And I had no idea where to begin looking for her. The crowd seemed to thicken rather than thin: a great eddying mass. I was weighed down by my many bags of shopping and I felt that heavy immobility one suffers as a young mother when one is still used to being encumbered by pregnancy or by lurching hand-held toddlers. I ran, I think, in small mindless circles, looking blindly behind nearby bales of silks and cotton fabrics and around the bundled mounds of coloured cloth set out in front of the neighbouring shops. I was afraid to move far in case she was here somewhere nearby, looking desperately for me. And I was imagining her little stricken face, pale with fright while the crowds lunged past her, buffeting her cheeks with a flurry of flapping skirts and *sherwals*. I imagined her being trampled underfoot, crying, shot at . . .

How long was it? Twenty seconds perhaps? Probably not much more than that, before I caught sight of her a few yards away, sitting in the middle of all the noise and chaos on top of a bale of cloth, looking as inscrutable as her pyjama-clad Iraqi at the bakery, watching the crowds stumbling by every which way, her legs dangling apart and her cheeks drawn in as she sucked *nargileh*-style on her thumb. Already, at six years old, securing her place out in front of the newly beginning Lebanese affray.

I used to feel uncomfortably claustrophobic in the *suks* for years after, but Elena pestered and pestered more than ever after that to be taken there.

And yet on the whole I did not have to worry a great deal about Elena. It was Yusef who was the mischievous and turbulent one, with his fierce temper, always getting himself into fights with other boys, or into scrapes from which I had to extricate him like sticky dough from a bowl; while Elena stood well clear of the mess, looking on with cheerful and almost priggish derision at his big-brotherly misdemeanours. Her father's daughter, I used to think sometimes. A little fair freckled English miss.

She was a fairly conventional child and a straightforward wholesome adolescent. She came skipping up to us at the tennis tournament in Zahleh, while she was waiting for her match to begin, and sat cross-legged on the grass in front of our chairs, twirling her racquet excitedly round and round and chattering away to us about the tennis and a host of other things: horses, swimming, good marks in exams. She must have been about thirteen then; it was one of the summers when we were all staying at the holiday villa there, near Zahleh, the one we shared with Najib and his family, tucked away in a valley beyond the town. Elena proudly pointed out her doubles partner, who was standing with his parents not far away, a tall boy in spotless white, one of those almost worryingly wholesome types, with eyes of a Teutonic blue, whom she had a knack of finding wherever she went. Then she jumped up, and off she sped, back towards the court, swinging her tennis racquet and calling to her friends. The pleats of her little white tennis dress bounced and bobbed.

'*C'est une jeune fille tout à fait comme il faut,*' said Marie-Claire, smiling after her. '*Tout à fait!*' She touched the back of my hand, in warm woman-to-woman approval.

I heard George saying to Najib, with delight in his voice, 'She's bright as a button, our little Lenni. Bright as a button.' And he combed his fingers proudly through his by then much thinned and receded hair. It was something he often used to say of her. In those days. Before his view – and her late adolescence – became tarnished by that bitter irritability which came with his worsening arteriosclerosis. Even then, that day, he somehow managed – I don't know how it happened, she was dreadfully hurt and disappointed – he somehow managed to miss her great tennis match by wandering off somewhere with Najib just at the wrong moment. I last saw them, when I shielded my eyes against the hot glare of the sun, striding heavily towards the pavilion, deep in conversation, their white shirts clinging to their backs with sweat.

Bright as a button. She was full of curiosity, just like George, though in her own different way: the same restless, relentless curiosity. So that later, as a university student, she tried out every new cult that was going, plunging herself in a spirit of experiment and universal empathy into other people's ways of doing things, presenting herself in the guise of one strange or exotic persona after another – down-and-out, artistic drop-out, yogi: the various fashionable student guises of the time – always with that same gregarious girl-guide enthusiasm, never quite carrying it off, remaining too much her bouncy self.

'Why Ethiopia?' I asked her when, in 1973 – sadly it was

after George had died – she made up her mind to go there to work. Sadly, because it was something he would have understood.

'I guess I just kinda like the idea,' was all she said. She was lying on her bed, in jeans and beads and moth-eaten fur, with her books strewn around her, chewing the end of her thumbnail and staring at the ceiling. I turned down the volume knob of her record player.

'But why?' I asked her. 'Why specially Ethiopia?'

She shrugged. '*Shoo be'arrifni* – dunno.' She looked sideways at me, without moving her head, and grinned sheepishly. 'Dunno.'

She was at the end of her final year at the American University. It was just before she took her economics degree, when that dreadful cult of inarticulateness was rife, all grunts and inaudible monosyllables. It was a belated import, I think, from the campuses of the American continent, left over from the Haight Ashbury, pot and hippy days of the late sixties. Thank goodness Elena didn't manage to confine herself to it for long. Not more than a month, at most. It was one of her least successful excursions, so completely at odds with her usual excited talkative style.

But the month was barely up when she went off on a student visit to Paris and there the traditional French sport of '*discuter, discuter, discuter . . .*' well into the night, in every student café in and around the Boulevard St Michel, was apparently irresistible. She wrote home in such tones of wonder! She was *bouleversée*!

'*C'est formidable!*' she wrote. 'The French students are great. There's a bunch of them who gather in one café or another every night, from about ten o'clock on. People keep arriving all the time, shaking hands all round and squeezing in where there's room.

'They're very hot on Arab Nationalism. "*Vive l'Algérie Arabe!*" They're with us on that every minute of the way, right into the small hours! And there's a bunch of black students, studying at the Sorbonne, from high places in French-speaking Central Africa. All government (or ex-government!) ministers' sons. Primed for power, you can tell. When they're talking you get the feeling of Africa; of political power in the big African cities, all hot and elemental, waiting to be grasped. You get the feeling that if you were only there, and got to grips with things . . .'

Then of course, from Paris, she went straight on to London to start her fieldwork training, so that I never did quite catch up on why it was she particularly wanted to go to Ethiopia. Except, I suppose, that the banners often look clearer and brighter on someone else's march for a just cause. And Ethiopia under Emperor Hailie Selassie (as it then was) was full of just causes.

And now it's Yusef, I thought – it's Yusef who has become the conventional one in most things he does: in his job, his marriage, his two properly-spaced children. While Elena has developed a definite taste for unconventionality and is embracing her own particular brand of it with increasing seriousness: driving with her convoys of supply lorries across the Ogaden.

Perhaps I do her an injustice, I thought. Perhaps the seeming flippancy of her bandwagon-hopping was only ever a figment of my over-mothering anxiety, of my frightened hopes for my very talented daughter. It may be – yes, almost certainly it's true – that she has been carefully and selectively gathering along the way the various components of an ideology, a commitment, into which she will be able to bounce finally, unreservedly, with both feet.

And she's happy, I thought. That's after all what matters. She's happy. And so beautiful in her way. Such a very lovely girl.

But also so fond of things which have just a suspicion of danger about them.

After I left Elena's Field Director, I went into a coffee shop on my way back to Knightsbridge and ordered a glass of lemon tea. Once inside it, the place was an unexpected delight: the polished oak tables, the plush intimate atmosphere. Women mostly, but some men too, were sitting over their afternoon coffee and slices of rich *gâteau*, talking in a babble of subdued but animated voices. I could hear snippets of foreign languages – Polish? Hungarian? – among the various conversations. It must be the gathering place of a circle of European *émigrés* who came here to while away the afternoon together.

I sat by myself at a small table by the wall, taking it all in. Everything – the arched ceiling, the red velvet upholstery, the carefully gathered velvet curtains draped beside the windows – everything reminded me of the big formal *aka* at home in the twenties where, as a child, on wonderful rare occasions, I had been allowed the awful thrill of sitting in on one of my mother's literary gatherings, tucked into a corner in my best blue organdie, with my hands clasped lovingly amongst the crisp blue mounds on my lap, listening to the readings in classical Arabic, English and French. The Islamic poets, Shakespeare, Racine, Stendhal, Ibsen too – I loved their wonderful unintelligibility, all the grandly uplifting sounds of great literature; while my mother presided in her high-collared black dress, which buttoned right up the front with two long rows of tiny buttons and which had such enviably puffed sleeves!

Such nostalgia! Which will get me nowhere, I thought. Such nostalgia for that far-off era, my mother's heyday, when she presided, all unsuspecting, over her admiring and enthusiastically creative literary circle.

I sipped my lemon tea, then I got out writing paper and a pen from my leather shoulder bag and cleared a space on the table in front of me. I positioned my pen as best I could in my right hand and began my attempt to write letters to Elena, one to each of the addresses the Field Director had given me. But how to begin writing? It was something I hadn't tried since my stroke, since Rashid's sad attempt to help me. And at first I was confused . . . whether – it was so stupid – I didn't know whether it was Arabic or English which should go from right to left . . . ? So that I had to try it out two or three times before I was sure, to get the feel of it, the flow of the Arabic lettering.

And my hand was so clumsy! My handwriting so humiliatingly jerky! My fingers couldn't make the necessary fine movements, which meant that I had to write from the shoulder and which made all the curves end up straight and angular. I struggled at it, hating it, trying hard for Elena's sake not to let this first news of my new sub-literate debility be too graphic; trying hard to hide my efforts from the politely curious glances of the two women at the next table. It was like being a child again, just beginning to learn to write: the same frustration at not being able to control the shape of the letters.

But why all these thoughts of childhood today? I wondered. First Elena's and now mine? It's that something is worrying me, something to do with what the Field Director was telling me. What made me remember that incident with Elena in the (now desolated) *suks*? The mental image of the child's – Elena's – stricken face: these themes have come to me before. Often. The sequence of thought repeats itself, like grinding wheels. Even back here, full circle, in this coffee-drinking setting of my mother's era, the cycle is apparent. From my mother's milking of every Western culture in her grand design for the revival of Arabic literature, to Elena's experimental riding along with every imported bandwagon going . . . Is this a connection of which I should for some reason beware? Oh, this stroke still! If I could only clear the fuzz in my brain. If I could only grasp . . . Perhaps if I saw Elena it would become clearer. But will she come? This boyfriend . . .

I took another sip of tea and to each of my rather brief letters I added (in what I gauged to be the right, not too demanding way) my cheerful hope that Elena would be able to visit me in London soon. Then I laboriously addressed each of the envelopes and sealed the letters.

So Elena has a boyfriend in Ethiopia, I thought. But, yes, of course she would have by now. Several even. Why not? And now Somalia. It rather pleased me that she was in Somalia because I liked what I knew about it, its homespun literacy drive, its habit of taking the overtures of the would-be aid-giving nations with a pinch of salt; its growing affinity with the Arab world. There's something about the Somalis, I thought, which will make Elena fit in very well there: a determination, in the end, to work out their own ways of doing things. They will like her, and also she cares so much about other people and how they see things. She'll be very welcome there.

I paid for my tea and went to a post office to buy stamps and post my letters. I was walking away again, from the post office, when . . . No, no, it wasn't enough. I turned round and went back inside. There I slowly wrote out telegrams to each of the four addresses saying: DO NOT REPEAT DO NOT FLY TO BEIRUT STOP TOO DANGEROUS STOP PLEASE CONFIRM STOP I AM AT ABOVE ADDRESS IN LONDON FOR SOME WEEKS STOP FONDEST LOVE.

And then because this was London and danger seemed so unbelievably remote, I decided I was being over-protective with my saturation-bombardment of messages and so I tore them up, not the letters of course, which were already posted, but all but one of the telegrams. Besides, if Elena was already thoroughly aware of the danger, as she must almost certainly be by now, she would only be irritated by being told so often. She became so bolshy and contrary when irritated. I tore up the last telegram and reluctantly left the post office.

Latifa rang, from Junieh.
'I'm going back,' she said.
'Back?'
'To Beirut.' Then, after a slight hesitation, 'To Yusef.'
After Christmas she had begun to ring me frequently, almost daily. The telecommunications people in Beirut were heroically working, in almost siege conditions it seemed, to keep the equipment in operation, in spite of the frequent bombing. And really, it was surprising how often one could get through now to Lebanon without much difficulty. I couldn't understand it though, this sudden need of Latifa's to talk to me, to her mother-in-law, across thousands of miles. And most of the time with really nothing very much to say. She had bought the little ones new fur-trimmed anoraks; they had been up to the ski-slopes and done a lot of falling over; her mother's friend, the one with the two yapping miniature terriers, thought she ought to engage a tutor to improve the children's English. She sounded careless and

vivacious, full of all the cultivated gaiety which I had so often seen her turn on quite unconsciously and which seemed to be the more intense whenever she was least certain of herself; the tinkling laughter. And I resented it now. No, no, I mean I was glad, very glad that she thought to ring me, but she seemed to have very little to say about Yusef, to be quite flippant about him, even when I asked her specific questions. 'Oh, you know what he's *like*!' – then a dismissive laugh and some other tit-bit of information from Junieh. I asked about his special little patient, Yacoub. 'Him? Oh, he got over his chest condition. He ought to, with all the attention he's been getting!'

And now suddenly this news that she intended to go back to Beirut. Which horrified me! She surely couldn't have understood what it would mean to be back there! She surely . . .

'Anyway I'm going, tomorrow,' she said. She threw it at me like that, petulantly. And then waited to hear how I would react. I knew by her petulance that her mother, her mother's friends, everybody had tried to argue her out of it; that she wasn't asking me for my opinion, only telling me stubbornly and wilfully that she was going.

'And the children?' I asked.

'I'm taking the children.'

'But –' My grandchildren! I took a slow breath. 'What does Yusef say?'

'He can't really stop me, can he?' And once again the bitter dismissive laugh.

I asked her to give him my love.

By explaining my credentials to an interested and sympathetic man behind a desk, I managed to acquire a reader's ticket which allowed me to use the British Museum reading room and I spent the next two or three days there – it was during a very cold spell at the beginning of January – sitting at a table in the 'pit' beneath the ascending circular tiers of leather-bound books. I was trying to catch up on the professional journals which had not been available while the troubles were wreaking their disruptions around me in

Beirut.

But it was like chewing cardboard, or counting up to fifteen thousand. Nothing I read grabbed my interest. I doodled, stretched, yawned. I thought of Latifa. My eyes circled slowly round the tiers of books above me, and I wondered again, is it the drugs? – the drugs I'm taking to reduce my blood pressure, which are numbing my intellect? Certainly my worries don't help. But I have had worries before and this yawning mental vacuity is something new.

Dr Khouri had told me I would get over my stroke *almost* completely. And I wondered now, why only *almost*? Was this what he meant? Was I never going to be able to think clearly again? Never be able to keep confidently abreast of my work? For a couple of days I had been trying to read up about the recent developments in educational provision in the United Arab Emirates, so that at least I could be useful to Rashid by feeding him with suggestions from a distance. But I couldn't, couldn't make the leap required to relate what I was reading to what Rashid had told me he was proposing to do. Couldn't connect the two. A piece of wiring in my brain seemed to have short-circuited.

I met Connie Maddox that afternoon, by arrangement, at the Tate Gallery. I had so many invitations from various people to do this or that, to go to dinner, to the theatre. But I refused most of them. I wasn't in the mood for sociability and I was afraid, as well, ridiculously afraid of settling into life in London, into the life of the London Lebanese. But there were one or two friends I was glad to be with, Connie in particular, whom I had known well in the days when she used to work amongst the desperately poor of the Middle East, travelling by camel to remote stricken villages – Connie, who could understand my silences.

We sat, she and I, on a seat in the middle of a roomful of luminescent Turners, quietly, companionably absorbed. She strode once or twice across to a particular picture, a watery scene of sunlight and mist, which she examined intently, standing in her brogues and tweeds, with her feet wide apart and her hands clasped behind her back. Her grey hair was cut to a puritanical bob. Then she came back and made some comment and we moved on together to the Braques, and the

Matisses, not saying much, just enjoying one another's presence. Passing, for me, the gaping anxious January hours.

On the way out we browsed round the gallery shop and I bought a reproduction to give to Elena, an Egyptian Hockney, full of desert sand and sun.

Latifa rang me most days from Beirut, or I rang her. Her bright gaiety was gone. Which wasn't surprising. Life in Beirut sounded harrowing. And Yusef was almost always away, working at the hospital.

'We've just spent the night in the basement bathroom,' she told me. 'All of us. Mathilde and the old housekeeper too.'

'In the bathroom!'

'Yes, we took our bedding in there. It was the only reasonably safe place. The children were screaming in their bedroom because of the noise and then a shell landed quite close by and brought some plaster down from their ceiling. Mathilde couldn't cope and I thought we'd better go down there. – The housekeeper's teeth chattered all night.'

'And now? What are the children doing now?'

'It's all right in the daytime. They've gone to school.' A pause. 'It's just the cold I mind,' she said in a small voice. 'It's ever so cold. The electricity's been off again for hours and hours.' Then, trying uncertainly to sound chatty and gay, she added, 'There's a rather sweet Phalangist guard who escorts all the children to school across the exposed road junctions. He doesn't really need to. The other mothers say there haven't been any snipers round here. But the children *adore* him!'

She sounded terribly young, telling me all this. Well, she was young, of course, just twenty-five and not really very mature, with her constant fluctuation between breezy giggling vivacity and on the other hand a pouting defensiveness when, so often, I used to see her cheeks fall and her black tossed-back curls hang limply forward down the sides of her hangdog face. Very young to have to manage two children in such circumstances, with an even younger nanny. I still didn't understand why she had come back to suffer all this in Beirut – to put the children at such risk – especially as she had seemed so apparently happy with her social whirl. But I couldn't ask her. Clearly I wasn't expected to ask. She must have come back in desperation about something. Something to do with Yusef, no doubt, or otherwise why would she so anxiously keep on ringing *me*? She really was not a very secure young woman.

Once or twice, to my joy, I got to speak to Yusef.

'Little mother, I'm so sorry – all this work – I haven't rung you for ages. I love you, little mother . . .' He sounded – vague. The way he often did when he was completely involved and passionate about something, completely preoccupied. Vague and very tired.

'My poor Yusef, how are things, at the hospital?'

'It's time, time's the problem. If I could only do more! There were two – three children who died this week whom normally we could have saved. I felt so bad, little mother! There was one little girl of four who bled to death simply because nobody had a moment to get to her, to give her a blood transfusion. If I'd only organised things differently! There were seven children, all quite small, who came in all at once. We saved the other six. But I felt so bad! It ought to have been possible.'

'My poor Yusef.' We talked a little longer about the hospital, about Yacoub who had just had some skin grafted on to his chest. 'And at home?' I asked anxiously. 'Is everything . . . Is there anything I can do? It must be worrying for you – now.'

'It's better Latifa should be here. I need her.' He was always stubbbornly, generously loyal, though I knew by his very stubbornness that he dearly wished her and the children safely and mercifully away.

'And is she coping, do you really think?'

A moment's silence.

'Keep ringing her for me, little mother, while I'm at the hospital, will you? Keep talking to her.'

'Of course. Yes, of course. As often as I can.'

All day. I would talk to her all day if it would help him.

Then one day in the middle of January, in the late afternoon, she rang me and her voice was so distraught I thought at first that something terrible, that Yusef . . .

'He shouldn't have come,' she wailed.

'What's happened?'

'He shouldn't have come, not if he was going to scream at me like that. He's at that precious hospital night after day after night and then when he does come . . . Well, I won't say any more. You wouldn't thank me if I told you half of what he said to me.' I could hear her injured held-back sobs. 'He's just – he's just a sunken-eyed evil-tempered . . . Well, you know what he's like when he's tired.'

Yes, I did know. I knew very well: he yells at everybody. He has always done that. Whenever he's terribly over-tired he goes into a rage and yells and yells.

'But you know not to take any notice of what he says when he's like that,' I told her. Surely she could support him just a little? – knowing how hard he was having to work, with the scores of maimed and injured children constantly being brought in. Not add to his troubles with the demands she was making upon him.

'What about his *own* children?' she asked. 'He only ever thinks about that precious boy with the collapsed lung. That – Yacoub or whatever his name is. It's Yacoub this, Yacoub that, night and day. And now today, he hadn't been home five minutes when there was a phonecall: would I ask him to go back because there was an emergency on? Al-Maslakh – that Shi'a slum area down by the slaughter-houses. The whole district's been captured and its up in flames. People arriving at the hospital by the score and now this phonecall: could he come at once? Well I was furious! I told them, no he couldn't, they could get someone else for a change. Like I said to him, if the hospital hasn't got the staff to deal with the casualties, it shouldn't accept them. Those people have got their own hospitals over in West Beirut, let them go there. Well, he didn't have to go stark raving screaming mad at me, did he? Insulting my mother on top of everything else. I was only thinking of him because he hadn't slept at all for two nights. I told him the hospital could go to hell as far as I was concerned, I ran and locked myself in the bedroom and I won't, I won't make it up, not when he treats me like that. He can go on pleading all he likes. Well, I'm right aren't I? It's only him I was thinking of. He'd got no right.'

'Where is he now?'

'Where do you think? At the hospital! Goodness knows when he'll next come back home or what lousy foul-tempered dead-alive state he'll be in!'

Rows, always rows. Tensions, not of one's own making, leading to sad, permanently hurtful rows. It was something that Yusef had inherited from George and me: this propensity for carrying on a rowdy marriage. And Latifa doesn't help, I thought. He's always so contrite and loving after a shouting fit, but Latifa is too insecure to open her arms to him. She harbours her resentment, so that by the next time it's worse.

I let her sob. 'I wish I wasn't on my own all the time,' she said.

'You could go back to Junieh.'

She started to cry then, properly. Miserably. And I knew of course, that to go back to Junieh wasn't an answer. She had always been so uncertainly perched between Yusef on the one hand and the world of her mother and her fashionable childhood friends on the other. She had been attracted initially by his intensity and caring, by his involvement with sick people who had no present use for dances and cocktail parties. But her mother had never approved of him. Never. And she made things far worse by encouraging Latifa's grumbles against him, by joining her in running him down. Now, just recently, Latifa had fled all that, she had come running back to Yusef in Beirut, needing him. But he was twenty times too busy at the hospital to be able to help her.

'Poor Latifa, I'm so sorry I'm not with you,' I said. 'I only wish I had come to you instead of to England.'

'I wish you had!'

She was fond of me. We got on well. It would have been easy then, at that stage, to mediate between them, to give them each the friendly support they needed. If I had only been there!

When she rang off her voice was still thick with sobbing.

It was time then for the early evening television news, and there it was – I could see the cranes and warehouses of the port in the background and in the foreground the closely huddled shacks, all those dilapidated erections of corrugated iron and canvas and bits of salvaged wood – al-Maslakh, where one of our literacy programmes had been based, in a Moslem school there. And they were ablaze, the shacks. Terror-stricken men and women were fleeing with few or no possessions and with their children and their tottering, dangerously slow old people in tow. They were being herded by Phalangist militiamen in jeeps who were shouting and firing over their heads and gleefully tossing grenades into the shacks as they were abandoned. There were spurts of flame, explosions, corpses . . . a shattered mass of burning homes and humanity.

Today the sack of al-Maslakh. And tomorrow? One could only imagine – and fail to imagine – what in the end would become of Beirut.

My poor, poor Yusef. To have gone back to the hospital to deal with the aftermath of this! He would be struggling harder than ever now and right through tonight, and tomorrow probably, and the next night, growing ever more tired, tired, sickly feverishly tired.

All the rest of the evening I felt overwhelmingly dismal. It seemed such a betrayal of the warmth and hectic joy of my past life with my children that my relationship with them now should consist solely of this helpless worrying. It was doing my blood pressure no good and it could do my children no good either to feel the weight of my continuous querulous worries upon them. I was usually so proud of Elena's adventurousness, proud of the work both she and Yusef were doing, proud of the exhaustingly intense fire with which he approached everything. But now I seemed to spend my time trying to rein in my children to my own encroaching limitations, splattering their positive young lives with loathsome doddering negativity. What else was there that I could do for them now though, except worry? In my gloriously undisturbed safety, my gallingly remote safety, there was nothing I could do at all. Except wait and wait, with my insatiable appetite for news.

You could become addicted to danger in a depraved sort of way. I almost felt like going out and walking right across Hyde Park Corner in the rush hour, right across the careering gyrating lanes of traffic, in order to feel part of things again.

If I could only be back in the thick of it, back where there was constant turmoil to offer me the prospect of coherence once again; the unity of conflict. Unity? What was I saying?

I tried on impulse to get through to Latifa again on the phone. She needed to be told that it was inevitable she and Yusef would argue in such tense and terrible circumstances, that she shouldn't mind. It didn't mean anything. She needed to be told that Yusef loved her, that he wasn't pushing her out by wanting her away from Beirut. He only wanted her and his children to be safe.

The old housekeeper answered the phone and told me through her loose-fitting teeth that Latifa was not there and was not expected back. She knew no more than that, she said. Yes, she thought she had gone to Junieh. *Ma'al owlad.* With the children, yes.

Well, I was the one who had suggested she should return to Junieh. Poor Latifa. When I rang her there her mother said she was resting and did not want to be disturbed.

Karen took me shopping at Liberty's, to buy clothes, to supplement the very few I had brought with me. I wouldn't have gone of my own accord, the need for clothes wasn't uppermost in my mind. But she took me there in a taxi and she had a gift for picking out the things I would like, clothes with sweeping flowing skirts and oriental colouring – though they weren't at all like her own plain style, not at all. She helped me choose two kaftans, one red, and the other – my favourite – in bright buttercup yellow and cream; and also a long patchwork skirt in a great jumble of colours and designs. It was a perfect match for the blouse which Yusef had given me as a parting present, all russets and golds and intricate patterns of olive and brown. Wearing it, I felt the stirrings of my old verve and flair, I felt almost myself. She knew how to woo me, that girl.

Then we spent an hour or two together at my flat, chatting, while she waited for Henry to come for her. I gave her the names of two or three books about the history of art and ideas in the Middle East, she was insistent on having them, though I couldn't imagine her reading them. One of them especially was a blatant uncompromising challenge to accepted thinking.

Henry arrived. He plunged through into my kitchen, straight to Marie-Claire's new salmon and white breakfast corner where he had sat the last time he visited me, when he had come to tell me how thrilled he was with his fund-raising: his Lebanese Appeal. 'Guess what, Aunt Samia!' he had said, bursting in, 'another twenty-five thousand pounds promised!' I had got the impression I was a reference point, as it were, an excuse almost for his boyish involvement in this new Lebanese adventure. He had seemed bursting to show off to me his suddenly expanding knowledge about Lebanon.

Today his face was full of indignant anger. He came in looking quite shaken.

'They've broken the siege at al-Damour!'

He sat down at the table, rumpling the salmon tablecloth where he caught its fringe against his leg. 'There's a massacre! Of the Christian inhabitants! Wholesale pillaging and killing. They're –' He looked sick, as if he might retch. He looked from one to the other of us, sick and appalled. 'The Palestinians and their friends – they're mutilating people. Cutting off people's ears and limbs and – and private parts!' Karen's sharp face turned pale and she stared down at her hands. 'You can find them – the bits I mean – lying in the road.'

And of course it had been inevitable, in revenge for al-Maslakh. Al-Damour, the little town where I used to take my grandchildren to the beach. For days past it had been a desperately besieged pocket of resistance, cut off there to the south of Beirut, behind the Islamo-Progressive and Palestinian lines. It had already been clear what would happen, a day or two ago, as Chamoun, that hoary ex-presidential warlord, had fled with his army from his magnificent residence there.

'Al-Maslakh? That was nothing,' said Henry. 'Compared to this, I mean. Just a few slum shacks. This is a whole Christian town! And people have got nowhere to escape to, they aren't being herded to safety like those people were. They're even swimming out to sea to try and get away before they can be gunned down.'

I should have pulled him up on that, on his lack of concern for the people of al-Maslakh, but his appalled pity for the inhabitants of al-Damour touched me. He was almost crying, his face was so contorted with indignation.

He sat and drank the tea which Karen gave him, tipping his chair backwards and waving his hand excitedly about, as he told me about the new plans to expand the fund-raising drive – 'for Yusef's hospital' – referring back continually to the plight of the people of al-Damour.

'But those people won't be sent to Yusef's hospital,' I interrupted him. 'Damour's ten or twelve miles south of Beirut. There's no way to get across from there now to the eastern side of Beirut where Yusef is.'

'Oh goodness, we're not only raising money for the hospital!' he said with a short irritable laugh. Then recovering, he said, 'Aunt Samia, the response to the appeal among the Lebanese here has been wonderful. Absolutely fantastic!' He took Karen's hand and gave it a husbandly squeeze. 'I can't tell you, Aunt Samia, how good everyone has been!'

But I felt more depressed after they had gone than ever before. That Lebanon's political troubles should have developed now into such a frenzy of sectarian hatred and vicious slaughter! When we had always prided ourselves on our easy-going religious toleration, on our ability to accept everybody – Palestinians, Armenians, refugees of every nation, Americans, Europeans – everybody; such a blend and variety of human beings. And now this narrow bigoted loathing! Well yes, it's true that there had always been sectarian grievances – political grievances: that the allocation of parliamentary seats and government posts according to religion and sect gave much too much power to the Maronites; and so on. But this!

I sat on at the kitchen table and tried to ease the strain I felt in my right side, the stiffness of the bunched muscles in my shoulder and upper arm. It was something I had not at all expected: the resentment I felt against these forgotten muscles which were thrusting themselves so uncompromisingly back upon my awareness with their aches and pains and their ill-coordinated ways of doing things. And the stiffness had been getting worse again during these past few days, not better. It was the tension of course, the physical toll of the war, causing the muscles to seize and ache, as if al-Maslakh – and now al-Damour too – were fought and laid waste within my own body. I would not start to get better again, I knew, so long as all this lasted.

I ate out that evening – I had to get out, to walk, to move – at a small Greek restaurant near Charlotte Street. I needed a place where I could sink my melancholy into the atmosphere, a place sympathetic, in its Mediterranean way, to the spirit of what I had lost.

I ordered *houmous* to start with, which came of course with all the necessary ingredients at last to turn wartime chickpea mush into a palatable dish. Then to follow that I ordered *kebabs*. The place was full of the smell of charcoal cookery, of Greek music, Greek faces, cheap formica-topped tables and students eating or squeezing to and fro in the cramped space. It reminded me of the places where Elena and her crowd used to go to eat, in Beirut, near the American University. Voices from the kitchen area jabbered urgently in Greek above the sizzling of the skewered *kebabs*. And there was plenty of heady '*Othello*' to wash the meal down, against doctors' orders. I began to feel much better, in a melancholy escapist way.

The proprietor took me for a Greek at first and later on, when things were a little less hectic, we got talking. He kept coming to sit down at my table whenever he had a minute, squeezing his cook's stomach in opposite me and he told me in a mixture of broken English and abominable Arabic about the business fortunes of his large Greek Cypriot family in various parts of the Middle East. He drank '*Othello*' with me and talked about Cyprus, with a sudden bitterness which was remarkable in such a genial man.

'And Lebanon,' he said. 'Lebanon is like Cyprus. Will be partition very soon now. After such terrible hate, just like Cyprus. Is the only thing possible.'

But no, I couldn't accept that – the parallel. I couldn't accept that Lebanon had two irreconcilable communities. As if this murderous sectarianism among the armed militias had anything to do with the feelings of ordinary people!

'No, no!' As if the very many conservative Moslems – the Sunni elders especially, with their urban prosperity and high standing – as if they would ever be able to see their way to allying themselves with the radicals and commandos! It was ludicrous. 'Impossible. No, no!' I looked down at my glass and I could feel on my face the scoured lines of age, etched deep as if in marble.

'But already you have like us now the Green Line, yes? The dividing line. Ker-chomp!' The proprietor made a downwards chopping gesture with his hand. 'And the whole populations now – each fleeing across. This way, that way.'

I did not argue. Could not argue. It was too painful; the partition of Lebanon was too frighteningly possible to discuss just then.

'Listen, I tell you –' He called across his two sons to come and back up his verdict. They all became very heated. Very emphatic. Again the proprietor made his chopping gesture, ker-chomp, to illustrate what partition had done to each of their lives.

'And you?' he asked me. 'In Lebanon. Which side you on?'

Side? 'But . . . you see – I have two sides!' I don't know why I did it, I put out both my arms. To demonstrate the fact, I suppose: you see, indisputably I have two sides. But while one arm thrust itself forward energetically, palm upwards, the other hung clumsily outwards with the fingers limply curled and the gesture only served to draw attention to the disjunction between the two; to how odd it was that I should be constrained to think of my body in terms of differing sides at all. And he noticed. The proprietor noticed. I saw the shrewd look in his eyes and he would have said something, but his wife called across to him from the kitchen area, scolding him loudly in Greek. The sons hurried, with a lot of busy plate-clattering, back to their work.

'She tell me is my business to make you cheerful. Is right. Is a different thing, Lebanon. No Greeks, no Turks. Is only a difference of Christian and Moslem. Is nothing. Will come to nothing. Pouff!'

He was not stupid. I was not stupid. We understood one another completely. But he was the genial host again and he seduced me skilfully with wine and ebullient good humour into talk of other things. He pressed more '*Othello*' on me and when finally I kept my hand firmly on top of my glass, he called to his wife and plied me with cup after tiny cup of thick sweet Greek coffee, on the house.

'And London,' he said, pushing his cook's belly well forward to make the space on the chair more comfortable for the rest of him. 'London is, well, O.K. But without your man, huh, not so good. You come here next time, I find you a man. You like?'

'Yes. Yes, of course!' I said, replete with the wine and the delicious Mediterranean emotionalism which wafted with the smoke from the skewered *kebabs* on the fire behind the counter.

'Yes? You like? Good!' he said and we laughed together in amicable disbelief.

I walked down through Soho, through the throngs of people disgorging from cinemas and restaurants, past narrow doorways and nightclubs pulsing with music. And it was true, I longed for . . . well, yes, for a man. For . . . Never mind my age and my stroke, never mind the slight imbalance in my walk, I noticed men's eyes on me as I walked and I knew I could be stunning still, with my flowing skirt and the fronds of Yusef's glorious hand-embroidery straying out in a billowing colourful cascade through the open front of my coat; with my soft silver-white hair and my very expensive perfume (a delightful gift from Marie-Claire).

But no, it was not a man that I longed for especially. That was to simplify things too much. It was not sex that Soho managed to suggest to me, in spite of the intended message of the posters outside a row of strip joints which I passed. It was not sex but physical proximity between people which I saw wherever I looked. With George here, life in London could have been fun. Theatres, restaurants, walks together arm in arm, watching the crowds go by . . . But no, it was not George whom I wanted to think about for the moment either. I felt an urgent need to touch, to be touched by somebody living. Somebody who could return the sensuality to my body which had been ousted by my stroke. What did it once feel like to be loved, cuddled, held, crashed into all day by a household of children? There was a certain responsiveness, a capacity for emotional expression missing from my right side which I would never get back through physiotherapy and exercises alone.

I wondered whether I should invite Latifa perhaps. To come here with my grandchildren. It would do us all good. Maybe . . . Maybe if she came Yusef might follow? No, it wasn't that I liked it here, but if they were to come . . . I could find a flat of my own, somewhere more permanent . . . a second home for my grandchildren, for little Mouna and Majid, away from the terrors of Lebanon. For Elena. A belated family home here. Yes, yes perhaps . . . Perhaps it was not too late, even now, to redress the balance?

I thought of George again in a rush of guilt and I could have wept at the bathos of my sudden urge to stay here. My poor George, if you only knew, after all we went through, how I have succumbed!

I took a taxi when I reached Shaftesbury Avenue – the wine and the walk had made me tired – and as soon as I was back in the flat I rang Rashid; an expensive unwarranted call.

'Samia! *Habeebti*!'

'It's not too late? Were you asleep?'

'Would it matter if I was? How are you, my very, very dear Samia?'

I told him about my stiffness. The physical burden of the war. 'And, I can't explain to you . . . What I need is sensuousness; people around me. If I could only be battered back together again. Part of the hurly-burly. I need to be pummelled, squeezed . . .'

'Samia, Samia. As incorrigible as ever!' He chuckled. 'Samia, *habeebti*!'

'Do I sound so mad?'

'Listen, *habeebti*. Imagine this. Imagine I am there with you, I have taken tight hold of you and we are dancing, barefooted on the carpet. Dancing, dancing –' His voice was very soft. 'Can you feel it? My arms are round you and I am bumping you here and there into the furniture. Treading on your right toe –' Again the quiet chuckle.

'Rashid, you're such a tease!'

But I loved him in that moment. Loved him. It was so

exactly the sort of thing I had wanted him to say. My very dear Rashid.

Rashid and Yusef. The two men who wanted to dance me round the room.

A telegram came from Rashid the following day: WILL FIX HOLIDAY FOR US BOTH STOP SUGGEST SWITZERLAND STOP LET ME KNOW DATES TO SUIT YOU STOP MY BEST LOVE.

A holiday with Rashid! I loved the idea. It would be cold in Switzerland, but never mind. I should enjoy walking with him in the snow, all muffled up together. Just as soon as I knew when to expect Elena . . .

I tried ringing Latifa again, but it seemed her mother still did not want me to speak to her.

A holiday with Rashid! The idea was perfect. It filled me with such hope.

Then, within a few days of the fall of al-Damour, what had scarcely seemed possible . . .

The combined forces of the Progressives, strengthened – greatly strengthened – by the Palestine Liberation Army, advanced in a broad sweep across Lebanon, with thousands of Christian refugees fleeing before them, in their cars, in lorries, on foot, cramming the roads out of al-Damour, al-Jiyeh, the Bekaa Valley. It was so unexpected, this breaking of the deadlock, this tipping of the balance of power. Clearly it was the full-scale involvement of the P.L.A. which made the difference, with their Syrian-trained fighters, their Syrian-provided arms and munitions; with the Syrian faces reportedly among the troops which were pouring down the Bekaa Valley and fanning out across the mountains. But what would come of it? I was not sure. It was something which perplexed me over the next few uncertain days, why there were no protests from outside Lebanon, from America and Israel particularly, at this massive influx of military aid from across the Syrian border; so that clearly there must have been some deal, some international arrangement. But what deal? It was something which, for the moment, I couldn't at all understand.

Then in the end the advance halted at the Green Line, leaving only East Beirut, and also the Maronite heartland of Mount Lebanon – leaving just this cherished fiercely-defended chunk in the hands of the Maronite-dominated militias. A Syrian delegation with (by now thoroughly official) international backing arrived to mediate and a peace agreement was duly formulated.

The war was – was it? could it be? – yes, surely. I blinked. I could not believe it. It had happened, in the end, so very quickly. The war was over!

Peace! It was wonderful. I skipped, hobbled, hopped for joy round Marie-Claire's brocade-cushioned sofa, pirouetting almost with the cushions clutched to my chest, then throwing them into the air in my delight. On the television news, fighters with bunches of flowers in the muzzles of their guns whooped and shouted, embracing men of their own side, of the opposite side, what did it matter? They were all friends now, compatriots, fellow workers from the same factories and offices once again. It was finished. It was over!

The doorbell rang and it was Najib, beaming, his thumb holding down the cork of a champagne bottle. I ran for glasses and he released the cork so that champagne spewed into each glass – spewed everywhere! We hugged and kissed each other, with the bottle and our brimming glasses clutched between us, and sipped, and hugged again. I was so happy! Najib bubbled on about his plans for a party (Najib! bubbling!) and Marie-Claire, dear Marie-Claire arrived too with bagfuls of food, enough for a feast. 'You don't mind? If I cook for you? A special celebration dinn*eur*?'

Friends rang up, one or two called in even. The flat was alive with people. Connie Maddox came stomping in and was pressed to stay for dinner, then Karen came, and Henry too. Henry shook my hand, a big up and down shake, then embraced me and kept on shaking my hand, looking awkwardly boyishly pleased. I sat in the middle of it all – it was the most wonderful dinner, the most wonderful evening – I sat, hardly knowing what I was doing, watching the bubbles rising in my champagne glass, drunk with joy and relief.

In the middle of February President Franjieh announced a programme of reforms; and also a revised and reaffirmed National Pact. That delightful old Lebanese institution, the National Pact! I wished I could have a copy of it to hang on the wall. (Was it ever in writing? I couldn't remember.) It would be appropriate above my bed perhaps, that good old Independence Day statement of the principles of nationhood: that Lebanon's constitution should be founded on a union, a marriage as it were, between our Arab and Western affinities; that every aspect of civil life should recognize and celebrate this life-giving duality.

The best of both worlds! It was a delightfully, quintessentially Lebanese solution: once again our affinity with Syria and the Palestinians – our sense of belonging to the Arab world – was to be cemented and confirmed and yet it was promised that the independent Christian spirit, the freedoms, the internationalism of Lebanon would remain unthreatened still.

It was crazy, wonderful. Everybody's rights and privileges were being guaranteed with warm handshakes and with loud and generous goodwill. I wanted to laugh and laugh for joy.

The National Pact! It was in 1943 that people used to go round talking about unity and National Pacts all the time: the year when George and I were engaged to be married.

Yes, it would look good on my wall.

Part III

TAKING SIDES

And then, at last, I had news of Elena.

The phone rang, in the flat. I was not expecting anybody in particular.

'Mama! *Marhaba*!' For a moment I could not . . . The Arabic . . . 'It's me, Lenni.'

'Elena, *ayni*! Oh, my love!' I had not heard her voice for well over a year. 'Where are you? Are you in London?'

'No, but I'm on my way. Poor mother, I'm dreadfully sorry! About your stroke, I mean. I've been away at the camps for three months and I only just got your letters and messages when I arrived back in Mogadishu on Monday. If I'd only known!' She sounded so upset for me, so sweet. Her lovely loving self. 'Anyway, I'll be with you the day after tomorrow.'

'And are you well? Where are you now?'

'I'm fine. I'm in Beirut. At Yusef's. I've just stopped off for a day or two on the way.'

'In Beirut!'

'Well don't sound so horrified!' She laughed. 'It's peacetime now, don't forget.'

'But –'

'Don't worry! It's *perfectly* safe.'

'You're sure?'

She laughed again. 'Latifa's coming back, with the children,' she said and there was a sort of catch in her breath after she said it, the nasal equivalent of a raised eyebrow. 'They'll be here after the weekend.'

'And . . . But were you coming to England anyway? Or just to see me?'

'Oh, I don't mind. There's plenty I could do there.'

'Are you sure? But wouldn't it be much more logical . . . I was planning a holiday with Rashid in any case, somewhere convenient for us both . . . Wouldn't you rather I came to the Middle East, to you?'

'I thought Yusef said you'd been banished from Lebanon.'

'Well, I didn't necessarily mean Lebanon. But if, as you say, the trouble really is all over – well yes, why not? There isn't any good reason why I shouln't come, just for a short time at least. Just to see you. Then after that Rashid and I could have our holiday together. Somewhere warm – Egypt perhaps. It would make so much more sense.'

'Well, it suits me. If you're sure you'd rather.'

'Yes. Yes, certainly. Why not?'

'O.K. I'll hang on here then. Let me know what you've fixed.'

It was rash of me. Of course it was rash. But I felt so well. Since the peace was declared I wanted to dance, dance, dance. My body felt altogether different. Much lighter, more lissom. It was a huge release from tension.

'Of course you should go,' said Connie Maddox that evening, standing flat-footed in the middle of the carpet with her arms folded. She was snorting with delighted jealousy. I couldn't imagine that she had ever let ill-health prevent her from going on one of her jaunts, one of her camel-trains across the Middle East.

'You don't think, though, that I should give it just a little longer, this convalescence?' I asked her.

'Do you?' She was practically defying me to stay.

And really, looking round the flat after she left, giving me her short dry kiss of affection and blessing – looking round the flat I could see how mad I had been to think that I could make some sort of home here for Elena. She could be very forthright sometimes and I could imagine her arriving here, standing looking round her with her hands on the hips of her jeans and her rucksack slung on the floor at her feet. I could see Marie-Claire's furnishings through her eyes: the candelabras, the fussy chintz and china excrucia. 'But mother, *albi*! How can you *stand* it?' And I could imagine her itching to slink off to the cheerful student pad in Fulham, where she usually stayed, with its communal sitting room strewn with gramophone records and young people and discarded coffee mugs.

Yes, I should enjoy being with her ten times more in Beirut, on our own ground. A hundred times more.

I rang Rashid, full of excitement.

'But Samia, *habeebti*, yes of course I shall be delighted to go to Egypt with you. Anywhere you like. But is it wise for you to come? Does Yusef know?'

'I suppose Elena will have told him. But I'm so well! There's absolutely no problem.'

'Do you want me to believe you?'

'Of course you have to believe me!'

'*Habeebti*, some people, myself included, will believe anything. Anything! – Samia, I only hope you're right.'

Najib looked pained when he came to collect me the next day, to drive me to the airport. While I put my last few things together, he stood looking at the ceiling, looking beyond me, looking everywhere but at me, just as he had stood when he was a boy, suffering because I was wild and would *not* be good. Poor Najib, he carried my baggage down to his car for me, then came back and gave me his arm, solicitously, checking with me that I hadn't forgotten anything, handing me out of the door and into the lift. It was something he had absolutely insisted on: that he should take the morning off work to see me to the airport and on to my plane. Bless him, I was very grateful, I couldn't have had better care taken of me.

He told me in the lift, 'I may be going to Lebanon too in a few days, on business. There's a lot to sort out, financially speaking.'

'You're going yourself!' Well then, it wasn't such a crime!

'I'll see you there then, perhaps. How nice!'

His solemn face brightened when he saw my smiles. 'Marie-Claire's thinking of coming with me, and Henry too perhaps. We thought . . . How would you like it if we were to hold that party there? That celebration party?'

'Yes, do! Yes!' I was full of happiness, of glad love for him at the generosity of his forgiveness. 'Yes, it would be so much more fun than having it here!'

As the lift started its last abrupt descent to the ground floor it seemed to me, from the look of pleasure on Najib's face, that not only his belly leapt with the motion, but also his staid soul.

I had just passed the customs desk at Beirut airport. I was not looking out for anyone, not expecting to be met. I hadn't let Yusef or Elena know exactly when I would be coming. Even now I didn't quite trust . . . I didn't want them to cross Beirut unnecessarily.

She was there, waiting for me at the barrier; standing with her hips on a slant and her thumbs hooked over the pockets of her jeans. When she caught my eye she smiled. Then as soon as I was through the barrier she ran to me and hugged and hugged me. I looked at her – I cried I think – I looked at her, taking in everything I had remembered and forgotten about her: her tanned face, lightly shadowed as always by strands of long sun-gilded hair; her taut arms locked around me in a girlish, almost painful embrace; the little noise of excited pleasure in her throat. My lovely, lovely daughter.

'Lenni! *Deeri balek*! – take care of your poor old mother or you'll squeeze the life out of me!'

Her arms slackened a little, she looked down into my face again, there was a shyness – 'Are you all right? Let me . . .'

And it was a cruel thing, which made us both wince: the way I had become just a little frail since we were last together, while she . . . She had blossomed, grown in confidence. There was something, in the way she held me: she had that warm strength which I had used to complain was still missing from her in her extended bumptious adolescence – that warm solid strength of a woman in the swing of life. So that what struck us both, I think, was how the feel of that old familiar hug had changed: I was in her arms now, rather than she in mine. And I felt once again that intense mixture of pleasure and pain (which I have so often felt with Elena) at this tangible proof that, since we had last met, I had moved on – we had both moved on – a generation. We would not now have the chance, which I had mistakenly looked forward to as I had watched her grow up, of tackling the world from the same perspective.

Then I was aware of a person so insistently facing us that I looked up and Rashid laughed at the look of astonishment on my face. Then there were more kisses and huge drowning embraces, he kissed me on each cheek, half a dozen – a dozen times over and . . .

'But you were in Damascus!'

'Yes, I *was*!' he said.

. . . and they were both laughing, each of them had an arm around me and they were chortling and laughing like a pair of lunatics.

'But how did you know which plane I would be on?'

'*Baseet*! Easy! There were two planes direct from London today,' Rashid said. 'You weren't on the first of them, but you were on this one.'

'You've been waiting for me since early morning!'

They looked at each other and laughed again, and they were all joy and warmth and mischievous complicity, prancing round me until I couldn't tell my brains from my nose.

Then Elena went on ahead to show the porter where to take my luggage and I was left to walk with Rashid. Of which I was glad. I could not have borne just yet, with my slight limp, to walk beside Elena. Rashid tucked my arm in his and he was so dear to me just then that . . . I . . .

I loved his face as he turned to look at me. He was so happy!

We lunched – I wasn't hungry, I had eaten in the plane, but they were both starving Elena told me and we ate a late snack lunch in one of the airport bars. Elena sat opposite us and in between hungry forkfuls of quiche and salad she chattered to us about Somalia. 'I've written you reams of letters,' she told me, 'though I don't suppose you've had a single one of them.

Absolute reams!' Rashid sat with his arm over the back of my chair, prompting her from time to time, reminding her of things she had told him earlier during their long morning's wait for me to arrive. At least they had been enjoying each other's company.

She was explaining about the famine in the Ogaden. 'It's the dry season now, the *Jilal*. The trouble is we didn't have a proper wet season again this year. The rains have largely failed for two or three years now and we've got 80,000 nomads in the Somali relief camps already, with more pouring across from the Ethiopian side of the border all the time. You come across them at the roadside, little groups of them, children, old people, women with their babies wrapped closely to them inside their brightly coloured shawls – hardly any men, they're all off at the front or somewhere. You usually end up with a whole load of skinny kids clinging to the sides of the truck once you get near to a camp – cadging a lift. You can imagine what they look like when they arrive, with the dust the tyres throw up in this drought! Then at the camp the refugees make their own little round *tukuls* – their huts, you know – built of sticks, in a couple of hours flat, and covered with a sort of brown tent-cloth. And there they stay. We just feed them on a subsistence ration of boiled wheat grain.' She shrugged and looked pensive. 'The trouble is with them being pastoralists, even if this coming year's rains are good, that still won't bring their animals back to life. You keep coming across them – bunches of bones by the roadside – dead camels, sheep, goats. Humans. Even the desert scrub is dying in places. It looks brown and skeletal everywhere. It hems you in like a cage of twigs on either side of the road, mile after endless mile of it.'

She seemed to spend a lot of time travelling across the Ogaden, between the camps.

'You just about see the whole of colonial history written on the landscape,' she told us. 'The old Italian milestones are still there with Mussolini's *fasces* on them – you know? – the bundle of rods with an axe in the middle. And further up near the front, so I'm told, you see abandoned army vehicles – American, Russian, Cuban, you name it – a sort of museum trail from all the different foreign armies that have been traipsing back and forth across the desert for God knows how long, with their own pacts and alliances and side-switchings that leave the local people absolutely clueless as to what it's all about anyway.'

'But you haven't been near the front?' I asked.

'No! – No thanks!' She laughed. 'You're likely to get shot at by both sides – just as a precaution! – if you stray within a couple of hundred miles of where it's all supposed to be happening.' She pushed her empty plate away and pulled her feet up, tucking them neatly on to the chair in front of her and holding them there crossed over, with her jeans tightly stretched. 'Then on the road back to Mogadishu it's the various foreign relief lorries that you see overturned where they've been trying to edge past one another with one wheel each on the soft verges either side. Alan and I counted four on the way back to Mog last week. There's nothing you can do if that happens, there aren't any recovery vehicles to be had to pull them out again.'

'Alan?' Rashid gave her a perceptive curious look.

She wrinkled her nose at him. 'Didn't I tell you about Alan?'

'No, you didn't. Not a word.'

'Oh, he's the one with the knack for making spare parts out of safety pins and things when we break down in the middle of nowhere. I mostly team up with him when I'm travelling round.'

'Purely for the sake of the safety pins.'

She grinned at him.

'Very wise,' he said. *'Ma'akool.* Very wise.' They broke again into gales of their crazy chortling.

Rashid went to fetch coffee for us all and we chatted some more. She told us about her job and the way she'd organised it so that the individual families in the camps could do their own budgeting of the food supply as far as possible. 'The women really appreciate it – it means they can do the traditionally polite thing and offer us back some of the grain cakes and things they've baked on their own fires.' She sounded full of her work, thoroughly absorbed in it. And I remember thinking that really I had no need to worry about her, that she would do well, with her caring and commitment, wherever she chose to work in the future.

'But have I dragged you away?' I asked her. 'Did you come away specially to see me?'

She gave me a big, very Elena-ish smile, full of cheerfulness. 'It's all right. It was quite convenient really. I'd only have been hanging around in Mogadishu anyway for the next two or three weeks, waiting for all the proper clearances from the secret police to take the next consignment of supplies up to the camps. Which is a big bore, if ever there was one. All we can do is sit around in deck-chairs at the British beach club, day after day, wishing there was somewhere else to go and having a good old moan with other aid workers in the same boat. The only consolation is the half-price beer! Heineken lager, practically on tap.' She tossed her hair back behind her shoulders. 'Anyway, Alan and I had both got some leave due and we were thinking of going to London in any case, to see some people about a certain scheme we've got in mind.'

'London!' And now I felt guilty. She had wanted to go there after all and here we were – 'But you didn't tell me on the phone that you wanted to go to London!'

'It's all right. It doesn't matter. There's time enough.'

'But where's Alan, now?'

'In London. He flew straight on there from Cairo.' She looked at my face. 'It's all right!'

I asked her about this scheme which she said she and Alan had in mind.

'The thing is –' She looked perplexed for a moment, uncertain how to begin to explain. She let one of her feet fall to the floor and sat curled slightly sideways, twiddling a fork on the table in front of her; glancing at Rashid, as if she hoped he might be able to help. 'The thing is, nobody's really given enough thought to what all these tens of thousands of nomads are going to want to do after they've spent the next couple of years sitting in the relief camps waiting for absolutely nothing to happen. The war – the mines and things – aren't going to disappear from their traditional stamping grounds in the short term, and half their men will be dead by then.' She paused, frowning, with her chin in her hands and her shoulders shrugged up to her ears. 'We've been

talking to some of the women and what we thought was –'
Again she hesitated.

'Go on.'

But she looked restless. 'Oh . . . I can't really go into it all now. It's . . . Anyway, oughtn't we to be getting back? Yusef's expecting me at the hospital at six.'

'Ah, yes. The hospital!' Rashid said. 'Have you heard –? She tells me she's been appointed head nurse already.'

'Oh, at least! – Yusef signed me on as general dogsbody practically the moment I arrived, they're so short-staffed now everyone's taking their leave at last. He'll have you roped in next,' she told me and I knew she was trying to be kind, to pretend my stroke had never happened. She stood up and reached for both my hands, pulling me to my feet too. '*Yallah*! Let's go.'

'Yes, I must get back and see about getting the flat in order,' I said.

'Yusef's expecting you. Your bed's made up.'

'No – no, I'd only be in the way there. Didn't you say Latifa will be back soon?'

'She's back. She arrived last night.' This time, at the mention of Latifa, she really did raise her eyebrows a fraction.

'Well then, we certainly shouldn't stay there. They need a chance to be on their own, those two. Without added complications.'

Elena and Rashid looked at one another.

'You're expected for supper,' Elena said.

'Yes, of course I'll go for supper, but –'

'Samia, *habeebti*!' Rashid put a hand on my shoulder. I could feel his fingers very gently caressing the side of my neck. '*Habeebti*, things aren't so simple. You can't just cross back and forth at all hours, when you feel like it.'

'Cross?'

'The Green Line.'

'But . . . I thought all that was finished with!'

'If you want to be with your children, *habeebti*, you'll have to *be* with them.'

They were both earnestly watching my face.

'Well then, all right. For a day or two anyway. After

that . . . And you, Rashid, what are you doing?'

'I'll be here for several days at least.' He smiled. 'I shan't be hard to find!'

We drove into Beirut, a small cavalcade, Elena and I in front in Yusef's car and Rashid behind. And there really was no problem, nothing to worry about. The barricades and the succession of military checkpoints on the road from the airport had all been taken down. The only evidence of them was a clutter of sandbags and wreckage here and there at the side of the road. We were passed three or four times by military trucks full of steel-helmeted soldiers ('P.L.A. regulars,' Elena said knowledgeably), and once by a patrol on motorbikes. But we saw nothing very remarkable. No gun emplacements, no sign of recent fighting. One thin wreath of smoke curled above the skyline way over in the eastern suburbs.

The warm moist February wind blew off the sea bringing with it the particular smells of Lebanon, of Mediterranean vegetation, of eucalyptus and pine, of dust and salty sand after the recent rain. There was a faint smell of engine oil as we drove into the outskirts of the city, of washing, of industrial chemicals, of rotting fruit and once – just once – a whiff of cordite. Women, dressed mostly in black, were going stolidly about their business wrapped in on themselves in black shawls or austerely-tied black headscarves. Two lads in tight jeans and open-necked white shirts were standing on a corner lazily inspecting the innards of a rifle. Jammering voices called out instructions to each other in Arabic across a building site which we passed. There was an atmosphere – a sense of currents and cross-currents – in the sound and pace of the traffic even, all of which was distinctly Lebanese. It brought back to me all the emotions, the intimate tense tangled emotions of home. I looked round and Rashid, in his car behind us, smiled and raised a hand to me. He was keeping determinedly close behind us all the way.

When we came near to the Avenue Abdallah Yafi, he hooted and flashed his headlights at us. We drew into the side of the road and he pulled up behind us.

'Our ways diverge,' he said, when he had walked round to my window. He bent down towards me. 'Elena's promised to bring you to lunch with me on Thursday. Will you come?'

'Of course.'

'Lunch is best, then we'll have plenty of time together, and you can still cross back with the traffic before evening.'

Again I was taken aback by the reference to crossing. But Elena explained, 'You're safe enough from snipers if you cross during the daytime when the road's chock-a-block.'

It was a revelation to me. This peace of Lebanon's was relative. Well, I should have known. But I had wanted to believe Elena when she told me over the phone that it was perfectly safe. Wanted so much the excuse to come.

'Oh, there aren't *many* snipers,' she said, seeing my face.

There was a commotion behind. We were blocking the traffic. With a light touch on my shoulder, Rashid was gone, to rescue his car. Elena threaded out into the streams of traffic heading for the Corniche.

We crossed. And again there really was no problem. We were waved through the first checkpoint – the P.L.A. checkpoint – with the rest of the traffic and it was a mere formality to show our identity cards to the Phalangist guard at the barrier on the other side. But in between, in the no man's land of shattered streets by the National Museum, the destruction was appalling. Every building was charred and holed. Walls were buckled and balconies hung perilously down. There were lopped and torn trees, lamp-posts leaning at wild angles and everywhere a huge debris of sandbags and ironmongery, of smashed vehicles, broken glass and concrete gun-bays, hastily botched together and desultorily, half-heartedly taken down. That Beirut was divided like this still, when hostilities were supposed to have been brought to an end, was a shock to me. It offended against my emotions of the past few days, against my sense of health and wholeness. As we filed with the queue of traffic slowly across, past gutted buildings where, according to Elena, snipers were known to lurk, I had a feeling in my head as of a twist of muscle fibres tightening. And it was only now that I noticed that this feeling, there in my head all last summer and autumn, had in the meantime gone away.

'*Cartes d'identité!*' snapped the *gendarme*, thrusting his hand demandingly in at the car window on Elena's side. It was the third time, in just the few hundred yards since we had made the crossing, that we had been stopped at a checkpoint. No, not a checkpoint this time. That's the wrong word. Nothing so military. This was just a local *gendarme*, patrolling the neighbourhood, keeping things in order. If he wasn't as polite as his colleague whom we had met two streets away, it was probably because he knew Yusef's car and was suspicious of what we were doing in it.

'*Cartes d'identité!*' He was getting impatient.

Elena turned slowly to me and asked me very loudly and deliberately, in Arabic, to pass over my card. He didn't like it, I could tell, the deliberate Arabic only increased his suspicions.

'*Où est-ce que vous allez?*'

'*Nomroo 47 – foke.*' She pointed ahead, indicating the precise house.

He looked at Elena with intense dislike and made a show of inspecting our cards minutely and mistrustfully. If it weren't for our surname, Gilbert – Yusef's surname – clearly in evidence, I think he would have given her a very hard time.

It was something I had noticed already, since we crossed, the way in which French had become definitely the official language over on this side. Arabic signs had been taken down from shops and hoardings and everywhere there were new notices in French, prominently displayed: notices about various curfews, about food shortages, instructions to residents about the new organisation of rubbish collections – almost pedantically precise notices, mostly issued by the Phalangist party, about every aspect of public order and control. And I was struck already by the way in which this 'East Beirut', this entity newly created by the Green Line, was taking on a character of its own. One could see it in the clothes people were wearing, in the neatly tailored lapels and skirt hems, in the women's trim high heels clicking along the pavements: the almost regulation *délicatesse* and good breeding.

This 'Christian Lebanon' had become a beleaguered provincial outpost, strictured, middle class, European. *Comme il faut*. Separated off like this from the busy living hubbub of the rest of Beirut it lacked . . . What was it? A certain capacity for emotional expression . . .

We were greeted in French at Yusef's house even, first by the young nanny, Mathilde, who laid her cool manicured hand limply in mine and bid us shyly and formally welcome, '*Bonjour Madame Gilbert, Mademoiselle Élèna, soyez les bienvenues.*' Then by the children, who bounced and tumbled down the stairs to throw themselves upon me, and tumbled excitedly up them again calling out, '*Maman! Maman! Regarde qui c'est!*'

Latifa appeared on the stairs and we could hear her admonishing them in French, '*Taisez-vous, les enfants! Il ne faut pas –*' before she caught herself and, with a furtive glance down at Elena, switched to Arabic – '*Majid, haddi balak!*'

Il faut, il ne faut pas . . . Poor Latifa, it was something I always noticed about her after she had been amongst her mother's circle for any length of time: this adherence to form, this anxious need to behave, to be seen to behave, just so.

'Do come and sit down. Yusef's at the hospital I'm afraid.' She led us through to the drawing room with as much awkward formality as if I had never been in the house before. 'Oh, it's wonderful to see you!' She tossed back her head and laughed gaily, but all the time that she was chattering to us and flitting back and forth to the kitchen to make sure that tea was on its way – all the time I kept noticing how her head was inclined to sink forward and downwards again and a stray black curl would hang damply over her pale cheeks. She glanced at us with an unhappy furtiveness, between her stiff bright smiles – at Elena especially. And she was alert all the time too for the moment when one of the children would need to be brought under control. They were clambering on me and running in and out to the garden and she was watching as Mouna cartwheeled back towards us across the terrace, one, two, three cartwheels, in at the doorway . . .

'Mouna, take care!' Latifa's voice wavered anxiously and, to my surprise, her face was full of fear.

Elena came round behind my chair and put her arms round my neck, with her cheek against mine. 'I'm off,' she said. 'To the hospital.'

Latifa said, 'But you haven't had tea!'

'It's all right thanks,' she said cheerfully. 'I promised Yusef I'd be there by six.' She slung her desert-worn canvas bag over her shoulder and off she went – still wearing her jeans. It seemed not to have occurred to her to change out of them first. The children followed her out into the hall and we could hear them clamouring to be taken with her.

Latifa, left standing in the middle of the floor, looked as if she were about to cry.

'Latifa, what –?'

'Just a moment . . .' She walked hurriedly out on to the terrace. I heard her calling, 'Mathilde! Mathilde, *viens t'occuper des enfants*!' When she came back she was gay and brittle again, full of chatter. The children came bounding back and the old housekeeper brought in tea for us all, with shiny glazed slices of *tarte aux pommes* from the *pâtisserie* for the children to bounce and exclaim over. I didn't get the opportunity again to ask what the matter was. It was one of the great pities of those brief ten or twelve days Elena and I spent in East Beirut that I didn't get the chance to talk to Latifa, to really talk, as we had done that once or twice on the phone.

Yusef hadn't appeared when I went to bed that night and he had already left again when I woke up in the morning. I found a note pinned to my pillow with a large safety pin: 'Kisses, kisses, kisses, little mother. Love and kisses!' There was a lingering smell in the room, it seemed to me, of sandalwood. I must have been very soundly asleep when he came.

I found Latifa in the nursery, sitting with little Majid on her lap, trying to persuade him into his clothes.

'Yusef asked you to go over there this morning, to the hospital,' she told me. 'With Elena. Just at the moment he's having to cover for one of the other doctors who's on leave, so he can't get away.' She looked at me, as if appealing to me. Then, turning back to Majid, 'Come on, darling, you must wear your sweat-shirt if you want to go out to play!' But there was too much pleading in her voice to convince him. He kept taking his arm out of the armhole again and again, grizzling and complaining. She struggled with him, her black curls falling forward. 'We always seem to have to go to the hospital if we want to see Yusef,' she said, so bitingly that Majid began to cry.

'Will you come with us?' I asked her.

'Oh, I . . .' Her voice tailed away reluctantly.

I beckoned to Majid to show me the picture on the front of his sweat-shirt. He stopped crying, and Latifa easily slipped his arm in. He ran across to me.

'Please do come. We'd like you to.'

'Oh, well . . . All right.' But I could tell she would rather have said no.

After breakfast she handed the children over to Mathilde. They were dressed ready for a walk in the public gardens, at Sioufi. We left, the three of us, for the hospital.

On the way up in the lift to the children's ward Elena warned me: 'You'll probably find Yusef wanted to see you so he can give you a plane ticket straight out of the country. He was absolutely furious with me for letting you come back to Beirut.' She hitched the strap of her bag higher on to her shoulder with a half-guilty, half-mocking shrug.

Certainly it was the first thing he said to me when he strode across to us, his chin thrust forward and his eyes fiercely intent: 'Little mother you shoudn't be here.' In the midst of all the kisses and greetings he kept repeating it. 'You shouldn't be here.'

He was casting his eyes around, looking for something . . . 'Little mother, I almost forgot –' He snatched up the flowers out of a vase on a neighbouring bed trolley, '– your flowers, little mother!' He was mad, wild, crazy, presenting them to me with solemn fiery joy. The little girl in the bed laughed as he thrust them at me, a big bunch of yellow jonquils and ferns. Water dripped down on to my shoes.

'Yusef, I –'

'And Latifa! And Elena!' Not to leave them out, he snatched another bunch for each of them from the trolley, vase and all and pushed them into their hands. All the children in the side-ward broke into giggles, six pale little momentarily-brightened faces. Crazy, he was quite crazy. The small owner of the flowers was delighted all over again, as if we were offering her a special gift, when Elena and I arranged her flowers back again for her in their place.

'Seriously, little mother, you shouldn't have come,' he said, with a fierce, brother's glance at Elena, as he strode out with us into the corridor. 'Beirut's no place to be.'

'But the fighting's over,' I said.

'Over? Over?' His brush of black hair shivered glossily under the corridor lights. 'Who told you it's over? You call this over?' He indicated three beds which were standing against the wall of the corridor while the porters were conferring with the ward sister. The children lying in them were bruised and variously bandaged: heads, arms, a strung-up leg. I had assumed, I suppose, seeing the children, that they had been involved in some commonplace accident, a car accident perhaps.

'We haven't heard of any new outbreak of fighting,' I said.

'Fighting? No of course you haven't. Everybody knows it's peace time! These children here – there wasn't any fighting where they happened to be playing. Of course not! It was just an unexploded hand-grenade they found. Anyone must realise that! But even if it was – even if it was just an accident . . . There'll be retaliation. This trickle of weapon-injured children every day – it can't just stop there, arbitrarily, as if it wasn't happening . . .'

But he was called away just then, by the ward sister, who had some queries about the newly arrived children.

'Elena – in there. If you'd just . . .' He went off, in mid-sentence, but Elena knew what he wanted her to do. We followed her, Latifa and I, into a side-ward where a very small child, unattended by anyone, was crying with fright. He was rubbing his bandaged palm across his mouth.

'He's trying to suck his thumb,' Elena said. 'He needs turning.'

I wondered if it wouldn't be possible to free his thumb from the bandage, but then I saw how thin the bandaged hand was. There was no bulge where the thumb should be. Elena turned him, freeing his good hand. She held the child's wrist gently while he began to quieten down, his only thumb in his mouth.

A light flashed urgently, out in the corridor, and a young nurse at a nearby bed said, 'Would you mind, *Sit Latifa*, making sure this girl doesn't turn on her back?' She hurried off leaving Latifa to manage her patient, a big heavy girl who was only half-conscious and was thrashing her limbs wildly. There was a murky stain on the pillow by her mouth. Latifa went and stood awkwardly by her, but when, almost immediately, the girl rolled on to her back, Latifa laid just a half-hearted hand on her to encourage her to turn over again. The nurse came back in a rush and thrust her into her former position. I helped Latifa then and we managed more or less to keep the child on her side – it wasn't easy, she had huge strength in those big limbs – but Latifa seemed, poor girl, to lose confidence, rather than gain it, in the process. Her shoulders drooped and her hand trailed limply on to the girl's upper arm.

Yusef was back and he got Elena to help him with one of the new children whose broken leg he wanted arranging just so, with supports and pulleys. I asked her where she had acquired her nursing skills. She wasn't the most likely-looking nurse, with her T-shirt and faded jeans.

'Oh, I'm always having to help out with the nursing in the camps.' She gave me her girl-guide grin. 'You can't help but learn when you've got an office full of overspill from the medical hut!'

The young nurse relieved us of our job with the girl and Yusef, suddenly celebrating the fact that here we all were, Latifa, myself, Elena, all with him together for the first time in – what? two years? – Yusef flung an arm round each of us and hugged us to him in turn, with his jaw thrust upwards and his face alight with pleasure. I laughed, Elena laughed and poked his ribs. She had been forgiven it seemed for bringing me. Latifa, with a sulky look at Elena, received her hug passively and tossed her head away with a little imitation laugh. Yusef touched her face gently, encouragingly. Her eyes flicked towards him, then away again, her lashes as sharp as pins.

Elena took hold of my arm and nudged me in the direction of the corridor. 'Come on. Come and meet Yacoub.' As we walked down to the next bay of beds she said, 'He's a smashing kid, he's always hobbling off round the ward with his funny lop-sided walk and sitting on the other kids' beds, telling them stories and jokes. He's terrific. Yusef's always coming to see him when he's got a moment.'

I recognised him at once, from her description, a small bony child with a chest that seemed to be caved right in, sitting, as she had said, cross-legged on another child's bed. He bounced up and down when he saw Elena, as if he were sitting on a spring.

'Listen to this one,' he called over to her. 'Listen to this one.' Then to the other child: 'Knock-knock!'

The child, who was very pale and had a drip connected to his arm, answered in a tiny voice, '*Meen*?'

'Karim.'

'Karim *meen*?'

Switching to very sweetly enunciated English, Yacoub said, 'Karim me back to my bed or I'll come in yours.' Then with a look of huge delight at Elena he rolled over – right over, deliberately – so that she had to catch him quickly to stop him tipping completely off the bed. She hoisted him high in her arms and carried him back to his own bed, a laughing, wriggling, mis-shapen ball of merriment.

Yusef came and showed me with huge loving pride the places where he had operated to remove shrapnel from Yacoub's chest and arms. 'And look, little mother, look,' – he showed me all the dressings round Yacoub's midriff – 'this is where a lot of skin and muscle was torn away and I've had to do graft after graft of skin, here and here . . .' He was so pleased and proud, showing me. And it really was wonderful – considering that he had never done anything like this before – the sheer determination to succeed.

Yacoub was enjoying the attention, thoroughly enjoying it, somersaulting on his bed. Yusef, with a deft flick, popped him under the bedclothes, head and all. The covers lifted into a mountain and Yusef patted its top. 'Now stay there,' he said, 'and watch out for those dressings!' I could understand why he wanted to do so much for this one child amidst the terrible raw-flesh-and-scalpel inhumanity of his casualty duty. Without Yacoub he would go completely spare.

Latifa was standing some distance away, by another

child's bed, watching us. When she saw that I had noticed her, she looked away quickly. She picked up a little toy bear which was lying on the floor at her feet and stared down at it, picking at its fur with her blush-red nails.

Yusef went over to her. He spoke to her – I didn't hear what he said. He put his arm around her shoulders and tried to draw her to him, but she shook her head. He persuaded her out into the corridor and, while Elena and I straightened the covers of a child who was lying half out of bed, we could see them, there, through the glass partition, Yusef cajoling and Latifa bursting out with short resentful sentences and casting bitter looks back in the direction of our side-ward. Elena, on the opposite side of the bed from me, raised her eyebrows and rolled her eyes in an eloquent arc.

But I could understand her resentment, poor Latifa. She had only just come home, just two nights ago. She must have come back with such hopes, such good intentions. And here he was, apparently just as thrilled with everybody else as he was with her. With me, for example. With Elena, and Yacoub: just as thrilled.

Yusef was standing holding her head between his hands, running his fingers through her curls. He took hold of her hands and, tiger-like, he looked as if he wanted to lick them, to nuzzle the thorns from her wounds. He was all love and tender concern. Then, with his arm around her, he led her off down the corridor. I didn't see where they went.

Later, when it was time for us to leave, Yusef beckoned Elena to him. 'Lenni, would you do something for me?'

'Yes, what?'

'We're thinking of sending Yacoub home and –'

'Home?' She couldn't believe it. 'Home?'

'Yes.'

'But yesterday you said –'

'The ward sister's anxious for us to send home as many children as we possibly can. We need to clear the ward. Especially if the fighting gets any worse, we're going to be in danger of having to turn children away again for want of beds.'

'But you told the sister yesterday he couldn't possibly go! I heard you. You said it wouldn't be safe to send him home yet.

Not to a tin shack. Not until his skin grafts are completely healed. You said he'd probably get some revolting infection and very likely die or something!'

Yusef looked unhappy. 'I'm not saying we'll definitely send him. It'll depend how well he can be looked after. But if you could just find out for me what sort of conditions his family are living in . . . We're not exactly sure where they are now, since January.'

'January?'

'Al-Maslakh. They used to live in al-Maslakh.'

'Oh.'

'One of the nurses thought they mentioned having gone to relations in Tal al-Zaatar. If you could just find them for me, Lenni. Wouldn't you? It might be a couple of weeks before they manage to visit again. Please?'

Elena stood with her weight on one foot and her thumbs tucked into the waistband of her jeans. I saw her give Latifa a very penetrating look. Latifa dropped her eyes to the ground.

'If it's just a matter of *finding* them,' Elena said.

'I still just can't believe it,' she said. We were in the car, just Elena and I, driving down towards the port. Towards al-Maslakh. Latifa had looked dismayed when I asked her if she wanted to come with us. She had given one of her little laughs and shaken her head in distaste.

The closer we came to the port, the more damage we saw. Here and there whole vistas opened up where buildings used to be.

'I just had no idea when I came that it would be like this,' Elena said. 'I mean, in the Ogaden there was a war on and yet I never saw it, not the slightest trace of it. You might just happen to hear the guns once or twice, miles and miles in the distance, but you could never be sure. All you heard was what other people told you about it, some of the nomads, maybe, who'd found themselves overtaken by one of the armies at some stage. But here in Beirut – well, there isn't even a war on, supposedly. It's supposed to be finished. And just look, look at them.'

Some men in combat jackets were unloading munitions

from a lorry: bundles of rifles, boxes of this and that – of ammunition, I suppose. There were cryptic-looking ciphers marked on the boxes: 5.6mm, 7.62mm, 0.50in. cal. We edged slowly past and I could see where somebody had scrawled with a finger in the dust on the side of the lorry: Avenge Damour. One of the men, standing just ahead of us, was testing a rifle. I had seen it coming: I had seen him load it and examine it as we approached, then point it at the sky. But our car jolted suddenly forwards as he fired, then came to a bumpy stop as Elena's foot slipped on the brake. The man looked in at us and laughed.

'Christ!' Elena said. 'No wonder everybody in Beirut's so jumpy.'

We turned down Chafaqa, past the electricity station where soldiers from the Army were re-arranging mountains of sandbags. From there we turned on to the Avenue Charles Helou and drove along behind the docks, past the cratered burned-out acres of warehouses and cranes. Various military trucks and armoured cars passed us, coming from the direction of the coast road. A group of militiamen, standing at the side of the road, cheered and fired a salute into the air as a contingent of their comrades drove by. Everywhere this afternoon there were guns, it seemed. Guns and more guns. A lorry came towards us with its headlights full on and an escort of motorbikes, four of them, weaving alongside with noisy importance. On the back was a massive recoilless rifle, openly, flagrantly on its way towards the Green Line. There was no attempt, even, to cover it or disguise it.

'Things like those,' Elena said, pointing. 'Fire one of them in the desert and a bit of sand flies up. Bits off some unfortunate tank maybe. That's about all. But surely nobody in their right mind would allow one of those to be let loose here! In the centre of a jam-packed city! It's incredible. And there seem to be scores of them, absolutely cramming the place out.'

'Yes.'

It was the first time today that she had mentioned the Ogaden, even obliquely. I had asked about it once at lunch time, but she had been busy thinking about Yacoub and had shrugged the subject off. I tried again now.

'The refugees in your camps – in Somalia,' I asked, 'how many of them do come from the area of the fighting?'

'Oh . . . quite a few.' She was looking for the right place to turn. 'I think if we go down here . . .'

We turned left. Then right, down past the building where one of our literacy classes used to be held. One more turning, and what should have been a street was . . . Wasn't. The road was blocked off, after a few yards, by mounds of earth and rubble. Here, where the dense jumble of the slum used to begin, where the shacks used to hem the street in closely on either side so that it was almost impossible to progress any further in the car through the crush of children and dogs, of washing hanging on lines, of rubbish bins, of men and women filling the road on bicycles or on foot, or sitting busily occupied on mats outside their homes – here was nothing. Just the bare mounds around us. And silence. We looked at one another. Elena drew the car into the side and switched off the engine. Silence.

We both got out. A light wind, smelling faintly fetid, blew dust and small scraps of paper off the mounds, around our feet. Elena scrambled, in just a couple of bounds, up on to one of the mounds and gave me her hand, to help me up beside her.

And . . . I was nowhere that I knew. Or rather, like a photomontage, it was the unknown and the familiar, impossibly superimposed. I was at the edge of a beach, or a dried mud-flat perhaps, I don't know what one would call it: a huge bare tract of land, stretching away to the grey shadowed hulks of what – yes, of what had to be the slaughterhouses, there dominating the skyline, and away to the sea beyond.

Al-Maslakh. It had clearly been bulldozed, the whole densely crowded expanse of it. There were the tracks of the bulldozers still imprinted in the soil. Here and there, where planks of charred wood and strips of rusted corrugated metal had refused to be buried, the bare earth had been scooped up against them in small heaps. Gulls swooped in from the sea, crying and foraging. One perched, not far from us, on a saucepan handle which projected from the ground and another bird, much smaller, a sparrow I think, hopped about a few yards from our feet. It pecked at a tuft of hair and, eyeing us warily, pulled it loose from the ground and carried it off in its beak.

Elena went across to where the sparrow had been and I saw her squat down and look closely at the ground. She looked up at me and I went across to see what she had found. There was some hair there still, quite a tuft of it, black and matted with dirt and it was attached to something, to a shred of rotting flesh on which a cluster of small flies were crawling. And I could see the curved yellow-white surface of bone beneath it, where the earth had been washed away by rain.

All at once I could see what our mound consisted of, our roadside mound, on which we were standing. There were fragments of cloth protruding too; of clothing. And several more pieces of bone, many more of them, their smashed splintered ends poking through the thin covering of earth and beginning to be whitened by the weather. That strange, sweet, fetid smell of the place: I could understand now what it was.

Elena straightened up next to me and we stood for a long time together, silently, beneath the cawing, circling gulls. The cawing was like my own anger. My powerless anger: as useless and thin in this vast place as the gulls' cries.

I felt suddenly old, as I had done when I was weak and decrepit after my stroke. The sight of this desecration, this hacking down of human life, filled me with physical helplessness, so that I suffered a shaky loss of footing on the bumpy ground. Elena had to take my arm and hold me firmly to her. Once again I felt, as I had felt when she met me at the airport, that shifting of the generations.

'If only I were properly well again,' I said. 'Well enough to work, to help the poor people who have survived this! If only I were your age!'

'Relax.' She squeezed my arm kindly. 'You can't always be responsible for everything. There are other people to do it, you know.'

'But who? Who?' I felt the old desperation, the churning urgency of my pre-stroke days.

She didn't answer. She stood staring ahead of her at the mounds, the bones, the corrugated iron. Looking at her, I was reminded of the way my own mother had looked at me that evening when she was combing out my hair for me in my bedroom, when I was roughly Elena's age: her face glowing in the lamplight, animated with her secret hope and pride. Looking at Elena now, at the determination in her face as she stared at the wasteland, I loved her with my mother's fervent special love. I loved her because she was what I might have been, a generation on.

We walked back to the car. Elena held on to me tightly on the way down the mound, taking care for me where I put my feet.

It was stuffy in the car, making my head feel thick and stale. As we drove away I wound down my window to try to disperse the lingering fetor, the rank slaughter-house sweetness, blowing in on the wind.

That night my nightmare came back. Errr-*oom*, errr-*oom* there was a bulldozer grinding along against the inside surface of my skull, the toothed edge of its scoop scraping and rasping across the bare bone. Elena was there in the dream, picking things up off the newly scraped earth and holding them up with exultant anger for me to see. But I couldn't see. She was caught up somehow behind the bulldozer, in the errr-*oom*, errr-*oom* of its tracks, and I was running, running helplessly on the rough ground, trying to keep up. I can't remember any more than that, but I know there was a tremendous sense of fear in the dream, of elation mixed with fear, whether hers or mine I don't know. I could no longer tell our emotions apart.

I had a throbbing headache and in the morning before he left, Yusef came in to me, in my bedroom, and insisted on a proper check of my blood pressure. He seemed quite happy with what he found, but he gave me something for my head and positively ordered me to spend the rest of the morning in bed.

'In luxury, little mother. With a good book, and cups of jasmine tea brought to you every hour. And all my love.' He bent over me as he said it, close to my ear, and I could feel his light soft kisses in my hair. My dear Yusef.

Towards the end of the afternoon, Elena returned from the

Palestinian refugee camp at Tal al-Zaatar, from her search for Yacoub's family. We were in the garden when she arrived back. It had been a warm spring day, warm enough for us all to be in short sleeves and bare sandalled feet and the air was wonderfully clear and fragrant with daffodils and hyacinths and with Yusef's abundance of sweet-smelling freesias, growing in their clumps below the terrace. Spring in the Middle East: which is something I have always loved – the intense blue of the sky, the riot of colour and of luxuriant green growth, the bright abiding soul-warming sunshine.

Mathilde was playing with the children at the bottom of the garden, down by the swings. Latifa was sitting where she had been all afternoon, on the swinging canopied seat in front of the trellis and, miraculously, Yusef was with us, he had managed to take the rest of the day off, and he was sitting beside Latifa, with his arms twined around her, as lovey-dovey as she could wish.

'What news?' he called, as Elena came trotting across the grass to us.

'I've found them!' She flopped down in the deck-chair next to my seat, throwing her canvas bag on the ground. 'I've got this method I devised for tracking people down in the Somali camps. It works a treat. What you do is you go round all the places like clinics and water points and food queues and so on and you spread the message that you're looking for a particular family. Or you pass the message down each row of huts or whatever. Then sure enough, when you go back round again later on, word has come back along the line telling you where the family is.' She lay back in the deck-chair, stretching her arms behind her head, looking thoroughly pleased with herself. 'It took a while, but anyway, I found them in the end.'

'*Azeem*!' Yusef said. 'Well done, my little Lenni.'

Latifa looked jubilant. 'So Yacoub can be sent home, then!' She smiled up at Yusef and snuggled closer to him, putting her arms round his chest.

Elena sat upright in a hurry. 'No he can *not*!'

'Pardon?' We all looked at her, startled by her vehemence.

'No chance. I went along to see them – his family. It's terrible where they are. They've only got a tiny tent, lent to them by UNWRA. It's not even what you'd call a tent, just a glorified bit of canvas pinned up against his aunt and uncle's leaky corrugated shack there. And the filth everywhere! They're squatting by the road, in the muck, with the nearest water tap a couple of hundred metres away. Yusef, it's just not on, he can't possibly go home until his skin grafts have completely taken! There's a little boy in the tent cheek by jowl up against theirs who's got the most revoltingly gungey impetigo all over him!'

'Well he'll have to go home all the same,' Latifa said sulkily. 'Everybody at the hospital says so.'

'Who? Who says?'

'The nurses. The sister. You've heard them talking.'

'Well, it's up to Yusef, isn't it?'

I was looking at Yusef. He was looking at me. My poor Yusef.

Latifa persisted, 'It's not right – they all say so – him taking up a bed all this time. Four months! Coming up to five! Back in January other children – Christian children – in a worse condition than him had to be turned away!'

'Oh, so that's it,' Elena said, full of scorn. 'Just because he's a Moslem!'

'Well? If they will harbour gunmen who maim and murder innocent people! If they will shell us night after night, what do they expect? I suppose they think they deserve five star treatment from us when their own children get injured for once!' Latifa's curls were snaking savagely.

'Oh yes? And what about your precious gunmen who are being harboured round here in droves? I suppose they're all sunshine and light.'

Yusef said, 'Elena, please!' He stroked Latifa's arm.

Elena turned on him as well, she was so angry. 'What do you understand? If you'd come with me today and seen the absolute grinding bloody misery . . .'

Latifa tucked her toes up on the garden seat and curled up close to Yusef again. 'They deserve everything they've got,' she said, with an aggrieved pout. 'And more. After what they've done they deserve to be ground into their own dirt and misery. They're as good as murderers, all of them. It serves them right!'

'Latifa Selim!' Elena said, using her maiden name, 'You bitch! You bloody bitch!'

Latifa yelped.

'Elena!' Yusef held Latifa to him, caressingly; as if she were a hurt and vulnerable child. 'Elena, you'll please be respectful in my house.' Poor Yusef, he looked so bewildered, finding himself inveigled all at once into Latifa's jealous tug of love.

I put a restraining hand on Elena's arm. I could see she was bursting to say more. She glanced at me and hesitated.

'It's true isn't it, Yusef-*rohi*,' said Latifa, smiling up at him, 'it's true they can't just expect to have an automatic right to a bed in our hospital? Not when there aren't even enough beds for our own people?'

I don't know what Yusef thought, whether he thought he could defuse the argument by telling us in a rather involved way how, if things got much worse, they might have to start choosing again who to treat and who to turn away. 'It all depends . . . We have to weigh up one person's chances of surviving outside the hospital against another's . . .'

'And Yacoub will have to go,' said Elena sarcastically.

Yusef looked wounded. He hadn't at all seen, I think, where his own argument was leading him. Latifa's hand was curled in his. She had nestled, like a small child, into the crook of his arm. He said, 'I suppose, yes, he'll have to go before the next round of fighting starts. Obviously we'll have to clear the wards of everybody whose life isn't strictly at risk.' There was a pause, then he said, 'Obviously.'

Elena, with more hope I think than cynicism, said, 'Well, you can always bring him home here, until the danger of infection is over.'

I saw a look steal over Yusef's face. Latifa saw it too and in a flash she sat up, taut with anxiety. 'As if Mathilde hasn't got enough to do! No, he can't come here. I *won't* have him.' Her curls shook with revulsion. 'Yusef? He can't. He can't! People would lynch us if they knew we were harbouring a Moslem. They'd kidnap Mouna and Majid!' She was trembling, practically hysterical.

'Rubbish,' said Elena. 'What absolute utter rubbish!'

'If you think that's rubbish, Elena Gilbert, then you haven't the first clue what's been going on here. Not a clue!

You haven't any idea what it's like . . . !' Her voice was rising in tight strained sobs. She got up and started to run indoors, but Yusef caught up with her. He held her and she was trying to fight him off, pushing him away . . .

He held her. In spite of her struggles he held her to him, and he was wild. Wild with Elena. Shouting at her with rage. 'How dare you, Lenni! What do you know? What do you know about what she's been through in this war?'

Latifa sobbed against him and I could see her face – she had it turned sideways, towards me, against his chest – and it was full of that fear again which I had seen on my first afternoon here, when she had been so worried for the children's safety while they were playing. It was the fear I had heard hiccuping through her bright social voice on the phone to London, when she was alone in the house with the children and Mathilde in the thick of the fighting; when the night-time bombardment here in al-Ashrafiyah was as bad as it ever was at my flat in al-Qantari. One doesn't lose such a fear, just like that, in the first deceptive peace of springtime.

She was clutched against him, gasping and at the same time trying to pummel him too with her tightly clutched fists. Yusef, fiercely loyal, was murmuring into her hair, 'Latifa *ayni*, my little soft furry love!' Then he turned to yell at Elena again, 'Go! Go away! I don't care where you go. Just go. Go!'

The children came running up the garden to see what was happening. Mouna clung to her mother and Majid clung to Yusef, then to me, wailing at the top of his voice. They both stared with wonder and dismay at Elena, who was muttering and shouting back at Yusef that she didn't care where she went either, but not to be such a bloody fool!

It was bedlam. She didn't make any move to go, she just lay back in her deck-chair abusing him, and Latifa too, with all the gusto of their childhood battles and letting his rage pour down on her head like desert rain. Which made him, as usual, more and more mad . . .

'You've got fifteen minutes,' he said, 'to pack up and leave this house. If you're not gone in fifteen minutes –'

Then he took Latifa limping and stumbling indoors and Mathilde hustled the children away for their bath. Elena muttered on to me about what an idiot he was, but I didn't say anything. I had seen too many such arguments before. I got up and went for a walk down the garden, wondering what the result of all this would be, in the end, for Yacoub.

When Yusef came out again after a short while, we were both at the bottom of the garden. I was sitting on the wooden seat amongst the clumps of white irises where the path ends. Elena was perched on one of the pair of swings, scuffing her foot to and fro along the ground. Yusef stalked down the garden. He passed me with a nodding toss of his head and then, after a few moments, sat down irritably on the remaining swing. His chin was thrust high and his eyes were still fierce and fiery. He sat there, saying nothing, using his foot to make the swing move in angry jolting circles. Gradually – if Latifa was watching them out of a window, she would be jealous, as always, of their closeness, of their easy reconciliations – gradually their swings began to move together; in rhythm. Back and forth, back and forth. They weren't conscious of it, I'm sure; just naturally falling into the same mood. Yusef's head had rolled morosely down on to his shoulder.

'We can always send some ointment for the child in the next tent, to get rid of the impetigo,' he said.

Elena looked dejectedly down at the ground. 'Oh, that – I already got him some,' she said.

Nothing more. Nothing more was said.

My poor Yusef. I hoped Latifa would deserve such loyalty.

Thursday. We were due at Rashid's for lunch and I was glad of the excuse to take Elena out of Latifa's way for the day; to keep her away from the hospital – from Yusef – rather than risk her sticking pins into Latifa's inadequacies again so soon.

'I'm sure Rashid doesn't really want me as well,' Elena said, with a smile. 'He'd much rather you went on your own!'

But I managed to persuade her to come. She had plenty of friends over there whom she had been wanting to call on. We could arrange to go early and drop in on one or two of them on the way.

I was struck once again by the contrast which the Green Line had somehow managed to create, as we left the staunch and righteous East behind and crossed to find ourselves amongst the multifarious humanity of West Beirut. This was much more the Beirut I loved, with its bustling pavements; its service-taxi drivers careering with twice the panache, it seemed, of their fellows in the east; the flamboyant bargaining beside pavement displays from overflowing shops. The streets were so alive; full of all the emotions of living.

But oh, I was impatient with this splitting of the city, so that to go just a few minutes journey across the town like this was a day's adventure! This idea of East Beirut, West Beirut – it was totally arbitrary, it bore no relation to how things used to be.

The Moslem side. But how could they call it that, in the foreign newspapers, on television? It was absurd. How could they lump together all this – the Jewish quarter, the American University, the big hotels and embassies, the internationally famous shopping streets – how could they lump together so much and call it the 'Moslem side'?

And yet – yes, in a way there was something more Moslem about it than before. Very many of the more affluent residents must have left, because those that remained were darker-skinned, poorer, more plainly dressed. And many people were in black, in mourning for somebody lost in the fighting, so that there was a sombreness in the clothes people were wearing which was reminiscent of a more Islamic country. And a sadness, amidst the ravages of war. All the emotions of living were here, and of ten thousand deaths.

While East Beirut, in spite of its shell-pitted façades, had an aura of neatness and affluence still, of anxious military orderliness, West Beirut on the other hand had somehow contrived to become tatty, ramshackle, totally chaotic. The squalor of the streets was striking. There seemed to have been very little organised effort here, even after a month or more of peace, to clear away the debris and wreckage, to set up any sort of civic administration. The rubbish piles were huge and the gutters ran with unsavoury-looking fluids. Many shops remained pessimistically boarded up and rubble from countless explosions lay uncleared at the sides of the road.

We passed what used to be a favourite mosque of mine, a pretty building whose arches, set at various angles, seemed to open the building out towards the street. I used to go past it often at the time of morning prayer, when the pavement would be covered with heaps of shoes and with men bowing their heads to the ground. Now it was the mosque itself which was spilled across the pavement and into the road so that we had to pull right out around it. Fragments of mosaic decorated the tumbled heap.

'Good stuff for making roads,' Elena said with a grimace, thinking no doubt of Somalia.

In al-Zarif, at the entrance to the street where her friend Khalida lived, we came upon an impromptu market. Expensive-looking tables and chests of drawers were stacked at the kerb-side, piled high with Persian carpets, statuettes, light fittings, brass and china ornaments, jewellery.

'But where on earth –?' I was astonished at the mountains of goods.

'All looted stuff,' Elena said knowledgeably.

'From the shops do you think?'

'Shops, abandoned flats . . .' She stopped abruptly. She was suddenly very busy concentrating on edging the car past the busy stalls.

I watched a woman gleefully running her hand over the most lovely red Bokhara carpet and I couldn't help looking at it carefully as the stall-holder rolled it up for her, wondering whether perhaps I might recognise . . .

'Here we are,' Elena said.

We had stopped a few yards from the narrow doorway to Khalida's building. The road just in front of us was cracking up from the pressure of a burst water-main. Water was spurting from fissures in the tarmac and swilling around the tyres of the passing traffic. An armoured car was parked across the pavement and two soldiers were standing prodding the humped tarmac with their boots. As we got out of the car and stepped across the torrent, we heard them arguing desultorily about what could be done. Elena shepherded me through the water-logged entrance and up the narrow stone stairs.

Khalida, dressed in some sort of baggy army trousers and a

green army jacket, opened the door to us. There were shouts and excited voices and two other girls came running, as soon as they heard who it was. I knew them, there was no need for introductions: fair-haired Mariam, wearing jeans and a shapely cotton shirt, who was Elena's soul-mate from college days, and Wajida, with her olive skin and her black bush of hair, the one who used to have harrowing boyfriend problems. They all fell on Elena, with much excited chatter, all vying to be the first one to kiss her.

There was a clatter, and a pile of Kalashnikovs, in the corner of the hallway, crashed to the floor. Khalida picked them up and stacked them again, leaning them one upon the other against the wall. With her foot she nudged a fallen ammunition belt in among them.

'We're just back from a training morning,' she said and grinned. 'Veterans' target practice.'

Her big bottom rolled inside the army trousers as she showed us into her bed-sitting room. There were cushions to sit on, strewn around a threadbare Afghan carpet. The walls had posters pinned to lengths of peasant-patterned cloth which hung in place of wallpaper.

'My parents are out,' she said to me, apologising. 'If you don't mind joining us in here . . . ?' She offered me the bed to sit on.

They all sprawled around on the cushions and I might not have been there, they were so absorbed in catching up on each other's news. I don't mean they weren't polite. They seemed very happy to have me there, not at all put out by my presence as they reminisced together about the old foursome they used to be in college days. Elena sat cross-legged on her cushion and I could see from her face that she found it delicious, quite delicious to be back.

Is it the rhythms of speech, I wonder, which make friendships so irresistible? The tones of voice, the innuendoes, the way that friends have of following on one after the other in their own particular pattern? I could hear how Elena seemed a little out of it at first, not quite catching the in-jokes, not quite pitching her remarks as they did. Not, even yet, quite reimbued with the rhythm and flow of the Arabic language after so long away. Then gradually, gradually she became enmeshed in the joy of being among friends. Her way of thinking began perceptibly to turn again round the old phrases and assumptions. Around the new phrases and assumptions which the girls had adopted in her absence.

'We've all joined up, quite a while ago now,' Khalida said when Elena asked about the rifles inside the front door. 'Quite a lot of us have, from our year.' It was strange to think of them with guns in their hands. Using them. Impossible to imagine them engaged in real fighting. They were just girls who used to come to our flat with their shoulder bags untidily stuffed with lecture notes and who sat around for hours talking indiscriminately about Arab Nationalism and what was on at the cinema, drinking instant coffee late at night and expecting to have careers and families. Mariam must be a qualified lawyer by now.

'Do you remember Rima?' Mariam asked, laying her long straight hair carefully back behind her shoulders. Rima was the girl, I remembered, who had carried off all the distinctions in their year. 'She was killed in December, by a shell. On the day the St Georges Hotel fell.'

And again it was inconceivable. The patterns of life had clearly altered while Elena had been away. She had quite some catching up to do. I saw her frown. Her finger was tracing a thin brown line along the markings on the carpet.

Khalida brought in platefuls of little biscuits and cakes and put them down on a large round tray in the middle of the floor. Her big breasts bobbed, as they used to do, swaying inside her army jacket in time to her walk. Her sandals slapped against her heels, rhythmically, flap-flap-flap as she went out a second time to fetch a jug of her homemade lemonade. Or rather, half a jug – the mains water had given out on her – but it was brimming with ice and quartered lemons. The music in the background was student fare, old Arabic and Moorish songs, some Beatles too, from Khalida's stack of worn tattered records in the corner; evocative, even for me, of all the people and places that were distinctly Beirut. I saw Elena's fingers on the carpet beginning to tap in time to an Arabic song which had been all the rage before she left. Mariam caught her eye and smiled.

'About half the people our age have joined up round where

I live,' said Wajida. She was smoking furiously and the smoke was wafting up through her tight black curls. 'More than half. Just about all the boys have been involved in the fighting.'

'They were landed right in it, in al-Naba'a,' Mariam explained. 'Practically surrounded.'

'What can you do?' Wajida shrugged. 'You can either sit squashed up all the time in one of the basement shelters and wait for the day when you get overrun and massacred by the Kata'ib, or you go out and help to fight them off. You fight, or you and your family get massacred. It's as simple as that.'

Of course, yes. I had forgotten Wajida lived in al-Naba'a, over there in the east, in one of those predominantly Moslem suburbs which, like al-Maslakh, had become increasingly isolated and under fire as the war went on. No wonder she smoked so much, a lot more than I remembered.

'Couldn't you –' Elena was frowning again. 'Couldn't you move out now, just in case? To somewhere safer?'

Wajida looked offended. I remembered what George had told me once, about the white feathers of his boyhood in the First World War, with which he had seen the girls taunting young men who hadn't gone to fight. In Beirut, in a place like al-Naba'a, it must be much more imperative still, with the war there, being won or lost in one's own home street.

'You'd be a jerk if you weren't prepared to fight,' Mariam said. 'You can't just go away and leave everyone else to it.' She was sitting on her cushion with one knee tucked under her arm and her knitting needles going vigorously. She had always knitted, in practically every available moment: great chunky pullovers. Now it looked like chain-mail armour that was growing, grey and as coarse as string, in her lap. 'Oh, not *you*, Lenni!' she added, seeing Elena rolling her lip between her teeth. 'I didn't mean you. You're needed where you are, in Africa. That's different.' She smiled at Elena again across her knitting, the affectionate friendly smile of their soul-mate days.

'You change your outlook,' Khalida said, rolling back the cuffs of her army jacket; and added, a touch heroically, 'You just don't think, any more, of preserving yourself for your three score and ten, like some precious commodity. That's not what it's all about.'

Mariam's knitting needles continued their steady clicket-clicket and Wajida puffed rhythmically on cigarette after cigarette, lighting each one from the stub of the one before. They all kept offering round the platefuls of little biscuits to nibble and talked on about what Elena was trying to achieve in the Ogaden and how it was basically the same here: it didn't matter whether you were a Moslem, or a Christian like Mariam, you were fighting for the people in the slums and refugee camps, trying bit by bit to get them a better deal. The new National Pact didn't change anything. Not a thing. There had been nothing but endless political shilly-shallying this last month and so long as Franjieh was President, there'd be no question of real reforms.

'The new Pact's just a repeat of the old one,' Khalida said, 'full of the same old illusions. It might have seemed the right thing a generation ago, but it certainly doesn't now.'

There was a slight glancing at me. Khalida gave a little smiling cough of apology.

Elena said tentatively, 'I'm beginning to think that the only way to achieve anything for the refugees in the Ogaden is to help back up their liberation movement. At the rate things are going they could be there, in the camps, for ever. If you could just help them to win the war quicker, so they can go safely back to their own territory and their men . . .'

I thought for a moment that she was going to tell us more, about her scheme perhaps, about what she and Alan had in mind. But the conversation moved away, cheerfully, inconsequentially, on to other things. The girls asked us about Yusef and, with big smiles, sent him their love. They had alway been fond of him, of Elena's fiery-eyed older brother who loved the girls. Wajida blew him some kisses into the air with her puffs of smoke. 'Tell him we need him in al-Naba'a,' she said with such doe-eyed longing that they all laughed merrily.

Khalida flap-flapped out to see if there was any water for more lemonade and Elena sat, hugging her knees and rocking to the old rhythms coming quietly from the record-player in the corner.

'What's it like in Africa?' Mariam asked her, pulling on her ball of wool. 'I mean – are you thoroughly enjoying it?'

'Yes, it's fine. It's O.K. I've got people I'm good friends with, there.' I noticed the emphasis she put on the word 'there', and I wondered again about Alan. It was as if she couldn't quite imagine being with him outside the context of Africa.

There was some attempt to talk of things that did not have to do directly with the war, of jobs and who was now living where. But – well yes, inevitably, the fighting entered into everything, into every consideration of who was doing what, and why. It was not the sort of war – as I knew so well – in which one could pretend that life carried on, regardless.

'It's a farce,' Wajida said and stopped to cough up the presumably smoky contents of her lungs. 'It's a farce, the idea that people have gone back to their jobs as usual since the peace. What jobs? I got a job as a librarian last year, but when I went to look for it last month, the library had gone.'

Mariam, who I remembered had wanted to be a civil rights lawyer, said there had been no legal system to speak of – no courts, nothing – for months past. 'I gave up trying to pretend there was, the day I went to visit a family who had been served with an eviction notice, down in Chiyah. When I got there I found them barricading themselves in as best they could against a couple of armed thugs who were playing a sort of cat-and-mouse game with them – firing through the windows but not coming in too close. They were waving their K'lashn's about and shooting at the feet of anybody in the street who came near, so I ended up borrowing a rifle from a woman living just a bit further down – I'd never used one before and neither had she – but anyway – at least I've got a steady hand!' Yes, that was exactly what she had. Mariam, the imperturbable knitter. I could imagine her calmly and serenely taking on any emergency without fuss. 'I hid in her doorway, then I fired over their heads to chase them off.'

'Did they go?' Elena asked.

'Fled! They couldn't tell where the shooting was coming from or anything. They just took to their heels and ran.' She laughed. 'It was the first useful thing I'd done in months!'

'What happened to the family?'

'They were O.K. The baby's carry-cot was riddled with

bullet holes, but the baby wasn't in it. I gave them a lift, with all their wordly goods, to relations in Ain al-Rummaneh.'

Elena sat with her chin resting on her knee. Again the smile passed between them and I thought, as I had often done in the past, how alike those two were, Elena and Mariam, with their casual good looks and their long light-coloured hair. They used to do everything together in college days.

Elena told them about Yacoub's family, squatting with relations in Tal al-Zaatar.

'I didn't know any people from al-Maslakh had gone there,' Mariam said. She spread her knitting out along the needle. 'I'm on the military committee here for the new refugees. I might pop over to Tal al-Zaatar one day and see whether they've got any of the people who are listed here as missing.'

'Perhaps you could come with us if we take Yacoub home,' Elena said.

'Yes! Let me know.'

They began to talk about the vulnerability of Tal al-Zaatar, militarily speaking, cut off there on the east. Like Wajida's nearby Naba'a. I looked at my watch. Just a few minutes more and we could begin to move on to Rashid's.

It was Khalida who suggested Elena should stay for lunch with them. 'It would be great. We'd have all afternoon then,' she said enthusiastically.

Elena looked as if she would jump at the chance, but she turned to me with a querying tilt of her head.

'Well, but –' I was apprehensive about leaving her – I couldn't quite say why, '– we'd have to ask Rashid, at least. He may have made special plans.'

When I got through to him on Khalida's phone, Rashid said, 'Tell her not to move a muscle. I'll come over and fetch you.'

'But –'

'But nothing, *habeebti*. It's no trouble. See you soon.'

The girls took to Rashid at once when he arrived with his ample supply of hugs and kisses for me, and for Elena too of course. Elena wrinkled her nose at him in mischievous fun.

'Samia, this daughter of yours does my heart good!'

The girls were all crowded in the hall once more, high spirited and laughing. They had after all, I thought, been perhaps just a little constrained by my presence. They would enjoy having the afternoon to themselves.

I have a last picture of them in my mind now, as they were when Rashid and I reached the stairs and I turned back to wave to them in the doorway. Mariam's string-thick grey knitting was hanging heavily from her needles, draping itself over the stack of Kalashnikovs, where they leaned against the wall. The metal of their barrels protruded gleaming through the large regular holes. And Elena was standing there, behind the grey mesh, behind the rifles, apparently knitted with them into the scene.

I should have been afraid – the image was so striking – if it weren't that the general happiness and good humour made fear seem inappropriate. I waved, they waved and, arm in arm, Rashid and I once again braved the floods down on the street below.

'Yes, please,' I said. 'I should love a cup of one of your delicious fragrant teas, but then I must go!' – though I would gladly have sat there with Rashid all afternoon, in the sunny archway where his house opened on to the paved courtyard.

'You must go. I see.' He looked at me with his worst rapturous teasing face, full of jollity and disdain. 'You've eaten my lunch, talked to me most politely and now you must go. Very good. Go where?'

'Back to pick up Elena.'

'Who is very happy being left exactly where she is. And what do you propose to do with her?'

'Well, before we cross back, I'd like to go home – to my flat. To see what can be done.'

'*Habeebti*!' I had stood up, I was restless now. He patted my chair until I sat down again. '*Habeebti*, just think. Here we are back in October – do you remember? That day we met up by chance in the office? When I tried to persuade you to come home to my house with me? – Here we are, once again, back with the same troubles plaguing Beirut, the same anxiety for Elena.' He was looking at me, wickedly. 'Let's see now, what point did we get to exactly? You'd just gone downstairs to send your telex message to Elena, summoning – isn't that right? – yes, summoning her to Beirut –'

'Rashid – !' I tried to protest, but he waved away my objections with a big exuberant wave, the sort of wave one might use for flagging down a bus.

'– summoning her here to Beirut. Then you stood in the entrance hall for just a few moments, staring out at the street; waiting. Then . . . Well anyway, here you are finally, in the safety of my house and do you think, *habeebti*, that having got you here at last, I'm going to let you rush straight out again, headlong, back to your flat?'

This time I shook both fists at him. He grabbed them both and his face was very close to mine. The sides of his fingers were lightly brushing my cheek. He was looking at me, looking . . .

'*Habeebti*,' he said slowly, 'when Mariam was telling you about her committee for the new refugees from the east, did she tell you where they were all living?'

'No, I don't think she did, but I've heard they've taken over all the beach huts.'

'There are a lot of refugees and not many beach huts. But never mind that now,' he said jumping up. 'Tea.'

He went to ask the old servant to bring tea, his dear devoted servant who, with her husband, had looked after the house for him right through the winter months of war, while he was away. She came through one of the doors on the opposite side of the courtyard, shuffling towards us on her plump varicosed legs, carrying a tray laid out with Fadwa's eggshell teapot, with tiny white napkins and slices of paper-fine lemon. There was a little vase of early orange blossom in the middle to heighten the scent of the tea. Rashid went to take the tray from her and she bobbed and smiled and shuffled away again the way she had come. He put it down on the low table in front of me.

'There,' he said. 'Now what was it we were talking about, in your office, before we were so rudely interrupted by that slight incident in the street – with the children, and you, and . . . those young men?'

'What were we talking about? Well, I was thinking that my bottle garden could do with a drop of your *araq*, and . . .' Not to be outdone by his outrageous humour I said, 'We were talking about proposals of marriage.'

'Proposals of marriage? Yes, I do believe we were!' He drew his chair up close to mine and there was something hugely delightful in the way he looked at me, his eyes brimming with merriment – with delicious fondness. He sat forwards on his chair, with one hand poised over the teapot and the other hovering – poised . . .

'Which is it to be first?' he asked. 'The proposals or the tea?'

I'm glad now that it wasn't the tea.

But I had to see my flat.

'Shall I tell you what's happened to it, or do you want to go and see for yourself?' Rashid asked me, very kindly and gently, when I raised the subject once again.

'Have you been there? Have you seen it?'

'Yes.'

'No, don't tell me. If you're sure you don't mind taking me . . . ?'

There was news on the car radio as we drove down there of the assassination of Brigadier-General Chehab, by men from Zgharta. Well, there was nothing special about it, in the few days I had been back in Beirut there seemed to have been nothing but news of kidnappings, murders, isolated outbreaks of fighting. But someone on the radio was warning of reprisals against Christians and suggesting that anyone who didn't need to be out should stay at home.

'Elena and I ought to cross back as early as we can,' I said to Rashid. Perhaps people were heeding the warnings because the streets, I thought, were a little emptier than they had been in the morning.

'Yes,' Rashid said. 'It might be as well if you do.' He reached across and patted my knee a little sorrowfully.

There was washing hanging from all the beautiful balconies and terraces of al-Qantari, where flowers and vines used to grow in abundance: worn and tattered strings of washing. There was rubbish and debris, shell-holes and crumbling roof-lines. We came to my own block and passed the entrance where I had been cowering with my dizzy aching head when Mustafa arrived so opportunely on squealing tyres. Rashid turned into the side-road into which my own flat faced. He stopped the car . . .

The rectangular pattern of windows and terraces, windows and balconies, of staggered interlocking groups of flats, was so frequently interrupted by damaged and missing portions that it was hard to recognise my own bit . . . There! Those were my sitting-room windows, but the glass was broken right down their whole height and there were now torn and haphazardly draped sheets where my woven jute blinds and bead hangings used to be. There was the big old fig on the terrace, but it was almost broken off, the trunk was sheared almost through, and it was hanging down the side of the building, covered in dust and fragments of rubble. And George's study, beyond that . . .

There was no study, nothing. Just a gap, where the projecting corner of the building had fallen away, taking with it the ceiling of the flat below. A woman with a baby, wrapped in a dirty shawl, was leaning on the balustrade – just next to where I always put my chair when I sat out – staring into the distance.

'I took the liberty of going up, a couple of days ago,' Rashid said. 'They were quite friendly – the squatters, I mean.' He nodded towards the woman on the terrace. 'They told me there was nothing in the flat when they arrived, *habeebti*, not a thing, the door was broken down and it was completely empty. They let me come in and I found this, though, look. Does it mean anything to you?' He unfolded a scuffed-looking piece of paper and handed it to me. It was Majid's little crayon drawing of Yusef.

'Where did you find it?'

'Tucked into the skirting. That was all there was. Nothing else.'

I looked at the drawing but, I don't know why, it didn't mean much to me any more. Perhaps because it was George I had lost with my flat, not my grandchildren. George: his books, his papers and drawings. Every memento I had of him.

'Do you want to go up?' Rashid asked doubtfully.

I shook my head. Then after we had sat for a few moments, I said, 'It's time we crossed back. Let's go for Elena.'

All the time Rashid's hand was on my arm, lightly holding my wrist. I was very, very glad that he was there.

Yusef's car was gone from where Elena had parked it and at first we thought nobody was in. But then we heard slow hesitant footsteps on the other side of the door. There was the scraping of bolts and locks, then the door opened a little and Khalida's father appeared in the chained gap.

'You want who? El-en-a?' He looked at us suspiciously and called to his wife.

The door opened just fractionally more. 'No,' she said, peering at us, keeping almost out of sight behind her husband, 'we're not expecting them back for an hour yet.' I noticed that the stack of Kalashnikovs was no longer there.

We weren't invited to wait. The chain was still firmly in place. I had only ever met them briefly, once or twice, and if I had aged as much as they had since then, it wasn't surprising they didn't recognise me.

It wasn't the sort of day to invite trouble by waiting around in the streets. The looters' market had packed up and gone. Water was still pouring from the cracks in the road, but nobody seemed to be bothering with it any more. There were no cafés nearby where we could sit. The only thing to do was to go back to Rashid's.

It was two hours before Elena rang. She was breathless.

'Sorry, we've only just got back. I heard you came. Mariam and Khalida were called out by their militia – emergency orders – and Wajida and I went along as well. Goodness knows what it was all about. It was all very secret. Everybody hung about for ages with rumours flying like mad, then finally they told everyone to go home again but to stand by in case.'

'But Elena! This late!'

'I'm sorry. They kept saying everyone would probably be able to go in a few minutes and I'd promised them a lift.'

'Should we risk crossing this late, do you think? I don't know . . .'

'We'll see anyway. I'll be with you soon. I'm just about to leave.'

Five minutes later she rang again: 'Turn on the television, quick! Channel 7.'

I gesticulated to Rashid, who turned the switches for me, on the other side of the room.

'Elena, what –'
'Listen!'

Someone called al-Ahdab, in the uniform of a high-ranking Army officer, was announcing the military take-over of Beirut and demanding the resignation of President Franjieh. From the bemused look on Rashid's face I gathered that he had heard of him before.

'It's a military coup,' Elena said into the ear against which I still held the telephone receiver. 'I can't come for the moment – he's just announced an immediate curfew.'

For the next hour – nothing happened. There was no sound from the streets, no fighting, no military activity of any sort. It was so quiet in fact that al-Ahdab (to much amused head-shaking from Rashid) declared the curfew lifted again. But should Elena risk coming to us? Certainly it wouldn't be wise to attempt the crossing this late. I rang Latifa to tell her not to expect us. Then I rang Elena again.

'I'll come over to you if you want me to,' she said. 'What do you think?'

It was already dark.

'Well, perhaps –'

We agreed – I didn't like it, but I agreed it would be best if she stayed put for the night. I could hear one of Khalida's records beating out its rhythm in the background.

I didn't like it.

'See you in the morning then,' she said.

'Yes.'

'It's all right, don't worry! I'll be there.'

Rashid came and cupped his hands reassuringly round mine. 'She'll be here,' he said.

She was; to my immense relief. She arrived at Rashid's house in the morning looking as if she had begun life anew, as if she could run twice round the world and do cartwheels over the sun. She flung her arms around me, full of the joys of this lovely spring day.

Wajida was with her.

'You don't mind, do you, if we give Wajida a lift back to al-Naba'a? – her militia's just cancelled her leave.'

'No, certainly.'

'She can drive the car as far as the crossing, so that if there's any trouble she can show her Moslem identity card. When we get to the other side we'll swap over.'

Rashid made one of his theatrical gestures with his hands as if we were all a little mad.

'*Ma'a salameh*. Take care, *habeebti*.' He held me back as the girls were going to the car and kissed me full on the lips. 'See you soon.'

'Very soon.'

He smiled. He knew, now, that I loved him.

We drove – Beirut seemed perfectly calm – we drove with a full car-load of Wajida's belongings: sleeping roll, combat jacket, ammunition belt, rucksack. She looked precisely (and alarmingly) as if she had been away on a military training exercise. Her Kalashnikov – I was horrified when I turned round and saw it there – was lying fully in evidence on the ledge behind the back seat. 'Elena! Please!' – I insisted it should be moved.

The girls talked constantly about yesterday's events, as I gathered they had been doing half the night too, speculating with the benefit of their slight inside knowledge of military developments. There was a rumour that Franjieh was going to refuse to resign. Factions were being declared within the Army – pro-Ahdab and pro-Franjieh.

'I bet Franjieh's spending today rounding up support,' Wajida said, applying the dashboard lighter to her cigarette. 'He won't be coming to *us*!'

A regular Army jeep drove past us and turned down in the direction of the radio station, the seat of al-Ahdab's take-over. On the back was a jaunty placard, daubed in white paint: Franjieh Out. In the back seat an Army soldier was polishing the barrel of his rifle. One of his companions waved at us and whistled.

'*Amma wakaha*,' Elena said cheerfully. 'Cheeky so-and-so.'

At the crossing back into East Beirut, Elena and Wajida changed places and Wajida's more military-looking belongings disappeared with her K'lashn' down out of sight behind the front seat.

Passing us in the opposite direction was a stream of refugees in their heavily-laden cars, Moslems presumably, fleeing the sectarian violence which was once again becoming commonplace on the eastern side. One family was standing, with despairing faces, round a steaming car which had boiled up under the weight and the heat of the journey.

But I was a refugee too, I realised all at once. My home was gone!

'What's the matter, Mama? You don't look too well.' Elena was looking at me from the driving seat, with concern.

'Just a headache again. It's nothing.' I lowered the shade above the windscreen, against the glare of the mid-morning sun. I thought of 1958 and how my house-hunting then had taken us in quite the opposite direction from the one in which my new homelessness was taking me now and I felt very anxious.

'I'm sorry about the flat and everything.' Elena leaned across to me and reached an arm around me for a brief moment. 'Very sorry.'

At the approaches to al-Naba'a, gangs of young men were at work frantically rebuilding the barricades after the events of the night, piling them high with sandbags, rubble and concrete blocks. Excited boys were climbing and leaping all over them. Wajida directed us along to a particular turning which was less impregnable than the others. She leaned out of the back window and as we drew up she was greeted with shouts and waves. A low barrier was immediately dismantled and we were cheered and waved gaily through.

We left her just outside the wide skirt of squatters' shacks which surrounded her cheerless granite-grey block of flats. Some children darted out from among the shacks to help her carry her bags and her K'lashn'. But she had to grab the K'lashn' quickly back from an over-enthusiastic boy who was pointing it, unwisely, at a wall and cocking it. The wall was covered in graffiti: great slogans of anti-Christian hate daubed in thick black paint. Also there were the graffiti of the war itself among the daubings: gouged areas where missiles of some sort had hit the wall; and chipped-out bullet holes too, scores of them. There was a spattering shower of brown stains at head height. Of blood? Yes, very probably.

A rat scurried behind Wajida, darting past the children's legs and into a hole.

'*Allah yewafkek*. All the best,' Elena said to her bravely, doubtfully.

A rattle of machine-gun fire exploded upon my ears, somewhere much too close for comfort. None of the children so much as flinched, they were busy chasing after the rat. I could see that this was one of the places Yusef had talked about where the war had never really been abandoned.

Wajida hoisted a bag on to her shoulder and raised a nicotine-stained hand. 'Chou. So long.'

It seemed wrong to leave her here.

We drove away. And I was frightened now. For Wajida; but also for Elena. It was madness for us to be here in Beirut. Madness! The war wasn't over. Of course it wasn't over!

'Lenni, we should leave here – today. Tomorrow at the latest. Before the fighting begins again in earnest. It's not safe –'

She grinned and wrinkled her nose at me. 'Chicken! We've only just come!' We were following a lorry out through the barriers of al-Naba'a. She wound up her window against the fumes. 'What are you worried about suddenly? Nothing's happened, nothing at all since yesterday. That's the whole crazy thing!'

'Even so –'

'What about dear old Uncle Najib's party? Had you forgotten that? It's only a few days away. He'll never forgive you if you miss that!'

'Surely he won't still be thinking of holding it.'

'Why not? Nothing's happened!'

'What about Alan, and your scheme. Isn't it time –'

'Oh, they can wait a few days. I'm not going yet!'

Well, I would speak to Najib . . .

When we got back to the house, Latifa was out. She had taken the children up the coast for a day at the beach. Towards tea time the children came running in, full of sand, sea air and sunshine, each with the first tan of summer beginning to colour their bare arms and their salt-splattered legs. Buckets and spades had to be brought in from the car, tea had to be organised. Baths, stories, bed.

I rang Najib, at the hotel in Junieh where he and Marie-Claire were staying.

'Yes, of course the party's still on!' he said. 'Isn't the weather wonderful? Really something to celebrate! Do you want to talk to Marie-Claire? She's been out getting –'

'But what about the situation? Al-Ahdab's coup?'

'Oh, that! Don't worry, it'll blow over.'

'Do you think so?' In Junieh, it seemed, there was no hint of war yet.

'Al-Ahdab himself isn't the problem, he's such an ineffectual man. Never mind that Parliament does look like backing him, Franjieh's quite determined to stand firm.' He said it with his businessman's weighty certainty.

'But don't you think, in that case –'

'Don't worry, the party will still be on, I promise you. Just a moment, I'll pass you over to Marie-Claire . . .'

Well, perhaps he was right. I didn't know.

The warm evening air coming in at the window was fragrant with jasmine. Beirut was very quiet. I really just did not know.

We were taking Yacoub home. He sat right on the edge of the back seat between Elena and Mariam, bouncing up and down as if the seat were a trampoline and he a caved-in rubber ball. He rattled on to us – to Mariam especially, who had arrived from the west to come with us – he rattled on about his aunts and his grannies, his brothers and sisters and everybody at home. I couldn't follow half of what he was saying, he was talking so excitedly. Even Elena was won over by his huge joy; her reluctance to take him home brightened into smiles and teasing tussles to keep him still.

Mariam kept nodding and asking him questions. He seemed very impressed by Mariam – by her long fair hair perhaps, by her serenity – certainly by her knitting, which had grown yards long and seemed to wind its way all over the back seat. She had to promise she would knit him a chain-mail vest next. 'To cover these bits and pieces,' he said, pointing to the dressings under his shirt.

Yusef sat beside me, in the driving seat, with a fire of

feverish excitement in his eyes. He hadn't intended to come, he had meant to leave it to Elena to take Yacoub home, but at the last minute he couldn't resist – just couldn't resist! – coming with us. All the way Yacoub's young head kept zooming around – ker-pow! – whenever there were any guns to look at anywhere. Holstered pistols, rifles, it didn't matter what, he kept an eager look-out for them and his throat rattled with sound-effects: ta-ta-ta! pee-ow! pee-ow! Yusef laughed. His hand reached back and he cuffed Yacoub round the head with indulgent affection.

At Tal al-Zaatar we called first at the nursing station near to where Yacoub's family were camped. Mariam left us to go and talk to people at the Fatah office a stone's throw away about her register of new refugees, and while Yusef took Yacoub into an inner room to consult with the doctor on duty, Elena and I stayed in the ante-room where two district nurses were clearing away after the morning's clinic. Elena immediately got into friendly conversation with them. She sat perched against the edge of a table, busily exchanging tips and knowledge with them about the various ways of tackling public health problems in their respective refugee camps, about milk feeds and inoculations, drain layouts and well-testing . . . I made a mental note to call on Elena's expertise if I ever did produce my radio survival series.

Yusef and Yacoub came back through to us, Yacoub looking as if he had just passed a test with flying colours, and we went, on foot, to find his new canvas home. Yusef and Elena were carrying between them the most enormous box, which we had brought with us in the car, full of bandages, swabs, ointments, antibiotics, everything Yacoub could conceivably need, and more. Yusef was taking no chances, no chances at all.

We were in a very shabby shanty area, some way from the permanent parts of the camp, crowded with a jumble of dilapidated huts and flapping canvas shelters. Elena obviously knew just where she was going, she seemed to have a practised ability to navigate her way through a refugee colony which was changing and transmuting before our very eyes: people were dismantling their huts, or re-erecting them, closing or creating pathways by the way they spread their belongings about them; a gang of men was digging a drainage ditch and mounding the soil where a muddy bog took up precious ground. Yacoub reached shyly up to hold my hand, to guide me along the rough path.

We passed a group of seeping squalid latrines and I knew we must be getting near, because a couple of children shouted out when they saw us, a woman looked up from her cooking and called to someone in the hut behind her, another woman shouted to a neighbour. In a moment or two we were surrounded on all sides. Yacoub's mother and father came running to embrace him, and his aunt too. His grandmother hobbled out of her shack, with tears pouring down her cheeks. Neighbours came. I don't know how many of the neighbours must have originated from the same part of al-Maslakh – everybody came crowding to see him. His mother pulled his shirt up to show off his wounds and his dressings and the children all stared, the boy with impetigo scabs among them. Yacoub giggled and hopped from foot to foot; then there was more exclaiming and hugging and crying with emotion. Yusef glowed, positively glowed, as if a candle were lit inside him; his face, his eyes, his black hair even, everything simply shone. His chin was thrust up so that his jaw-line caught the sun, he was so proud and pleased.

We were invited in, as guests of honour, to sit on mats and mattresses in the aunt's superior hut of corrugated iron and sacking. Everybody crammed in with us who could, all his family, young and old. Yacoub, looking impishly pleased, was passed from one adult to another to be held and hugged again and little cups of strong coffee were handed round, with much talking and with warm expressions of praise and thanks to Allah, in celebration of his safe healthy return.

His mother wailed and deplored the dreadful conditions to which we were having to return him. 'In al-Maslakh I kept a clean house,' she said, shaking her head and rocking Yacoub in her arms. 'We didn't have much, of course. Just one room, but it was clean. But here,' – she turned to her sister, who shook her head too – 'what can we do? The drains run across the floor when it rains, there's no way to keep out the flies. We've only got a piece of canvas to live under, next door to this.'

There was a lot of shaking of heads and telling of stories – obviously much-recounted stories – about what had been lost at the sack of al-Maslakh.

When it was time for us to go, Elena told Yacoub's mother, 'I'll try to come and see him again, before I leave Beirut – to check how things are going. Or if I can't, I'll send a friend at least.' Yacoub put his arms up to her, as far as he could with his concave chest, to clasp her – and then Yusef – round the neck.

'Thank you, Dr Yusef,' he said.

As we came away, Yusef's jaw lost its proud thrust and there were grey patches under his eyes which I had not noticed until then. 'Little mother,' he murmured, when I took his arm in sympathy. 'Little mother.'

Mariam was standing waiting for us outside the Fatah office, her white voile shirt rippling in the wind. On her face was the quiet flicker of a smile.

'How did you get on?' Elena asked her.

'Fine. I came across an old school friend, who's promised to act as a link with us over the new refugees. In fact they were all very friendly. We had a long chat – apparently they know quite a lot of people from our militia. I felt like some honoured envoy, from the neighbouring army, come to cement allied relations!'

We walked across to the car and she slid in beside her knitting on the back seat. Elena asked her if she would keep an eye on Yacoub if she came back here again.

'Yes, of course! If the crossing stays open I'll come again in a week of two. Or whenever you like. Of course!'

A little beyond the gates of Tal al-Zaatar, past a row of concrete bunkers, Yusef stopped the car at the side of the road and reached forward into the front pocket for a pair of binoculars. He looked across – I couldn't see at what particularly – towards al-Ashrafiyah, perched on the opposite slopes. Down in the valley between, I watched a contingent of the Army, a division loyal to Franjieh presumably, heading along the road towards Baabda and the Presidential Palace; a snaking line of troop-trucks and armoured vehicles.

'Look,' Yusef said. He passed me the binoculars. 'Look, there, on the skyline.' I couldn't see anything where he was pointing, with or without the binoculars, except the chequered pattern of the buildings of al-Ashrafiyah against the hill. 'The cannons,' he said. 'Look.'

I thought, yes, maybe I saw them, I wasn't sure. But I believed him anyway. Glancing back, I thought how isolated Tal al-Zaatar looked, with its fenced-in jumble of buildings, tall and small; a beleaguered encampment perched there on the fringe of East Beirut. It was the only remaining Palestinian stronghold on this side of the Green Line and I knew, as well as Yusef did, that it was no place for Yacoub to be.

Najib had excelled himself. The setting for the party was beautiful, quite beautiful. The penthouse terrace was flood-lit and fragrant. Frangipane and violet-blue-flowered clematis trailed from high trellises down across the marble balustrades. There were creamy water-lilies, miraculously in full bloom, resting cupped upon the dark water of a ferny ornamental pond. Rashid and I stood together looking over the balustrade to where, far down below, the harbour lights of Junieh glistened on the water. They lit up here and there, with the last glimmers of twilight, a cross-hatched pattern of masts and rigging, a complicated shining tracery. The air was warm, very warm, with the promise of summer. Very warm and dry and clear. Najib couldn't have chosen a better night.

Back through the wide, open archway, in the frescoed interior, we watched more guests arriving. Henry was there already, and Karen (who had joined him on this business trip), talking to Yusef and Elena. And there were many, many other people whom we each knew: from business circles, from government circles, from the compact interlocking circles of Lebanese life. Latifa, in a pale grey evening dress and long silver earrings which dangled limply from her ears, was talking with brittle animation to a group of acquaintances – people she knew from Junieh itself. There was the chink of glasses, there were party laughs and champagne-sparkling voices raised to party pitch. The room beyond the archway glittered with fractured light off mirrors and jewels and gleamed with the sheen of deeply coloured silks.

Najib was, for the moment, nowhere to be seen. 'It's not like him,' I told Rashid. 'He's always so particular about the duties of a host.' For perhaps ten or fifteen minutes, Marie-Claire had been alone at the door, beside the head butler, charmingly welcoming every new group of guests as they were announced.

'There he is!' Rashid pointed, and I saw Najib walk in briskly, full of apologies and wide-embracing benevolence. Immediately he was the centre of a circle of people, talking amiably in their midst.

The party billowed out on to the terrace to surround us, a gay silken throng. And there was something – there was a roll of distant thunder, somewhere away to the south – and at the same time a *frisson*, a preliminary ripple of excitement among the guests . . . A woman's laugh rang out, high and clear, with an edge to it, an almost hysterical edge.

Rashid and I each accepted another asparagus *canapé* from the silver salver which a waiter in green and gold-braid livery held out to us with a half bow.

'Samia! Samia, there you are!' Najib stepped out on to the terrace, raising his glass. He called me over to the middle of the throng and insisted on pronouncing a toast: 'To Lebanon!' His chest was puffed out with the pomp of the occasion. 'To Lebanon! And also to my dear sister Samia, in whose honour this party was planned. To the health of both! *Sihtek!*'

Everybody raised their glassed to me – '*Sihtek!*' – and Najib kissed me formally on both cheeks. Elena too came and gave me an affectionate squeeze round the waist. Dear Elena, looking nicer than anyone, I thought, in the simplest Indian cotton blouse, with a long wrap-around skirt striped a dozen shades of red.

With a host's deft skill, Najib was introducing people all around, grouping them in little knots of conversation. Rashid raised his hands and eyebrows, looking at me with ironic merriment as he too was whisked away.

'Samia!' Najib drew me aside, back to a corner of the terrace where we wouldn't be overheard; the same corner, by the balustrade, where Rashid and I had been standing a few minutes earlier. 'Listen, my dear Samia. I've just had news from Beirut. I've been on the phone – several calls – there's trouble. It's not quite clear yet what's happening, but I've taken the precaution of booking us all a flight out of Lebanon first thing in the morning. Elena too, of course. It's all under control.' He almost beamed, he was so pleased with himself, with the shrewdness of his timing. He had been absolutely right when he assured me that tonight's party would be on; perfectly, precisely right. By tomorrow . . . 'There's no need for alarm,' he said. 'I just thought you'd be glad to know, we leave for London in the morning.'

'London!' I looked wildly past him, hoping to catch Rashid's eye, but he was firmly lodged in one of the conversational groupings. And to contradict Najib, at such a moment . . .

I closed my eyes, I think, taking the plunge. 'I'm sorry, Najib, but Elena and I have already made other plans. We're going with Rashid to Damascus tomorrow, by car. Elena's flying on from there.'

'Impossible. Out of the question. You'd never get through. The Bekaa Valley's sealed off by a massing of troops –'

There was another roll of distant thunder, from away down the coast.

'– my family – my responsibility –' Najib was smiling on me, benignly. I don't know quite what else he was telling me, I was too distracted to listen properly, but I did hear him say, 'Your one certain chance to ensure Elena's safety.' He was saying it reassuringly, confidently, as if I were an anxious child. He kept his hand resting on my shoulder, as if he thought I might be afraid of the thunder. We stood against the balustrade listening to it rolling away in the darkness. It was unexpected, that there should be thunder, when the air was so clear and dry.

He left me to think it over and went to circulate among the guests, carrying on with his correct and dignified introductions. I was aware of a stirring after he had gone, the guests near to me at the balustrade shuffled and rustled. While they carried on their breathless chatter they kept glancing, almost unconsciously, in the direction from which the thunder had come, as if uncertain of its effect on their own mood. As if . . . A group of young men whooped and descended on another of the liveried waiters, relieving him of his whole tray-load of freshly charged glasses, within seconds. I heard someone whisper, 'Don't tell Najib, we don't want to spoil the party, but there's news from Beirut of a major offensive –' The whisper circulated around the terrace like a tiny under-current, a tiny stormy electric charge.

Lina Bashoura stood beside me, beneath a bower of starry-white clematis, looking out across the light-spangled waters of the harbour. 'Isn't it lovely?' With a sweep of her arm she took in the whole setting: the garlanded terrace, the party, the frescoed Raphaelesque interior.

'Yes.' It was so extravagantly lovely, it really was quite beautiful. 'But at the same time it makes me just a little sad,' I said. 'I share Elena's sadness that not everyone has the chance to enjoy such opulence tonight.'

She smiled. She was – what could I call her? – a conservative feminist? She was a woman of my own age, whom I had known for a long time; one of Lebanon's aristocrats, a well-known woman doctor, with a husband who was a Cabinet Minister. Her grey hair was drawn up and back in an aristocratic sweep and held in place by diamond-studded pins.

She smiled. 'Yes, you're right, my dear Samia. *Ma'ek haq.* You're right to be proud of a daughter like Elena.' She looked across to where Elena was standing talking to Henry and Karen. 'At her age, if one's not angry about these things, one has no heart . . .'

'But?' I could see there was a 'but', that there was something else she wanted to say.

'But you and I, my dear, are too old to go on blindly enjoying the sweet music in our own ears while Lebanon burns.'

'Meaning?' There was what looked like a flash of lightning further down the coast, out at sea. And another. In a group near us, by the balustrade, voices were raised in excited laughter.

'Look at the allies Elena's friends keep. Look at the allies your good-hearted friends the Progressives have to keep, to get the arms they badly need. What do you want – for Lebanon? The grinding blinkered armoured-tank style of politics of the Syrian military state? Or the *Jihad* of the Shi'a – the holy Koran-thumping war of Islam?' She hesitated. 'You and I . . .' A gentle breath of air wafted the strands of clematis above us so that the flowers caught the light, like white flickering stars. ' . . . We people who like to think of ourselves as liberal, open-minded – able to see all sides – the salt of the earth – I'm afraid we really do have to make our choice.'

'You mean a military choice?'

Somebody called to her. She looked at me with a twinge of delicacy, of liberal open-minded doubt. And nodded. Her hand gestured once more towards the fragile beauty of the light-stippled harbour. She excused herself and slipped away.

Elena came over to me. She had seen us looking at her. I asked her how she would like the idea of going direct to London tomorrow, compliments of Najib.

'Oh! All right, yes, if you like. I don't mind.' She shrugged, surprised but willing enough. 'I'm still starving, can I get you anything?' She went off again, in search of one of the waiters.

I found Karen leaning on the balustrade, just a yard or two away, sniffing the unfamiliar scents of the Lebanese night. Just as I turned to her, Henry came pounding over, in a hurry, stopping only for a second to give instructions to a waiter with an empty drinks tray – full of his duties as Najib's son; as self-appointed master of ceremonies. He took Karen by the arm.

'I think I might make my announcement soon, don't you, now that everybody's here?'

'What announcement?' she asked.

'You know. The results of the fund-raising.'

'For goodness sake, can't you just tell people quietly? It's not exactly the most tactful thing to go shouting out when not everybody agrees with –' She looked doubtfully at me.

'Oh, come off it, love. This is a party! Don't let's go through all that again! What am I supposed to do? Jack in the whole campaign just because of what Elena was saying just now?' I wondered what Elena had been saying. Henry looked at me and gave a hearty over-vigorous laugh. 'Just because Aunt Samia's invited a Moslem here tonight!' He laughed again, boisterously, to show it was meant as a joke, I suppose. I wondered how he had managed to avoid inheriting any of Marie-Claire's Lebanese grace.

Then he spotted Yusef and he was off, edging past the clusters of people, grabbing a little *mahshi* and a *vol-au-vent* from a waiter's proffered tray as he passed. He and Yusef strolled away, deep in conversation, Henry's arm around Yusef's neck. I knew what they would be talking about. They had been in cahoots with one another since early evening, jubilant about the funds which Henry had raised for the hospital. Yusef's stride was quick and taut with excitement.

'Ah, Samia, there you are!' Najib descended on us; it is not the privilege of a guest of honour to remain quietly in a corner. 'And Karen too! Come and let me introduce you to Ramzi Rahman.'

He shepherded us across to the lily pond, where a group of young people were gathered, looking as ornamental in their beauty as the pond itself. Two of the young women there, sisters from the Bakhara banking family, sat in light gauzy dresses on the edge of the pond, trailing their fingers in the water. The fountain was gushing, sending water flowing in rivulets down over the sculptured marble forms of romping children and leaping fishes. Ramzi Rahman, wearing a dinner jacket and a brilliant emerald frilled shirt, with a matching cummerbund, was quite as handsome as his reputation; and conscious of it too, I had no doubt at all. I hadn't met him before, though I knew of him, of course. As the son of one of the feudal lords of Mount Lebanon, he already had his own small fiefdom, so I had heard; and his own army. After he had shaken hands with us, and graciously offered me a marble plinth to sit on, he leaned back with his arm lightly embracing the thigh of a statue: a life-size Venus on a pedestal, who held a garland of frangipane aloft on her cupped hand.

They had all been speaking French before we joined them, but they switched to English, out of politeness to Karen, when we were introduced. Ramzi was looking at Karen, but then slowly his gaze shifted back to Latifa, who was standing by the Bakhara sisters. She was aware his eyes were on her, I think, though she didn't look at him; she was holding her head on one side so that her curls danced and shone and her laughter became, if anything, more high-pitched. I noticed too something else in her manner: a too-fixed brightness in her facial expression, a tendency to raise her glass to her lips much, much too often. She was, I could see, a little drunk.

There was a young man next to her, a studious-looking young man, talking about the political situation in grave tones. 'It's terrible,' he said – the Bakhara sisters nodded and trickled water through their fingers – 'terrible the way the Palestinians have been allowed simply to take over half our country.' Latifa gave a breathy little laugh. 'If they're allowed to retain control on a permanent basis it will be the end for us. Finish. Israel can't afford to let the Palestinians become that powerful, at such close quarters. They'll have no alternative but to strike back at the Palestinian positions wherever they are in Lebanon. In the heart of Beirut itself. Quite possibly they'll invade –'

He was thumped on the back by a couple of the men, who raised their glasses in loud and hearty agreement.

Latifa was ecstatic. 'Exactly, yes, exactly! That's exactly what everyone's been saying!' Her curls bobbed and twirled into ringlets, scattering the light. 'Exactly!' I saw her cast a malevolent, challenging look towards Elena, who was standing across on the other side of the pond, with Rashid.

Elena stared curiously back. Together she and Rashid began to make their way round the pond towards us, through the press of people. And I was thinking how the young man was, in some ways, very probably right – though he was not happy, clearly not happy with the raucous party mood which greeted his remarks. He tried to break in again . . .

'We've got to flush out the Palestinian guerrillas wherever they are,' someone else was saying. 'A concerted military attack –'

'Yusef! Yusef!' Latifa called out shrilly. She had caught sight of him not far away, still wrapped in conversation with Henry. Her pale cheeks had blushed pink under Ramzi Rahman's continued gaze. His hand had moved to the buttocks of his Venus. 'Yusef, do come and listen to this!' She turned and said to the men of the group in general, 'I do wish you'd tell my husband what you've just been saying. He's such a darling! He's so sentimental about the Palestinian families!' She tipped back her wine glass and gazed triumphantly across the pond, her eyes searching for Elena.

Yusef, with a bemused frown, was dragged into the group. Ramzi Rahman had him by the arm and was pressing him to have a drink from the very special-looking, dust-encrusted bottle he kept between the feet of his Venus. Meanwhile Najib, with the alert anticipation of the perfect host, had arrived to pour oil before the first ripple of discord could develop. He had waylaid Elena and involved her in conversation with Marie-Claire. Marie-Claire was gesturing, with her gentle French-drawing-room grace, towards the frescoed interior, which looked lovelier than ever now that the night had deepened outside, and I saw Elena smile and heard her chattering to her, in her prim girlish French. *Une jeune fille tout à fait comme il faut.*

Ramzi Rahman was telling Yusef, in much earthier French, how he thought that partition was the only answer for Lebanon. 'The National Pact, pouff! *C'est fini. Foutu!*' He tossed his hand, the one holding his wine glass, up into the air as if it were a puff of smoke. Yusef nodded. He had an absent frown. 'The rest of Lebanon,' Ramzi said, '*je m'en fous*! Let *Mont Liban* be free of it . . . *débarrassé* . . .'

Listening to his clannish territorialism, I wondered if Lina Bashoura was any more pleased with her own chosen allies than she was with those of the Progressives. And I knew that of course she wasn't. No more than I would be. Which made her choice – her fear for the beauty, the humanism, the infinite open-armed diversity of Lebanon – all at once more poignant, more compelling.

Everyone round the pond helped themselves from a heaped tray of pastries which a waiter brought round. There were *baklawas* and *ghraibehs*, *éclairs* and *petits-fours* and there was brandy too, in bowls as big as the water lilies. The gauzy Bakhara sisters were doing their best, with much finger-licking, to eat collapsible *mille-feuilles*. They were showering the surface of the pond with tiny flakes of pastry. Everybody watched and exclaimed as scores of colourful fish came up for the fallen flakes, diving and re-emerging in a continuous golden-orange cascade. Somebody who had just arrived late at the party from up in the mountains, said that the shoal of fish was the colour of the sky he had seen tonight, over Beirut. 'Glowing orange,' he said, 'with shooting sparks. Like fireworks.' Latifa gave a thin shrieking laugh. She reached out towards the back of Yusef's arm, but it was just out of reach and her own arm dropped loosely to her side again. She lowered her nose, and a stray curl, into her brandy bowl.

Three of the women, bending low over the pond, murmured over a thin under-nourished fish which was lurking away from the rest, partly hidden under a lily pad. '*Le pauvre! Qu'il est maigre! Pierre, regarde, donne-lui à manger!*' They trailed their hands in the water again, itching to stroke it.

Rashid had come to join me and I whispered to him about Najib's plane booking to London.

He looked at me.

'What do you want to do, *habeebti?*'

'*Allah biyi'lam* . . . To be a fish, I think,' I whispered. 'To hide away down in the watery dark.'

'*Habeebti,*' he said mockingly, cherishingly, into my hair, 'sometimes you can be so cool!' I could have hugged him, if this weren't Najib's party, hugged him with laughter and passion.

'A veritable Lorelei!' Rashid whispered, with gleaming mischievousness, seeing me hold back.

'Henry!' Finding Henry come to reclaim Yusef, Latifa took hold of his arm. 'Henry, it's so good of you,' she said, in emphatic English, leaning up against him and raising her voice, it seemed to me, in the direction of Ramzi Rahman, 'you've done wonderfully well with your fund-raising for Yusef's hospital. Wonderfully well! We're *so* grateful. Yusef's absolutely over the moon!'

'Oh, that's nothing,' said Henry, with pleased bluster. 'Of course, the money for the hospital's only a fraction of the total we've raised in the campaign so far.'

'What campaign is that?' asked Rashid.

Karen, glad to find a conversation in English again at last, said, 'Henry's worked terribly hard in London, canvassing all the people and firms with business interests in Lebanon. Terribly hard.'

'I was thinking, you know,' Henry was saying to Latifa confidingly, 'I ought to make an announcement. Let everybody here know the total amount raised to date –'

'Yes, you should! You should!' Latifa cried, and again she couldn't resist a glance across to where Elena was politely, if distractedly, listening to two matrons of Marie-Claire's acquaintance. 'I'll tell everyone. Everyone!' But Ramzi Rahman, busy telling Yusef about his army, responded only by the vaguest passing look. She did her best not to look disappointed. 'All the Junieh people will be thrilled! An announcement! I'll call them over, now, this minute. This very minute . . .' She trailed away, unsteadily, glass in hand, to round up her friends. 'Listen everyone, listen . . .'

Karen frowned urgently at Henry, who called doubtfully after her, 'Latifa! Latifa!'

My poor Latifa. I wondered, should I take her aside? Well, if it weren't that I was her mother-in-law! Or prise Yusef free from Ramzi Rahman to go to her . . .?

Rashid said to Henry, 'You're raising funds to help the victims of the fighting, is that right?' And he waited, with a look so shrewd, but at the same time full of such . . . such disarming, such typically Rashid-like innocence that there was no evading him.

'Well, yes, to help them too, to some extent,' Henry said, stalling. He looked embarrassed. He looked for Latifa. Looked everywhere except at the waiter whose tray of drinks he nearly knocked over with his flailing elbow. 'Apologies! – Aunt Samia, and Mr Errh . . . – Excuse me –'

He had enough to do, what with the waiter, and wanting to run off to restrain Latifa. Or maybe to encourage her, I don't know. More likely, I thought, he would end up encouraging her. She had found her Junieh crowd. We could see her standing among them while glasses were being raised, and voices too. Somebody exultantly called out a toast. 'To the war effort!'

There was a shout. From over at the balustrade. And a flash, the second in only a few moments, away to the south. More shouts. Somebody, pointing out to sea, called out something about a ship and I saw a pair of binoculars being passed from hand to hand. Voices all over the terrace were raised excitedly and people began to flock towards the balustrade. The thunder rolled faintly towards us and there was another flash, a smaller one, from the mountains inland. Ramzi Rahman, with a sudden urgent look on his face, let go of his Venus. Muttering something to Yusef about using the telephone, he excused himself and slipped indoors, stopping only to bow swiftly and gallantly to a young girl who had stepped aside in the archway to let him pass. Najib, coming out with the rest of the people from the interior to see what was happening, was held back by the head butler who, grave-faced, took him aside and passed him a folded message on a silver tray.

There was another flash out at sea and this time we all saw it quite clearly – unmistakably, the silvery outline of a ship, lit up for a few moments against the darkness of the sea and sky. Then the answering flash, the much bigger flash, several miles to the south-west of us, illuminating the smoking orange-stained sky above Beirut. I turned and took Rashid's hand and it came again, rolling towards us, the far-away sound, the rumbling thunderous sound of the pounding of Beirut. The party broke into wild, scared, exultant chatter. Faces reddened, the drink flowed. The next lightning flash was accompanied by a peal of Latifa's manic laughter.

Below us in the streets of Junieh there was a whooping and hallooing. The news came from somewhere and was passed quickly, excitedly around the terrace that a full-scale bombardment was being mounted against 'rebel positions' in West Beirut.

'Think of it,' I heard Henry say, 'they've got hold of some cannons from the regular Army! 155 millimetre shells! What a bang!'

From all over the town below us came the loud sharp cracks of celebratory rifle fire. I felt sick. Old. I sat down, and Rashid sat next to me, on a protruding ledge of the balustrade. Elena was standing not far away from us, tense and nearly in tears. Beirut – West Beirut – exploded once more, far away, in a smoking orange glare.

Yusef, his brush of black hair bristling with the fierceness of his anxiety, said, 'I must go. The hospital –'

Henry clapped him on the shoulder. 'It's O.K. Dad's

checked it out, it's definitely not your area. Anyway, we need you! I haven't presented you with the cheque yet!' He looked quickly about him and called to a waiter, 'Champagne! Bring champagne!' Seeing that everybody was gathered in one place, Henry found himself a perch, a podium on which to stand, on one of the trellis mountings, beside a pot of trailing ivy and lobelia.

'Champagne! Champagne!' The cry was taken up all around. People hugged each other with emotion, with fear and frenzied excitement. 'Champagne!' The liveried waiters came hurrying, five or six of them, with trays full of brimming glasses.

'Quiet, everyone, please! I'd like to take this opportunity –' Henry, swaying with bumptious self-importance on his precarious perch, made a warm-hearted presentation to Yusef of his forty-thousand-pound cheque for the hospital. Then he jumped down and he and Yusef hugged each other again and again.

'Speech!'

My poor Yusef. His eyes were on fire with anxiety; with gratitude; with fear for the consequences of this massive new attack. His jaw was up-thrust, his face hollow and strained with compassion. 'Thank you. Thank you. This money will be invaluable,' he said. He told Henry, 'We need it to buy more equipment – ventilators, monitors, drugs – all the drugs we can get hold of. Morphine, anaesthetics, *mukhadderat* . . .' He switched back from English to Arabic, unaware where he was or who he was talking to, bound up in the intensity of his concern.

Latifa's voice rang out again, excited, intoxicated: 'The announcement!'

'And also –' Henry leaped back on to his podium. He glanced at Najib to check for his assent and raised his hand for silence again. 'And also, I have to announce the total amount raised so far by our Lebanese campaign in London: just over three million pounds!'

There were cries and gasps. More hugs, more frenzy. A waiter offered me champagne, but I refused. I asked Rashid quickly, 'Do you want to leave?'

Rashid waved the waiter away. His answer, if he gave one

was drowned in the toast: 'Lebanon! *Le Liban*!' It was shouted on all sides. Somebody cried, 'The war effort!'

Ramzi Rahman, who had returned to the terrace, climbed jubilantly on to the podium beside Henry and, with a twirling flourish of his glass, cried, 'The defence of Lebanon!'

Then in the moment of silence while everybody drank came Elena's voice, sober and short, 'Three million pounds to buy what?'

Glasses stopped in mid-air. People stared at this defiant figure, standing in their midst, her hand on the hip of her Indian skirt. The skin of Najib's full beneficent face contracted as if he had been slapped. Henry, startled, tried to wriggle out of her question with his blustering laugh.

She asked again, doggedly, 'Three million pounds to buy what?'

'To buy arms.' It was Najib who answered her and I had to admire the calm assurance with which he tackled her; Najib who had spent a life-time smoothing the ructions of everyday business life. His genial frankness would have appeased anybody. Anybody except Elena. 'Arms to defend Lebanon against the presence of outside forces on our soil,' he said. 'To defend the newly reaffirmed National Pact, and the Lebanese tradition of sharing and toleration enshrined within it, against all those who want to undermine it. Against all those insurgents and terrorists who have leapt in to destroy all semblance of normal life in Lebanon for their own ends. Arms,' he said, giving Elena his final commanding word on the subject, 'to regain our country so that the Lebanese people can hope to repair the damage done and live together again in peace. Please, everybody, help yourselves. There's champagne, liqueurs, chocolate truffles . . .'

There were cheers and murmurs of admiration. A general relieved hubbub . . .

'Arms for use against which targets?'

I was shocked. My heart leaped for her. There was silence again. Everybody waited.

Najib's chest swelled to its full broad expanse as he slowly took in breath. He was not obliged to answer such impertinence. But there was in Najib that deep-rooted concern for mutual consideration . . . There was his need to support

Henry, to whom the honours of the moment were due. 'For use against the insurgents wherever they've taken up their positions.'

'Against the Palestinian refugee camps? Against Tal al-Zaatar?'

'If necessary.'

'But there are women and children there! Whole families crammed closely together!'

Henry leaped in. 'Oh come on, Elena, that's hardly our fault! It's up to the Palestinian commandos to make sure they don't set up their military bases right in amongst their own women and children.'

Elena turned to Yusef. 'Yusef, listen, it's a farce them giving you that money. You've heard what they want to do with the rest of it.' She was boiling, shaking with anger. She took hold of him and squeezed her arms round him with the fervour of when they were children together. 'Tear up the cheque. You can't accept it. Yusef, think of Yacoub!'

Yusef stood there, bewildered. He didn't know where to look. He tried uncertainly to loosen her grip.

Najib was incensed. His face was purple. He strode over and took Elena's elbow, standing where he could hide her, her dishonour, from the gathered crowd. He said in a very stern restrained voice, 'Elena, I think you should remember this is not an occasion when –'

'All right, Uncle Najib,' she said, turning on him. 'No need to employ the bouncers. I'm just leaving.' Her lips stretched into an acid smile. 'Thank you for the party!' She almost ran from the terrace, head down, and I felt with her the welling pain; I felt – for all the world as if I were her, as if my legs were running in hers – her heartburn anger, her girlish aching shame.

There was polite uproar. There were murmurs of outrage and cries of sympathy for Najib; and for Henry, who grinned and laughed it off. Ramzi Rahman jumped down over the lobelia pot and thumped him heartily on the back. Latifa's Junieh friends gathered round her in commiseration.

Rashid and I glanced at one another, he touched my wrist and went out at once, after Elena. But I didn't know – should I follow him? Or stay with poor Yusef? But there were people gathered round Yusef and he was replying warmly to them, he was so pleased – in spite of himself, in spite of Elena – so pleased still with his cheque! He was already explaining again to those around him what the money would pay for; how many more lives it would help to save.

And it was true Elena had behaved unforgivably. Whatever her feelings. One achieves nothing by offending people. By causing, in Najib's hour of bounty, such gross offence.

I saw Lina Bashoura standing, with her grey elevated head, not far away. She was looking at me; queryingly. Her champagne glass was raised to her lips and there was that look of irony in her eye. Of amused, intellectual irony.

The lightning flashed again, out at sea, and from the mountains too, behind Beirut. People all around me talked loudly and volubly and my head was aching, just as if the air really were close and thundery. I was thinking: so, if Najib has his way, the day after tomorrow I shall be with him in England. Even if I have my holiday with Rashid, he'll expect me back there afterwards. We'll sit politely, Sunday after Sunday, over lunch in Berkhamsted, as if nothing at all were amiss; ignoring, with the best of good manners, the fact that his son is helping to buy arms to fight, perhaps to kill, my daughter's closest friends . . .

As if Rashid and I had never considered proposals over tea.

I arrived in the ante-room to the penthouse suite at the same time as Najib. The commissionaire was just bringing Elena's jacket. Rashid was leaning on the cloakroom counter-top, talking to her.

With his formal, pained dignity, Najib said, 'Come, come Elena, I know you regret your behaviour. You've said nothing so bad that it can't be forgiven. Come back and join the party.'

Elena shook her head so that her hair flew. 'Uncle Najib, there are people at your party who are cheering because families across in West Beirut are being wiped from this earth at this very moment. I'm sorry, but I can't stomach your party!'

He drew in his breath and stiffened, as one does with indigestion. 'All that's required is that you should manage a smile.'

'A smile!'

And it made me angry too, so angry, his obligatory forgiveness, his lack of grasp of what was at stake.

'Najib —' No I would *not* apologise for her. I would not.

Elena said, 'And I won't need your plane ticket tomorrow thank you. I'll make my own way.'

He said, 'You'd be foolish not to take it. There'll be little hope of getting out of Lebanon otherwise.'

'I'll take a chance.'

Rashid helped her into her jacket and stood behind her with his hands holding her shoulders. All at once she turned round and took him impulsively by the hands. 'Rashid, you go, instead of me! Go on the flight to London and then take mother off somewhere — anywhere — wherever it was you were going on that holiday of yours. Won't you? Please!'

I saw the discomposure, the impeccably polite discomfort with which Najib looked at Rashid. Rashid saw it too. He smiled at her — at me — a wistful smile.

'But if we leave tomorrow without you — what would you do?' I asked her.

'Oh, I'll be O.K.'

'But where? Where will you go?' She shrugged noncommittally. 'How will you leave Lebanon?'

Yusef had meanwhile come rushing, looking for his coat, in a hurry to get back to the hospital. He heard my doubts.

'You must go, little mother. Tomorrow, with Najib. Doctor's orders.' He murmured in my ear, 'You must, little mother, you must!'

But I had been in this position before! I had been pushed once before into a plane journey to London which I did not want. I had lain in hospital amidst the chrome and whiteness, stroke-ridden; Rashid had been there beside my bed, blowing his nose copiously on my embossed private-wing paper handkerchiefs, on the point of going his separate way to Damascus. And I had felt such a longing, then, for the power of speech! To be able to speak out, to assert myself, to plunge headlong . . .

'Yusef, my dear Yusef, I'm so sorry, but no . . .'

I said to Rashid, 'What do you think? Do you think we'll still manage to get through to Damascus by road?'

He smiled. Such a smile.

'We'll try,' he said. 'We can certainly try.'

Whether it was the alcohol, I don't know – or the combination of the alcohol and my blood pressure drugs perhaps – my night was full of wakeful images: of Yusef saying good-bye to us, to Elena and me, with such a perturbed unhappy face; of Najib looking appalled, pained, blue from his bruised and buffeted honour. Najib, the only person now living who had loved me and cared for me from the beginning. The night was full of images and half-awake fitful thoughts: what happens, I wondered, to the person who has one foot firmly in each camp, when the two camps move apart?

The wheels were rolling and grinding against the inside surface of my skull. There were two of them this time, rolling slowly outwards, away from each other, until they were grinding and pressing against opposite sides of my head. Pressing, pressing . . .

Part IV

BATTLE JOINED

It was impossible – to get to Damascus, I mean. Impossible to think of going by road. The shelling was still continuing, on and off, when we arrived in Beirut next day. Now and then an explosion made the whole city shake – which was something new, previously there had always been a daytime respite from the night-long bombardments – and we were told that the fighting was worse if anything in the mountains, up along the Damascus road and in the Bekaa Valley. There was talk that the Progressives had launched a major offensive there – a final bid to unseat Franjieh, to force a reformist administration. If they could only seize the advantage now, while the military balance – and the tide of feeling, the parliamentary vote against Franjieh – were in their favour. If they could only overrun the small part of the country, across the Damascus road, which was still in the hands of the 'isolationist' militias . . .

There was no question, if we were in our right minds, of making our way across the shifting hidden lines of fire.

We could have gone to the airport and queued, I suppose, along with a milling mass of other people, in the hope of a flight. Or gone with Najib after all – which Elena refused, still absolutely refused even to consider. But it was in any case so much safer, once we had reached Rashid's house, to stay put there, where things were relatively quiet.

We called at Yusef's on our way back through East Beirut; to pick up our belongings. Only the old housekeeper was in, muttering anxiously to herself as she brought us our laundered clothes. Yusef was at the hospital and it wasn't until we had packed and were almost ready to leave that Elena and I heard Latifa in the hall below, arriving back from Junieh. When we came down she was in the drawing room, sitting perched on the edge of an armchair with her legs pressed tightly together, talking uncomfortably to Rashid, though he was smiling at her, doing his best to put her at ease.

The children were not with her.

'I've left them and Mathilde at my mother's,' she said. 'This is no place to bring them . . .' Her mother's words. She looked pale after the night before. Her hair had lost its lustre. She wouldn't look at Elena.

'It'll be good for you not to have to worry about them for a little while,' I said, encouragingly I hoped. 'To have Yusef to yourself when he's home.'

'Oh, yes! When he's home!' She wouldn't look at me either. Her eyes flickered warily towards Rashid, then she tossed her head away and stared out into the garden.

When we left I gave her my love – sent my fondest love to Yusef – and said I would telephone. And Elena threw her arms around her, awkwardly, in an impulsive parting squeeze. But I felt guilty about her as soon as we had gone. I thought of her spending her days in the empty house, alone except for the housekeeper. It would do her no good. No good at all. I was suddenly conscious of how little I had done to help her while we had been staying with her. I had barely sat down with her. We should not be leaving her now with no other choice, if the shelling drove her away, except to go back to her mother in Junieh.

We stayed put. We were at Rashid's house for two weeks almost. Two weeks in which we were in a world which was – how can I describe it? – enclosed, absorbing, intensely strange. West Beirut was cut off like a plague city, and we were isolated within it, in the house, shut off in a close nest of precarious unreality. As in a plague city we lived from moment to moment; surviving, simply, for another day. At night I couldn't sleep. I watched the sky over the city and it was like a mediaeval hell, with streaking comets, explosions, belching billows of blackest smoke and fiery luminescence. One could believe, in one's demented sleep-starved brain, in the whole mediaeval theatre of demons, devils and damnation. Then every morning the night-time's dead were carried out of shell-shattered buildings and counted in scores, in lorry-loads of corpses. They trundled by under our windows: cargoes of flesh-filled clothing and interlocking limbs.

The weather was often damp and still, and in Rashid's inner courtyard the air was tinged at times a putrid green. Why green, I don't know. Something to do with the reflection of the viburnum leaves against the white walls, perhaps, in the smog-filtered light, but one could smell the unwholesome pestilence of the city, the fetid stench of garbage and of putrifying corpses lying rotting beneath collapsed buildings. The old servant's husband hobbled across the yard with a clanking pail. One of the drains was blocked.

I was not well. Rashid persuaded a doctor to come, but there was nothing wrong, nothing wrong with my blood pressure. It was high, yes – it's always high – but not dangerously so. I was ill with the tension, the nausea, the aching strain of the war. With the limited tolerance of creeping age. I had a taut fraught sense of imminence. Of grief and dread. It was something I was getting used to, that while the war lasted I would never feel well.

But at the same time those days were peculiarly sweet. I was with Rashid – and Elena too – and there was nothing, nothing at all to do except to be together. To talk and talk. With such pleasure. There had never been time before to talk so much. Elena went out in the daytime, perhaps three or four times altogether, to see her friends; whenever in her opinion – never mine – it was safe enough. Rashid and I stayed, sitting in the big *akd* which opened on to the courtyard, wrapped together in fondness. We talked about things which mattered intensely; and things which didn't matter at all. About his life in Egypt, about music, magic, about George.

My right side ached and I half lay on a sofa, propped, at Rashid's insistence, against a mound of pillows. I protested, 'But I'm not an invalid!'

'Not an invalid, no.' He chuckled. 'Certainly not an invalid!'

He brought a large silk shawl which he put over me, tucking it in gently, round my hips – my waist . . . my . . . 'If you only knew, *habeebti*, how tempted I was in the hospital to tuck you in softly like this, when that terrible starched sheet was drawn tight across your chest as if you were a corpse, or a mummy. How tempted I was to take away that poor stiffness –'

And it was true, under his hands I felt an easing, a softening. A happiness. 'They would have turned you out,' I said.

I closed my eyes. I could feel the warmth of his hand where it rested against me. The warmth of his breath.

He must have been looking at the expression on my face. 'They would have turned *you* out,' he said, with the lightest chuckle.

As for the war . . .

Elena came back from spending the afternoon with Mariam and Khalida, bristling with indignation. She had been helping Mariam with the job of collecting and supplying blankets to yet another wave of homeless people who were bedding down in churches and make-shift shelters. And she was full of it, full of what she had been doing. Rashid helped her to large piles of vegetables – there was once again no bread to be had in Beirut – and in between her hungry mouthfuls she told us every detail of her afternoon; every tale Khalida had brought back of her stints manning the barricades.

Then, remembering, in the middle of a thirsty drink of water, she gulped and said, 'It's incredible, though – have you heard? About Assad?'

It was something Rashid and I had been talking about, on and off all afternoon: the news that Assad was withdrawing Syrian support, just at the moment when the troops of the

Progressive alliance were almost there, when victory seemed so close; when Assad could have handed it to them on a plate. Just another few days and there could have been a definitive outcome at last. The end of the war!

'What on earth's he playing at?' Elena asked. 'He's completely starving our fighting units of supplies!'

I shook my head. Rashid turned out his hands and shrugged. It was a mystery – a mystery to all of us – what was going on. It was one of those days when one didn't know what news to believe – what or who (al-Ahdab-style) was in the ascendant next. There were so many contradictions in what one heard.

The girls – Mariam, Khalida, their friends – had all been seething all day. – 'Absolutely hopping mad,' Elena said. On the radio people were talking nineteen to the dozen. There was once again so much emotion. Such anger and confusion.

Elena seemed moody. Which wasn't like her. Her leave was almost ended and she was due back in Somalia in a few days time. A (Syrian mediated) ceasefire had been negotiated and the plan was that she would go with us to Damascus and fly on from there.

She seemed . . . not depressed exactly. I found her sitting on one of the mats in the courtyard, in the twilight, the evening before we were to leave, with one leg drawn up to her chin. Her finger-nails were picking and chafing at the seams of her jeans.

'What's the matter, Lenni?'

She shrugged her shoulders up to her ears. 'Oh, nothing.'

The evening was very warm still and filled with the scent of orange blossom. I sat down on a chair beside her and we stayed for a while, in silence, listening to the doves crooning themselves to sleep in the trees and to the sporadic desultory rattle of machine-gun fire enlivening the ceasefire somewhere in the distance.

I had heard her earlier, in the kitchen with Rashid, talking as they so often did through the ins and outs, the ups and downs of development aid. It was the old servant's evening off and Elena had been washing up while Rashid made coffee.

There had been an obtuse disgruntled merriment about her, she was gesticulating with the dish-mop, being deliberately provocative. Which Rashid loved. There was nothing he liked better than provocation! They were both being outrageous, I could hear, and I had stayed well out of the way.

I said to her now, gently, 'What about your scheme, Lenni? You still haven't told me about your scheme.'

'Oh –' She ran her fingers round the hem of her jeans, thoughtfully, as if measuring the seam . . . 'The thing is, relief work's all very well – It's great, I enjoy it enormously, working in the camps and watching the little stick-limbs of the kids fill out,' – for a moment her face brightened – 'seeing them get back the energy to run about and brush the flies off. But like I told you, what the refugees need in the long term is land. Communal pastoral land. So Alan and I thought, if our people in London would let us organise some independent funding –' She stopped. She just sat there, twisting the hem of her jeans round her index finger, round and round.

'What's the matter?'

'It's just a complete non-starter,' she said. 'A total waste of time.'

'Why? Is that what Alan thinks?'

She hunched her shoulders and let them drop again, seeming irritated. 'It's not a matter of what Alan thinks, the only way these people will ever get their patch of the Ogaden back is to bloody well fight for it. Back-up for the fighting is what they need most. When I get back to the Ogaden I want to go up-front and –'

'But Lenni! You said yourself – the risk! What can you achieve, do you think, that's worth the risk?'

'Well, for goodness sake, I never noticed *you* chickening out of any of your literacy projects because of the risks! What about when you were on the West Bank during the June War? You didn't exactly turn tail and flee.' I had not known her be so outspokenly aggressive towards me since her teenage years, when her anger at George sometimes used to spill over into everything else she said.

'But if you were only sure of what it is you want to do,' I said. 'You worry me, you seem so unhappy about it. Why this? Why have you chosen suddenly to get involved in this particular fight? Aren't you really just one more colonialist, muscling in, with your own particular axe to grind?'

'I'm not a colonialist. I'm an Arab – an Arab nationalist.'

'So then why this?'

She scowled, saying nothing. It was growing dark. A solitary owl hooted in a neighbouring garden. Regretfully we left the orange-blossom-laden night to go indoors.

Elena came and plumped down on the sofa beside me in Rashid's tiled and carpet-scattered *akd*. A moment later she slipped her arm through mine and snuggled up against me, burying her knees under the folds of my grey silk kaftan. She looked tired and pale. Her young arms around me felt as soft as they had done when she was a child. They looked smooth and beautiful in contrast to my own drying, lightly crinkling skin.

'Isn't she the perfect English rose?'

Even now the memory jars, making something twist tightly in my head. 'Isn't she the perfect English rose?'

Elena used to be made such a fuss of at her grandmother's house in England. Visitors praised her so much for her fair skin and her pretty light brown hair. ('You'd never realise, would you, that George married *overseas*!') She used to sit curled in the chair that had been her grandfather's, allowing herself to be stuffed with sweets and cakes by her doting grandmother, reading her way through piles of sentimental classics about moral and spirited Victorian misses, loving it all, gorging herself on the petting and the xenophobic compliments until . . . She loved it and then, as always, by the second day . . .

'Your father would have been proud of you, Elly dear, if he'd known you were going to work in Africa. He always wanted to be a missionary when he was a boy.'

Elena gave her grandmother such a look! A missionary! – when we blamed the missionaries for so much of what had gone wrong in the Middle East! And in any case Elena still resented everything to do with her father! She writhed in her chair in grimacing overgrown-teenage discomfort. She stood up and fiddled restlessly with the china dancing-figures on the mantelpiece, her toes scuffing around within an inch of sending the fire-irons clattering. No, she didn't want to play cards. She didn't feel like a walk round the village just now.

Her grandmother must have seen that little glance of Elena's into the mirror behind the china figures because she leaned her forearms on her splayed knees and said to me, with emphasis, 'Isn't she the perfect English rose? Nobody would know any different, would they?'

'Granny please! If you say that again I shall scream.'

'Well, it's only the truth, Elly dear.'

And I thought: no, no, please, it's not the sort of thing one says to Elena; you don't know what it can cause.

'I'm not an English rose or an English anything!' Elena said. And, with that youthful need of hers to get everything quite clear, to the point of brutal frankness, 'I'm an Arab.'

'Elly dear! Now don't say that!' She pivotted her weight on her old mottled forearms and turned to me. 'Isn't she though? Isn't she the perfect —'

There is some hurt in Elena, a prickliness . . .

I think perhaps, for all her bandwagon cults, she never has been able to tolerate the notion of a synthesis; the ideal of a final triumphant fusion of the heritages of East and West. She has seen in her lifetime, in my generation and my mother's too, so much failure. So much flagrant conflict. What with that, and also being brought up in the rift of my marriage to George . . .

There is some hurt in Elena, a prickliness, a spikyness.

My poor Anglo-Arab.

Damascus.

Perhaps if I had come with Rashid initially – back in November, following my stroke – I might have been able to relax here, in the sedate stillness of his aunt's house. Or out in the sunshine beneath the ochre walls of her garden. I might have been able to cut my mind off from Lebanon then, when Damascus itself was cut off from it by the fighting in the intervening countryside.

But now, when everything that happened in Lebanon was initiated in Damascus first: all the negotiations, the manipulations, the manoeuvrings. After the Syrian invasion of Lebanon in early June especially, the Damascus road was opened up to a constant flow of troops, personnel, officials, armoured carriers, tanks, supplies. With the closing of Beirut airport it became almost the only way in and out of Lebanon – a constant thoroughfare of Lebanese military freight and Lebanese affairs. Then at the end of June, when the border once more became passable by civilians, floods of refugees came pouring through. Whole convoys of foreign evacuees arrived from Beirut in their buses and official cars, with their escort of Arab League soldiers in white helmets and full battle dress and their national flags flying – the union jack; the stars and stripes covering the hearse of the murdered American ambassador. Every other face one saw in the street, it seemed, was a face from Beirut.

It was impossible not to be involved. Constantly bound up, mentally and emotionally, in the war in Lebanon. Impossible, in those few days at the end of June when the Bekaa Valley was safe once again, not to contemplate a short foray . . . Just for a few hours, I thought. To comfort Yusef . . .

Alan was to spend a night in Damascus on his way back to Somalia; it was too late now, after we had been held up in Beirut for so long, for Elena to go to join him in London. I asked her if she would fly back to Africa with him.

'I don't know,' she said. She was biting off a rough corner of her thumb nail. 'I've still got a few days leave yet. I'll see.'

I liked Alan. I took to him at once. He was not at all the camp-fire adventure-scout, the rugged bearded explorer, which for some reason I had expected from what Elena had told me about him. He was a very urbane and charming young man, exceptionally articulate about the work, the aid work, he was doing in Africa, clearly very hard-headed and intelligent. Sitting with him on a seat beneath the garden wall on the morning of his arrival, it was surprising how time flew by while we talked. He had big gold-rimmed glasses, the sort George used to wear in middle age, only they had become fashionable again now, with their owl-eyed outdoor-intellectual look. He was handsome in them, with his curling fair hair.

In the afternoon Rashid lent us his car and we took Alan sight-seeing. We wove our honking winding way through the sand pale streets of the old town, past the crush of traders, past the shoe-shine boys, the laden pick-up trucks. We went on foot through the covered *suks*, where Alan and Elena, with their English faces and English-speaking voices, were pressed and harried to buy necklaces, loquats, lengths of silk, bags of pistachios.

We visited the Omayyad Mosque, with its pleasing domes and minarets, then drove out of the city and walked a little way up the hill of B——, to where we could see the white walls and roofs of Damascus spread out below us, nestling in the hills of the surrounding countryside. 'The landscape of the Bible lands,' Alan called it, appreciatively, shading his eyes against the sun.

He seemed very fond of Elena; he kept giving her quiet caresses as we walked, the way one does to somebody one has been attached to for a long time, lifting back the hair which strayed across her face in the wind, and keeping his hand resting for a moment in the small of her back.

'My mother was brought up in this part of the world,' he told me. 'In Palestine.' We were walking back to the car through an olive grove. A boy was running barefoot along the track in front of us, goading his donkey forwards with a stick. 'We've got family connections there still.' He said it, I thought, with a touch of pride. Even that, then. He aroused such hopes in me. Such hopes.

Elena's attitude to him was – well, it was hard to say. She was fond of him, certainly. She seemed very much used to him, in a friendly comfortable way, walking arm in arm with him down the path. I could see they had spent a lot of time together.

Later on, when we were alone in our room, I told Elena how much I liked him.

'I *thought* you would!' she said, with a reluctant smile.

'Why, what's the matter?'

'Nothing, it's just . . . Oh, never mind!'

She was unpacking the remainder of my clothes for me, folding them into an ancient chest. I was already in bed, watching her from my pillows; the sight-seeing had been too much for me – the tiring to-ing and fro-ing in the car from place to place, the walking, the crowds in the *suks*. I was feeling sick too, from the motion of the car. But so long as I stayed lying down, my queasiness was not too bad.

At the bottom of my suitcase, Elena came across the rolled Hockney reproduction which I had bought for her in London and forgotten until now to give to her.

'What's this?'

'Unroll it and see. It's for you.'

She was at once full of sparkle, 'Oh, this one!' She held it up for us both to see. There were two figures against a scorched yellow desert sky: an Egyptian bride in classical ancient-Egyptian profile and gloriously colourful persona and beside her the bridegroom – to me he was a European. He was grey-clothed and ill at ease; blotched pale and sickly strawberry-red in the unaccustomed heat. A hot Arab sun shone behind them and a grey tombstone stood before their feet. The mismatch between the couple was disturbing. I could almost feel it as I lay there in the bed: a clanging resonant dissonance.

'It's terrific,' Elena said laughing. '*Azeem*! I love it!'

She wanted to hang it above the clothes chest, with a bit of elastoplast from her sponge bag, but I wouldn't let her. I was afraid she would damage the wallpaper. So she tied a piece of string through it instead and hung it from the lamp bracket. Then she stood back to admire it with her arms crossed and her weight on one hip and said gleefully, 'It's fabulous! It just about sums it up!'

'Sums what up?'

'Oh, you know – everything! Everything!'

'I'm not spoiling anything between you and Rashid, am I, by staying on here for my last few days leave?' Elena looked from one to the other of us, queryingly. She was just back from the airport, after seeing Alan off.

'Now what exactly might you be spoiling?' Rashid asked with an audacious twinkle, 'under the virtuous Syrian eyes of my maiden aunt?'

He and Elena were both laughing. She seemed happy. Much happier – more certain of herself – than she had been for a while past. I imagined that she must have made up her mind to rejoin Alan and the scheme when she returned to Somalia in a few days time and I was very glad for her.

It was too late now, after being held up so long in Beirut, for Rashid and me to go on our much longed for holiday together. For the moment, anyway. The Literacy Centre needed him after his absence. There were various problems. He couldn't get away again just yet.

He took Elena and me with him when he drove a few miles out of Damascus, to al-Majat, to see how Haya was getting on with her women's literacy course there in the village school – the course which I myself had set up, the year before last. She was training women to run their own classes in the surrounding villages.

Haya was waiting for us in the school porch. She stepped down into the dusty yard to greet us, with outstretched hands. Something made her start when she clasped hold of me. I don't know what it was – something in my face perhaps. She hadn't seen me since before my stroke. Since I was the busy Organising Director. And I was thinking that I hadn't noticed before that Haya's hair was tinged with so much grey.

She introduced us to a man who was standing in the shadow of the porch, dressed in a plain brown suit. He was 'from the government,' she explained. She smiled at him formally. 'He's come to help us.' So that I knew at once why we had to talk in convolutions.

The problem was over reading materials. The women were arriving at the various classes with birth control leaflets, personal letters, one young woman from a refugee settlement was trying to read the diary of her Palestinian grandmother. 'We like to encourage the women to bring along things of their own which they want to be able to read,' Haya said, 'But of course so much of what they bring is unsuitable.'

Rashid nodded wisely. I nodded wisely.

'Unsuitable?' Elena looked aghast. 'But surely,' – I could see her struggling for the polite words to inquire of Haya – 'surely the whole point –'

'Is to provide materials suitable for their own circumstances,' said Haya nimbly. 'Exactly. Which is why so much of what we ourselves provide through the Literacy Centre, from outside this country, no longer meets with approval . . .' She gave the merest flicker of a glance in the direction of the government official.

I turned the pages of one of the new approved readers which were stacked neatly on Haya's desk. I had to smile at what I can only call the abundance of government words. Poor Haya. It used to be second nature to me to deal with such a situation: to support and encourage Haya and at the same time build up the trust and good-willed co-operation of the government concerned so that we could agree on materials appropriate to our task. But today . . . I listened to Rashid and Haya talking, to Rashid and the government official, I listened and the words turned over in circles in my mind. My mind was full of lists, incipient anxious lists of books, of processes to be gone through, churning inaccessibly in lazy rhythmic circles. Lists from another age.

The 'government official' – looking almost too much the part with his plain brown bureaucratic demeanour – had been watching Elena and now, while Rashid and Haya were talking, he walked casually (too casually) across to her where she was standing leafing through one of the readers with a scornful smile on her face.

'From Lebanon?' he asked.

'Yes.'

'Well, well, what a business there, eh? And what do you think of Assad's – er – peacekeeping efforts, eh?' – he lowered his voice so that I only just heard – 'Not quite the thing?' He winked at her. Definitely, he winked.

I saw in Elena's face all the answers she would love to give him, paraded before him in her outspoken eyes. Surely she wouldn't . . . – she must be used by now to such people in Ethiopia and Somalia – he was so clumsy, surely she wouldn't . . .

Rashid's voice boomed out, 'Peace in Lebanon? *Ma'ak haq*.

Just what's needed!' I didn't know he was listening, but it was like Rashid to gauge exactly what was going on, even when his back was turned. He strode over and clapped the official on the back, with preposterous wicked enjoyment. 'Just what's needed!' And all at once he was talking about Assad's new glittering – yes, glittering – role in the Middle East, in such highflown language that we were all left standing and Elena couldn't get a word in edgeways even if she tried. Dear Rashid. I was very, very grateful.

But it was something I found hard to take, while we were in Syria: the restraints, the curbs on one's freedom of speech, the need to be constantly alert to who was listening. I was aware all the time of the influence of the military; of the orderly ranks of soldiers outside every official building. Aware of the dourness, the regimental lack of humour which they somehow imposed. In the past, working in Syria, the restrictions had never bothered me. One works, in any job, within constraints. They are part of the challenge, the parameters which form the basis for thoughts and ideas. But now that I had no other base anywhere, nowhere else to go . . .

Sipping my night-cap of iced water in my room, I thought of Lebanon in peacetime: the freedom to be oneself, to do . . . anything – anything! To eat out in a thousand places, to drink; to relish the unpredictability of things. I thought of Lina Bashoura and her dread of Syrianisation, and I was with her in spirit and soul, in the ache of my head and the pressing, grinding anxiety of my mind . . .

Two days after Alan left, I fell ill. For once it wasn't my blood pressure which was causing the trouble. I had a fever, a 'flu perhaps. Probably my resistance was low after the sleeplessness and stress of my stay in Lebanon. For days I ached all over and I was hot and shivering in turn. Elena nursed me – there was no doubt she was an excellent nurse: cheerful, willing, dosing me regularly with pills and drinks and tempting soups; changing my sweat-sodden sheets. She sat beside me, reading to me from various books which she borrowed from Rashid's aunt: soothing poetic writings which dipped in and out of my fevered consciousness.

But I was worried for her when, after four or five days, she was still here looking after me. Her leave had run out. She should be back in Somalia by now.

'It's O.K. I've rung London. Everyone's very understanding – about you losing the flat and everything. They said I can take unpaid leave for a while if I like.'

She sounded altogether too cheerful about it. Too cheerful.

'You're not keen to go back.'

'Oh, it's not that –'

What could I say? I needed her. I couldn't put upon Rashid's very good aunt or her household to nurse me. I couldn't, in all modesty or friendship, allow the burden of caring for me to fall upon Rashid. But more than that, I needed Elena emotionally. I ached with the misery of my homelessness. Of having nowhere – nowhere at all to belong. At my age! She was home and family to me in this small room. She pattered around me in her jeans and bare feet, nursing me with her girlish bright love.

When I was better – Elena still insisted, for whatever motives of her own, that she couldn't leave me just yet – we were made welcome, more than welcome, down in the main part of the house. I loved Rashid's aunt's house. I loved the atmosphere there of . . . of prayerfulness. The cloistered tranquility, such as one might expect to find in a house of religious retreat. The main *akd* was dimly lit. Its walls were panelled in warm mahogany and there were tapestried cushions on the seats round the edges of the room. Woven friezes and hangings, and red Eastern carpets, covered every surface, and intricately beaded curtains swayed gently in the arched doorways. The women of the house sat quietly there for hours, working at their sewing or their various tasks and occasionally talking in subdued voices. There was an atmosphere of hushed timeless meditation, of smiling openheartedness, of warm vibrant Eastern spirituality. It was the spirit, the underlying spirit of Islam, though it might equally have been of Eastern Orthodoxy or of Buddhism. It was – would have been – the perfect place in which to recoup; to unravel. In which to find, with Rashid, new beginnings.

Or, simply, to accept. With *islam* – with resignation. Peacefully. To be. So that I felt, at times, that same shame I had felt in the presence of Fadwa, Rashid's late wife: shame at my own impatience, my itching to act, to create complexities, to know what on earth would *happen*! Shame at my urge, urge, urgent need –

Perhaps, if Elena had not been with me . . . Or just supposing, I thought sometimes – just supposing that instead of all that had happened in my life, I had been, right from the beginning, a Moslem . . .

Rashid was unhappy with the way the work of the Literacy Centre was going.

'It's not only Haya's classes. There are just so many, many difficulties, *habeebti*. What can we do? Without proper buildings, proper facilities . . . All our materials – everything's in Beirut. Without the necessary people –' He looked at me as he said that, sidelong. Wistfully. But he wouldn't let me get involved, not after the day with Haya. He wouldn't let me too near. 'In July I'll close the Centre. For the summer. Then after that – maybe . . .' He paused. I felt the calm of the house suffusing the panelled room, like incense. 'Maybe – it's just possible I suppose – that things in Beirut will have settled down by the autumn. If not . . .' Again, a long contemplative moment of quiet.

'But Rashid! What are you saying? That from July onwards the Centre will cease to operate? Nothing – absolutely nothing – will be done?'

'*Habeebti*, there *is* nothing we can do for the moment, so why rush around tying ourselves in frustrated knots pretending there is? And if it takes us a year or two to get back to Beirut, or to set up properly elsewhere, what does it matter? The same illiterate people will still be waiting for us –' That teasing twinkle!

'Rashid! But how can you say such a thing – a year or two!'

'To listen to you, *habeebti*, one would think that the centre of our operations was suffering a bout of the hiccups, not a rain of 155 millimetre shells!' We were on our own, his aunt wasn't in the room. He took my chin in his hand. 'Samia, my love, I'm as incapable as you are. Things won't go back to how they were. Not again.' He smiled. His hand moved to touch my neck, my shoulder. To me it was a painful thing, his warm capacity for happiness.

'In July we'll have our holiday together, *habeebti*. 'We'll have all the time in the world.'

I might perhaps have managed it – managed to accept; to wait, patiently, for July. In spite of the milling presence in Damascus of tanks and soldiers ominously on the move, in spite of the news hoardings and excited rumours, I might have found sufficient peace within the walls of Rashid's aunt's house to enable me just to wait. Calmly and quietly. Perhaps. If it weren't for . . .

Elena was through in the little study, on the phone to her friends in Beirut – by the sound of her answers they were all on different extensions, all talking to her at once – bursting with anger at the latest news. The news of the Syrian invasion of Lebanon.

'It's incredible! With full international backing! I know – protecting endangered Christian towns, my foot! – Yes. – Yes, I know. *Ba'raf*. I heard. – What, you mean actually shelling the Palestinian refugee camps? *Ya Allah*! But that's incredible! – It's Black September all over again. Another bloody Jordan! It's unbelievable, the Maronites must be absolutely laughing up their sleeves!'

I went through into the study.

'Elena! Shhhh!' I was terrified for her. With Lebanese people known to be staying in the house, with Elena perhaps already under suspicion, who could be sure the phone wasn't tapped? There had been a spate of arrests already. 'Shhhh! You can't say those things!'

She glanced at me, and said into the phone, 'Yes. Incredible! Yes – Look, I'll have to go now. Ring me again. Let me know what I can do. – Yes. Yes. – *Ma'a salameh*.'

'Elena, you know very well you can't talk like that!'

She shrugged. She knew. But . . . For a few days we were as bad as each other, Elena and I. Not caring who heard. Full of such crying anger. And I wondered at the irony of it: Syrian domination of Lebanon no longer a threat but a virtual reality, and in the name of protecting the Christians! What side, I wondered, would Lina Bashoura be on now?

Elena did her best to tone down what she said on the phone after that. Just a little. For Rashid's aunt's sake if not her own. Her friends were more cautious too, afraid of inadvertently divulging military secrets, knowing full well that the conversation might be overheard. Mariam couldn't come to the phone, Khalida told her. She'd volunteered to join a relief party elsewhere. Khalida couldn't say where.

'Elena,' I said anxiously, 'Oughtn't you to get back to Somalia?' She kept putting off her return – for just a few more days. 'Surely you ought to be doing *something*?'

Then after the middle of June came the news from South Africa of the Soweto riots – the mowing down of black schoolchildren by police bullets. And there was a general anger then, it seemed to me; a widely-shared anger which became the mood of the hot summer of '76. A burning impatient anger.

'Little mother!'

'Yusef, my love!'

'Little mother . . .'

There was nothing strange about him ringing me. He had been doing so regularly, almost daily, since I had been in Damascus. With everything else he had to think about, still he managed, devotedly, to make time. But today . . .

'Yusef, what is it?' Because I knew – I always knew at once with him – when something was wrong.

'Nothing, little mother. You shouldn't worry. Really, truly –' Then all at once, in spite of his resolutions, his misery was welling up in thick hiccupping sobs. He was crying and crying down the phone. 'Latifa, she's gone. Gone. To Junieh, yes. But I don't mean just . . . Little mother, it's finished. Between me and Latifa.' Then there were no more words which were intelligible through such a thickness of weeping.

'Yusef, where are you? Is anyone with you?'

'I'm at home. Sister Nadine sent me. I wasn't any use to anyone on the ward. No use at all!'

'When did Latifa go?'

'Yesterday? I don't know.' My poor Yusef, I could imagine him distraught beyond the means to lift his head.

'Have you eaten?'

'There's no food in the house. It doesn't matter. I took some pills –'

'What pills? How many?'

'Pills? Oh – I don't remember.'

'You should have someone with you.' In that state he would be lying somewhere upstairs, forgetting to protect himself against the shelling . . . !

'What does it matter? I'm finished. – Little mother, I loved them – Latifa and my children. I loved them!'

I was desolated for him.

'I'll go to him,' said Elena, when I told her what had happened. And it was so obvious that someone must go that, for a moment, I almost agreed.

'Yes – No, no, you can't go!' But someone must. In my mind's eye I was already in a car, speeding on my way, back past the columns of refugees heading this way.

'We could both go,' Elena said. 'There's no problem, now the Bekaa Valley's safe.' And I remember thinking, with a surge of genuine relief: well at least, once we're across the Syrian border, she'll be safe from being jailed for her treasonable outspokenness.

Rashid looked from one to the other of us. He was quite appalled. 'So. Two seconds is all the time it takes you to talk yourselves into going. And with such economy of excuses! Now how long will you allow me to talk you out of it?'

'Everyone says how quiet it is on the road.'

'Samia, in less than two weeks now you and I are free to go away on our holiday together.'

'But we'll be back long before then! We'll stay just one or two nights. Two at most, to be back here before the trouble flares up again.'

'*Habeebti*!' Rashid shook his head. With such reproach. But I knew that once we could get Yusef to plunge himself back into his work, the crisis would be over. He would have no energy to spare for himself. And he would have the nurses to pamper him, and sleeken his rumpled tiger fur. If we could just get him, safely, through the next day or two.

We ought to leave as soon as possible, as soon as our bags were packed. 'Elena, if you would kindly –'

Rashid looked at me. With wistful resignation. With sadness.

He cupped my face in his hands.

'Samia, *habeebti*, my *gallivanteuse*. Is there no changing you?'

Our taxi driver, throwing open the door for us, asked, 'You're in a hurry to get to Beirut?'

'Not specially,' I said. I had no intention of encouraging a taxi driver, of all people, into more haste than absolutely necessary.

But it had been a rhetorical question. Nobody, it seemed, asked to go to Beirut without an urgent, compelling reason. He slammed the door shut, leaped into his seat and we were away, at a speed which would have left even Mustafa behind. As Elena and I lurched into each other round corners and bends, I thought one last regretful time of Rashid's aunt's placid house and wondered what new, what crazy repeated madness this was on which we were embarked.

At the Lebanese customs post there were Syrian tanks and armoured cars pulled over on to the rough ground beside the road. Soldiers were to-ing and fro-ing amongst them under the burning June sun, calling and barking orders. There were just two civilian cars in front of us at the barrier. We watched as the driver of the front one was ordered out and made to stand with his hands above his head while a young soldier took him by the collar and frisked him. Two other soldiers covered him with their rifles, ready to fire at his head.

'Maybe –' I felt, all at once, faint-hearted. I suggested tentatively to our driver, '– do you think we should turn round?'

'Turn round!' He swore, a Syrian dialect oath. 'Do you want us suspected of complicity with that pimp? Do you want us shot?' But I thought his eye was as much on his fare as it was on the rifles. He pulled out past the two waiting cars and accelerated up to the barrier, with an imperious blast on his horn. He showed his identity card. Our passports were flicked over by a Syrian army guard. – We were waved casually through. Elena and I stared back at the guard. And laughed. With relief. It was so simple. As the car gathered speed, the breeze blowing in through the open windows ruffled my hair and I had a sudden feeling of exhilaration. Fields and ditches flashed by, shimmering in the noon heat. A row of soldiers, lounging against the side of their tank in the open countryside, smiled and waved to us. It was true, there was peace, perfect peace in the Bekaa Valley.

Near Chtaura we came upon fields full of tanks, dug in near the road and protected from the mountains by earth ramparts, on top of which flocks of gulls were lazily flapping their wings and foraging for worms. Nobody bothered us. Cars passed us going in the opposite direction, but we had our side of the road to ourselves. We climbed up to the pass and a moment later we were looking out across the coastal strip, homewards, towards Beirut and the shining blue of the sea.

'East Beirut?' Our driver shook his head. We had come through innumerable barricades on the way down into Beirut, past the last of the Syrian lines and through the confusing ranks of blockades manned successively by the P.L.A., by Saiqa, by the Mourabitun; by different splinter-groups of the regular Army. He got us through all of them by his same imperious hooting. But crossing the Green Line was apparently something else again. He would have nothing to do with it. Elena's attempts at persuasion made him quite angry. 'What do you think I am? Some idiot son of a ——?' We had to make do with being dropped at Khalida's flat instead, where he took off in noisy aggravation, in search no doubt of a lucrative car-load of evacuees to take back to Damascus.

Khalida was dubious too. She pushed the cuffs of her army jacket up above her elbows and shook her head. 'Even the Museum crossing's closed now. It's like the Berlin Wall. Though – I'll tell you what –' She turned and walked ahead of us into the sitting room, to the phone, her sandals slapping her heels, flap-flap-flap. There was just one Kalashnikov, I noticed, in the hall. 'I'll find out whether UNWRA or the Red Cross are getting through. Mariam knows their people through her refugee work. – Hang on –'

She gestured to me to sit down and began to struggle with the phone, dialling, banging it, shaking it, sitting with her elbows on her thighs and frustratedly scratching her knee through her baggy army trousers. I could hear her parents moving around somewhere, in another room. At last she got through, left a message, tried another number . . .

Elena, leaning patiently over the back of a chair, asked, 'So where is Mariam?'

'You'll never guess!'

'You said on the phone she'd volunteered for some secret relief party.'

'Yes, secreted through two enemy lines! You could give her a call, while you're over at Yusef's. She's helping defend Tal al-Zaatar. – Hello? Hello? Red Cross? Yes, I'll hang on. – Mariam got quite involved there one way and another after she went to visit that kid of yours. Of course, her mother's a Palestinian. – Hello?'

An hour later, thanks to Khalida's most effective efforts on the telephone, we were in a Red Cross van, driving past rank after rank of gun emplacements and across the no man's land once more to East Beirut.

'Idiot! Ass! *Hmara*! Are you out of your mind?'

Yusef was raving at Elena. He was pacing up and down with his fists clenched so hard they jerked at her in angry spasms. His jaw was clenched too so that the bone and sinew stood out like a serrated lower edge to his hollowed cheeks. I was shocked at the sight of him – at what I could see of him by the thin chinks of light which came through the closed shutters. His eyes were black and bruised round about from lack of sleep, the rest of his skin was sickly winter-white and his once so shiny black hair stood out from his head in a dull dry brush. His white shirt was sticking to his ribs in the clammy heat of the afternoon and he looked as skeletal and harrowed as a ghost.

'Are you out of your mind, bringing mother here?' he said. 'With her high blood pressure! Don't you realise the danger to her? You silly little fool! You –'

'Keep your hair on,' Elena said lightly. 'We've only come for a day or two. What's the harm in that?'

Yusef burst into tears. He leaned against the wall, hiding his face in his arms.

I did what I could to comfort him. He was like a child again in my arms, rocking with grief. 'I keep ringing her, little mother – in Junieh. But her mother won't let me talk to her. She just tells me Latifa doesn't ever want to speak to me again. And now they've taken the phone off the hook.' He went on crying, inconsolably. I stroked his poor matted hair. 'I've lost my children. She's taken away my children!'

Elena hovered by the window of his room – his study. She opened the shutters a little to let the breeze shift the stifling air in the room. I warned her to stay well away from the opening.

Yusef, seeing her hovering there, kept looking at her with anger and distress and I wondered if he blamed her partly for Latifa going. Certainly her presence in March hadn't helped.

'Anyway,' Elena said, turning up her nose at his fierce looks, 'I'm famished. I'm going to see about getting us something to eat.' She sounded as priggishly complacent as she used to do at the age of twelve whenever Yusef was carrying on at her in one of his rages.

But it was quite true what he had told me on the phone – there was nothing to eat. Literally nothing. Nothing in the house. We found the old housekeeper huddled in a dark corner of the basement kitchen, muttering prayers or lamentations, I don't know which. She looked very old and alone. She had grown thinner, like Yusef – her double chin was sagging into pendulous flaps of skin.

When I suggested she should go out at once to buy food, she clasped her hands together and shook her head.

'Out? Out? *Im Yusef*, have mercy!' The gaps round her loose-fitting teeth whistled. 'They took a Moslem servant from down the road last week and cut off his ears. Then they put a bayonet through his belly! *Shafaka ya rab*! *Allah* have mercy!' She wailed and rocked, wringing her hands. We found that she had been leaving the shopping entirely to Latifa. She hadn't stepped out of the door for weeks.

Elena and I organised food. We managed to buy tinned meat and packets of noodles from a nearby shop. And a little tin of artichoke hearts – the only vegetable to be had. Then while I was persuading the old housekeeper to cook what we had bought, Elena went back up to the study, to phone

Mariam in Tal al-Zaatar, at the number Khalida had given her.

When I came upstairs ten or fifteen minutes later she was still on the phone, sitting at Yusef's desk and jotting something down on a pad. 'O.K., I'll see what I can do. I'll get back to you.'

'How's Mariam?' I asked her, when she had rung off.

'She's fine. Apparently there's a desperate shortage of supplies at all the medical stations up there. The Red Cross are having trouble getting anything through to them.' She looked uncertainly at her jottings and then glanced across at Yusef who was lying where we had left him, on the black leather sofa. 'Mariam wondered if there was anything I could do . . . She's given me a list.'

Yusef's eyes continued to stare, out of their grey-black pouches, at the ceiling.

'She's been to visit Yacoub. Apparently he's got a skin infection.' Yusef's eyes still did not waver, but I had taken his hand in mine and I felt it twitch. 'They're almost out of ointment for him.'

He said nothing, but I could feel he was very tense. It was something he could never bear – the aftermath of quarrels, the way his fiercely loving loyalties lay torn all ways.

Elena wondered aloud about how some supplies could be got to Tal al-Zaatar. 'I'll go over there in the morning to see Mariam and suss things out,' she said.

Yusef was furious again. 'You'll go straight back to Damascus in the morning, first thing!'

But she put out her tongue at him. 'I'll take some of Yacoub's ointment over with me,' she said, undeterred. She was leaning with her elbows on the back of the sofa and I saw her mark one of the items on her list with a big asterisk.

Once more Yusef shouted at her in a fit of tearful anger. 'It's no good. I can't be bothered with Yacoub, why should I? There are other children, you know, hundreds of them! I can't give all my time – all our precious supplies – to just one.' He started up. 'I have to get back – to the hospital. I can't stay away so long –'

I clung to his hand. 'Yusef!'

'Don't be ridiculous!' Elena pushed him firmly and cheerfully down again into the cushions.

He was fit for nothing, he turned his face down into the cushions and sobbed. All over again we comforted him, I was hugging him and consoling him as best I could. My poor loving Yusef – always prey to such a furore of emotions; battling now with his anger and his loyalty to Latifa. He drifted, for a few minutes, into an exhausted doze.

The end of the day was still sticky hot and Elena sat beside him brushing away the flies which were attracted by his sweat and tears. He opened his eyes and stared out of the window, murmuring something which I didn't catch.

'What was that?'

Yusef didn't answer me, but Elena's smile was impish. 'There's a different ointment he wants to try – on Yacoub.' She began to flick the flies off him with a swatting motion, off his hair, his chest, his shoulder, his cheek. 'You soft old thing!' Backwards and forwards, flies or no flies, she kept playfully swatting and slapping him until he had to draw his knees up to his chest and raise his arms to defend himself. It was like one of the mock fights they used to have as children, when they were playing Elena's favourite invented game of Turks and Arabs. 'You great soft thing!'

After we had eaten an early meal, we persuaded Yusef into the safety of his basement bed. He slept for almost fifteen hours, right through the night-time racket of machine-guns and shell bursts: the traditional lethal fireworks from the same old familiar fronts. He slept until the sun was high and hot again in a smoky mustard sky.

In the morning we arranged that Elena and I would set off back to Damascus after an early lunch. Meanwhile, Yusef grudgingly agreed to lend her his car to drive to Tal al-Zaatar.

'If you must,' he said, shrugging. His mind was already back at the hospital, I think – on the ward. He was striding about, looking so much better after his long sleep – intent, preoccupied. Well enough for us to agree to leave him. 'Little mother . . .' He came impulsively to kiss my forehead.

Elena said, 'About Mariam's list of drugs and things –'

He was reluctant to talk about it. 'I don't know about that

– you'll have to come up to the hospital –' He wouldn't commit himself. 'Be quick, though, if you're coming,' he said impatiently. 'I have to go.'

But I was touched by the way that, a moment later, he was holding her back, 'Look, about that ointment . . .' He seemed excited, he was waving a bit of paper around, on which he was writing some notes for her to take to the nursing station at Tal al-Zaatar, and at the same time he was getting her to repeat the instructions he was giving her, eagerly concerned (in spite of his protests to the contrary) about the care of his much loved Yacoub.

Elena turned to me. 'Are you coming too?'

'You go. I'll stay and do some shopping, to make sure there's some food in the house before we leave.'

'O.K., if you like.'

And so I let her go. She was twenty-four. It was something I had to struggle constantly to do: to keep myself from forcing my anxious fears on my children.

'Don't worry,' she said, throwing her arms around me in her cheerful affectionate way. 'I'll be back by lunchtime.'

I scoured the depleted shelves of the neighbourhood shops and brought back what little food the siege conditions in Beirut allowed – some rice, some beans and oil; half a kilo of small green unripe figs. I talked to the old housekeeper sternly. Yusef could eat at the hospital, but if she didn't go out she would starve.

She rolled one of the small green figs wonderingly between her fingers. She didn't believe me. God would provide.

I had lunch ready for Elena, on the table. Just before half past twelve she rang me.

'Where are you?'

'At Tal al-Zaatar. Look, I'll be a bit late. I had to go through the Kata'ib lines to get in here and they pinched all the stuff I'd brought, and –'

'What, you mean all your medical supplies?'

'Yes, I told them they were urgently needed – for people who are seriously ill! – but they didn't give a damn. I was stopped by this kid in uniform, with a baby moustache. He said there was a blockade and I couldn't just roll in and out with whatever I liked. The sergeant came over and ordered him to search the car and pile everything up at the side of the road. Then they just carried it all off. I was livid!'

'But they let you in.'

'They weren't going to – I had to make a fuss about having come to pick up some patients to take to hospital. Finally they did let me through, but the trouble is, I've now got to scout round finding myself some patients before they'll let me out again. I'm just waiting for Mariam to call back from one of the casualty stations to let me know if there's anyone there that I could take.'

'And Yacoub's ointment –'

'It was in my shoulder bag. They didn't search that!' I could hear the glee in her voice. 'You can tell Yusef it's already been safely delivered and Yacoub's fine. I saw him. The infected area's very small – it should clear up in no time.'

'Thank goodness for that at least.'

'But honestly, the state of things here! It makes me so angry! Just imagine – they're not letting any food through and the electricity and water are both cut off. It's chaotic. I'm just giving a hand at the moment helping to get a system going for controlling what food stocks there are, so the food can be rationed out evenly – in case the blockade continues. There's nobody else here who's ever had experience of doing that on a large enough scale, so Mariam volunteered me for the job as soon as I appeared! There are anything up to twenty thousand mouths to feed in the camp. Maybe more.'

'But listen, Elena, if Mariam can't find you any patients quickly enough, couldn't you just take anybody who wants to leave? Put bandages round their heads or something?'

'Don't worry, there won't be any problem. I'll be as quick as I can.'

I don't know why I sat by the phone that afternoon waiting to hear from her, rather than by the window looking out for her to arrive. I sat. Nothing in me moved – not a muscle.

I sat. I waited. She didn't ring again.

Evening came and it grew dark. I could no longer make out my hands where they rested on my lap. All over Beirut the sound of machine-guns started up in earnest, barking into life

– the nightly cacophony. I saw the trail of a rocket blazing up into the sky. She wouldn't come now. She wouldn't get through the Phalangist lines now.

I rang Yusef, at the hospital.

'I thought you'd gone!' he said. 'Back to Damascus! I've been in theatre all afternoon, I'd no idea . . . Hang on, I'll borrow someone's car and come straight over.'

I went to the window and looked out. Suddenly from quite close at hand, so close that it made my heart lurch with fright, there came the most enormous screaming whoosh, like a jet plane going over, barely skimming the roof tops. Then another and another. A dazzle of flashing brilliance was lighting up the sky at the top of the slopes of al-Ashrafiyah, not more than three or four hundred metres away. I'd seen nothing like it before: a whole host of rockets, three separate groups of them, flaring forth in rapid blazing sequence. Then the silence . . . After a few moments I heard them land, over there towards the south-east, where the moon had just risen large and yellow over the roof tops. – Over in that direction, about three kilometres away, lay Tal al-Zaatar. There was the most terrific crash, boom, boom, boom, making the air reverberate, even at this distance. Presently I saw a bright orange glow over the hill and thick black smoke belched across the face of the moon.

Yusef pulled up in the road outside, driving a car I hadn't seen before. He leaped out and up the steps into the house. Then he came into the room where I was and we stood beside one another in the window. Watching. Yusef's fists were pressed tightly together. He blamed himself, I think, for Elena going there. We both blamed ourselves.

That night the Phalangists launched a massive attack on Tal al-Zaatar. The din went on all through the night, the return shells and rockets from Tal al-Zaatar's limited husbanded supply whacking at intervals into the buildings of al-Ashrafiyah, just up the slope from us, near where the missile launchers were placed. In the morning – Yusef had already long since returned to the hospital – the news came that the attackers had tightened the blockade, all the phone lines to Tal al-Zaatar were now cut and there was no question of anyone getting in or out. Even the Red Cross were turned back when they wanted to evacuate the wounded. Tal al-Zaatar was completely sealed off.

I waited, hoping.

There was no question of going back to Damascus. I had to be at hand.

All that day the shelling continued. In the early stages of the war, even as late as March when we were trapped at Rashid's house, there had always been a relative daytime lull, a rise and fall, a rhythm to the fighting which somehow corresponded – comfortingly, it seemed to me in retrospect – to the patterns of normality. But today there was just this relentless exhausting summer madness, so that within a few hours I had already forgotten that I'd had any other life but this in the interval since last October. And it was not only the battle of Tal al-Zaatar which raged all day. All over the city, shells were lobbed about in endless profusion, courtesy of the outside world, killing people randomly, at every moment.

I sat in Yusef's study at his desk, doing nothing; in the end thinking of nothing. Fear for my own safety was unsustainable I found, when the shelling was so dispersed and unpredictable. Emotion was unsustainable. I sat, and there was nothing beyond this moment, nothing which could be reliably anticipated. There was no perspective. No July. I sat with my head resting on the desk top, on my arms, while my mind jumbled randomly through the heat and stickiness of the day, dipping in and out of a listless sleep.

Footsteps echoed in the corridor of the empty house. Echoed in my memory. The door opened. I jerked my head up. 'Rashid?'

It was the old housekeeper.

'*Im Yusef*, whatever's the matter?' She came hurrying across to me and bent her wrinkled face over mine. 'You're as white as a sheet.'

'Perhaps – would you help me? – I think I ought to lie down. – If you'd kindly fetch me some brandy.'

My head felt cold, very cold, right inside, although my brow was damp with a hot sweat. But the brandy revived me. I felt a little better. I must, I suppose, have been suffering from shock.

I tried, for perhaps the third or fourth time, to get through to Tal al-Zaatar on the phone; knowing of course that the line was dead. I asked the operator what the chances were of it being reconnected.

'It's nothing to do with us, *ayni*. Ask the Kata'ib.'
'I have to get in touch with my daughter.'
'Sorry, love. Talk to the Kata'ib. Perhaps for you they'll tie the lines together again. They won't listen to me!' Then, after a pause, 'Your daughter, did you say?'
'Yes.'
He whistled with sympathy. 'Very sorry, *ayni*.'

I went out. I walked round the corner and up the avenue, under the shade of the eucalyptus trees, and over the brow of the rise, to where I could see Tal al-Zaatar, perched on its hill top across the river valley. It was a-dazzle in the afternoon sun. Sunlight glared off its white surfaces and shimmering yellow fires flickered here and there, tonguing their flames into the white-hot sky where plumes of smoke rose, high above the mountains, into the upper atmosphere.

There was another screeching whizz of sound from nearby and, a few seconds later, yet another explosion came booming across the valley. Another bright flare and belch of smoke started out of the burning midst of the camp. I put on my sunglasses against the general summer glare, and tried to make out buildings, landmarks . . . But my vision was blurred. There was a prickling of heat behind my eyes. I couldn't quite see . . . I remembered that I was on my last jar of pills – my pills to keep my blood pressure within bounds. I must not forget to ask Yusef to get me some more.

No, it was no use, I couldn't make out any details so far away. Next time I must be sure to bring Yusef's binoculars with me.

Back at the house I tried the phone again. This time I rang Rashid's aunt's number, in Damascus.

It was Rashid himself who answered.

'*Habeebti!*'

I cried. I couldn't help it. I cried and cried.

It was late afternoon and Yusef had just arrived back from the hospital.

'Little mother!' I hadn't seen him for almost two days. 'I've just come to see how you are and to kip down for a couple of hours while there's a lull.'

'A couple of hours!' He looked exhausted again. Frenetic. Pacing about. 'But when do you plan to sleep?'

He shook his head. 'Listen, little mother, I can't just walk out leaving critically injured children waiting in casualty – children who'll very likely be dead by the time I get back. What do you want me to do? Say to their parents: "Tough. I'm off to get my beauty sleep. See you in a while."?'

'But Yusef, you must sleep.'

'I'll maybe manage to snatch another hour or two later on tonight.' But his eyes were dull. He tumbled into a chair, looking flaked out. He knew – he knew as well as I did that he couldn't do his best if he treated his body with such erratic disregard. He was undoing the top button of his shirt, fumbling. His surgeon's hand trembled with tiredness.

And so I persuaded him into a routine of coming home at midday to eat and sleep, before the nightly rush of casualties. But I couldn't persuade him to slow down any more than that. He was full of the tension of his work – still! After more than a year of almost continuous war! And he was constantly on the phone to Junieh. Sometimes – just sometimes he managed to speak to Latifa. 'Little mother, she loves me, I could hear it in her voice! –' He wore me out with his wild hopeful excitement; then, the next time, with his lugubrious despair; with his constant yo-yo expectations as to whether she would eventually come back to him. With his demanding demonstrative love, – 'little mother! – ' leaning his tired head against me, sucking me into the whirlpool of his passions. Quickening my heart beat, my breathing. Raising my blood pressure. 'Little mother, it was my job to make the decision on casualty last night, which patients we could treat and which ones we would have to leave to die. There was a mother of young children – with her intestines ripped apart. We could have saved her – easily – with a lot of time and a lot of intensive nursing. But it was her or ten others. I gave her morphine and she spent three hours fighting not to die. I watched her, little mother. I watched her and let her die!'

He hid his face against me with the shame.

I fell into my own routine of shopping while Yusef was asleep – it meant a daily forage round the nearby shops to snatch up whatever scarce food had found its way through the various battle lines blockading Beirut – a routine of helping the old housekeeper to decide what plain dish to prepare, then of helping her to cook it. She shook her head and mumbled imprecations and words of misgiving over the little gas picnic stove, on which we were forced to cook. The main electricity generating station had been put out of action by an exploding shell on about my second day back in Beirut, and while the bombardment of that area continued day and night there was no way the damage could be repaired. We would just have to manage, like everyone else. But at each attempt to set the gas flame at the right height, or to perch the pan on its flimsy stand, the housekeeper sat down with a sigh and fanned her face with a weary flopping hand.

I left her to it, I wouldn't be drawn into taking over that job too, even though it meant the dinner would yet again be burned or only partly cooked. I had enough to do. Poor Latifa, no wonder she fled two such impossibly draining house companions. I took the plastic bottles and went out into the hot wind and the swirling biting dust, the dust of countless explosions, to fetch water. Because, of course, without electricity there were no pumps and without pumps . . .

The queue snaked its way from the standpipe in the street and I joined it for perhaps the fourth wearying time today. We needed water yet again for drinking, for washing, for washing up, for flushing the toilet – every drop of water we used had to be fetched in buckets and plastic containers, which of course were so heavy for me to carry that I had to bring home just a little at a time and trudge back to queue again and again. I didn't mind in a way – it was a purposeful enough thing to do – except that my head ached from the din of the cannons just over the rise. Ached and ached out there in the hot sun.

Sometimes in the morning I went to help on the ward, doing little things – fetching bed-pans, talking to the children. I was a grey grandmotherly figure in my son's domain, amongst his band of maimed saddened children.

I could see across to Tal al-Zaatar from parts of the ward. Perhaps I should have stayed away. It must have taken its toll on me, to watch the shells falling and bursting there, day after day, like an explosive rain. Every day the skyline altered, sometimes in a moment, before my eyes. Buildings vanished, and looking through Yusef's binoculars, from the visitors' waiting room at the end of the ward, I could see that more and more concrete structures had appeared behind the crumbling periphery. Existing walls had been reinforced and openings plugged, until Tal al-Zaatar was a gaunt fortress. Once, standing at the window, I counted over a hundred shells falling – in perhaps five or ten minutes. And I kept thinking: that one – maybe that one . . . The father of one of the children, waiting there, told me he had heard on the radio that three thousand shells had fallen on the camp, earlier in the day, in the space of three hours.

By the time a fortnight had passed the skyline was levelled and rounded and a thousand people were reported to have died in Tal al-Zaatar.

Then one day, miraculously, a letter came. From Elena! It was delivered by hand, by a ragged boy of perhaps about thirteen or fourteen, who accepted a note or two from my purse, muttered his thanks in what sounded like Armenian, and was gone – before I had thought to ask him any questions.

I took it through to the drawing room, opening the envelope as I went.

Tal al-Zaatar,
July 6th

'Dear Mother,

'I don't know whether this letter will reach you, but

anyway – I'll give it to one of the Armenian fruit-sellers who sometimes manage to creep in and out of the camp at night, and I'll hope for the best. They tell us they get in through the surrounding orchards, though how they manage it I don't know. If it weren't for them, I doubt if we'd be able to hold out much longer. Food stocks are getting pretty low.

'What can I say? I'm O.K. – I expect you gathered, when I didn't turn up, that I'd stayed on here for a bit longer to help sort things out. It's scarey with all the shelling, but we keep to the basements most of the time and there's so much rubble lying up above us that we reckon we're probably safe in our basement, even from a direct hit. All the smoke gets to you sometimes when you have to go above ground to collect firewood from the rubble, or empty the toilet-buckets or anything. Some nurses have been round from the casualty clinic in the next basement, teaching everybody how to clear their lungs.

'Of course the noise is *phenomenal*! The basement vibrates to the low-frequency rumble of the shelling and you get so you'd do anything to stop your head vibrating with it. The stink's pretty awful down here too – like sick and pus mixed with old socks! We're very overcrowded. At least it's not completely dark, we've got enough candles to keep one burning all the time and somehow most people seem to manage to keep a sense of humour. I'm in with Mariam's unit – she and I share her sleeping roll. We're all pretty excited at the moment because, as I expect you know, there's a relief column fighting its way through, over the hills, so we shouldn't be cut off for much longer now.

'The other day the Kata'ib made it right to the gates of the camp, but it was all hands to the guns and we managed to drive them back. We were so pleased we practically had a party – almost half a bottle of beer each! We've got some terrific fighters in the camp (Mariam included!), some absolutely A1 professional marksmen. Morale's amazingly high, considering. It's just when I have to recalculate the food allocation each day according to how many people in our adminstrative section have been killed – I must say that gets to me. And the same when you go up above to help in a burial party and there are faces you know – like last night there was a boy from our unit whom I'd been speaking to not long since.

'Today I helped a man who was scrabbling with his bare hands in the rubble, trying to dig out his wife and his mother. We found them both alive – just – but it was pretty awful picking out the bits of debris where their legs were badly mashed up. There's no morphine or anything left.

'Tell Yusef that Yacoub's skin grafts have completely healed. The infection's cleared up and he's amazingly well. His family's homeless again, needless to say, but we've squeezed them into a corner of our basement, next to Mariam and me. They're ever so grateful, they shared their last bag of sweets with us yesterday. Yacoub's bouncing on us at this very moment. Hence the messy writing! He keeps us sane with his absolutely lunatic jokes. Crazy boy, he's a smasher. All the children are. It makes it human having so many families in with us. In spite of the occasional bedlam!

'I'm O.K., really I am. Try not to worry. I seem to be able to take it better than a lot of people. It's partly having Mariam here. I'd be really lonely without her. She keeps calm and cheerful whatever. The other day when I felt low she bought an egg for me off a woman in a bunker not far from here who's still got two hens! Mariam paid the earth for it, I know. We boiled it and she insisted I should have it. She only accepted a spoonful, just to taste. It was out of this world! *Lazeez!*

'Mariam's got the runs at the moment, which sends her bolting for the bucket every five seconds, poor girl. She looks awful! She's not the only one either. There's practically an epidemic of it.

'We'll be all right when the relief column gets here and opens up our supply lines again for food and medicines – and arms of course. Most of the families will probably be evacuated. I'll be all right. Really I will!

'I love you. xxx Lenni xxx'

* * *

Then, just a few days later, Henry rang me.

It was so unexpected that for perhaps half a minute I couldn't think who he was. Henry . . . ?

'I thought I'd let you know, I'm flying out to Nicosia tomorrow. Actually, we're all staying with Mum and Dad at the moment, Karen and the kids as well, while we've got the decorators in . . . By the way, I've resigned as treasurer.'

'Treasurer?'

'Of our group. Of the fund raising for the war effort.'

Najib's son, of course! I recognized his voice now. It was the sort of voice which burst at me down the telephone, seeming almost to bump my ear when he spoke louder to make me understand what he was trying to say: '– It's just that it mightn't seem quite ethical if I carried on.'

'Ethical?' Why was he ringing? What was all this to me?

'My company's got the contract for buying and shipping the arms, you see – the arms paid for by the campaign – French SS11 missiles, recoilless rifles – you know the sort of thing. That's why I'm flying to Nicosia actually – to see someone about getting hold of some of those ground-to-ground missiles – the sort the Leftists are using as well. Perhaps you've seen them, have you? Multiple tubes of high explosive, a couple of yards long – they make a terrific fireworks when they go off.'

I felt sick. I should put the phone down.

'Henry, perhaps you don't realise, those missiles of yours are being used against Tal al-Zaatar – where Elena is.'

'Look, Aunt Samia, I'm terribly sorry about Elena. I . . .' His voice was full of friendly clumsy sympathy. '– That's why I'm ringing actually. You see, well now that I've got contacts with people at the front in Beirut, I thought . . . I thought I might be able to arrange for her to get safe conduct out of Tal al-Zaatar. When I get to Nicosia I could get someone to put in a special word . . .'

'Henry, I don't think you understand. Everybody's tried – the government, everybody – tried to evacuate the civilians there. Even the Red Cross has failed two or three times to get through to help the wounded. Even though both sides had agreed to let them pass.'

'Maybe the British Foreign Office could help in Elena's case.'

I could hardly hold the receiver. Like his voice, it was bumping against my ear.

'Aunt Samia, please don't misunderstand.' He sounded hurt. *He* sounded hurt! 'Only with the Soviets getting their oar into Lebanon, through Syria and the P.L.A. and so on – it's like Kissinger says –' He started to tell me – I don't know what. I wondered what he thought this war was about.

'Look, Aunt Samia, I'll do my very best to get Elena out.'
'And Mariam?'
'Pardon?'
'Elena's friend Mariam.'
'I'll do what I can.'
'And Yacoub? And Yacoub's family? And –'

He gave a braying laugh. 'I don't know that I can quite do all that! But I'll do what I can. – Hello? Aunt Samia? Are you there? Hello?'

But I had dropped the phone and was rushing over to the basin in the corner of Yusef's study. I was sick, then sick again. The receiver had toppled over the edge of the desk. I watched it spinning on the end of its coiled cord. – 'Hello? hello?' – The cord was wringing one way, then spinning back and wringing the other way, wring, wring, wring. – 'Hello? hello?' – Henry's strangled voice. Wring, wring, wring.

I was sick again. And sick. And sick, until there was nothing left in me to come up. And sick. And sick.

By the end of July the heat in Beirut was fierce, with a stifling humidity which made my unwashed sweat itch and brought me out in rashes down my sides and under my breasts. Without adequate water for washing, my bright buttercup-yellow kaftan was streaked and dulled with dirt and wear. I scratched my underarms again. I had already put on perfume four – five? – times today to keep the smells of my body at bay. It was all too much – the squalor everywhere, the sweltering heat, the small lumpy helpings of noodles day after day, the boiling of every drop of water we drank, the bombing, the despair – It made me so old! So tremulous and old. As if I had aged by half a lifetime since July began. The pail quaked when I picked it up in the kitchen entry. My right foot faltered on the sill. I was all at once of the same ilk as the old housekeeper, lurking along next to the emotionally protective walls of the kitchen yard, taking care that when my vision blurred I wouldn't stumble. I made my way slowly down the road to join the sullen queue at the tap and half-filled my pail with the erratic reluctant flow. The weight of the pail reminded me that I would have to ask Yusef to carry our rubbish bin out to the road later today.

July – endlessly passing.

'*Habeebti*, it's all right,' Rashid said on the phone, 'we'll have our holiday when we can, that's all. Just so long as you're safe and sound.' The dearness and nearness of his voice! 'Samia, my *habeebti*!'

But I was a scoured-faced worn *habeebti* now, sitting around in lank and greasy clothes. A hopeless *habeebti*, with all warmth erased. As marble-hard as a tomb amidst so much death.

Five hundred people – old men, women, children – were trapped in their basement shelter on the perimeter of Tal al-Zaatar. A building had collapsed on top of them. So far rescue had been impossible because of the intensity of the shelling. I listened to the radio news bulletins and to the continuous pounding din of the cannons just over the rise. The noise went on without let-up into the night and through the following day. After two days, 'Voice of Palestine' radio reported that the cries of the four hundred survivors could still be heard from under the rubble. After three days, one hundred and fifty of the bodies had been recovered. There were no more cries.

I didn't know which basement shelter it had been.

My ears imploded with the most painful bang, glass tinkled and crashed all over the house and I watched the front of the house diagonally opposite sway and collapse in a cloud of dust.

For an hour or more the area round about us had been

coming under continuous shell-fire from Tal al-Zaatar. It was something which didn't happen very often any more. I got the impression that the few remaining shells there were being used only for special crises. The intention was presumably, as always, to disable the cannons and missile-launchers just over the rise. But many of the shells were badly over-reaching their target this time. Houses all along this side of the ridge were being hit. I fled to my own small bed-corner of the basement.

Then just as suddenly as it had begun, the bombardment stopped.

Five minutes. Ten. Fifteen. My lungs began to expand with relief. Twenty minutes. I began to feel safe.

And anxious. Why the silence? For over a week, people had been saying that Tal al-Zaatar couldn't be expected to hold out much longer – a day or two more now, at most. The Palestinians were losing the war. They and the Progressive forces had been beaten back on several fronts in the mountains. The relief column, headed round through the hills towards Tal al-Zaatar, stood very little chance now of getting through. We heard that people were beginning to die in the camp from starvation and from dysentery. From diseases contracted by drinking sewage-polluted well water. From infected wounds and gangrene.

So this sudden battering assault had been it, I thought: the final desperado chucking of the remaining shells; and now . . .

Thirty minutes. Then, boom, the house shook with the crash of a piece of furniture falling over somewhere in the upper storeys. My head was split, boom, boom. Split between fright and hope.

At the beginning of August some fugitives, diseased and dying, fled Tal al-Zaatar and managed – some of them – to evade the Phalangists and cross to hospital in West Beirut. Well, if it was possible, why didn't Elena steal away somehow? Just run. Run!!!

We had no news of her. Nothing.

My pills, to control my blood pressure, had finally run out.

Yusef was a-jitter with anxiety for me.

'Why didn't you tell me sooner? We're completely out of them at the hospital! Goodness knows where we'll be able to get any.'

'It didn't seem important – compared to everything else.'

I had given him just a few days warning – not enough apparently. The hospital pharmacy simply wasn't getting supplies of the usual range of drugs along with the emergency shipments. Yusef had one of the hospital administrators ringing round half Beirut for me, trying to find some remaining cache, so that I felt terribly ashamed, to be causing so much trouble; when they had other people to deal with, in a much more critical state. In the end a reluctant pharmacist was persuaded to go and search in his boarded-up, bomb-damaged shop and a little bottle appeared in Yusef's office one morning when I was there, with a (no doubt exorbitant) bill.

But by then I had already been without my pills for a week. Over a week. Yusef measured my blood pressure – yet again. And wouldn't tell me the reading.

'Little mother, you should be in a bed here in hospital – for observation.' Except that the hospital at the moment, with its crush of casualties, was no place for someone with high blood pressure.

'Where do you want to put me?' I asked him. 'Head to toe on a mattress with one of the wounded?'

'Little mother, this won't do. It won't do at all.' He was looking out through the cracked window of his office, on to the ward, shaking his head – over me, or over the children – I don't know which. He ran his fingers upwards through his hair in exasperated frustration.

The ward was like the impromptu field hospital I had once seen set up in a crowded bus station in Gaza, packed with people in all attitudes of lying, sitting, walking, waiting, rushing. A humane desperate shambles. There were children vomiting, crying, curled in the foetal position, obsessively rocking to and fro, back and forth. Some were on mattresses in the corridors, or on mats under other beds. Some were on life-saving respirators but there were not enough – not nearly enough – nurses to keep a constant continuous watch on each critical dial. A jumble of miscellaneous parents and helpers did what they could. There was a constant hectic flurry among the nurses; a quick swish of an obscuring curtain round a bed as they attended frantically to an emergency bleep; a constant hauling off of soiled bed linen. Some of the children were roaming round, too ill to smile, looking lost and shocked. One boy was raptly spoon-feeding dinner to a smaller child with whom he shared a bed, end to end. In a corner of the ward near to us was a heap of rubble and dust where a ceiling had fallen in under the impact of an explosion during the previous night. The beds were pulled out higgeldy-piggeldy around it and a fine white mask of dust had formed on the face of one child who lay motionless, with vacant eyes.

'Little mother.' Yusef held me to him with my wrists against his flushed cheeks, shaking his head. 'Little mother . . .'

I thought of my private room in Dr Khouri's hospital at the end of October – the gentle quiet stillness. I could hear again the intermittent squeak of foorsteps across the expanse of gleaming floor; the soft rustle of starch. I fancied I could smell the flowers and the clinical cleanliness and see the sunshine sparkling off the chrome trolleys. There was my cut-glass water jug, my box of embossed paper handkerchiefs, the vermillion butterfly on the window ledge.

Back in October there had been such a thing as professional excellence, there had been my work to think about – and service taxis – and a full bottle of *araq*. There had been a radio series, and people who were not dead or gone or too isolated even to think of producing it.

There had been Dr Khouri saying, 'You will get over it almost completely.' Almost. You will not work again.

I went home. The hospital ward was heart-rending, but I had no capacity to help there any more. No coherent ability left, after I got back to the house, to think of fetching water. I went to bed. I lay very still.

Memories.

It was the anniversary of my mother's death and I was

delirious, I think, with heat and poor health, with thirst and lack of food – it was as if I were back in my mother's room, watching her die. Today the wind was off Tal al-Zaatar bringing with it, quite distinctly, the reek of decomposing bodies, rotting in the sun. I could smell again my mother's putrefying lungs.

She died on the most suffocatingly humid day of the Beirut summer, that summer of 1958, the summer of the civil riots, when I was making last-minute plans to cart the family through the tense streets to our new home in a more 'Arab' quarter; the summer when Elena had sat inscrutably on her bale of cloth, in the middle of the gun fight in the *suks*.

The windows of the sickroom were all open, but still the stench of death was insufferable, belching out of her lungs as she lay, railing accusingly in her most proud and cultured classical Arabic against all the excesses of that summer.

'Move? Move house? Where to?' She could be scornful – rancorous in her old age. She had never understood why her followers had drifted away in recent years, breaking up her venerable literary circle, rallying instead to the banner of Nasser – the new, the modern champion of Arabism. She could not tolerate any political philosophy which made it expedient to pass over the great literatures of France, of England, of Russia, as if they were an irrelevance. To her it was literary suicide, Arab-national suicide, to ignore such a wealth of sources.

She railed at me on her deathbed, with her seemingly mad extravagance. 'Move? Move house? Where to? You can't escape it, European literature is in the turn of your tongue and the surface-texture of your retina. You can't choose that it should be otherwise.' She was given to these (to me, painful) flights of literary metaphor. 'You can't choose.'

Then her cheeks sank back again into their hollows and her cold stiff fingers scraped around on the covers, searching, until I gave her my hand to hold. To grip, fearfully, as a child does.

Truly a little mad. Or deluded at least. A little deluded to suppose that through literacy one might create that great synthesis in the Arab world, the final embracing quintessential Arabness . . .

Literacy? Who am I talking about? Which generation? Which civil war? Truly a little delirious.

There was a bump. Little Elena had crept in earlier to my mother's room and had been sitting, quietly forgotten, on top of a pile of cushions which she had heaped up for herself in the window corner. Now, with her arms pressed and squeezed tightly across her eyes, she rolled off her perch and behind the curtain in a small contorted heap. Dust from the curtain's decaying fabric flew in a cloud against the light. Elena had always squirmed and shrunk away in my mother's presence. She felt, I think, in the way that children sense these things, that all this vaunted disillusion somehow reflected on her. I picked her up and led her out for one of the willing servants to take care of, in the kitchen.

My mother lay that afternoon looking strange and wild as the sunlight filtered through her curtained bed, casting angular shadows from her nose and cheek-bones across her livid face. She appeared to be sinking, but then she would toss her head and rail again, feebly but angrily, against her illness. 'I won't see Dr Khouri, I won't see him!' She clawed again, in fear, at my hand. 'He'll take away my power!'

He had been her doctor as well of course. He had looked after her while she was dying, bowing over her and gently laying on his hands, performing his elegant, tenderly thoughtful rites, just as he did much later, after my first stroke, for me. At the time my mother said it, I thought it an absurd thing to say of such a mild and quietly respectful man. But I understood now how she had felt about what she called her power, and about Dr Khouri's gentle capacity to tell her, quite simply, that it was gone. – You will not work again. She would never be queen of Araby; there was no Araby.

Then a man in exceptionally evil-smelling clothes came to the door. His face was covered in red-purple boils and the whites of his eyes were a bright liverish yellow. He held out a dirty wad of paper and blurted at me that he wanted fifty Lebanese pounds. I would have given him a hundred, two hundred. I could see Elena's handwriting on the paper, among the smudges.

'Please, wait a minute,' I said, as he was edging away with his money. 'Could you take a message back to Tal al-Zaatar for me?'

He looked aghast. And fled. One of his feet dragged behind him, bumping against the edges of the paving slabs in his hurry.

9th August 76

'Dear Mother,

'I've been talking to you in my head all the time. Non-stop, for days past. I thought if I wrote you this letter, at least I could imagine that maybe you might get to read it. I can't keep back the tears, Mama. I've lost Mariam.

'One of our last candles is alight, over at the opposite side where a woman called Ghada is trying to rebandage her daughter's arm, and I can just about see to write. I'm sitting on Mariam's rolled sleeping mat with my back against the wall. The floor's crammed with people.

'I'll have to move Yacoub soon so I can get up – one of my legs has gone to sleep – but it hurts him when I shift his head. He's lying with his head in the crook of my knee as usual. He came over to me the other day when his mother had stopped noticing him and curled up against me. She's been in a high fever for a few days now. I don't know if Yacoub realises she's dying. He hardly moves. He just lies quietly hour after hour with his lips all cracked and splitting and his tongue shrivelled to a hard lump. He's just dehydrated, that's all – through diarrhoea. It's easily treated, if you can get hold of some water. In the Somali camps we just keep giving the children small amounts of water with a spot of sugar and salt. They're right as rain in a few days.

'There's just one well now that's any use, across a field down towards the Kata'ib lines. I expect it'll be dark enough any minute now for them to start the relay of people creeping down there. If there's any for our basement tonight, apart from what's needed to cook the lentils, I'll give him some. If we can both just moisten our mouths the dryness won't be so painful. Yacoub's skin grafts are absolutely and completely healed! All he needs is water.

'I keep Mariam's knitting tucked round him, like a blanket. It's sweltering in here, but he gets shivery sometimes. Mariam was meaning it to be a vest for him, but it's a bit on the large side! He kept his monkey eye on her all the time she was making it, checking she'd got each hole the right size by stuffing his fingers into it. They had great discussions about it, him and Mariam. By now though you could practically get his poor little sunken chest through one of the holes, he's got so thin. His shoulders and elbows are sticking through at this very moment! Mariam would be glad he's got it. My Mariam.

'A couple of the men are just beginning to carry today's dead over to the bottom of the stair well. I'll get up and help in a minute, when I can get my leg to move! I can tell whose body that is they're struggling with now by the shape of her shadow against the candlelight. It's the fat woman, nick-named Baboushka, who used to keep the children amused with games and things all day, before they all got too ill to want to do anything.

'Everybody's beginning to move about now – those who can – gathering their things off the floor. We used to swill the place down once a day with a bucket of water – (water!!) – but now someone just scrapes the worst of the vomit and stuff off with a shovel and we hope for the best. Then after that's done and the dead have been taken away, we fetch any wood from the rubble that's not already burned to a cinder and we cook up the day's food ration – one saucepanful of lentils – here in the middle of the room. The smoke seems to clear the air a bit – it funnels its way up the stair well – and for a while after that it doesn't smell quite so bad.

'There's a woman over there, sitting with her knees drawn up and her toes turned in, shrieking at the women who are trying to prise her child's body off her. The little girl's gone stiff in just the position she was in when she died this morning, moulded to her mother, behind her knees. I'll go over in a second and persuade her to bring the child upstairs herself and hand her over at the grave. That's usually the best way, I find. Provided you can be sure she won't start wailing up there and draw –

'Draw fire, I was going to say. But suddenly I felt the runs coming on urgently and I had to rush off up to the shit trench. After it was over I felt so weak and completely hollowed out inside that I just had to lie down somewhere. Anywhere. I felt absolutely gutted. I came over here, where there's a sort of bomb shelter of rubble and I lay down – God knows on what. – It ponged a bit. But I just felt so sick and parched and revolting, I didn't care about anything.

'There are a lot of people creeping about up here now. The starlight's a bit bright for comfort again tonight. It generally is. And the explosions pick out people's silhouettes clear as clear. They always step up the artillery bombardment at this time of night when they know everyone's out. There's the massive crash of the air thudding against me each time a shell explodes anywhere near, and in between times I can hear them quietly reciting from the Koran over where we heap the corpses into the shell holes, just beyond the road.

'Mariam used to leap about like a mad thing as soon as we came up here each night. It was such bliss after being cramped in a squash of people for hours on end.

'Mama, I don't know how to tell you about Mariam.

'She cut her hand on a knife, opening one of the flour sacks. Nothing special. But after a few days it began to ooze pus and get hot. Then her whole arm swelled up. We were both frightened. She went very hot. Then her eyes glazed and she spent three days and nights writhing beside me on the mat in a puddle of sweat. I knew if I could give her gallons and gallons of water to drink, she might be all right. There were no antibiotics left anywhere for love or money, but if I could just get her enough water! I was desperate, begging for her to be allowed extra. I gave her all mine and four or five people in our basement gave her some of theirs as well, but it wasn't nearly enough. She just peed once in the last three days – a dark brown thimbleful. Then the fourth day she lay quiet. I couldn't see her, it was pitch dark down here, but I was lying beside her cuddling her and I felt her going colder and colder. I could tell she wasn't there any more. I had to tuck in one of her hands because it was going stiff at a funny angle. Then later when the candles were lit, one of the boys came and said sorry and took her away.

'It was all right when I'd got Mariam. I could stand it all then, somehow. Now the grief's the worst thing, mother. Worse by far than the diarrhoea and the heat and the grating thirst. I can't make myself move. I can't bear her to be dead.

'I just don't understand why we're not surrendering. It's some policy or other – to do with morale – I don't know whose. It's got nothing to do with us here in the camp. I thought when I came here and got a proper system going for making the food last out, I'd be helping to save lives. But all I've done is help us to hold out longer, so that people can die more slowly and horribly. Like so many thousands of diseased flies. Whatever it's all supposed to be for, it wasn't worth Mariam dying for it!

'I could get up, I suppose. I could see if there's any water for Yacoub. If I didn't feel so completely torpid. One polluted well, for fifteen thousand people.

*

'I did get up eventually. Someone had scraped the stairs with a shovel when I got back, but there was some slippery squitter on them again already. I've been caught like that myself a couple of times. It just runs out without any warning. And as for the people down here who are too far gone to move from their mats – whenever they lose control of their bowels the stench is terrible. It made me retch again when I came back in, in spite of the smoke from the cooking. That stinking soupy smell of rotten guts and yuck and death.

'They've all finished eating ages since, but I don't care. I'm not hungry anyway. Only vilely viciously thirsty. Yacoub hadn't moved when I got back, but his mother's shawl was drawn up, over her face, and his aunt was wailing beside her. I sat down again here on Mariam's sleeping roll and took Yacoub's head on my lap. He was pleased I was back – he put his arms round me and tried to say something, but it turned into a cracked cough. His throat's so dry that he coughs up flecks of hard blood-stained scab. – There's a bit more room since they took today's dead up-top. I can stretch my legs right out.

'Nobody talks to anyone else now, if they don't have to. It hurts too much when your throat's turned completely to sandpaper. Yacoub's aunt has given up wailing. One of her children is vomiting.

'There's another candle burning, I don't know why. Perhaps because we'll all die of thirst before we die of lack of candles. I keep picking at Yacoub's scalp when there's any light to see by. He likes that. It's full of bits of scurf and grot and every so often I find a fat louse. If you squash them in your mouth you can feel just the tiniest drop of moisture on your tongue.

'It feels nice having Yacoub's rumpled old head tucked under my arm – it's like we're a little family, him and me. I'll keep him with me when all this is over. Tell Yusef he and I could both look after him, now his own children are gone.

'Now I come to think of it, I was supposed to report to the military office this evening for defence duty. I think. Was I? I don't remember. I'll go up in a bit and see. If it's worth it. If Yacoub can be left, that is.

'All my love.
xxxx Lenni.'

Henry rang.
'Aunt Samia! I'm in Junieh, on business. I slipped across in one of the supply boats, from Nicosia. I gather the war's practically over where you are too.'

'Is it? I don't know. Perhaps.'

'Are you all right, Aunt Samia? You don't sound too well.'

'I –'

'Look, about Elena. I've been given the name of a man to get in touch with at the headquarters of the besieging forces outside Tal al-Zaatar. I'm quite hopeful –'

'Please, yes! If there's anything you think you can do,' I said.

'I'll do my best.'

'But quickly. Quickly!'

On August 12th, just the morning after I received Elena's letter, I awoke a little before dawn. To silence. The light of day was just creeping into the sky over the rise and there was a vast silence over the whole of Beirut. The shelling had stopped. Not a single machine-gun broke the stillness. There was just the faintest tentative sound of birds fluffing themselves awake in the tree outside my window. Peace.

I watched the light slowly growing in the east and I had no emotion left to weep. Only to accept. To pray. God's will be done.

I watched, and the sun rose over the hill, in all its expansive Middle Eastern beauty, colouring the street with a clear glowing brightness, drenching the remaining white houses opposite in sunshine. And still there was perfect peace.

I was thinking; thinking that, yes, the Western mode of rational analysis is right: one can chart the causes of this civil war. But they are legion, ten a penny. A destined effect can always find some causes to help it on its way. The Third World War will not have to look far. And look at Elena. She found causes in Somalia, in East Beirut, in Junieh, in West Beirut, in Damascus – in Lifcote End – to propel her to where she is now. What are we but the instruments of Allah's will?

I felt the calm in me, the quiet of the morning. Resignation. If you were a Moslem . . .

I thought of ringing Rashid – but it was too early yet in any case – to ring and say: Look at me, I'm a Moslem now. I could hear the far-off echo of Rashid's chuckle. Light laughter rose up in me at the thought of what he would say to see the sort of Moslem I might think myself to be, sitting here in my sullied but smug Christian enclave, in the lap of one-time Phoenician splendour. How can anybody belong to just one side or the other? There is no simplicity in the Middle East.

I heard again Rashid's chuckle and I could feel the light laughter welling, welling . . . Tumbling upwards into my throat. How can anybody be one-sided?

Then, with a thunderous din which made the window frames shake and the blood rush pounding into my ears, the south-eastern sky erupted in flares and flashes of light, spurting like a second angry sun over the hill. The cannons crashed and boomed on top of the rise, firing one after the other in an almost continuous volley of deafening sound.

It went on for – how long? Half an hour? An hour even, I don't know. There was no let-up in the intensity of the bombardment. I watched as, over in the direction of Tal al-Zaatar, the sky blazed and fizzed. The smoke, pouring upwards, shimmered and trembled in the white growing heat of the sun.

Then all at once the shelling stopped. I hurried unsteadily up the avenue – there was no danger, there had been no return of fire reaching anywhere like this far. I hurried up to the top of the rise, to the point where Tal al-Zaatar came into view. From across the intervening valley I could hear what sounded like a great shouting and shrieking. Machine-guns and rifles bayed and barked in the distance like excited dogs, and through the binoculars I saw figures streaming up the hill towards the camp, a whole mass of them, finally covering the hill and swarming over the ramparts.

How it happens I don't know, but somehow one finds oneself busy with this and that, even when there's only one thing in the world that matters and when one is helpless, for the moment, to do anything about it at all. The morning passed.

Henry rang. He was still in Junieh, but he was coming over to Beirut at once, he said, to see what he could do. 'Tell Yusef to leave it to me.'

I listened to the news bulletins on the radio. I fetched

water. Yusef rang me from the hospital to tell me that the Red Cross were still being barred from the camp by the fighting, but they'd promised to let him know as soon as it was possible to get through.

I rang Rashid.

'*Habeebti*! What's happening?'

'I don't know. I'm not sure. They stormed the camp, early this morning. There's –' Why was it so hard to speak? To get the words to come? 'There's mews of a nacassre.'

'*What did you say?*'

What had I said? I didn't know. They were saying on the radio now that the war might be over. 'There's talk of mass killings at Tal al-Zaatar,' I told him. 'Solehale murder. They're gunning everybody down.'

'*Habeebti*, listen, don't do anything. Just stay where you are. I'm coming at once.'

'Rashid –'

'Promise me you won't go out – not even for water. I'll find out from Yusef what drugs I should bring for you. I'll be with you in two hours – two and a half at most.'

He shouldn't come. In all dignity, he had no obligation to come to me again, after I had gone from him – twice (three times?) already. 'Rashid, I'm so sorry. So very sorry –'

'My poor *habeebti*, don't lose hope. I've great faith in your daughter. Great faith!' He sounded definitely as if he believed it. 'Just sit tight, *habeebti*. I'll be with you soon. Don't try to do a thing.'

Afternoon. And still no news. But how long *would* it take – for her to get in touch I mean – if she was still alive? How long before someone – the Red Cross perhaps – would tell us they had come across her body? – her name on a roll of the dead?

Then Henry rang yet again and suddenly, from such an unlikely source, there was hope.

'I'm at the military headquarters just outside Tal al-Zaatar. They're being very helpful. I think I may just be able to track Elena down.'

'You think it's possible?'

'There's an officer here who thinks he knows where she's

likely to be. They're just arranging an escort now to take me into the camp.' There was a trace of self-importance in his voice, but I was touched, in spite of it, by his busy boisterous concern for Elena. 'Anyway, just to let you know,' he said. 'I'll be in touch.' And I was overwhelmingly grateful that there was after all something which might be done and that he was doing it.

I waited. Waited. If Rashid would only arrive! . . .

Then perhaps an hour later a girl, a secretary, rang me, relaying a brief message from Henry: Would I meet him at the main entrance to Yusef's hospital, in twenty minutes time?

Twenty minutes! But I couldn't wait a moment and I was rushing – rushing to order a taxi. Then when it came – a taxi! with petrol! just sometimes in Beirut miracles were still possible! – when it came I was running to get into it. Running . . . and like in a nightmare I almost couldn't make it. One of my legs was trying to melt away like jelly underneath me, so that I was clutching on to the door frame, the railings – at whatever would keep me from falling.

Don't try to do a thing . . .

Rashid! Of course, I must leave a message for him! Of all the places he was afraid I might go gallivanting, surely he would be relieved to find me going to the hospital! And I was struggling to run back again, to tell the housekeeper.

'*Im Yusef! Im Yusef!*' While I was looking for her, she was coming through the hall, calling to me, '*Im Yusef*! Your friend – from Damascus – he's just rung. He says to tell you he's arrived in West Beirut. He's setting out for the crossing, thanks to Miss Elena's friend Khalida he says. – In an Arab League convoy.'

So he had come! Rashid! He had made it to Beirut!

'You'll be sure to answer the door to him when he arrives? You'll be sure to tell him where I am?' I didn't trust her. When the taxi-driver had rung the bell just a few moments earlier, she had cowered and stalled, staying well back from the door, afraid even to look through the spyhole for fear of getting a bullet in her eye. I had to go to open it myself. 'You promise?' I said to her now. 'You'll be absolutely sure to tell him? At once? – At once?'

She was nervously fingering the miniature Koran on her

neck-chain. She promised.

After so many explosions, the hospital forecourt was strewn with stones and debris, like a beach at high tide. I waited there in the taxi, hesitating. I was suddenly frail again, uncertain what to do. Should I . . . ? I didn't know where I would find Henry and the entrance area was crowded with people. Better perhaps, if my impatience could stand it, to stay where I was with the firmness of a seat under me, and let him look out for me. In any case I was a few minutes early.

'If we could just wait here . . .' I said to the taxi driver.

He scowled and turned on his radio in protest, filling the car with loud music.

A military lorry arrived in the forecourt, its large wheels crunching across the rubble. It pulled up some distance from us and a man jumped down from the passenger side of the cab. He stood and I saw him wave, then come striding rapidly over. I didn't recognise him until he had come quite close, my vision was once again more blurred than it should be.

'Aunt Samia! Good to see you.' It was Henry. 'Look, I've just arrived with a lorry-load of children, from Tal al-Zaatar. They're all in quite a bad way. I found them being loaded up to take them to hospital in West Beirut, but I thought it would be quicker to come here. I knew Yusef would look after them. If you don't mind hanging on just a moment –'

'But Elena – is she with you?'

'Well . . . No, I saw her, but –'

'You saw her!'

'Yes, she's fine. She's fine, don't worry. She's O.K. Look, I'll be with you in a few minutes. I'll just go and let the hospital know the children are here.'

'But – Elena –'

He rushed off, striding across the debris. He could be cruel, that young man, in his busy unthinking haste. I couldn't bring myself to believe . . . Not until I heard more. I was in an agony of anxious dawning joy.

Two other men jumped down from the cab and stood idly around, smoking and scuffing the rubble with their feet. If only my sight had not been so poor, if I had seen the particular military insignia on the lorry . . . I think if I had been able to see for certain what uniforms they were wearing, if I had been able to make out the expressions on their faces, something might have registered with me – I might have raised the alarm. But I wasn't aware – I wasn't thinking. Or rather, I was thinking of Elena.

My taxi driver turned off the music abruptly. He revved his engine several times and drummed his fingers, in an irritable staccato rhythm, on the wheel.

After perhaps five minutes Henry came back. He said something to the men and walked across to me.

'I got hold of Yusef. He'll be down in a minute.'

But by now I was worried. The men had made no attempt to open the lorry doors. I had heard nothing of the children. 'Oughtn't you to take them straight round to the casualty entrance?' I asked Henry.

'Yes, maybe. I don't know . . .'

At that moment Yusef came running, with two or three nurses. One of the men from the lorry strolled round to the back to join them, out of my view. There was the sound of activity there, behind the lorry, the grating of metal fastenings.

Henry opened my door and offered me his arm. He paid off the taxi driver. He was excited, babbling on to me about the successfulness of his day. 'The thing is about someone like me,' he was saying, 'coming as I do from outside Lebanon, I see myself being very useful as a mediator –'

'But Henry, what about Elena? Tell me – please! What news?'

'She's fine, she's still at the camp. – She's skin and bone like they all are – and she's chopped her hair down to a short stubble because of the dirt and vermin. But she's in good shape considering–'

There was a cry from Yusef. It sounded like rage. I saw the hand of one of the nurses fly to her open mouth. As we came round to the back of the lorry, Yusef was taking the limp body of a child and laying it out gently on the ground. I looked inside and the lorry was packed high. Packed with children. They were crouched or lying on top of one another, even towards the roof there was hardly a space. They were all very still, each cramped figure fixed and silent. Yusef lifted down another child, whose emaciated limbs fell loosely from her as she was freed from the crush, and I was shocked to see that she was dead, though the flush of life had not yet drained from her face. The nurses too had each begun to take the children out, laying them one by one on the ground. I reached out to touch the girl Yusef was holding. Her face was still warm.

'I don't understand it,' said Henry, looking aghast. 'They were all more or less O.K. when I was helping the first ones in.' I saw the driver and his companion look away, drawing deeply on their cigarettes.

Attracted by the commotion, people began to flood out of the hospital entrance and across the forecourt towards us. They crowded around, peering over one another's shoulders to see what was going on. I felt faint. In my head was a swirling . . . Still Yusef and the nurses were unloading the children from their huddled stacks and laying them tenderly in rows across the ground. Every one of them was scrawny and lifeless. Their heads and limp limbs hung from their carriers' arms, like those of children picked up in the depths of sleep. Then one of the nurses called out something and I saw her quickly cup her mouth over that of the child she was carrying, a small boy, soiled and ragged. One of his stick-like legs twitched. I saw her gasp and lower her mouth again, trying desperately to force air into his lungs while she laid him on the ground and pumped his chest up and down with the flat of her hand.

The crowd broke up and reformed. People closed in around us, exclaiming to one another and angling for a better look. The vendors in the hospital entrance must have reappeared today, with fresh stocks, because many of the bystanders were carrying plastic cups and beakers and they looked almost as if they might have been called from a wedding, I heard so many shouts of good cheer amongst those still milling round the hospital doors. It had been a day of good cheer in East Beirut: the last enemy enclave had fallen, the partitioning off of the east was safely complete. A day to shut eyes and ears and make merry.

The nurse was still struggling to revive the child, but I could see she had almost given up. Her face was running with tears. Some technicians arrived at a canter wheeling resuscitation equipment, and took over from her. They were very efficient, helping Yusef and the nurses, going round the children systematically, one after another, doing the things that might have saved them.

'I just don't understand what can have happened,' Henry said to me in distress. 'Do you think they've suffocated or something?'

Then there was a howl from Yusef, from inside the back of the lorry. He climbed out carrying the body of a child, a boy, aged perhaps about ten, dressed in a torn pair of shorts and a T-shirt so caked in muck and filth that it was impossible to tell what colour it might once have been. He was trailing a coarse string-like shawl. The boy's eyes were staring wide within their bony protuberant sockets. His lips were deeply cracked and scabbed and a dried, purple tongue lolled out of his mouth. He was as thin as all the other children, thinner even, or rather he seemed it because of his caved-in unnaturally sunken chest.

Yusef looked towards me and I saw his lips mouth the words, 'Little mother . . .'

My poor Yusef. He stood there, clutching Yacoub's body to him and howling with all his tiger-like anger, a ululating stricken howl. The crowd fell silent. People looked at the ground and began to move away. One of the nurses went forward and rested her hand and her cheek on Yusef's shoulder to comfort him; and I moved to take a step . . . but dared not. I had no faith that my legs would hold me if I shifted my balance. Yacoub's face lolled towards me, skeletal and scabbed beyond recognition.

'Cretin!' Yusef turned on Henry, holding Yacoub's body in front of him like an accusation. The driver and his mate were nowhere to be seen. 'Idiot! Cretin! How did this happen?'

'Elena gave him to me to take care of. She said he was very special. She asked me to bring him to you.' He was shaking his head with uncomprehending contrition.

'Elena! You saw her! Where is she?'

'She wouldn't come. She was helping some people who were too ill to get away. She insisted on staying.'

'You mean you saw her, but you went away and left her there? In Tal al-Zaatar!'

'It's all right. She'd been taken prisoner, they'd got her locked into a fenced yard with some other women, but I told the military that she was my cousin, she'd been trapped in Tal al-Zaatar by mistake. They let her out when I came.'

'But they're lining up the nurses and doctors even, and shooting them.'

'It's O.K. They were very friendly about it. They're letting her organise a safe haven for people who are too weak to get out. Really it's O.K. She's not a Palestinian.'

Yusef looked rapidly for someone in whose arms to lay the body of Yacoub. He came to me, came and handed him gently, very gently over. 'Little mother . . .' His poor eyes! They were more bruised-looking than ever in his grief.

At first I thought I wouldn't manage to hold . . . But the body was much less heavy than I would have thought, lying lightly in my clasped arms.

'Little mother . . .' Yusef kissed me, then ran; ran round to the cab of the lorry and climbed in. He started up the engine.

Henry rushed to hold on to the open cab door, remonstrating. The driver and his companion were still nowhere in sight.

'I'll get those murderers!' Yusef shouted, wrenching the door out of Henry's grasp. 'Idiot girl, entrusting him to you! I'll get those murderers!'

He revved the engine and the lorry jerked forward across the forecourt. Some rubbish – a few oddments of clothing and a child's skipping rope fell out of the back and the doors swung shut with a clatter. Yusef turned the lorry in a wide circle and came back again towards us, making for the exit. Henry was running after, trying to stop him, but he had to jump out of the way quickly when Yusef, with the horn blaring, accelerated towards him. He tripped and tumbled, then came limping back towards me, looking shaken.

'What does he think he's doing? He could have killed me!'

'For goodness sake, go with him!' I called to him. In my mind's eye was the image of Yusef with his outraged love, pummelling his fists into the big teenage bully of long ago.

Ending up then with a bloodied nose, and now . . .

Yusef was slowing down in front of me.

'For goodness sake, go! Go with him! Go!' Henry was still standing clumsily undecided.

Yusef slowed to a stop and leaned down to me from the cab window. 'I'll find her, little mother. I'll find her and bring her.'

'Henry, go!'

Henry ran round to the other side of the cab. I saw him haul himself up on the passenger side.

There was something strange happening in my head. A sort of whirr. A gushing. Across at the road entrance to the forecourt I saw a contingent of Arab League soldiers in their white helmets arriving on motorbikes . . . escorting a car, I thought – but they disappeared into a dizzy blob of sightlessness.

Yusef stretched his arms down towards me. I only half heard what he was saying, above the roar of the engine – the rushing in my head. ' . . . Lenni . . . very soon.' He waved.

For a moment, in my imagination, Elena was there – vividly – as she had been that day at the airport: in her jeans and with her arms lovingly locked around me, the little noise of excited pleasure in her throat; breaking away to smile at me with her young woman's bright warmth. Once again I could feel in her embrace my own, increasing, frailty. Her strength. It was an image full of hope.

The lorry moved past me and away, its wheels crunching and grinding once more across the rubble. Yacoub's weight was becoming heavy, sagging inwards between my arms. If only Rashid would come! I felt the slight remaining warmth of Yacoub's small body against my solar plexus. I looked down at his filth-encrusted T-shirt, his wide eyes; the eyes of the boy with the open mouth, George's eyes, Elena's eyes, beseeching me . . .

'Go, go to her! Go!' . . .

I had a sense of events telescoping; of time collapsing down into a single instant. I lost all sense of up and of down, right and left, of coming or going. I felt just a sudden lightening of weight, a painful scraping against my knees and against my unclasped hands; glimpsed a car's metal underbelly. I heard the last disjointed sounds of voices – one familiar voice – around me. Silence.

That was all.

Rashid?